Iniquity

THE PREMONITION SERIES
VOLUME 5

AMY A. BARTOL

Also By Amy A. Bartol

Inescapable: The Premonition Series Volume 1

Intuition: The Premonition Series Volume 2

Indebted: The Premonition Series Volume 3

Incendiary: The Premonition Series Volume 4

Copyright © 2015 Amy A. Bartol

All rights reserved.

ISBN-10: 0991292537

ISBN-13: 9780991292530

For my mom, Gloria Lutz. I love you.

Contents

CHAPTER 1	MY HEART WITHOUT YOU	1
CHAPTER 2	I WANT TO	9
CHAPTER 3	TAKE THE WORLD	25
CHAPTER 4	THE INVITATION	43
CHAPTER 5	HISTORY	55
CHAPTER 6	YER RULER	67
CHAPTER 7	GUESS WHO DIED	73
CHAPTER 8	DIVENIRE	85
CHAPTER 9	RIGHT RODE AWAY	95
CHAPTER 10	PAST IS PRESENT	105
CHAPTER 11	STRIPPED DOWN	127
CHAPTER 12	THINGS I SHOULDN'T KNOW	141
CHAPTER 13	HEAR DA WIND CONFESS	155
CHAPTER 14	KISS ME SO I REMEMBER	163
CHAPTER 15	THE WORLD KEEPS SPINNING	175
CHAPTER 16	THE WORLD BELOW ZERO	187
CHAPTER 17	FASCINATION STREET	203
CHAPTER 18	DEBT TO INIQUITY	209
CHAPTER 19	CHAMPION	221

CHAPTER 20	UNTIL THE END OF TIME	239
CHAPTER 21	FATE CALLS	253
CHAPTER 22	FADE INTO YOU	259
CHAPTER 23	THE QUEEN OF HEARTS	273
CHAPTER 24	RED SKY	287
CHAPTER 25	SURRENDER	303
CHAPTER 26	THE BATTLEFIELD	319
CHAPTER 27	DA FAERIES	329
CHAPTER 28	I AM THE MESSENGER	343
ACKNOWLEDGEMENTS		353
GLOSSARY		355
ABOUT THE AUTHOR		357

Evie

CHAPTER 1
My Heart Without You

EVIE

Soft whispering touches cascade against my cheek, so light that they're almost a shadow against my eyelashes. I stir in bed, stretching my arm to Reed, searching for my angel even in my half-conscious state. My arms come up empty as my fingertips touch damp earth. I open my eyes to the hazy sense of wrongness. My fingers trip over the silky softness of my feathers. The acrid smell of smoke is all around me as my head lies against the grassy ground. Above me, angels are flying, moving chaotically.

Fire rains across the dusky skyline, turning what is left of the blue filament to red and orange as giant rockets burst and riot. The explosions make the ground tremble. There is a pain in my belly; fear twists it. A shrill roar causes all the hairs on my body to stand up at once. I've never heard its like and I dread seeing what is capable of making such a sound.

As I sit up, my head throbs painfully. Using my trembling hands, I rest my head in them, hoping that the world will stop spinning. From the corner of my eye, I see an armored-clad Power angel flying low to the ground near me. His forward trajectory switches in the sky as a hulking Seraph broadsides him. They rapidly lose altitude, plummeting towards me.

When the warring angels tumble to the ground only a few feet away, my hands go up to cover my head and I brace myself for their impact. Rather than being crushed by them, I'm scooped up and thrown over someone's shoulder. My cheek rests against his strong, blood-colored wing. Yelling in Angel echoes in the air as carnage from the war waging around me litters the ground.

"Mo chroí" the soft voice echoes in my skull like it's being amplified.

No longer slung over an angel's shoulder, I awake in my bed, but I'm not in my room in Crestwood. The bed is in the middle of the battlefield. A thin, white sheet barely covers me as I sit up against the pillows with a jerk.

I feel Brennus in my bones before I ever see him. I breathe him in; his exotic scent makes my skin dance to touch him. I could paint him red and he wouldn't be anymore startling to me. Brennus' black, velvety wings float around him as dark as a shadow in the night. They're nearly as black as his hair.

His iridescent green eyes drink in every inch of me. I clutch the stark white sheet to my breasts to cover them, only to find as I look down that it's nearly translucent. I push my long auburn hair over my shoulders to cover them. "Ach, Genevieve, have I na told ye before dat yer attempts ta hide yer beauty from me are made in vain? Ye only succeed in looking more seductive."

"Where are we?" I ask. I'm still in my bed, but I'm far from my room.

"Ye tell me, 'tis yer dream," Brennus smiles nefariously as I gaze around in trepidation. "As soon as I entered dis nightmare, it began to crash down around me—Heaven is secretive, but I was able ta discern enough."

"What did you see?" I ask him.

I shiver and he smiles. "'Tis na a pleasant future. Welcome ta da new age, eh? 'Twould appear dat tomorrow has been cancelled." Brennus lifts his eyebrow, looking around as the dreamscape surrounding us is changing, turning from catastrophic destruction to a haze and blur of shapes. Dust swirls in the wasteland.

"How did you enter my dream?" I ask, deciding to focus on the least scary of everything I'm seeing around me.

"I was worried dat da other wouldna be able ta save ye. I have been ta da aingeal house, but dere are layers of magic surrounding it. I couldn't be certain it was yer magic. Da other has a similar scent ta his spells."

"Magic has a scent?" I ask.

"It does," he nods. "Yers is exotic—intoxicating."

"You didn't know I survived?" I finch. He's been here at the house studying us.

"I've been going out of me mind wi' worry over it. Me yearning for ye was so strong dat I had ta find a way ta quench it. I retrieved one of da perfume bottles ye gave ta me."

"The ones with my blood?" My heart skips beats.

"The moment I tasted ye on me tongue, I felt ye. I shut me eyes and tought o' ye. I tought of da way ye smile, da way ye walk, da turn yer eyebrow takes when ye're angry. It made me chest ache. I was afraid ye died. Dere was a pull within me...here." He lays his hand over his heart, "I followed me heart...ta ye—ta dis place." Opening his arms, he looks around at the contours of my dreamscape. "I ache without ye."

I'm an idiot, I think. I gave him a gift that provides him a means to reach me—to get inside my head—my dreams.

"It's a cruel world, Brennus. Imagine how my heart felt when you tried to kill me." I watch him warily as he turns toward me. He smiles again.

"'Tis a violent world, Genevieve. Dat's why I'm here. I've found out a few tings. Tings ye need ta know."

"Oh?" I stall for time so I can try to figure out how to wake up from this nightmare. I pinch my arm hard, but nothing happens except now my arm hurts.

"Have ye na learned yet dat 'tis us against dem?"

My mouth hangs open until I snap it closed. "No, I thought it was me against you."

Brennus' brow puckers. "'Tis na. We're on the same side. Ye're me queen."

"I'm not your queen! You tried to kill me. I'm divorcing you or dethroning you—whatever! We're done!"

"Ye really hurt me. No one has hurt me like dat—ever." Brennus looms near me. His skin is a softer color; it's not just the lighting. His bare chest is like that of an angel's. It's almost like he burns brighter now. His wings move with an elegance that would be hard to copy. He notices me staring at them. A crooked smile crosses his lips. "But, den, ye gave me back me wings...dey're na da same color as was born ta me—dey once were white."

"Do they work? Can you use them?" I have an impulse to go to him and pet his wings to see if they're soft like velvet—black velvet.

"Oh, dey work grand. Dey're stronger dan me old ones. Finn is envious."

"Finn...he's alive?" Something within me exalts knowing that I didn't kill Finn when I'd unleashed my wrath of energy against Brennus and his soldiers.

"He was na among dem." He sees my relief and tries to suppress a smile. "He is yet undead and more dan a wee bit angry wi' me, truth be told. He blames me for losin' ye again. He tinks dis is all me fault."

"It's not your fault. I just love someone else," I breathe.

"Ye love me, too—ye love me da most."

"I don't—"

"Ye do love me da most. Ye have ta fight it, shift it ta hate because ye fear it. Ye only hate me because I will na play by yer rules. I make ye abide moin."

"I hate you for what you did to Reed," I snarl.

"I let him live," he seethes with his jaw clenching. "He'll na be so fortunate should he try ta come between us again."

"I love—"

"Ye just met him first. But ye'll need a god o' war if ye intend ta survive and so ye've made one. Me. Ye made me stronger wi' new found power."

"That was an accident, Brennus. I was trying to kill you, like I killed all of your men."

"Den we're even and so we can begin again—and ye only emptied da cradle. Dat was but a few of me newest warriors ye ended, na even close ta all o' dem. Ye can na drown da fire wi'out me. Ye feel it now? 'Tis na cold between ye and me—'tis fire."

He's right; the closer he gets to me, the warmer it becomes between us. He sits on the sheet as I draw up my legs away from him. The bed sags under his weight. He's really here in my dream. He has a physical presence; he's not just a ghostly shape, but is as real as I am.

Barely breathing, I watch him reach for my sheet, tugging it lightly so that I have to clutch it to keep myself covered. The supple fabric trails over my flesh anyway, feeding his hungry eyes. I pull harder on it, but Brennus flicks his hands and my arms splay wide and are tied behind me to the headboard of the bed.

My eyes narrow as I glare at him, feeling the sheet slip lower on my breasts as I struggle against the binding on my wrists.

Brennus' eyes go from sultry to frustrated when he pulls the sheet lower only to find me fully clothed in a baggy t-shirt and jeans, brought about by my hastily cast spell. Smirking at him, he pouts as he looks into my eyes. I rub my wrist that I unbound using my own magic.

"Dat's no fun, Genevieve." He flicks his hand at me, and when I look down at myself I'm attired in a silky black corset pulled tight enough to crack my ribs. Skimpy black panties and black-gartered stockings complete the ensemble.

He reaches for me, but I growl and flick my hand at him. He is thrust backward to the wooden poster of the bed. His hands are bound behind him and a metal manacle around his throat keeps his head from turning away from me.

"Is that fun?" I ask, getting up off the bed and approaching him with my hands on my corseted hips.

"Honestly?" he asks me with a raise of his eyebrow. "'Tis, mo chroí." Then he smiles his wicked smile that touches me everywhere. I conjure a black trench coat and hastily tie the belt at my waist.

I turn away from him, not wanting him to see how he affects me; the ache to touch him is there, just under the surface. Brennus' arms slip around my waist from behind, startling me, not only because he freed himself from my spell, but also because his arms are warm against me, not cold. They cause a riot inside of me.

"Brennus," his name falls from my lips in surprise.

"Do na fight me, Genevieve. I have someting important ta tell ye and it can na wait."

I allow him to hug me as I grow still. "What do you need to tell me?" I know him, he's calm on the outside, but his voice betrays something...it sounds like concern—deep concern.

"I was wrong about ye," he brushes my hair away from my neck, breathing in the scent of it.

"This is bad. You rarely admit to being wrong."

"And ye're very stubborn. Ye rarely relent ta listen ta yer demon, unless ye need him...and ye do," he says, running his fingertips over the curve of my throat.

"You're my demon?" I ask.

"I am," he affirms. "Yers and no other's."

"You keep shifting on me, demon, and I can't keep you happy," I wait for him to coil in retort, but he doesn't. "You're ruthless."

"Yer love is ruthless," he breathes against my cheek. "Hush, now. We can argue about it later. I was wrong ta tink ye're like Persephone," he admits as he explains. "Dat portrait blinded me ta whah ye are. Dere is another name dat suits ye better." He turns me around so that he can look into my eyes. His green eyes shine with ancient fire. "Ye've begun a havoc in Sheol. 'Tis yer face," he uses his thumb to rub my cheek tenderly. "Beauty wi' grace. 'Tis a face worthy of launching a tousand ships. Ye're na Persephone atall ta da ones dat hunt ye now...ye're Helen."

"What?" my voice shakes as I whisper.

"'Twas Finn who learned da truth—Molly really. She has developed a taste for Fallen. She attracts dem with a certain skill. 'Tis her air of innocence dat draws dem in. 'Tis like milk and honey ta dem. She stumbled across quite an interesting bird."

"Interesting how?" I ask.

"One dat knew a great deal about ye." His eyes are a slow burn as he watches me. "'Twas Finn dat made him elaborate on whah he knew."

"Which is?" I murmur, feeling all the blood draining away from my cheeks.

"We were wrong when we tought dat ye're da only hybrid human-angel."

"I know I'm not the only one—there's Russell..."

He slowly shakes his head at me. "I'm na speaking of da other. Sheol has found a way ta create deir own version of yer kind...and dey want ye ta meet him. Ye're very special, Genevieve, special in that ye're still the only one—da only female."

"How can you be sure your source wasn't lying?" The need to deny what he's telling me is so strong that I can taste the fear on my tongue.

"Our source was interrogated by Finn. He told Finn anyting he wanted ta know just for the pleasure of his touch."

"What does this mean?" I ask as my hands rest against his chest for support. I feel like my legs might give out on me at any moment. "What do they want?"

"Yer enemies, da Fallen, have decided dat ye're worth a war. Dey're gathering da means ta wage dat war. Every demon is now deciding whether dey'll play a part."

"And what part do you intend to play?" I ask.

His neck bends and his lips hover inches from mine. "The part that allows us ta survive, of course. Da Fallen would like ta introduce ye ta deir spawn. Dat does na fit inta me plans."

"What if the price becomes too high," I wonder aloud, "for your plans?"

"Ye have me marrow in yer bones, mo chroí. And I've yers. I will lay down me life ta protect ye," he promises. "We have ta strike a truce. I can na fight ye and dem, too."

"I don't trust you. There can be no truce."

"I'll love ye in yer dreams until ye do," he says in a husky voice. "'Tis yers ta decide. Do I have ye in da day or in da night? Either way, I will have ye."

Brennus lowers his head then, kissing me roughly and causing an ache for him to spread inside of me. His hands entwine in my hair, keeping my lips to his. I shiver at the craving for him he generates with his intoxicating kisses. Stroking my hair, he murmurs against my lips, "I love ye, Genevieve. I'll protect ye from yer nightmares."

My twisting sense of fate abruptly ends when Reed's voice whispers, "Evie," breaking the fever growing within me.

"Evie...love?" Reed says again, less distant. My eyes flutter open to find Reed reclining next to me on our bed in our room. "Good morning," he murmurs, brushing his lips to mine, but it's not Reed that I taste on my tongue...it's Brennus.

CHAPTER 2
I Want To

Stay wi' me, Genevieve... I hear Brennus' deep voice whisper in my mind before it fades away and is gone.

The darkness between my heart and my soul swells, pushing them further apart, making room for Brennus. *I'm the light to his darkness. There's no escape; he's a part of me.* I close my eyes. *Pick a side, demon,* I inwardly scold, speaking silently to my own black heart. *His kiss was sweet like cinnamon...*

My lips move over Reed's now, and as I grow more awake, so too does the desire for the one who has me in his arms, my *aspire*. Light and smooth he teases; it increases the tension that coils within me for him. It warms me, teaching my skin by touch about love. I breathe him in.

The fire inside stirs, stokes, and then burns me. I open my eyes to see perfect green ones above me. Pleasure spreads; it finds new places I hadn't known existed. Gravity begins to win; it pulls me to Reed with magnetic stirrings of yearning. I want to fade into him, fit myself under his skin.

My fingertips reach up behind his ear, entangling in his dark brown hair, tussling it as I draw him closer to me. Our lips part to taste one another. I groan softly. Reed reacts; his wings unfold violently from him with a *snap*. The darkest gray feathers splay out thrillingly behind him. His arm goes behind me, pulling me nearer as my legs wrap around him. He lifts his lips from mine. Our cheeks brush against one another's. The sensation of it vibrates through me, reaching that dark place in my heart. I feel the darkness retreat for a moment before it fights back, surging forward with the blackest desire.

My fingernails tense on Reed's scalp. The white sheet around me is unbearably constricting. My bare leg slips beneath the sheet to rub against Reed's skin. All of a sudden, I feel a desperate ache to consume him. I want to make Reed bleed. I want to make him bleed for me—only for me. My fingers shift in his hair, sliding to the back of his neck. The sharpest points of my teeth follow the column of his throat downward, grazing the smooth perfection of his skin. His grasp tightens on my hips.

I feel the beat of his arterial pulse beneath my tongue. His hand threads under the mass of my hair at the base of my neck while his thumb caresses my throat in gentle circles. The greedy desire recedes for a moment as my love for him swells. I sigh against his skin in relief, freed from the strange impulse.

Something grows in me, a malicious wave of anger flows out of the dark place in my heart, like poison, it winds its way through my veins. I lose my breath. My skin chills as coldness seeps outward from my core. The poison races on, weaving through me. My lips slacken and rest on Reed's shoulder. This dark elixir travels up my throat and into my eyes. My irises recede to blackness while I take a shallow breath.

Reed must feel the change in me because he tenses in my arms. A deep point stabs me where I join the darkness, like two lines meeting. I lift my lips from him. A smile spreads them thin. My mouth opens wide before I clamp down hard on his shoulder. Impaling his flesh, sinking in. The iron taste of his blood fills my mouth, the shock of which registers in my mind, but my jaw remains rigidly clenched.

Reed grunts and flinches as he exhales. His fingers tighten on the back of my neck in an attempt to pull me back from him. "Evie?" He breathes in and it catches in his chest before he exhales. He growls out one word, "Brennus."

A rumble of laughter rolls up from my chest. My jaw eases and my teeth slide out of Reed's shoulder. Blood collects at the corners of my mouth, sliding down my chin to drip onto the white sheet pressed between us. I feel something inside of me stir, making me pull back from Reed. When I catch sight of his face, his expression is grim.

My eyebrows pull together as my eyes narrow. "Whah part of 'moin' do ye na understand, aingeal?" I hear myself say.

Reed grips both my shoulders, steadying me and holding me in place so that he can look into my eyes. "Fight him, Evie," Reed orders with a sharp shake to rattle me to action. His jaw is tense. His fingers dig into my biceps with an urgency that is as palatable as the aftertaste of his blood. Charcoal wings ruffle behind him showing his agitation in ways that no words can.

"Da dark seeks out darkness," I say, but it's not me. "And she needs me."

"She needs to kill you, Brennus." Reed shakes me hard again. "Kill him, Evie!"

"She'll na do it. She loves me so."

"You haunt her. It isn't love; it's decimation."

The laugh that comes from me is condescending and not mine at all. "I'm da footing for her between ripe and ruin. She can na stop dem, aingeal. Na wi'out me."

"She'll bury them and you." Something about the way Reed says that causes me to shiver. I turn inward as I search for the ache, the point where the swirling dark has collected. I pull energy to me, the higher frequency energy; the kind that Brennus has no control over. The darkness recoils from the sting of it, allowing me to gain ground within my own self.

Reed grasps my chin. "Evie?" his eyes search mine.

Striking against the blackness of Brennus inside my veins, I grunt. "Brennus! GET OUT!" Reed breathes a small sigh because he hears me, but the command I've gained over my body is tenuous at best.

Brennus pulls a sea of high and low energy to us that forces me back. It makes the sound of a wave, rushing in my ears. "Reed," I pant in confusion, wildly looking around the room for a means of escaping my own self before I'm drowned in it. Brennus no longer controls just low energy. He controls it all...and he's much better at it than I am.

Reed's fingers dig into my chin, forcing me to focus on him again. "Evie, don't be his toy! Expel him like a clone!"

A wicked smile spreads over my lips. "I told ye dat I'd come for her. Do ye fancy some blood sport, aingeal?" My chin pulls away from Reed's grasp.

Brennus controls me, making me lunge sidelong for the dagger on the bedside table, the one Reed used to pledge his loyalty to me yesterday. Grasping the heavy hilt in my palm, I pivot back toward Reed. My wings spread wide to use their force to outmaneuver him. He tackles me, wresting me back onto the mattress. Involuntarily, I struggle against him as Brennus inside of me holds the dagger just out of Reed's reach with one of my hands.

Reed's knee digs into my chest as he pins me, and subsequently Brennus, down on the bed. He reaches for the ancient blade in my fist to pry it away. Brennus hisses and snarls, struggling beneath Reed's weight. The undead faerie inside of me manages to free my other hand. Raising it, Brennus hurls deadly energy from it. Hit by the hellfire, Reed explodes off of me. He crashes into the wall, scattering books from the shelves. My body crawls forward over the mattress. Red wings snap and wave behind me as pennants in the wind. Brennus uses my body to stalk Reed around the room. We engage in a stealthy dance. Whistling swipes of the knife cutting through the air makes Reed turn away in order to avoid being shredded.

Brennus! Stop! I scream in my mind, but no words form on my lips. Brennus ignores me entirely, choosing to focus his attention on Reed instead.

Reed refuses to fight back in any way, knowing that if he does, he'll be hurting me. I struggle harder within the prison of iniquity; the wickedness swirls around me in paralyzing waves. I follow it down because Brennus has me by my heart.

"Wake up, Evie," Reed says, searching my face for any sign from me.

"She's na asleep," Brennus enlightens. "She made me stronger and she gave me her blood so dat I could find her ta face her black future wi' her. Ye're in me way. I plan ta keep her all ta me."

"Too. Late! She binds to me. *Always* to me."

"So ye must die so dat she'll be moin alone."

Reed strikes quickly, backhanding us. My face jerks sideways. Brennus licks the blood that collects at the corner of my mouth.

"Mmmm, she tastes like whah I imagine daylight would taste like—da sweetest flame."

Reed growls and shifts to avoid the dagger thrust from Brennus that would've cut him in half.

"I tought ye were going ta kill me," Brennus taunts.

"Jump out of her body and it's done."

"Dere's so much power within her. More dan I realized. 'Tis as if I have da world at me fingertips. I'll have ta teach her how ta harness all dis power."

Brennus lowers my brows over my eyes in a razor-sharp look. My lips move in strange ways, forming words that have never before twisted my tongue. Brennus puckers my lips, as if I'll blow Reed a kiss. Glittering breath emits from my mouth; it sparkles like particles of rock dust, floating and spreading wide. Reed ducks away from the winking light reflecting in the cloud, dodging it. It catches his arm and the swirling mist shreds his skin with tiny glass-like shards. Blood wells up in tears from him.

When Reed glances down at his forearm, Brennus reacts quickly, throwing the dagger in my hand in Reed's direction. Reed's green eyes track it. He sidesteps the blade, evading its sharp point. The dagger shoots by him. Then, the ancient blade pauses. Instead of embedding in the wall behind Reed, the dagger chooses to turn abruptly, pursuing Reed with a relentless persistence. My outstretched hand tracts Reed, directing the dagger with a magical spell that Brennus murmurs from my swollen lips.

I use all my strength to shut my gob, hoping to break Brennus' magic, but it does nothing. Brennus still shifts the dagger to slice at Reed, missing him by inches. Reed blurs around the room at supernatural speed, trying to avoid death.

Zephyr appears at the threshold of our room, watching in confusion as I try to kill Reed. His blue eyes pierce me. He shivers when he sees the darkness within mine. His light brown angel wings launch from his back in a flurry of feathers. They spread wide and serrate with aggression. His confusion is written on his face. He senses danger, but he doesn't know from where it's originating.

The dagger Brennus magically wields cuts Reed's shoulder; blood spurts and stains his charcoal wing with speckles of red. Zephyr growls and barks, "Evie?"

My face turns toward Zephyr momentarily. Brennus lifts my other hand and the door between us immediately slams and seals shut. Muffled bangs and yelling from Zephyr can be heard on the other side, but he's unable to break through it. I hear him yell to someone, "FIND RUSSELL."

I'm like a tourist in my own body, I think.

The dagger hasn't stopped, but continues to pursue Reed relentlessly. In desperation, I concentrate on moving my fingers of my left hand. Energy spirals down my arm. I focus hard; my fingers twitch, and then bend. Lifting my left arm with effort, I bring it towards my face, covering my eyes with my hand. The clatter of the dagger is shockingly loud against the hardwood floor. I exhale a deep breath at its noise.

"Evie?" Reed says my name in question as his heavy breathing draws nearer while I war with Brennus inside me. The cold darkness races and bumps up against what I know to be me in my veins. It grips my skin unseen.

In the next moment, my right hand covers my left, ruthlessly prying them from my eyes, uncovering them. The sharp, unpolished metal of the dagger lifts from the floor and catapults in a whiplash toward Reed. He catches the hilt of it as the dagger point continues to drive on. Reed is propelled backward. His teeth clench and sweat breaks out on his brow as he struggles with the knife. My outstretched right hand glows brighter, forcing energy into the weapon. The tip of the dagger lurches onward to press up against Reed's bare chest where the image of my wings are branded above his heart.

Fear, like an accelerant, ignites inside of me. I flail my left arm, compelling all the fear and energy I can find into it. This is my heart and it burns for Reed. I'm never going to be the one to hurt him. Inside of me, fire meets ice. The dagger that's a breath away from cutting into Reed, with a lurch, abruptly changes direction. Reed continues to hold on to its hilt, but now he's struggling to keep it from crossing the room to me.

Wind from the powerful beat of Reed's wings causes my hair to blow away from my face. He's dragged across the floor toward me by the ancient metal in his hands. A deep growl snarls from his lips when the dagger continues its path to me. The deadly point pierces my skin, blood wells from the charcoal-colored wings etched above my heart.

A bead of sweat rolls down from the side of Reed's face. "NO," Reed yells at me. "EVIE! DON'T!" He's so close to me that I can kiss his lips. I don't, instead I concentrate on the energy controlling the dagger. "BRENNUS!" Reed snarls as he digs his heels into the floor, attempting to keep the blade from entering my heart. "SHE'LL KILL HERSELF!" Pain floods my senses. I focus on Reed's hands. The tension in them translates to his forearms as he violently resists my will. The dagger buries deeper.

The ice in my veins recedes. It flows backward to collect in the dark place between my heart and my soul. I'm disoriented. The room spins. An image of Brennus, not unlike one of my clones, lifts from me. Brennus glows, shimmering. His ethereal light fades to a normal hue of his skin—or his "new normal". His skin is much more golden now. His black wings unfold around him, large and menacing. But with the loss of my energy to sustain him, Brennus' glow fades, but he still remains.

"Do na kill yerself, mo *chroí*," Brennus pants as he sags a bit like someone who has just run an excruciating race. "'Tis weak."

With a firm grip still on the dagger, Reed draws it out of me. I fall forward to be caught in Reed's arms as he rests me against his chest. He flips the dagger in his hand before throwing it. The blade passes through the shape of Brennus to stick in the wall behind him.

I grit my teeth as Reed rips the edge of the sheet that I have wrapped around me and uses it to stanch the flow of blood coming from my stab wound. "It was the only way to stop you, Brennus. I'm your weakness," I pant against the pain. "Your *tristitiae*—I'm your sorrow."

"No," Brennus says with his eyes softening for a moment. "Ye're me love."

"How did you possess her?" Reed asks while his deft fingers bind and tie the makeshift bandages to me.

"We're connected trough blood. She gave hers to me."

Reed's fingers pause and clench into fists. He glances at Brennus. "I will kill you."

Brennus' eyes narrow at Reed. "Ye can na kill me! Ye're WEAK! Ye make her WEAK, *aingeal*! Dat's why ye have ta die." Brennus replies in disgust. "Do ye na see dat, *mo chroí*? He'll let ye be his martyr—he'll let ye die for him. Ye can na win dis wi' him. Ye have ta be ruthless! If ye're meek da aingeals will forsake ye. I know dis ta be true!"

"HOW DO YOU KNOW?" I retort. My blood smears on Reed's chest as I twist to look at Brennus.

"I KNOW BECAUSE I WAS FORSAKEN! 'TIS WHAH DEY DO! I prayed for Finn—for me—dat day when Aodh made me his *sclábhaí*! DA *AINGEALS* DID NA LIFT A FINGER TA HELP US!" He points his finger accusingly at Reed. "I'LL NA HAVE DAT FOR YE! I will na," he says the last part quietly, shaking his head with a grim expression.

"You have to stop trying to save me, Brennus!" I growl. "I don't want you to save me."

"I'm na concerned wi' whah ye want. Dere's opposition to yer very existence everywhere now. Ye tink da Werree wanted ye before? Dey covet ye, ta be sure, but dat is nuting compared ta whah dey want ta do ta ye now. Dey know dat if da fallen get ye, ye'll annihilate da Divine and da Fallen will control everyting on Earth and in Sheol. No one wants dat; jus as we do na want da

Divine ta have dat much power. Once da aingeal war ends, if dey were ta stop fighting one another, whosoever wins will focus on us—da na so divine craiturs. Dey'll reign down on whoever is left. So every craitur will either have ta begin ta choose sides so that dey have a chance of surviving whah comes after, or dey take ye out demselves."

I flinch at this information. "I'm not your problem. I thought we covered this in my dream."

"Dat's where ye're wrong. Ye're everyone's problem, but I take care o' whah's moin."

"I'm not YOURS!"

"Ye are. Moin and no other's. Dere will come a time when ye'll need me more dan ye need him. When dat day comes, I'll be dere for ye."

"It's not today," I state with heat.

Brennus' smile is iniquitous. "Den I'll see ye tonight and every night dereafter. Maybe 'twill be one o' dem."

"Until my blood runs out you mean. You don't have an endless supply, just two small vials. It won't last forever."

"'Twill last long enough, and who knows?" His eyebrow rises cunningly. "Do ye forget dat I know where ye live? Perhaps ye'll see a way ta give me more."

The shattering of glass from the bedroom window behind us hardly registers before Zephyr is beside Brennus, slashing a sword in broad strokes through his shadowy form. Brennus ripples; his image distorts and roils but it does little to Brennus but make him angry. Zephyr stops swinging at him when it becomes apparent that it's ineffective.

A moment later, Russell crashes through the bedroom door. He scowls as he enters the room assessing us all. His unfurled red angel wings make him look even bigger than six foot five. "Brennus, you maggot! Come here and let me kill you."

Brennus smiles. "Da other," he says, "ye get a bye dis time, but only because ye healed Genevieve. When I'm ready, however, ye best be, too."

Russell comes to stand next to Zephyr; his wings brush up

against light brown ones to form a wall of angel. "Oh, I'm ready," Russell responds, but his brown eyes are on me. He sees the blood-soaked bandage on my chest that covers Reed's binding mark. "I bought scented candles for the occasion."

Brennus' smile widens. "He's amusing, mo *chroí*, except for when he's na." He glances at Russell. "Do na worry, someone must get hurt soon—it will na be me. Half of ye will na make it. Care ta take wagers on yer Anya being among da casualties?" Brennus asks before he turns his sultry smile back to me. "We'll take dis world. Ye'll have no choice."

"There's always a choice," I whisper.

"Dere is. Either ye run tings or dey will. I'll see ye tonight, *mo síorghrá*."

Brennus' image falls apart like a dry sandcastle, running in grains onto the wood floor. A cloud of dusty smoke stirs up, and then fades away to nothing.

"He was with you while you slept?" Reed picks me up in his arms.

I wince, avoiding his eyes. "He showed up in my dream. I thought he was gone when I woke up—"

"He took possession of you, Evie," Reed masks his emotions. He lays me on the bed. I can no longer avoid his eyes.

"It wasn't me trying to kill you, it was him. I tried to stop him."

He touches my hair. "I know, but you weren't trying to kill him. You were trying to kill yourself."

"It was the only way I could see to make him leave before he hurt you. I'm *his* weakness. He won't let me die."

"That was a gamble, Evie," Zephyr says from behind Reed. He eyes my bandage. It's soaked through. He walks to the foot of the bed and squeezes my foot lightly. "Maybe you should have just pushed him out of you."

"He wouldn't go! I couldn't afford to let him stay one second longer and risk him gaining control of me again.

"What if he decided not to go?" Reed asks.

"He couldn't stay if I was dead," I murmur.

Reed's face completely changes from calm to stormy in a few breaths. His hand, resting on the wrought-iron headboard, crushes it with the whiny squeak of bending metal. He takes a deep breath. "And you thought that was an option?"

"It worked."

Reed's nostrils flare as he attempts composure. "Killing yourself is never an option. Are we clear?"

I glance at Zephyr. It's always been in my mind that if I ever need a way out of this, an alternative fate, he'd be who I'd go to for that kind of help. Not to live, but to die. "I protect what's mine," I say, sounding very much like Brennus.

"With your life?" Reed asks.

"With my life," I nod.

"Then Brennus is right. I make you weak," he says bitterly. "You can't end your life because you're afraid of what will happen to me."

I put my hand on his cheek. "You are my life. It begins and ends with you."

Reed pulls away from me. "Don't say that, Evie, or I'll be forced to leave."

I pale. "What?" I ask and an ache more painful than the stab I just endured squeezes my heart.

"I won't be the one who makes you weak." The conviction in his tone makes me shiver.

"Then don't be. Never leave me," I say, reaching out and touching his arm.

Russell snorts in derision. "Shoooot. Like you two could stay away from each other. Tell her another fairytale, Reed."

Reed ignores Russell as he touches his hand to his chest. "I'm a Power—an assassin. I don't need you to protect me. I've been hunting and killing creatures like Brennus for so long that you'd think it was forever. I won't let him touch me again."

Russell chimes in, "Reed and Zee are Prostat Powers, Red. You didn't get to see them stalk the Gancanagh while you were Brennus' queen. They freaking owned those evil freaks. So can you be a little less ridiculous and start explainin' what Brennus meant by 'see ye tonight?'" Russell asks while doing his best Brennus impression at the end.

"He's not the same, Russell," I say quietly. "Brennus is even more powerful now. His magic works on angels."

Russell walks to the bed and sits beside me on the opposite side from Reed. I push myself up on my pillow and wince as pain makes me dizzy. Russell frowns and reaches toward the bandage. His hand begins to glow. My eyes narrow as my hand leaves Reed's arm to knock Russell's away from me.

"Don't!" I prevent Russell from healing me with the magical power that we both share. I don't want to watch him transfer my wound to himself and see his chest break open and bleed. "I'm fine. I'll heal soon."

"I don't like seein' you in pain."

"I know, but just because you're my soul mate doesn't mean you have to take my pain from me."

Russell's eyes soften. "What about because I'm your best friend?"

"Nope. Not even then."

Russell sighs. "Then spill your guts and tell me what Brennus was doin' inside you." Russell pulls his hand through his tawny hair in agitation.

"Here's the short version. He drank my blood and wandered into my dream. I think he was a little surprised that he got there."

"And he had your blood because...oh yeah, that's right! Because you gave it to him. You freakin' let that vampire in!" He points an accusing finger at me.

"Thanks, Russell." Sarcasm drips from me as I frown, but I'm secretly grateful to fight with him. It prevents me from seeing how Reed is taking this. "I'll deal with it."

"How?" Russell asks, not giving me an inch.

"I don't know yet," I mumble, sitting up and dragging my feet to the edge of the bed so that my back is to Reed and Russell. "I'll figure it out."

"What did he do in your dream world?" Reed asks.

I glance over my shoulder at him before I look away. "He

warned me that the Fallen plan to go to war over me. He thinks there's another half-breed just like me...well, not *just* like me...a...err, a male..." I trail off, but the silence is short lived.

"How does he know?" Reed asks and it sounds suspiciously like his interrogator voice.

"Molly came across a fallen angel. Finn questioned him and found they're planning a war."

"Over you?" Reed asks.

"For me," I affirm.

"And Brennus is your ally?' Reed asks.

"I don't know what he is. He's my enemy one minute, and then he saves me from a fate worse than death in the next and I..." I look at Reed helplessly.

Russell's wings flair out in agitation. "You trust him!"

My eyes narrow. "I trust that he wants me. I don't trust him. There's a difference."

"There is a difference," Zephyr agrees. "Just make sure you know it."

Delayed shock sets in and I tremble. "I know it," I whisper. My hand manages to gesture toward my sore chest. The wound has healed over now, but it's still painful and raw. "I also know that the enemy of my enemy is my friend." *And my "frenemy" is coming back again tonight when I close my eyes.*

My stomach clenches in fear, making me nauseated. With the bed sheet still wrapped around me, I stumble to the bathroom. I make it just in time to vomit most of what I've eaten recently into the toilet. "Uhh," I groan the sick sound people make when they finish puking. My wings retreat into my back, refusing to remain out.

Reaching for the handle, I push it down. As I rise from the floor, Reed's hand grasps my elbow, helping me to my feet. Without a word, he leads me to the shower, turning it on. He pulls my sheet and bandages off before helping me into it, but he doesn't join me. Instead, he walks to the sink, finds a toothbrush and smears a liberal amount of toothpaste on it. He hands it to me in the shower. Then, he closes the shower door and walks back to the sink, leaning against it with his arms crossed as he waits for me to finish. The loose-fitting pajama bottoms ride low on his hips. He's obscenely handsome in a way that makes me feel weak for him.

I let the water rain down on me, parting my lips to wash away the taste of fear in my mouth. I glance at the shower wall where the broken tiles spider in a seductive pattern. Reaching out, my fingers glide over their rough texture. At the memory of how Reed and I made that mark, a small glow warms me, chasing away the bitterness.

The feeling is so unexpected, given what has already happened today. I turn the water off and open the glass door. Reed is there with a black robe. He takes the toothbrush from me and helps me into it. As I turn to look at him, I see his dried blood on his shoulder, the only remaining sign from where Brennus bit him, or I bit him, depending on how one looks at it. Frowning, I take his hand in mine and lead him to the sink. I wash away the blood from the bite and the other cuts that Brennus had made during the struggle. When I'm finished, I say softly, "I'm sorry."

"That wasn't you," Reed replies.

"No, it wasn't me," I agree. "This is me." I lean forward and kiss the spot on his shoulder where he was bitten, even though it's gone now. Reed grows still. "And this is me," I trail another kiss along his throat. "And this," I say as my lips find his and kiss him gently, with love rather than passion.

Reed's fingertips touch my cheek and trail a line down the sensitive part of my neck. It grips my skin. I shiver again with desire. His eyes darken at my response to his touch. The silk of my robe glides over me and slips off of my shoulder at Reed's urging. His hand moves downward, tracing the side of my breast before it travels to my hip. I gasp as Reed jerks me to him possessively. I feel the fire for him everywhere.

He turns me to face away from him. My hands rest on the marble countertop next to the sink. I see him behind me in the mirror. He reaches around me, untying the belt of my robe and parting it. The slick fabric licks my arms as it slips to my elbows. I straighten them and the robe falls off of me to pool on the floor. My abdomen tightens as I yearn for him to touch me.

Reed's hand sweeps my hair aside before it goes to the drawer next to us. Something glimmers in the mirror. I watch as he reaches in front of me and places the red diamond necklace he gave me for my birthday around my neck. The pendant is cool against my skin. It lies next to the ring that I gave him for our first Christmas—my uncle's ring.

"Wait," I breathe, stilling his hands before he can close the clasp. I work the ring off the necklace. It's heavy in my hand. "Okay."

Reed fastens the clasp. He leans forward, kissing me just behind my ear, causing every molecule in my body to come alive. His arms wrap around my waist. My hand covers his as I slip the ring on his finger.

"I missed my ring," he murmurs as his hands move to my bottom. I find it hard to breathe; my wings shoot out of my back. They press against his chest, not to push him away, but more to seductively play against him. I'm not exactly aware of what they're doing, they act in ways I can't explain, but I think he likes it because it elicits a sexy groan from him. As soon as I hear it, I want to find a way to make him groan like that again.

His reflection in the mirror smiles temptingly, while his wings spread out around him to mimic what mine are doing. His arm wraps around my waist as he pulls me against him. The deep green eyes in the mirror have my pulse racing. My arms reach up to thread my fingers into his dark hair. He bends forward, nuzzling my neck. My heartbeat is spinning. I want no other life than the one I have with Reed.

Before I know that I'm saying it, I whisper, "Stay with me." His threat earlier to leave me is still raw. I don't know if he meant it, but it scares me.

Reed's voice is sexy and soothing as he speaks to me in Angel. His mouth is so close to my ear that his warm breath does crazy things to me. The tip of his finger finds the binding mark on my heart: his wings. He traces the shape while he whispers something to me that I can't understand, but it sounds like another vow.

"I could no more leave you than the earth could leave the sun. You'll always draw me back to you," Reed says as he switches from his language to mine. I close my eyes, savoring his words.

I turn in his arms and kiss him in a way that will let him know that he means everything to me. "You're my one true love," I whisper.

Reed picks me up and deposits me on the countertop. My legs wrap around his waist and we fit together as one. I lose myself in him and he in me, each completely vulnerable to the other's cravings. My heart soars, all but the dark place between my heart and my soul; that place sorely rebels while it vows to make an enemy of me.

CHAPTER 3
Take The World

"We need a strategy meeting, Evie," Reed says as I rifle through my clothes. Finding a pair of designer jeans and a t-shirt, I shrug into them. I pull on leather boots that reach my knees.

"Are you worried about our position now that Brennus knows we're still in Crestwood?" I ask. I don't want to leave here. This is the closest thing to home that I've had in a long time. We've only been here for a couple of days but we've been able to fortify it with spells that have kept evil at bay until Brennus hijacked me and took over.

"I'm not worried about him knowing our location. It's moot," he murmurs. "Geography is irrelevant. He'll find you now as soon as you close your eyes."

The reality of what he says sends chills through me. "What can our strategy possibly be? Assemble an army while we fight off Brennus so we can wait for the Fallen to attack? And that's if Tau doesn't find me first."

"An army is where we start," Reed says with a smile meant to reassure me. He takes my hand and leads me from the closet into our room. The mess has been cleaned up. Russell must've used magic to reassemble the shards of glass from the broken window. It still looks shattered, but now it's all back and housed within its frame.

"You think we should bring them to Crestwood?" I lift my hand and murmur a spell, smoothing the glass of the window.

Reed watches with interest. "It's a decent position..." he trails off when he sees my face growing pale. "What's wrong?"

His eyes follow mine to the end of the long driveway, which happens to be where my barrier of magic that protects the house is located. Just beyond the closed gate is a parked car. Leaning against the vehicle with his arms crossed is Xavier. Snow falls on his bright, golden-blond hair. His deep-red Seraphim wings are hidden from sight. I can't see his mismatched eyes very well from this distance, but the set of his jaw tells me that they're stormy.

Had this been high school, my heart would've thrilled at seeing Xavier outside my bedroom window. But, this isn't and I'm not that girl who thought she was in love with him. I never even really knew him. *He has been lying to me since the day we met.* I refuse to consider anything beyond that—no past lifetimes before I was born when Xavier was my guardian angel...when he was *my* angel. I don't remember it.

I glance at Reed and see that he's studying me. My frown deepens, "You knew he'd be here." It's a statement of fact.

"If we wanted to avoid him, we should've left almost the moment we arrived here."

"I'd like to avoid him." I look at Xavier again.

"I would've done the same thing just a little while ago." My eyebrow arches in question so Reed clarifies, "I would've tried to stop you from facing Brennus."

"And now?" I ask.

He reaches for me; his shoulders cave in towards me with an air of protection. "Now, I'll always find a way to help you."

"What's changed?" I put my finger on his chest, absently tracing a heart over his heart.

"You. You've changed."

"Me?" I lift my eyes to his.

Reed's hand cups my cheek. "You're extremely resourceful, love," his lips are firm against mine as he kisses me, "resolute," he breathes before kissing me again, "intrepid. I trust your instincts."

"I couldn't breathe without you. I had no other thought but to get you back."

Reed smiles as he looks into my eyes. "And you did. Here I am." He kisses me again. My heart beats harder as I blush with pleasure at his touch.

"What do I do about Xavier?" I glance out the window to see him still there watching the house.

"Nothing. He'll challenge me soon and I'll take care of him," Reed says as if the expectation has been there all along. He sees the worry in my eyes. Leaning down, he kisses me again. His lips are gentle, meant to reassure me, but our kiss quickly turns into more. I want him to kiss me everywhere and feel his skin against mine. My arms wrap around the back of Reed's neck as I press against him. The butterflies that stir when he's near are rioting, insisting that I get closer.

Zephyr clears his throat. "Problem." Reed reluctantly straightens and looks to Zee in the doorway with a questioning look. "The Reapers took it upon themselves to leave the house."

"Buns and Brownie are gone?" Fear races through me.

Zephyr turns his icy-blue eyes on me. "They felt a soul in need of reaping."

"So you just let them go?" I demand.

"*I* did not let them go. *I* told them *no*." Zephyr answers. He turns to glare at Russell next to him who has managed not to say a word so far.

Shamefaced, Russell says, "Ahh, don't be mad, Zee! They told me it hurts them to ignore a soul who needs help ascendin'." When Zephyr just glowers at him, his expression turns desperate. "They ganged up on me—you've seen them!" His hands extend imploringly. "They're relentless. I had to let them past the barrier. They'll call when they're done and I'll let 'em back in!" He holds up his cell phone.

Zephyr growls and it raises goose bumps on my arms. "That is *if* the Fallen haven't set them up, Russell. You should've told me. I would've gone with them." He's seriously scary when he's angry. I haven't seen him like this since he tried to kill me when we first met.

"I know," Russell admits, scrubbing his eyes in frustration.

"They have this way of workin' on me—I can't think when they team up. It's brutal."

"Where's Anya?" Reed asks, probably trying to lessen some of the tension in the air.

Russell points his thumb over his shoulder. "She's in the library ignorin' the *hell* outta me."

Anya appears soundlessly behind Russell. "Now I'm here, continuing to ignore you," Anya says with a slight raise of her eyebrow. "The hell is welcome to stay where it is." She looks to Reed in question. "Do you need me?" Her long, black hair is swept back in a ponytail. Even in a pair of jeans and a loose sweater, she's flawless. How she'll pass as human, I don't know. Her skin is luminous without one imperfection.

Startled, Russell scowls at Anya, "Gahh! Don't sneak up on me! You're like a cat!"

Anya's eyes narrow to match Russell's. "I'm a *Throne*. I sneak up on people—karmic retribution is what I do. *It's my job*," Anya replies with absolute sincerity, describing her angelic role in the universe.

Reed smiles at Anya; he has a soft spot for her: not only because she was integral in saving him from Brennus, but also because they understand one another on a very visceral level. They're each in love with corresponding mated souls. "Have you heard from Buns or Brownie?"

Anya shakes her head. "No, but I know where they are."

"You do?" Russell's eyebrows rise while his shoulders sag in relief. "Where are they?"

Anya points toward the window. "They're with Xavier."

I take a shallow breath. Buns and Brownie are seated on the hood of Xavier's car. Their hands and wings are restrained, but they look like they're unharmed. Zephyr is out of our bedroom an instant later. Reed and Russell follow him immediately.

When I catch up to them, Zephyr's standing just on our side of the barrier. Xavier is eye to eye with him on the other side. Zephyr growls low as his wings spread out menacingly. Xavier's expression is blank. He doesn't even display his wings.

We're all right, sweetie," Buns calls to Zephyr from her seat on the hood of Xavier's black Aston Martin. The car looks like Xavier: ferocious and beautiful. "Xavier's just being a jackhole."

Snow falls lightly, covering us all in soft shapes of white. "Release them," Zephyr says from between his teeth.

Xavier's stoic gaze shifts to me. "I'm not here to hurt them. I need to speak to you."

"Russell, let me out so he can speak to me," Zephyr says, all business.

Xavier's eyes lock with mine as his jaw tightens. Slowly, he pulls down the zipper of his black leather coat. Snow catches on his elegant scarf as he reaches into his coat and extracts spade-like blades; they don't have handles, but notch-like finger grips. They look very much like the weapons Reed used to kill Pagan.

"Xavier!" I put out both my hands. My heavy breathing is evident by the white curls of smoky air coming from me. "I'll talk to you. Just let Brownie and Buns go."

Reed is next to me in a second. With his back to Xavier, he says in my ear, "You don't need to do this. I can take care of him."

I stiffen. My anger with Xavier is bone-deep. He crossed so many lines with me that I don't know if I'll ever be able to forgive him. Even with that, I'll never welcome his death. I loved him in high school; a part of me knows I loved him way before that. "We have to try to sway the Seraphim to our side, right? If I can convince Xavier to help me with Tau, then we can build our army quicker." Reed studies my eyes. "I've learned from the Gancanagh to never hold a grudge. Your enemy one day will be your ally the next."

"Evil will always betray you, Evie. Remember that." A sexy smile develops on Reed's lips. "Xavier isn't your enemy." Using his finger he brushes the auburn tendril of my hair away from my face. "He's mine."

"He's ours. We're one. That makes us on the same side. Always."

"It does." Reed agrees and kisses me. "If he attempts anything, use your power. Fry him. Give no quarter."

I straighten my shoulders. Reed steps aside for me and I approach the barrier, the energy from which sways back and forth within its dry riverbed like a swing of a pendulum. Zephyr is at my side; his fingers twitch in anticipation. He has every intention of joining me on the other side of the barrier.

"Zee, I got this," I say softly.

Zephyr frowns. "That is *my* angel he has threatened. Twice."

Despite the seriousness of the situation, I feel a rush of warmth over Zephyr's need to protect Buns. "I know." I lay my hand on his shoulder. "We need him alive. He has my father's trust." I need to build an army so that what Brennus said this morning doesn't happen. I won't survive losing a member of my family. I have to protect us.

The war is in his eyes. Finally, he says, "He lives...for now. Do not kill him. I want the pleasure."

I breathe a small sigh. "I promise I won't kill Xavier."

I face Xavier. "I'll come out after they're in."

Xavier studies me for a moment, and then he nods, trusting my word. He lifts Brownie down from the hood. Moving behind her, he unties the angel hair ropes around her wings and hands. It's a good thing that Preben isn't here to see this, but left the night we returned to begin recruiting angels for our cause. I'm not sure I could've reasoned with him like I had with Zephyr.

"You're a douche, Xavier," Brownie says as she rubs her wrists where the rope has fallen away. She touches her hand to her white-blond hair smoothing it away from her face as her russet-colored, Monarch-like wings wave away the snow that collected on them.

"You're a Reaper," Xavier frowns, "you should've followed my orders."

He moves on to untie Buns. "We don't answer to you," Buns says to him over her shoulder. Her golden butterfly wings give an uncharacteristic *snap*. "We pledged our loyalty to the Seraph over there." She waves her hand in my direction. "You're just static to us." I think for a second that Buns is going to stick her tongue out at him, but instead, she waits for Xavier to turn his back before she flips him off.

Xavier just misses catching her when he glances over his shoulder to give her a poisonous look. "That Seraph over there answers to me."

"Prove it," Brownie says in a singsong voice.

"In time," Xavier frowns.

"We need our—" Brownie says something in Angel as she glares at Xavier with hands on her hips. Xavier lifts the chrome handle of the passenger door. He extracts two golden field hockey-like sticks from his car, handing them to her. The sharp blades of their Reaper scythes gleam even in the gray, overcast light of winter.

Xavier's expression turns dark, like he has no more patience for them. "Go," he orders.

Buns locks arms with Brownie and they move Tweedledee and Tweedledum fashion toward us. Holding up my hand, I whisper words that softly blow from my lips to swirl around the energy that drizzles from my fingertips. The barrier glows, shimmering with a spectral light. Pieces of it break away, becoming iridescent, glass-like butterflies that float around in a haphazard flock while the girls slip through the opening it leaves in the wall.

They hug me. "Oh, sweetie, you need to run from that one. He has a caveman complex," Buns says when her eyes meet mine. Then she points at Reed, "You. We're upping your training regimen. You're not losing that challenge!" A smile flickers on Reed's lips as he tries to hide it.

"Evie," Xavier says impatiently.

Taking my time, I walk through the break in my magic. The magical butterflies mesh back into the wall when I'm through. I approach him warily, wondering what his reaction to me will be.

Xavier's eyes study my face, like he's memorizing it. He frowns when I shiver as the frigid air stirs my hair. Shrugging off his coat he says, "Retract your wings."

"I'm fine," I lie.

"You're not fine; you're freezing. You never take care of yourself. Now retract your wings!"

"I take care of myself."

The stubborn set of his jaw lets me know he's not going to take no from me on this, so in the spirit of expediting this parley, I retract my wings and allow him to drape it over my shoulders. He pulls the lapels of his coat close, engulfing me in his residual warmth and scent. It's almost Pavlovian, my physical reaction to it. A deep-seated yearning erupts in my core. I beat it down. *He's a liar. He broke your heart and left you here alone,* my ruthless inner voice reminds me. *And I love Reed.*

Xavier jerks open the passenger door for me. "We can talk in the car." He waits until I get in before he slams the door shut with more force than necessary. In less than a moment, he's seated next to me, having about crushed his own door. I pale at his anger. He's breathing heavy, like he's trying to contain the rage he feels. I've never seen him like this. He's been mad at me before—frustrated—but this isn't the same thing. He's livid. He starts the car with his jaw tensing.

"I'm taking you with me now," he states, his hand curls around the stick shift to put it in gear.

I wave my hand and the car engine dies. "No."

Tension shows in his profile. He crushes the knob of the stick shift in his hand, leaving finger indents in it when he lets go of it. "You're exposed here, Evie. Right now, you either have to have an army to protect you or be hidden better than a key beneath the doormat."

"Who am I hiding from?" I need to know if Dominion is my enemy now.

His eyebrow lifts over his blue eye. "From whom are you *not* hiding?"

I sigh heavily in response to his anger. "I'm not hiding from you, but I'm also not your problem anymore—"

"You've never been a problem; you're a pain in the ass, but you're not a problem. Problems get eliminated. That's never going to happen to you. I'm here."

"For how long?" I ask. My heart squeezes tight. I have to blink my eyes to clear them. I hadn't expected that reaction.

"For as long as you are."

"You don't belong here anymore unless you're interested in the army I plan to lead. If not, we've nothing to discuss."

"You're not ready to lead an army, Evie." Xavier looks up at the roof of the car in exasperation. "You still can't distinguish the difference between good and evil." He turns his head and glares at me, making me press deeper into my seat.

"Your definition of evil is not the same as mine. Maybe there's a reason for that."

Xavier exhales in frustration. "We don't have time for this. Will you come with me now or not?"

I look up like I'm thinking. "Um...hmmm. Not."

"You have something that I want," Xavier growls.

My eyes widen. "What?"

"I've searched Jim's house for it—"

"You've been to my house?" I ask, hardly able to breathe.

"Technically, it's my house now. I bought it—searched it, but most of your things are gone. I tore apart Brennus' estate—it wasn't in your dorm room either." He glances at me with little emotion on his face as he assesses my reaction.

"You own my house?" I say in shock, trying to understand what possessed him to do that.

"It was supposed to be our house," he mutters. "I bought it back for you, but you don't care about the past."

My heart aches as I try not to think about my old house or what it was like to be there with him. "And you broke into my old dorm room?"

"I wasn't just a shadow on the wall this time," he says bitterly. I cringe.

"What are you looking for?"

"You remember when I gave you my ring? I put it on a chain and gave it to you as a necklace...did you lose it?"

My face floods with color. "I tried to give it back, remember, when *you* broke up with *me*?"

Xavier looks away. "I wanted you to keep it, but circumstances have changed and now I need it back."

My eyebrow arches. "You need it?"

"Did you lose it?"

I shake my head. "No."

"The ring that looks like a sword? You still have it?" he asks with some relief.

I duck my head. "Sort of. Why do you need it? I mean, it's beautiful, don't get me wrong, but you can buy anything you want."

His eyes soften for just a moment. "It means something to me, Evie, or I wouldn't have given it to you." His hand inches nearer to mine on the console between us. It stops a breath away. I feel his body heat reaching out to me and I move my hand to my lap.

Suddenly the car lacks oxygen. "I know where it is," I say, not meeting his eyes.

"Where?"

"I'll tell you if you answer a few questions for me."

"Tell me where it is!"

"What will it take for Tau to join us?"

He shakes his head. "It won't happen. He leads."

"There's a tipping point in every situation. What's Tau's?"

"Be grateful that I could convince him to let me come here alone. How long do you expect him to let this go on?"

I laugh without humor. "He doesn't really have a choice, does he?"

Xavier gives me a sidelong look. "He's trying to find a way to gain your compliance without crushing you, but crushing you is still an option."

"He's welcome to try," I respond, sounding like Brennus.

"When he does, your friends go away," he threatens. "Anya is a traitor. Dominion will deal with her."

"She's not going anywhere—neither are they. You just need to remember that it was *you* who left *me* for dead."

"And you've paid me back for it. A hundredfold," Xavier counters venomously.

I sigh, trying to calm myself. "It wasn't payback, X. I fell in love with Reed. It has nothing to do with you."

"It has everything to do with me! Tell me where my ring is. I'll let Tau know that you wouldn't come with me willingly."

"What will he do?"

"Don't worry about what he'll do. It's what *I'm* going to do that should worry you."

"What are you going to do?"

"Learn my secrets, Evie," he says, "if you want to stay ahead of me."

"Tell me why I'm here or I'm not telling you anything. What's my mission?"

Xavier grips the steering wheel in front of him, bending it. "You came here for me."

"Why would I do that?"

"It was the only way we could be together. You made some kind of deal—you agreed to come here for one last lifetime, and then...then we're together forever—that's what you told me before you came here."

"Just like that? I push Russell away, like I never loved him? Like our lifetimes together meant nothing?"

"Not just like that. I've been your guardian from the day you were created. You've no idea what we've endured to be together. I'll do whatever it takes. You're worth it to me."

My chest feels tight. "What's the deal I made exactly? I said I wanted to be with you? I negotiated that?"

"I'm not sure exactly. You couldn't tell me. I just know you promised to come here so that you could have a love of your own choosing."

I hold up my hand. "Whoa. Hold up. You mean I didn't name you?"

"You meant me," he says with absolute certainty. "It's me you love. I was with you in every one of your lifetimes. When you died and Russell stayed on Earth, we were together in Paradise. When he died first, I always stayed with you in the shadows, watching, waiting. Now, it will be you and me until the end of time."

I don't want to believe him. I push that aside. "What, exactly, am I supposed to do here? What is the goal of my mission?" I raise my arms and look around. "What did I have to agree to so that I could be with you?"

"You had to come here and you did that. You don't have to do anything else. I'll do the rest."

"But if I was sent here—"

Xavier rubs his forehead in irritation. "No one is playing by the rules anymore, Evie," he growls. "I'm not going to lose you because they might see a compromise as the better option."

"Who are they—Heaven? I've been told Heaven doesn't compromise. Brennus believes there's another like me—a half-breed human angel with a soul—and I'm not talking about Russell."

Xavier looks murderous, as if I've just delivered the worst news of his life. "Brennus cannot be trusted."

"I believe him. He has connections and his connections say that Sheol has created a half-breed angel—a male version of me."

"If it's true, I'll kill the spawn," he replies.

My eyes widen at the slur. "The spawn?"

"The demon half-breed—Sheol's abomination."

"You think I'm an abomination?"

Xavier scowls at me. "You're nothing like the monster from Sheol. You're a *divine* half-angel, not a fallen demon's offspring with a corrupted soul. When did Brennus tell you about the evil half-breed? Was it while he was attempting to murder you at his castle?"

His derision isn't lost on me. "Not exactly," I fumble. I don't want to explain how I was given this information. "Why did Heaven make you ascend, and then let you come back?"

"Sheol adapts." A humorless smile spreads as his lips thin. "Heaven had to adapt as well. You needed to learn certain skills that they were sure would be taught more effectively by others, at least that's what they told me when I was taken back."

"Like what?" I whisper. "What did I need to learn?"

"Survival." He drops his chin as he confesses, "I sent you Jim...in the cave in Houghton—when Brennus nearly killed you. I thought your uncle would help. Did he?" Instantly, my eyes brighten with tears. I fight them and manage not to shed any, but I'm only capable of responding with a nod. Xavier looks away from me, out the window at some distant memory. "I didn't know what to do. Your dying meant your soul would come back to me...but then we'd never be allowed to be together. Whatever your mission is, you have to win it no matter what. If you don't, you and I will be separated. I will no longer be your guardian angel.

"I became too emotional after that. From then on, they cut me out of most of the intel on you. Tau was the only one who'd tell me what was happening with you, but they weren't giving out much information to him either."

"Why kill the other half-breed angel—"

His eyes snap back to mine. "I told you, he's not a half-breed angel. He's a demon—spawned from a fallen angel with a thoroughly damned soul."

"How am I supposed to find him?"

"I'll find him."

I shiver. "Why does he have to die? He could've so easily been me. There was a time when I thought that I was an evil demon half-breed, X," I whisper my confession, looking at my hands in my lap before glancing at him.

Sadness shows in his eyes. "How could you think that, Evie? There's nothing evil about you."

I force a shrug as I say in a small voice, "I just did."

With quiet rage, Xavier says, "If I'd been here, you'd never have thought that. Not for one moment."

"But you weren't here—it was Reed who helped me see who I am. He's been here for me. I can't let you close again. It's too late."

"I'm not letting you go." Xavier's gravelly voice bleeds with despair. "I'll challenge him for you."

I find it hard to breathe as I warn, "Xavier, if you hurt Reed, I'll kill you."

"You're the one who'll hurt him if you don't let him go. You're in a brutal world here, Evie, and he can't dig you out of it. It'll bury him. YOU will bury him. You've built this family around you that you can't possibly protect. When the spawn finds them, and he will, he'll use them against you. Why do you think Russell was supposed to die? He would've been a liability to you as a human. You wanted it that way—you insisted that he be taken out of this mission early—so that he wouldn't suffer—so there'd be no chance of his damnation."

"Why didn't I just insist he stay in Heaven?"

"He was bent on coming when he learned you accepted a mission."

"So Russell was always supposed to die and go back to Anya? He was never supposed to be a part of this?"

"He and Anya were allowed to be together because of the deal you made—the deal you would never fully explain to any of us. You pushed your soul mate away. You had them cut the tie that bound you to him. I thought you did it solely for me, but now I believe you did it for this mission. You only told us pieces of what you have to do, but never the goal of the mission—that you said you were prohibited from discussing. You were adamant that Russell was to leave this life when you began to evolve angelic abilities. You wanted all ties to your soul mate to be severed from you. I think you did it to protect him, a just-in-case measure."

"In case of what?"

"In case you fall from grace."

I blanch. "You mean, in case my soul becomes the property of Sheol?"

"Yes."

"Oh." I feel nauseated.

"It's not even a possibility, Evie. I've been with you in your lifetimes. They'll never turn you. You'll destroy them."

"What else do you know?"

"After you made this deal to return for another life, Russell and Anya fell in love with one another. They've been together since just after your return from being Simone in France."

"Were they happy together?"

"They seemed to be, but he still felt an obligation to you. He insisted upon joining you for this mission. Not that he had much of a choice. Heaven requires soul mates to have a chance to meet one another in a lifetime. He had to return with you, but he didn't have to stay. Your soul mate was separated from Anya when he was born as Russell. You followed him here soon after. Your evolution into Angel started the countdown for his death. He would've died some other way if not on the floor of the 7-Eleven to be with her."

Guilt makes my throat feel tight. "But Heaven was telling me to save him in my dreams."

"They were presenting you with the option."

My stomach clenches. "Why did they change the plan and take you away from me?"

"I can only speculate. I was not allowed to know the mission other than that I was assigned to protect you as your guardian, like I always am. When I was taken from you, I know that without me to advise you otherwise, you clung to Russell. You made the choice to keep him—to change him—to make him like you. Heaven didn't break their promise to you not to let him stay here...you let them out of it."

I nearly push the door from the hinges as I fling it open in my attempt to get away from what he's telling me. Exiting the car, Xavier rounds the hood and is in front of me in a moment. He pulls off his shirt, his muscles flex as they come into sight. Scarlet-colored wings punch their way from his back. I glance beyond him to Reed who already has his shirt off as his dark gray wings match the aggressive expanse of Xavier's.

Xavier grasps me by my upper arms, forcing me to look at him again. "You have to come with me now, before you get them all killed."

"Russell," Reed calls out, "let me out!"

Russell hesitates in indecision, watching the sky as it darkens. The gray overcast day changes. Black clouds move, roiling like waves. "Y'all, I'm not makin' the sky do that! Can you smell the magic, Red?" Russell goes to Anya, getting in front of her; his wings extend to shield her. Anya turns away from him, her black wings serrate to full extension, as she makes ready to protect his back.

"Russell!" Reed's hands press against the stout field of energy holding him at bay.

Zephyr pulls knives from holsters strapped to his thighs. "Buns, take Brownie inside."

Buns shakes her head. "We have our sticks. We'll be fine." Zephyr growls a warning at her, which she chooses to ignore.

When I glance back at Xavier, his face is turned toward the sky beyond his car. He moves to me so fast he becomes a blur. His arm slips around my waist. He pulls me close to him, whispering in my ear, "Run on now, honey, back behind your wall before the devils see you go." He nudges me in the direction of where I came through to meet him. His macabre words chill me, leaving me frozen in place. *I can't leave him here.*

Eerie whistling sounds from the sky surround Reed's manor house. The wild calls come from all sides—in stereo; they carry with them a sickening lullaby that raises goose bumps on my arms. The sun is gone like an unwanted guest. Its absence makes my feet heavy with fear.

"Where's my ring, Evie?" Xavier demands. His lips brush the shell of my ear. "Tell me quickly, and then slip back in and I'll lead them away from you."

I quake as I grab his hand, tugging it. I try to make him move with me back toward the barrier. "You're not staying out here alone. I'll protect you—"

But all at once, the freak show begins. The wicked black-winged shapes of *reconnoîtres*, demon scouts from Sheol, pour out of the shadows of the clouds. Hundreds of them fly like migrating birds, following swirling wind patterns and shifting in geometric formations until they dive en masse. Black leathery wings puncture the air with moaning soughs that disturb the gravity of snowflakes. A group of these creatures break formation from the rest to circle Xavier and me; wings blur by with the reek of brimstone trailing them in a rancid haze.

Next to me Xavier rips from my grasp. Nearly obscured from

my sight by black monsters, his wings are forced wide by sharp talons. The reconnoîtres lift him into the air. He fights back with his spade-shaped blades, slicing limbs and wings from the ones in front of him. Yellow-colored pus blood spews out of them while shrill screams hurl from the reconnoître's ghoulish, taffy-puller mouths.

CHAPTER 4
The Invitation

A dark flurry of reconnoîtres snatch Xavier into mid-air. He kicks like a mule, sending a few of them tumbling away from him. As they go, they claw feathers from his wings that swirl in the air and compete with snowflakes for supremacy.

A slash to my ribcage makes me suck in my breath as a reconnoître's long, silvery talons dig under my skin. They're not faceless like I had thought. The space above this one's jagged mouth is covered with a dozen camouflaged eyes. Pools of black barely contrast against his skin as they blink at staggered intervals so that he never lacks a moment of sight. The scent of sulfur wafts from his gaping maw as he leans forward, presumably to eat me. His forked tongue hisses out as saliva drips from several rows of bared teeth. Suppressing the urge to scream, I hold up my hands, expelling bursts of light from them. Blood-curdling shrieks fly from him as overripe-tomato eyes pop and yellow blood mists the air. His skin runs like melted wax before he drops to the ground, writhing from pain.

"Evie," Reed's rough voice makes me glance his way. He uses his forearms to push against the magic keeping him protected. "LET. ME. OUT!" The ring on Reed's hand begins to glow with blue fire; the center of which becomes a beacon. Light cuts through the film of magic in front of Reed, allowing him to plunge through the barrier. Seeing him emerge on my side of the wall, my mouth hangs open in shock.

At a run, Reed kicks into the air. Using the same kind of blades that Xavier has, he slices through reconnoîtres, sending pieces of them to the ground. Smoke rises from the carnage he creates; severed limbs turn to ash, dirtying the pristine white of the new-fallen snow.

I concentrate, collecting energy from all around. It flows, filling me with the sizzle of electricity. When I release it, it punches holes in the black clouds. Light shines through to batter the same-sized holes in the flocks of flying Sheol scouts amassed beneath white-capped clouds. It kills all the demons it touches, turning them to ashes.

The golden glow of Russell's clone rushes past me. It enters the body of a reconnoître poised to cleave me in two with his moon-shaped blade. The black figure convulses in agony; beams of light burst from inside him before firecracker-like flames turn him to dust in a shimmer of sparks. Similar things are happening to the reconnoîtres closest to us as hundreds of Russell's brilliantly lit images render them to dust.

Following his lead, I go down on one knee, forcing clones from me. Hundreds of them branch out in gold-colored streams of light to kill my enemies. I almost smile as the harrowing, black creatures ignite around me, but when I stand, the sky changes again. A new wave of darkness settles over us, the holes in the clouds fill in. Cold wind shifts from it, blowing my hair away from my face. My eyes circle the area. Russell is guarding Anya, Zephyr is doing the same to Buns and Brownie, but they're all still protected near the house. Claw marks bleed in Xavier's skin, lending an air of authenticity to his homicidal expression while he mutilates reconnoîtres with impunity. Reed is just in front of me, acting as my shield, but there are thousands of hellish scouts swarming in. We're going to be overrun soon.

I try to bring more energy to me, but it retreats, shifting perceptibly to dance over my skin; it continues to draw away from me across the snow-covered lawn to the wooded area just beyond. There's someone there, someone powerful enough to divert energy from me. There's a scent, too, a mark left in the air, which at once seems so morbidly familiar that it makes me recoil from it in revulsion. All my instincts alert me to the presence just beyond the tree line—it's someone who, if my heart can be believed, scares me to death.

Before I can react though, I hear a loud *whoosh*, like a gas stove being lit. A carpet of flames rolls out from the woods. The fire hits us in seconds, and because I expect fire to have intense heat, I'm confused that it's not burning me. Instead, it's like gale-force wind. Twisting bodies of reconnoîtres blow like dead leaves in its current. The ground trembles as a shockwave rumbles outward, tearing up the frozen ground. It hits me with the force of a moving train, making me close my eyes. As it quiets, a familiar voice whispers in my mind, "I've missed you, Simone. You're more achingly beautiful than ever. Perhaps I will let you live long enough to give me the child you stole from me that night."

When I open my eyes, I'm on the ground in the snow looking up at the gray sky. Black clouds are slowly ebbing. The reconnoîtres are gone. Soft, black petals float down to fall upon my cheeks. Reed's gray wings brush up against my shoulder just before I'm clutched to his chest. His warm hands explore me, checking to see the extent of my injuries as he speaks to me in Angel. He sounds worried, but I can't think of why at the moment.

I search the area over Reed's shoulder; everyone I love is on the ground. Black rose petals fall upon them, covering them like a blanket. Russell stirs; he brings his hand to his forehead to rub it. When he looks around in confusion, he sees Anya on the frozen earth beside him. He lurches to her, pulling her limp body up into his arms. He rocks her, wiping black petals from her pale cheeks. She coughs, and then gasps for breath, winded.

My eyes go to Zephyr who's kneeling by Brownie. He has Buns in his arms already and he's trying to help Brownie sit up. It takes me another moment to realize that the barrier of magic that had been protecting them is gone.

I turn my head and search for Xavier, finding him near me. He's getting to his feet, holding his ribs. Black petals cling to his blond hair. My focus returns to Reed who, unlike everyone else, is unscathed by what just happened. "That was magic, Reed. Someone just stole it all from Russell and me—they used it against us."

"Are you hurt?" Reed's expression is grim.

I move a little and feel the ache of bruises, but nothing seems broken. I shake my head. "No. You?"

"It never touched me," he says. "The fire-wind blew in and knocked all of you to the ground. It wiped out your magic protecting the house. The reconnoîtres that were surrounding us they...changed."

"Changed? Changed, how?"

He scoops up a handful of petals and crushes them in his fist. "This is what is left of them."

I groan in disgust, brushing all the petals off of me as I shiver.

Xavier squats down next to me and looks me in the eyes. His tone is one of accusation as he asks, "You gave him Jim's ring?"

"Um..." I look at him in confusion, "what?"

"Where's *my* ring?" Xavier grasps my shoulders; his fingers tighten on me painfully. "Tell me where it is!"

The hurt in his eyes speaks to me more than the pressure on my arms and I blurt out, "Backyard. It's in the backyard—buried near the tree where you first kissed me—"

Xavier silences me with his lips as they crush mine. He lets me go abruptly before I even think to protest. The growl from Reed says that it was long enough for him to die. Xavier's face turns toward Reed as he straightens. He holds up his hand to Reed and says, "Soon." With that, he turns and strides away to the car he came in. The black frame is now dotted with petals as it lies on its side, having been blown there by whatever magic had come at us across the snow-covered lawn.

He pushes the car over, righting it. The screech of metal rubbing metal hurts my ears when Xavier nearly tears the door open and gets in. It takes him a couple of slams to get it to close again. The engine roars to life just before the tires kick up clods of snow, dirt, and roses. The car fishtails onto the driveway as Xavier speeds away from us.

"What the HELL was that all about?" Russell yells to us from where he's helping Anya up from the ground.

"Russell, figure out a way to protect the house until we relocate." Reed doesn't try to explain further, but sprints to the separate garage where he keeps his cars. Disappearing inside, one of the doors lifts slowly, revealing a white Lamborghini. Before the door is all the way open, the car lurches from the darkness and flies across the drive to where I've gotten to my feet.

"Please get in," Reed says to me through the open window. As I retract my wings and comply, Zephyr appears at Reed's window. "Be ready to leave when I call."

Zephyr doesn't smile when he says, "I will make the arrangements."

"Shut the door, Evie," Reed says with his hand on the stick shift. When I do, the car rockets down the driveway. Instead of applying the foot break near the end of it, Reed pulls the emergency break as he turns the wheel. The car slides sideways onto the street; he releases the hand break, and pushes down on the accelerator, burying the needle. We swerve dangerously on the road every so often as we hit patches of ice on our way out of Crestwood. Reed immediately corrects the wheel so that we hardly lose any speed.

"Where are we going?" I ask as I scramble to put on my seatbelt.

"We're trying to catch up to Xavier," Reed replies. I want to ask him to slow down, but I can see by the tension in his forearms that he'd be going faster if it were at all possible. "We have to get to what's buried in the backyard before he does."

"Why?'

"Because Xavier wants it bad enough to leave you with me until he gets it. It's a ring, right? Like this one?" Reed holds up his hand, displaying my uncle's class ring, which I now have serious doubts about it truly ever having been a class ring.

I nod. "It's a ring. It's *his* ring," I clarify, "but it doesn't look like that one."

"Do you have any idea what it does?"

I shake my head. "How do you know it does something?"

Reed ignores my questions and counters. "How did you come by it?"

"He asked me to wear it."

"For protection?"

My face reddens. "No. It was because he was my friend. We were friends—"

"Friends?" Reed asks skeptically.

My cheeks flush more. "He was sort of my boyfriend when he gave it to me—but he was so weird about it," I try to explain. "He was so hot and cold all the time that I was never really sure where I stood with him...but he insisted that I wear it on a chain around my neck, like a pendant."

"This ring that you gave me, Evie, it just protected me."

"It did?"

"It lit up with a blue glow. It cut through your magic when I needed to get to you. I fell right through your magic barrier to the other side."

"How did it do that?"

"I don't know, but it fought off the evil invitation Sheol just sent you. Whatever was controlling that magic couldn't harm me the way it did the rest of you," Reed says. "I can only assume it was because of this ring. Xavier recognized it. He must know what it does."

We pass by a frozen lake on our way out of town. "Invitation? How can you say that was an invitation? They were trying to kill us."

"But they backed off. It was an invitation to you, presented with a warning, and wrapped—" reaching toward me, Reed pulls a petal from my hair and shows it to me, "—in a love letter. Sheol just invited you to join them."

A bone-deep chill runs through me. "Or everyone I love dies," I say with a hollow voice.

"Not everyone. I have Jim's ring. We need that other ring. We can't let Xavier get it, not until we know what it does."

My heavy breathing fogs the windshield. Reed turns on the defroster, and as the glass becomes clearer, red taillights shine in front of us. Reed tries to pass the battered Aston Martin on the icy road, but the car in front of us swerves into the passing lane, blocking us.

Reed applies more pressure to the accelerator and our car lurches forward, crashing into Xavier's bumper. Our white car shakes violently as it pushes against the black one, nudging it aside. Xavier's car begins to spin out; it circles to the right as Reed moves the wheel to neatly avoid it on the left. And just like that, we're clear of the Aston Martin.

I look out the back window, seeing Xavier's car regain the road from the shoulder and pursue us. The fogged windshield of the Aston Martin cracks and shatters violently as Xavier's booted foot kicks it away. When it bows out in pieces, he drops his leg and uses his arm to begin clearing away the glass.

"What's he doing?" My eyes go to Reed who's watching the rearview mirror.

Reed frowns grimly, "Evie, get to that ring as fast as you can. Don't stop for anything. When you have it, find a safe place to hide and call me. I'll find you." He opens the sunroof with a touch of a button. "Here, take the wheel."

"You're kidding, right?" I ask with a squeak, my eyes widening.

"We have to stop Xavier from getting there first." He grasps my limp hand and puts it on the steering wheel.

My eyes stray to the rear window again in time to see Xavier break the windshield out completely. He lunges through the opening onto the hood of his car, taking two running steps with his red wings spread wide. Leaping forward from the hood, he glides through the air and lands on the back of our car as his vehicle spins off into a ditch. The Lamborghini bounces hard upon impact, and then it decelerates rapidly. Xavier's powerful wings beat the air, lifting the back tires off the ground. I have no time to protest as Reed climbs out through the sunroof. His dark, ashen wings open wide as he emerges from the car and lofts into the air. He catches Xavier around the throat with his forearm and yanks him off our car.

The tires swerve over the road when the back ones thump onto the ground again. I manage to hold onto the wheel, scrambling into the driver's seat. I touch the brake, coming to a stop. Shifting the car into neutral and engaging the safety brake, I turn to look out the rear window. Snow drifts in anaconda patterns over the barren pavement. With both of my hands gripping the seatback, I watch Reed's wings thrash. He locks arms with Xavier whose wings serrate to red dagger points, and it's clear that both angels are trying to rip the other's arms off.

Like a revolving door, Reed spins free from Xavier's strong fists. He runs at our car, hitting the back end; it slides forward on the road despite the brake. "GO!" Reed shouts at me. Then he turns back, catching Xavier around his waist before he can move to my door. Reed throws him back. Xavier tumbles across the ground, skidding to a stop. Growling, he rises to his feet, running at Reed with weapons in his hands.

I jump out of the car as Xavier uses his spade-shaped blades to slash at Reed. He misses with the one in his right hand, but not with the other in his left. The razor edge connects with Reed's cheek, cutting it from his lips to his ear. My wings eject from me as I scream. Reed rears back from Xavier. I lift my hand, making Xavier's car rise into the air from the ditch; it crashes down on the pavement directly behind him. Before Xavier can hurt Reed again, his feet leave the ground as he's thrust back through the empty windscreen of his car. He lands hard in the driver's seat, staring at me with a murderous expression. The shattered glass on the pavement collects and finds its way to the front of the car, settling into place and smoothing to transparency.

Xavier pounds his fist against it trying to break it out again, but the glass holds. "Evie!" His muffled voice is barely discernible above the sounds of his thrashing. When it still doesn't break, he slams his shoulder against the door. It doesn't open either. He beats the window, leaving smears of blood on it from his fists.

I walk to Reed who holds his hand to his face to stem his

blood. "Are you okay?" I ask worriedly, as I touch his other cheek.

"It's not bad," he says, reaching out and wrapping his hand around the back of my neck, pulling me to him. He hugs me in an attempt to comfort me. "We need to go."

"Okay, just a second." I pull away from Reed and go to the driver's side of Xavier's car. When I near his window, I bend toward it, steaming it with my breath. Using my finger, I write: UOY ETAH I.

Pain shows in Xavier's mismatched eyes. He leans to the glass and fogs it with his breath. He pulls back, and with his finger, he writes: COME BACK TO ME. He rests his palm against the window. My heart squeezes tight, leaving no room for my blood to breathe. I feel hopeless as my eyes meet his again. *I hate this.* My hand twitches with the urge to meet his on the glass.

Reed backs our car next to me. I back away from Xavier's window and bump up against the door, blindly searching for the handle. When the door slides open, I retract my wings and scramble into my seat, refusing to look at Xavier again. Reed drives in the direction of my house. *Xavier's house,* my mind corrects.

Reed gazes in the rearview mirror. "He's not following us."

"He can't. I killed his car and locked him in. The spell should last for a little while, but the farther away I get, the weaker it'll become. He'll be out soon. How's your face?"

He pulls away a torn piece of fabric and I hiss at the violence of the wound. *I should've killed him,* I think.

Reed tries to smile but winces. "It'll be gone in a few minutes, love."

Opening the console, I'm not at all surprised to find a small first aid kit there. "I know. I'm so glad you heal faster than me," I murmur, unwrapping a gauze bandage and dabbing it lightly to his cheek.

"You shouldn't have stopped us, Evie. Xavier and I will have to face one another."

"Maybe not, Reed. Time can change anything." My hand stills.

I panic. *Time could change us, like it had with Xavier and me.* I feel like my heart unravels, but I don't let him see it. "One day, Reed," I begin dabbing at his cheek again, "you and I will get in the car and just drive. We'll wander from silver cities to golden coasts." I use an alcohol swab to clean the blood from his cheek. "We'll sleep when we're tired. When we wake, I'll find a way to make you laugh and I'll live in the sound of it." My throat gets tight because I long for that day to be now. "We'll find somewhere you've never been and we'll make it ours—fill it with memories of us. That's what I want." I finish with the alcohol swab. Leaning close, I gently blow on his healing wound to ease the sting.

Reed takes my hand and brings it to his lips, kissing it tenderly. "And when we get that sleep, there will never be a your side or a my side of the bed—we'll always meet in the middle. And when I hold you there, in our bed, you'll let me rest my lips here." Reed lets go of my hand to move his thumb to caress the sensitive skin of my neck just beneath my ear. I get swept up in him: my body his with one touch. I turn and rub my cheek gently against his palm.

"And we won't rush...ever," I murmur, forgetting to be scared. I want that future with him.

"The world can spin around us but we'll take our time, savor every moment."

My head rests on his shoulder. "Just you and me."

He kisses the top of my head. "I doubt Buns or Brownie will allow that."

He has somehow found a way to make me smile. "Do you know where you're going?"

"Detroit—to your childhood home," Reed answers. "I've been there."

"That's right," I murmur as I remember that he went there to take care of things after Freddie killed my Uncle Jim.

"I've been there several times when I was looking for you after you left Crestwood."

Once we reach the highway, the rest of the trip to Detroit passes quickly as Reed flies by cars like they're standing still.

When we exit, he weaves in and out of traffic on the icy two-lane roads. We enter my neighborhood and Reed is forced to slow the car. Garlands decorate doors shrouded by iron bars. People are getting ready to celebrate the winter holidays and the familiarity of it all seems foreign to me—my life prior to Crestwood is so far removed from the one I have now.

Everything in this city is the same, which shocks me. Maybe it's because I've changed so much since I was here that I expected it to have changed as well. But it hasn't. It's the same. The rectangular-shaped storefronts and restaurants hide behind growing piles of plowed and shoveled snow. People with scarf-wrapped necks and gloved hands hold shopping bags as their boots hurry toward parked cars to get out of the cold.

After we pass the fire station, we turn right onto the street where I grew up. It's all single-family, two-story dwellings with postage-stamp lawns and open front porches. Reed avoids the driveway and pulls up to the curb in front of my childhood house, parking beneath the snow-covered branches of the elm tree. It had belonged to Uncle Jim's parents, my grandparents. He'd inherited it when they died. I don't remember them at all—they were gone before I was born.

The red brick façade, black-shuttered windows, and bright red front door of my house cause my throat to tighten and close. I have to take shallow breaths—I can't afford tears right now. "Someone replaced the net," I murmur, gesturing to the basketball hoop affixed to the detached garage. I open my door and step out of the car; Reed is by my side immediately. "We always kept shovels in there." I point to the small potting shed beside the garage as I walk up the driveway that has been snowplowed recently.

Reed goes to it and finds a shovel inside. Taking it, he follows me to the fenced-in backyard. After I open the gate, it's immediately apparent that we're too late. A hole and small pile of dirt beneath the base of the enormous oak tree makes that painfully clear, not to mention the tracks in the snow leading to and from the house. The back door of the house opens and Xavier steps out onto the deck wearing the ring that I haven't seen since high school.

CHAPTER 5
History

Reed takes my hand and we turn to go, but there are at least ten Powers walking up the driveway toward us. None of them display their wings, but I know them to be Powers—Dominions. It's in their stride, the military way in which they carry themselves. All of a sudden, it feels like the house itself is bearing down on me. I turn back to face Xavier and find my father has joined him. Tau's gray eyes, so much like my own, are on me and I'm struck by our resemblance to one another, though we look more like brother and sister than father and daughter. I had thought once that I shared my Uncle Jim's eyes. I was wrong. They're my father's.

My heart gives a lurch and I panic. I drop Reed's hand as I raise mine. I let energy pulse out from it, the force of which connects with Tau. The smell of burnt cotton is in the air at the fury I unleash on him. The railing in front of him cracks, and then explodes, shattering. Tau cringes upon impact, but he absorbs the energy that should've easily lifted him off of his feet and thrown him back. He staggers a step, but then holds his ground as the windows behind him are blown out. As Tau's hands curl into fists, I notice the wink and shimmer of a platinum ring on his finger. I can't be sure, but from this distance it looks very similar to the one that Xavier now wears—like the ring that I buried in the yard.

"They work," Tau growls through his teeth to Xavier.

Cole materializes from the house and stands beside Tau. With his crimson Seraphim wings out, he's ready to defend his leader. Assessing the situation, he frowns at Tau. "Stings, huh?"

Tau exhales a deep breath. "A bit."

"EVIE!" Xavier barks my name. I flinch at his obvious censure, my panic doubles. I raise both my hands with my fingers spread out wide, whispering a hasty spell. Closing my fingers, I pull my fists toward me. I wait a second hoping to see them drop to the ground as magic squeezes oxygen from their lungs. Xavier, Tau, and Cole each grasp their chests, struggling to take a breath, but none of them fall to the ground as I'd intended. Inhaling deep gulps of air, they manage to stave off my charm. It only serves to infuriate them.

Reed has moved behind me to protect me from the Powers who continue to approach us with cautious strides. He pulls the spade-shaped blades from his pockets, gripping the notched handles in his fists. I close my eyes, pushing energy outward. It creates a barrier surrounding Reed and me; the Powers come up short when they bump into it, becoming unintentional mimes. A flood of relief swamps me that my spell works on them, rendering them useless in this arena. Reed, recognizing the shift in power, turns and faces the Seraphim, moving in front of me to protect me from them.

"So those rings protect you from me?" I want to scream at how unfair that is.

Tau holds his hand up, displaying a platinum band fashioned into an intricate sword over a shield, much like Xavier's ring. "They're divine; they make us impervious to all types of magic. Do you know where I found mine?"

I shake my head.

"It was outside your window at school, lodged between the wall and the rusting hull of your fire escape in Crestwood."

"How did it get there?"

"I lost it when I ascended—the day you moved in. It must have fallen off me right after you cut your hand. Cole's was harder to find. It came off him in the front yard of this house.

Someone found it and pawned it. We suspect one or more of the Murphy boys next door. It took us awhile to track it down. Then, all that was left was to find Xavier's."

I school my features to reflect Tau's blasé mask. "Can't leave that stuff laying around."

"Come inside, I'll explain it to you."

"No, thanks. We're good right here." I cross my arms in front of me.

"What I need to impart requires secrecy for *your* protection," Tau says with a neutral stare.

"I don't want to hear anything you have to say."

"You're still such a child," Tau sighs. He gives me a dismissive look before speaking to Reed in Angel.

Reed takes my hand in his again, warm fingers weaving between mine causing a current of love to swell in my heart. "I'm afraid I can't comply with your orders. My allegiance is to Evie. I swore a blood vow to her. We won't be willingly separated again."

Xavier tenses before taking a threatening step toward us. Tau puts his hand on Xavier's arm and stays him, before giving Reed a pitying look. Xavier is barely restraining himself as he rocks from foot to foot like a caged animal. "She has a hold on you. She builds like floodwater until you drown in her."

"I'm not drowning," Reed replies. "I've only just begun to live."

Xavier grows still. "You should remember that you're here for one purpose: to kill fallen, not to interfere with our mission."

Reed doesn't back down. "She's my mission. That couldn't be more plain to me if it were written in the stars."

Tau speaks again in Angel, this time to the Powers behind us. They retreat, seeming to dematerialize at the speed with which they depart, and just like that, Reed and I are alone with Cole, Tau, and Xavier.

"What did he say?" I ask Reed.

"He ordered them to await him at the chateau."

"Why?"

"I don't know. He didn't say."

Tau gives me a small smile. "If only you'd obey my orders like them."

I don't return his smile. "Hold your breath for that to happen."

"It will happen. I'm not here to be your friend. You'll need to learn to obey me."

"Any hope of that died when you wouldn't help me in Ireland. You think you can make me obey you now?" I scoff.

Tau smiles again. "Not me. Xavier. I have an army to lead. Reed will accompany me and be my right hand in that for now."

"Why would he do that?" I ask with a sinking feeling.

"Because he doesn't want me to hurt you," Tau replies, "so don't make me."

Something shifts inside of me. I start looking for weaknesses in him. "We may share some of the same DNA, you and I, but Reed is my family. Try to separate us and it'll be war with no winners. Are we clear?"

"I think I understand you," he replies in a relaxed tone. He holds up his hand—the one with the ring on it—for me to see. "These rings don't just serve to protect us...they also protect a secret."

I begin to fear what he'll say next. Reed feels it because he inches in front of me. Tau grasps the hilt of the tiny, silvery sword in his ring that pierces the shield diagonally from top to bottom. He twists the sword, turning it over within the shield. Suddenly, the sword loosens and he pulls it free from the shield base. He reinserts the sword into the shield from bottom to top, and lifting it up, he opens the surface of the ring to reveal a hidden compartment within it.

He waits for Cole and Xavier to open their rings. Cole's brown eyes watch mine as he reaches into his ring, extracting a round silver ball a little smaller than a marble. It's flat on top with a hole hollowed out. He hands the orb to Tau. Tau pulls a flat, silver square from his ring. It's a trifold of metal. When he straightens it, the hinges lock it in place, creating a single rectangle only a few inches long. Xavier removes a delicate, silver hollowed-out cylinder. He pulls the ends apart and the cylinder expands to become a small, arcing pipe. One end is cut at an angle and the other end has a lip on it.

Reed and I watch Tau deftly assemble the pieces, fitting them together. Reed whispers to me, "It's a whistle—a boatswain pipe. Cole had the buoy, Tau had the base—'the keel', and Xavier had the pipe—'the gun.'"

I exhale in relief. "A whistle."

Tau smiles. "It's a very special boatswain, Evie. It's a key."

"A key to what?" I ask.

"Sheol," Tau responds.

Reed tenses, whispering, "Evie, leave now. I'll be right behind you."

"Not without you."

"Together then." Reed's eyes lift to the sky, indicating that we should fly.

Xavier calls something out loudly in Angel. The word is familiar; I recognize it from my time at Dominion's chateau when Reed had declared himself my protector in order to fight for me. He'd said the same word then, before just about every Angel there repeated it—it means "Champion."

Reed stills before he glances at me. "Go, Evie, contact Zephyr and Russell—I'll meet you after."

"After what? I'm *not* leaving you."

"You don't want to see this," Reed murmurs. "Xavier has challenged me. I cannot refuse to fight him."

I inhale sharply, before I say, "Yes, you can. Come with me now." I tug his hand in desperation, but he doesn't move. The wind stirs his dark feathers, showing the crimson one that lies between them.

"I won't lose," Reed promises. His thumb caresses my hand, but I barely feel it.

My eyes leave Reed's green ones to shift to Xavier's imposing stare. "Xavier, don't do this."

"It's done," he says grimly. "I can't hold out forever. I've been dreaming of you—of us. I need you with me."

"This won't fix what's broken between us."

"When you remember me, he won't matter, Evie," Xavier's face darkens in its earnestness.

The sky turns gray with overcast clouds that threaten the daylight, as if Heaven disapproves. Reed lets go of my hand and I feel the loss of it more deeply than just the cold air turning my fingers to ice.

Xavier leaves the deck like a charging bull and hurls himself at Reed. Tau is next to me in less than a second; his arms engulf me. He holds me back when I would jump into the fight to pull them apart. I struggle in Tau's arms. "You have to stop this!"

"What worries you the most...that Reed will lose...or that that he'll win?"

I still. Blood runs from Reed's blade, spraying the white snow in violent patterns of red from a slash above Xavier's left eye. They stalk one another like wild things. Xavier counters with a gory slice from Reed's neck that mists the air with an iron scent. My eyes turn to Tau's; for a moment I discern sadness in them. My heart squeezes with a terrible ache as I beg, "Stop them. Please. For that little girl you once loved!"

He hides all emotion behind a blank stare. "They won't thank you for interfering."

"Please," I beg again, "do something!"

"No," he frowns and shakes his head. "This has to happen—"

I whimper in agony. "You don't know what we are to one another!"

Tau's eyes stray to the fight again. "Are you referring to Reed...or Xavier? I may have a clearer view than you do of that. This is a blessing in disguise for you. Now you don't have to choose."

"This is a curse," I retort to the sky, unable to pull free from Tau. "Let go of me so I can stop them!" Tau's arms around me only tighten.

"No."

In desperation I mutter a spell, "Hide the sun from my skin." My flesh becomes cold to the touch. Bristling out, my skin elongates to a thousand sharp icicle points that cut into Tau's arms. He flinches from the fleshy needles jabbing him while his own skin frosts over in a fine sheen of ice. It forces him to let go of me. My skin smoothes over and returns to normal.

The boatswain he had clutched in his grasp slips from his frozen fingers. Landing in the snow, the whistle gleams like a prism of refracted light. In a daze, I reach down and retrieve it. It warms in my hand. It has been waiting for me. Only me. Lifting it in my palm, its power surges into me like fuel to a fire.

Something grips me—some distant memory. Words fall from my lips unbidden, "In your hideaway, towers grow, so far away, in the dark of Sheol." I place the whistle to my lips, my cheeks puff out as I blow; the sound of a thousand tormented voices howl in my head—they're waiting for me to set them free.

Immediately, a rending tear forms in the air. It's as if a sliver of the night sky has ruptured a hole in the fabric of our world. It stands open, a doorway in front of me to a wretched cityscape of dark, twisting towers. A vile, reeking stench bleeds into the air as fumes emit from the breech between worlds. Unbalanced and disoriented from the pain of howling voices, I stumble. An invisible force drags me toward the desolate gateway ahead.

The boatswain is stripped from my fingertips by Tau. He raises it to his lips. Darkness leaps up from the ground to pounce upon me when another few short wails from the whistle roll over me. I raise my hands to my ears; certain the shrill screams have made them bleed. I stagger as the offal reek of Hell flows back, ebbing and receding, a horrifying smudge of evil upon the landscape of home. The whistle shrieks again and I'm on my knees in the snow, retching and writhing in pain from the sound of it. The gateway to Sheol takes the shape of angel wings spread wide. Another long whistle blows and I'm swept away in the sound. I curl back into its resonance of the noise and spiral down. The sky goes black for me. My eyes roll upward. I fall towards the ground, but I never feel it.

"SIMONE...*Si-moe-ohhnnn*, wo gehst du hin?" *Emil's teasing voice calls to me in Deutsche, singing my name and asking me where I'm going. The playfulness of his words scares me more than anything has ever frightened me in my life. He only sings to those he plans to torture...or play with, which really amounts to the same thing.*

Does he know? I ask myself. *Fear makes my extremities heavy.*

I glance over my shoulder at Emil. The waning light of day reflects off the crowns embossed on the brass buttons of his gray officer's uniform. Having just come from giving his orders to his men, he looks impeccable in his knee-high black boots and single-breasted tunic. The black visor of his Deutsche Luftstreitkräfte cap hides the strawberry tones of his blond hair and casts a shadow over his eyes. I know his eyes without having to see them. They're hooded, almost to the point of looking lazy, but they are anything but unobservant. The blue of them misses nothing, and of late, the only person they seem to seek out is me. They stalk me.

Some of the other German air force pilots are pulling out of Lille within a fortnight. British and American troops are pushing them out of France. By the end of 1918, the city should be liberated after years of German occupation; the tragedy is that there's not much of it left standing to free. Emil thinks he can take me with him to his next position. He's wrong. I'm leaving tonight. I just needed to find out where they planned to move. Now that I have the information, I no longer need to stay. I can be finished with this place forever—done spying on my enemies and leave with Xavier, my British contact, for Paris.

"*Schätzchen*," *he calls me "sweetheart," as if he's a lovesick fool, but we both know he's incapable of the emotion. He's without feeling, devoid of kindness or charity...or mercy. I don't stop, but cross the red brick driveway from our main residence toward the carriage house. I need to collect my bicycle and be by the river at dusk.*

"Simone, your rules should no longer apply since I have a very clear grasp of English now. Can we not speak in Deutsche? You need to work on your accent, *Schätzchen*," *He switches from playful German to amused English as he trails me. He has lost most of his accent; he sounds almost flawless. Deadly. I taught him English when he ordered me to* never again speak to him in French or German. He knows it's not my rule, but it amuses him to make it seem like it is. He makes all the rules.

When I don't stop, but continue to hurry toward the gabled doors of the stables where I've stowed my bicycle, his voice turns stern. "Simone!"

I stop immediately, my feet as lead, and turn toward him to wait. He leans on the silver, wolf-shaped handle of his black cane; his left foot drags as he moves toward me on the drive. His limp is the second thing I noticed when I had met him. The first was that he has the face of an angel.

Emil had been a pilot early on in the war, but was wounded when British forces shot up his plane. He managed to make it back to his base and salvage his aircraft, a feat for which he earned a commendation. His award means nothing to him. It only serves as a reminder to him that he'll never be allowed to fly another combat mission; a fact that causes him as much agony as the bullet still lodged in his leg. He has been working in intelligence ever since—stationed in Lille.

That's how I met Emil. He needed a nursemaid—someone who could see to his wound and help him with his daily activities. I had been hand picked by him. He had found me when German infantry soldiers forced me, and many French citizens, into the streets of Lille on an April morning. The young and able-bodied women of Lille were to be transported to German labor camps by the order of General von Graevenitz. Emil had been there and had addressed the assembled crowd as carts pulled up to take us to waiting trains.

Emil announced that he needed someone who could speak and read English, someone who could also dress wounds and help him with his rehabilitation. Being the niece of a physician, my aunt pushed me forward from the crowd, thinking she was saving me from the slavery of a work camp. She frantically announced that I had trained under her husband to assist him in his medical practice, which was almost a complete fabrication. I'd been helping her treat minor ailments in the absence of my uncle, but I was not properly trained. Had she known what would happen next, I know she wouldn't have spoken up. She didn't know then that she was delivering me to the devil.

"What kind of girl is she?" Emil had asked my aunt, giving me a cool, assessing stare, like he was discussing a calf in the marketplace.

My aunt was only too eager to tell him, "She's bright. She knows English—her father is French and her mother is British. Her mother taught her several languages—and the piano. She plays the piano like an angel."

"An angel you say?" Emil had smiled. "How is her disposition? Is she skittish?"

"Skittish?" My aunt had asked. "Why no. She's a very sensible young lady."

Emil had slowly taken his pistol from his side holster and held the barrel to my forehead. The gunmetal was cold against my skin. I didn't move as I gazed into his hooded blue eyes. My aunt beside me was aflutter, sputtering and gasping in her consternation. I barely heard her shrieks, my only thought in that moment was that I'd never see Nicolas' beautiful brown eyes again or his boyish grin.

With Emil's eyes still on me, his arm pivoted, removing the gun from my head to point it at my aunt beside me. The sound of the shot had made me flinch. My eyes strayed from his to my aunt's body in the gutter. Blood had exploded onto the faces of the women who had been behind my aunt. They were all wailing now, screaming in terror, but I could hardly hear them as the shot had deafened me. I didn't make a sound. I just stood there in shock, wondering numbly how that could happen. Emil took off his officer jacket and wrapped it gently around my shoulders as I trembled. He then pulled my wedding ring from my finger and tossed it upon the body of my aunt. "You are mine now," he had said before he led me away to his waiting car.

"Is a ghost whispering in your ear?" Emil asks me now. He touches my cheek gently. "You've gone quite pale."

"I was just on my way to Olympia to see if they have any more of the jam you like. We've run completely out, and I thought you might want it for the journey," I lie.

He has a faraway look. "You're just as you were on the morning I found you—so pale—so beautiful. Has it really been more than two years ago?"

"Almost two and a half," I murmur.

"The needle in the hay, that's what you were, Simone, and I found you.'"

"I hardly remember that day," I lie. It's etched in my brain. I have nightmares of it often.

Emil smiles at me now in admiration as he had then. "Nothing breaks your heart. You're bulletproof. You're like me—we both keep so many secrets."

"If I don't go now, it will be closed."

My excuse to meet Xavier slips away from me the moment I see his scowl. "I don't want your French jam. It will taste like the bitterest defeat now. I'll never eat it again." He watches me for a moment. His thumb comes up to trace my lips. I drop my chin. He lifts the silver wolf head of his cane beneath my chin, raising it so that he can see my eyes. "Do you know what I want?" he asks.

"No."

"I'd like a kiss."

I show no emotion as I lift my lips to his cheek and press them lightly against his skin. As I pull away, my eyes meet his."

"You belong to me, Simone. You know that, don't you?"

"Yes."

He touches the lace of my collar, admiring the fine detail of the day dress he chose for me. "Good. Come, I want to hear you play while the staff packs." He takes my hand and leads me back toward the grandeur of the main house. I don't resist. Entering through the kitchen, I nearly stumble to a halt as I see the blood-spattered wall and lifeless body of Tomas, the head chef, near the cast iron stove. Emil's hand gestures toward the blood pooling on the floor. "Tomas cannot come with us to our next location. I will miss him; I enjoyed his soufflé."

I avert my eyes at once. Death is a regular occurrence here. I had thought Tomas had a better chance than most of surviving the German occupation. I was wrong.

Emil leads me to the music room. He opens the enormous doors, spreads them wide, and allows me to enter before him. The room is arranged with opulent furniture: centuries old carved mahogany chairs, gold silk-covered sofas, and a light-blue, silk tufted settee among others. Most of the artwork that had adorned this space has been removed, shipped to the Fatherland to be hoarded by relatives of the officers who reside here. Large, discolored patches of plaster remain as a testament to where they had been.

We cross the immaculate blue and gold carpet to the black-stained bench placed in front of the piano of the same hue. All of the silver frames near the piano have images of the family who had once lived here. I don't know what happened to them, but they're richer by far for not having to remain.

As I settle on the bench, I lift my eyes to Emil's blue ones. The strawberry-blond highlights in his hair shine in the waning sun from the window as he doffs his officer's cap. "What would you like to hear?" I ask.

"Play Johann Pachelbel's 'Canon in D,'" Emil smiles. He drops his cap on the chair near us.

I remove my white gloves and take my hat from my hair, placing the gloves inside of it. Emil takes them from me and puts them on the chair beside his. As I rest my fingertips on the smooth ivory keys, gunshots explode from the floors above. My eyes rise to look at the ceiling, hearing the violent, high-pitched screams of women's voices and the heavy pounding of running feet. "It's just a bit of housekeeping, Simone. The staff cannot come with us; we have to be sure they won't see something that they shouldn't. I've given orders that they be...retired." His hand rests heavily on my shoulder.

"You'll kill them all?" I choke on the words.

"All but you, Simone. I have spared you." He caresses my cheek before he urges, "Now play for me." I hesitate for a moment, trying to think of a way to convince him to spare the lives of the staff. Emil leans close to my ear and growls, "Play!"

The first staggering notes are hardly discernable above the chaos and clamor. The pistol reports shatter the very air. Agnes, one of the chambermaids, pleads for her life, but her terrified cry is cut short. I concentrate on the keys so that my fingers won't shake and I fade away into the music. I hide in the notes, momentarily free from the terror of the Lille chateau. It's only when the song ends that I begin to pray.

I cannot stay here a moment longer...I can't stay...Xavier, please come, Xavier, please...

Emil whispers in my ear, "Again, Simone."

CHAPTER 6
Yer Ruler

The pressure of Emil's hand on my shoulder lifts. I continue to play the piano, frightened that if I stop he'll change his mind and kill me, too.

"Dat's lovely, mo chroí," Brennus' deep voice murmurs from just over my shoulder.

My hands fall on the ivory keys, making a horrible, discordant sound. "Brennus," I rasp. I turn on the bench and find him behind me, a dark blessing in this place. My arms go around his waist as I clutch him. The soft, white fabric of his dress shirt soothes me. One of his arms pulls me tighter to him as he strokes my hair with the other.

"Whah is it? Whah has happened?"

"He has killed them all!" I sob. "All of them!"

"Who has killed who?"

"Emil. He gave orders to kill the staff!" I lift my eyes to Brennus' phosphorous green ones.

"Shh...don't ye cry." Brennus' thumb wipes a tear way as it slides down my cheek. "Dis Emil, is he here now?"

"He's..." I glance around the room, but it's empty. "He was here..."

Brennus scoops me up in his arms and holds me to him. My hands go around the back of his neck and brush up against his velvet-soft black wings. He takes me to a gold silk-covered sofa. Magically retracting his massive wings, he sits down on the cushions with me on his lap.

Brennus pulls the pins out of my hair one by one. It spills down my back with each lock he frees. "Emil might come back, Brennus." My eyes dart to at the double doors still wide open. Brennus sees my fear and lifts his hand in that direction. The doors slam closed. "Better?" His eyebrow lifts.

I raise my hand and the furniture near the door slides across the floor and piles in front of it. I exhale and nod.

"Dat's da way I came in, mo chroí. Dere is nuting out dere but an empty house and empty streets. I tink it's jus da two o' us here now. And whah are ye afraid of?" he asks as he wipes the rest of my tears with his immaculate sleeve. "Ye're one of da most powerful craiturs in existence. I tought ye had learned dat by now."

"It wasn't like this before you came in. I wasn't me—I couldn't do magic—I didn't even know magic existed! It was like I was living a memory...I mean, I was me...but I wasn't really me."

"Ye were na really ye?"

I shake my head. "No, I was her."

"Eh?"

"Simone. I was Simone. She was me and I was her, but I'm just me now."

"So now ye're Genevieve?"

"Yes."

"Good. Ye're da one I like," he smiles, still playing with my hair. He looks around. "So. Dis is a crap place ye're livin' in. From da outside, dere appears ta be a war going on...empty trenches, missing bridges, debris wherever I looked."

"Big war." I nod.

"Got caught in da middle of dat, had ye?" he asks. "By da look of tings, dis may be Europe."

"It's Lille, France."

"Ahh. 'Tis." He nods in understanding. "Dis Simone was French?"

"Oui,"

"Tings go bad for her?"

"I think so. You showed up before I got to the end. I didn't have to find out what Emil had planned for me."

"'Tis a pity he could na stay. I'd have liked to have met him."

I shiver. "Why are you being so nice to me?" Now that my intense fear of Emil is waning to an acceptable level, the very real threat of Brennus being here takes over.

"'Cuz I love ye. I'll banjax yer enemies. I swear it."

"I can't trust you. You see everyone I love as a threat to me."

"True, because dey are. I've gotten reports from yer house, mo chroí. Someting happened dere. Ye want ta tell me whah 'twas? Da fellas say dere were hordes of demons at yer door—in da daylight no less! Did ye take care of dem?"

"No. Something else did."

"Someting? Or Someone?"

"Something's stalking me, Brenn." I whisper.

"Powerful?" he asks and I nod.

"Powerful enough to suck all the energy from me and use it against us."

He growls in anger. "Genevieve! Ye need ta work on yer defensive spells! Ye should be wi' me! I'll teach ye how ta take power instead of give it!"

I scramble off his lap. "I'm with you right now!"

"Only because I came looking for ye!" He rises from the sofa as well, his hands in fists at his side. "Someting feels wrong about dis place. It's almost as if ye're na sleeping. 'Tis too real: I can smell da burnt food in da kitchen. Dis place lacks da haziness of da divine nightmare we shared jus dis morning."

I pace in an attempt to stave off my growing panic. He's right. It's absolutely too real here.

"I do na have ta try ta keep ye here. Ye canna leave, can ye?" he asks in an accusatory tone. "Whah's wrong? Why can ye na leave?"

"I'm not sleeping, Brennus. I...I don't know. I may be unconscious. As soon as I wake up, I'll be able to leave...I think." I wring my hands as I glance at his hostile face.

Brennus takes a deep breath. His voice has the illusion of calm as he asks, "Where are ye now? I will send da fellas to collect ye."

"No."

"Whah? No? De ye jus say no ta me?"

"That's right. I said no. You're not allowed to come get me."

His fangs engage with a click. "Genevieve..."

"And put your fangs away! I've had it with being bullied!" I rub my forehead as it begins to ache.

Brennus retracts his fangs. His voice holds a note of concern. "Why are ye unconscious?"

"You want to help me Brennus? Teach me some of your defensive spells."

He takes a step toward me and I straighten in uncertainty. He pauses, seeing my reaction. "May I approach ye?" he asks.

"Why?"

"Humor me."

I incline my head and he comes to me and takes my hand in his. With his other hand he sweeps his arm wide. Every piece of furniture in the middle of the room moves against the far wall.

"What are you doing?" I ask with a cynical raise of my brow.

"I'm going ta teach ye how ta take someone's energy. Before I can do dat, ye first have ta learn ta accept someone else's energy—"

"I know how to do that."

"Do ye?" he asks. "From whah I've seen, ye never accept energy as yer own. Ye pass it on—ye get rid of it as fast as ye can. Ye never hold on ta it. Ye never claim it as yer due for being a powerful craitur."

"My due?" I ask skeptically.

"Yer due." He takes me in his arms then.

"What are you doing?" I squeak as I try to pull away from him.

"I'm getting ye used ta accepting energy from someone else."

I try to squirm out of his arms. "Isn't there another way?"

"Do ye want me help or na?" Brennus asks.

I stop squirming. "Yes."

"Foin," he nods. "Dis may be easier for ye if we move. Ye're fidgety."

"I'm uncomfortable. This is awkward."

He glances around the room and his eyes rest on an elegant wooden cabinet in the corner. A wicked smile plays upon his lips as he waves his hand at it. The lid opens. It's a Victrola. The crank on the side of the contraption moves on its own. The arm of the record player magically drops to the turntable. The music begins. The first few notes have Brennus laughing like he's heard the funniest joke of his life.

"What?" I ask, unable to keep my smile from showing as he grins at me.

"'Tis 'L'Amour Est un Oiseau Rebelle'—Habanera...'Tis da aria from Carmen...da opera..." I shake my head in confusion, unfamiliar with the song.

As it plays, I listen to a woman sing. "L'amour est un oiseau rebelle...Love is a rebellious bird?" I translate, seeing that the joke is on me.

His eyes glow with green fire. "Indeed, she is."

"Did you see this opera when it opened?" I ask, taking a jab at his age.

He ignores it. "I'll take ye ta see it. Ye'll love it." He holds me close in his arms. We begin to dance. One of his hands travels up my side, infusing me with the raw power of his energy as it goes. I gasp as the current flows under my skin. I bite down on my lip as pleasure-pain makes me breathe deep.

Brennus murmurs in my ear, "Bite down hard, it feels better."

He's right. I clench my teeth. He guides me around the room; we skip ahead at supernatural speed for a few moments. His energy spreads through me, first from my heart, through the roadmap of my veins, to places I never wanted Brennus to go. I gasp as my body involuntarily curls toward him like a flower to the sun, for the pleasure of it. He holds me close to him. His nose grazes the length of my neck. He breathes me in. I feel the roar and rush of my heartbeat. I'm his toy; his energy streams into me. He winds the invisible key in my back and the euphoria ratchets and coils inside of me: tick...tick...tick...

We slow to a human pace. He bends me in a dip; my back arches. I feel the heat of him. His hand holds my back while the other one traces over my side. I respond to his light touch; my skin becomes a magnet drawn to his. He straightens me again with a snap, pulling me close. His fingertips travel from the side of my breast to my back. Another wicked surge of energy flows from him into me. Pain. Pleasure. Bliss. My jaw unclenches as my lips part. I make a small, breathy sound as we dance.

Brennus responds with something close to a growl. "Ye're killing me, mo chroí," he murmurs. His hand moves down my back infusing me with a golden glow of power. My wings punch violently from me, tearing a hole in my day dress. My wings spread wide, like a red stain beyond my pale skin. I'm dancing now for the thrill of it. I follow his lead.

Iniquity

As the song comes to an end, Brennus kisses my throat. He whispers in my ear, "When ye get back, come find me, mo chroí. I've healed ye...now wake up and banjax whoever banished ye here..."

CHAPTER 7
Guess Who Died

My eyes fly open and I sit up, finding myself in a bed. Energy is overpowering me and it's all I can do to keep from bursting into flames. My hands and arms are glowing golden with power and I'm unaware of where I am until Xavier says my name.

I glance at the foot of my bed and realize I'm in my room in my old house. Xavier rises from the upholstered chair by the window with a vigilant look in his eyes.

I groan in pain, feeling like an overstuffed plush animal, the taut seams of which might tear open at any moment. Hoping not to be disemboweled by the energy inside me, I say urgently, "Open the window!"

Xavier stares at me like I've grown fangs. "What? Evie, how are y—"

"Now!" I cry, "Open it now!"

At supernatural speed, he moves from his chair and slides open the sash. As soon as he steps away from it, I let go of some of the energy that Brennus infused in me. It shines out of my pores in a concentrated, golden beam, hitting the snow-covered tree in the backyard. The snow melts instantly; the tree bursts into flames and is reduced to a pile of ash around a stump within seconds.

Now that I can control the remaining energy pulsing inside me, I turn my attention to Xavier. His hand is bare. "You're not wearing your ring," I observe.

He reaches for the pocket of his dark blue jeans that are slung low on his hips. I don't give him a chance to slip his ring on. Using magic, I lift him off his feet and pin him to the ceiling of my room.

"Where's Reed?" I demand. I can't feel butterflies inside me. He isn't near. "Did you hurt him?" My stomach aches at the thought that Xavier might have killed him.

"What would you do if I did?" There's sadness in his eyes.

It feels like he used his nails to scratch my heart. "Did you?" I croak.

Another surge of magical energy from me presses him harder into the plaster. He pants in anger, "He's alive—he's with your father." Xavier tries to move his arms, but they're pinned to the ceiling.

Relief makes me feel weak. "And where's that," I probe.

He stubbornly closes his mouth. I retract the energy holding him up and let him drop a couple of feet before I thrust him back toward the ceiling again with it. The impact causes cracks to snake out in the plaster as it crumbles against the onslaught. Xavier grits his teeth.

"Where are they?" I repeat. He doesn't say a word so I drop him again, farther this time, and then brutally slam him back to the ceiling. He hits it hard and scowls in pain. I have to force my next question from my lips. "Did you defeat him?"

Xavier's smile is one of bitterness. "We stopped fighting when you fell. We both believed the whistle had killed you."

I close my eyes and thank God before I manage to say, "You look like you're surprised by what happened."

He pauses and something enters his eyes. Fear. But it's only there for a moment before it disappears. "It's supposed to be a key, Evie, not a weapon. You have no idea what you looked like, do you? When I saw you on the ground, I expected to see your soul rise from you at any moment. You were bleeding from your eyes and your ears—I could hear your lungs filling—you were drowning in blood internally."

"I'm fine," I say to the morbid question I see in his eyes.

"How are you fine? I thought you were dying."

Brennus' last few words resonate within me: *I've healed ye...now wake up and banjax whoever banished ye here...*

I give him a ghost of a smile. "You don't know everything about me. Learn my secrets if you want to stay ahead of me."

That makes him angry. "You shouldn't have opened the doorway to Sheol! It could've sucked you in."

"I didn't know what it was."

"Your father told you it was a key!"

"He failed to mention it would possess me the moment I touched it!" I retort.

"None of us knew you'd react to it as you did. Heaven has been keeping secrets from us all!"

"Welcome to my world, Xavier."

"You knew the tone to use to open the doorway! Tau said you whispered something just before you used the key."

I rub my forehead anxiously. "I...when I picked it up...I knew the way to enter. I wanted to go, but it made me sick at the same time—but I knew I had to go. They need me."

"Who needs you?"

I shake my head. "I don't know."

"Do you remember what you said?"

I think for a second. "In your hideaway, towers grow, so far away, in the dark of Sheol..." I groan, and look around like I've lost something. "There's more...it's on the tip of my tongue...arrrghhh," I growl in frustration.

"Using the key to close the door almost killed you. It's like you were meant to go to Sheol and the fact that you remained here almost destroyed you."

"Why would I need a key anyway? Don't angels go in and out of Sheol all the time?"

He looks at me like I'm completely naïve. "There are gateways between this world and Sheol but they're all known to us. We guard them from this side and Sheol guards them from the other side. Sometimes there are tears in the fabric between your world in which demons and Fallen slip through. But mostly, there's balance—small doors that close and don't open again for long periods of time. The boatswain creates a gateway where none existed. You could theoretically control the flow of beings in and out of Sheol with it."

"What does that mean?"

"It means if you were to open the gateway big enough, you could march an army through it."

I shiver as all the hair on my body stands on end because he's speaking the truth. "Where's Reed?" Pieces of the ceiling fall to the bedroom floor as I force Xavier harder against it in panic. "I need him." He's the only person that can drive away the fear that threatens to overwhelm me.

The set of Xavier's jaw indicates that he's done talking.

"You don't like that question? Here's a different one: Where were you?" I ask, choking on betrayal.

His expression loses some of its defiance. "When?" he asks.

"When I was Simone and being tortured by Emil." I hiss. "You made me go back to him in Lille. You wouldn't let me leave Emil until I found out his next position, would you? Even with everything you knew about him! You knew he was a complete monster! You knew what he was doing to me! The brutality I suffered at his hands!"

A smile forms on Xavier's lips "You remember me—you remember us?" His elation is eclipsing his pain.

"I remember being tortured by Emil and abandoned by you! It's a theme with you!"

His smile is gone. "I never abandoned you! I've never walked away from you!"

"You let him have me," I whisper, wretched with the knowledge of what he allowed to happen to me.

"It was our purpose, Evie! It's what we do. We subvert evil. I couldn't touch him in that lifetime—I'm an angel and he was human. It had to be you, human verses human. It's how things are done. You knew going into that lifetime what could happen to you. What ALWAYS happens!"

"And what always happens, Xavier?"

"There is always a consequence—a price to pay! You die at the end. Period. Every time. You were human and that's how it always ends."

"Simone didn't know that though, did she?" I ask. "She had no idea she was there to take one for the team. She thought you were her savior—her *human* British soldier who'd rescue her from the sociopath who wanted to destroy her—to take her apart piece by piece—inch by inch. You abandoned her to Emil—to that evil bastard!"

"You used to understand that once you were sent to Earth to live a life, I couldn't reveal who or what I really am to you. This is the ONLY lifetime in which that no longer applies. This was going to be the first time I could reveal who I am to you while on Earth because you're angelic now, too," he explains. "But to answer your question: NO! My plan was to extract Simone before he killed you. I never meant to leave you there with Emil. Our plan went wrong. Evil won that time. Some missions end that way, Evie. You used to know that!"

I feel so hurt by him that I'm nearly overwhelmed by it. "I must've forgotten, Xavier, but you know what? Screw your missions! I don't care about your missions! This is about you and me."

"You're exactly right! It *is* about you and me. It's about you *being* with me. And it has everything to do with this assignment and Emil!" I release Xavier from the magic that has him pinned to the ceiling. He falls toward the floor, but his wings unfurl from his back, shredding off his shirt; they beat hard, saving him from crashing into the floor. He hovers for a moment in the air before touching down at the foot of my bed.

"Emil is back, isn't he?" I ask, as fear starts to choke me.

"He was just at the house in Crestwood," he affirms. "You didn't recognize him?"

"His particular brand of darkness was familiar," I admit, "but I didn't know who Emil was until Tau blew that whistle and sent me into my memory."

"You scared me when you were unconscious. I thought you were never going to wake up," he says, inching closer, touching the footboard of my bed. He looks so dangerous without his shirt on to hide the sinew and power beneath his skin.

"The last whistle blow—the one that closed the door to Sheol—it made me go back—I was Simone again. I was living her memories."

"You had a dream?"

"No. I was her—I was there—in Simone's body."

"What did you see?"

I feel bleak. "I saw how Emil was with me—obsessed, but not with love—with hate."

"He saw his opposite in you and pretended that you were the same—that he was like you. He always tried so hard to break you—to terrify you, but you'd been through it all before—pain, slaughter, death—you have lifetimes of experience with it."

"What happened to her? To me?" I amend. "How did Simone die?"

Xavier tenses. "I don't know. I was hoping you could tell me," he says with an urgency that startles me.

"Why don't you know?" I ask in confusion.

"I was called back at almost the same moment that Simone died. When I arrived in Paradise, you wouldn't tell me what happened between you and Emil in the last hours of your life and I couldn't remember much of that last day there."

"Why not?"

"Something went more wrong than just you dying—it was like you were protecting something—a secret. I asked you to tell me—begged you. You wouldn't say—no, it was more like you *couldn't* say. You were called then—soon after."

"Called?" I ask.

He smiles again and my heart beats faster. I want to be indifferent to him, but I'm not. There's so much between us; I can sense it, the weight of it. It's in every look, every nuance of his expressions. I know them well—bone deep, I know them. This is the smile he uses when he's hurt and doesn't want me to know. I don't know how I know that, I just do. "You were called for another assignment and you went to discuss it alone."

"My going alone, is that unusual?" I probe.

"I always go with you," he replies. "Russell is often there as well, but I'm always by your side."

"As my guardian angel?"

"Yes—as your partner for missions, but this time when you met, I wasn't invited to the discussion."

"I must have told you what it was about—"

"You said that this was it for you—this was going to be your final mission. You wanted to be with me forever. Just me," he explains, but then he frowns.

I read his look. "You didn't believe me—"

He turns away from me. "Of course I believed you. You loved me as much as I loved you."

"But there was something more," I assess.

"You had a look," he admits, his shoulders caving in a little.

"What look?"

"The sacrifice-your-soul look," he replies. "I know it well. I've seen you wear it often."

"What reason would I have to sacrifice my soul?" I wonder aloud. "Revenge? Emil was sadistic. Do you think I'd come back for revenge?"

He shakes is head. "You're not vengeful, you're forgiving. Can you think of another reason?" he asks me, probing my memory.

"I don't know," I mutter. I put my hands to my temples, trying to see inside my mind for the answer that eludes me.

"Emil is endowed with power like I've never seen until you—until now. Why was he granted such power? What happened between you and Emil in those last hours that would entitle him to acquire so much power?"

"I don't understand," I murmur. "Are you saying I did something wrong on my last mission?"

His jaw eases for a moment as he scans my eyes. He shakes his head and says quietly, "No, there's nothing you could've done to have given the Fallen the ability to bestow such power on him. It couldn't have been you—"

I bound out of my bed and pace the room in agitation. "Then

what could've gone wrong?"

"I don't know," he admits, equally frustrated. "What I do know is it's Emil's soul who's back. He has deadly powers, and we have to make him cease to be. Annihilate his soul so that it can never return."

"Is that possible?"

"Not without your help. I thought that I could do it alone, but after what he showed us today, I'll need you. You were remade for just this purpose. A special killer."

"If I'm a killer, why was I given a conscience?"

His eyes darken with a grim shadow. "So you won't fail."

I feel as if he's burying me alive. "I need to talk to Reed." Anguish and fear at the discovery that I'm here to kill Emil is doing bad things to me.

Xavier is by my side, pulling me into his arms. "Breathe," he murmurs in my ear as he rubs my back. "You can do this. You've trained for it in every one of your past lifetimes."

"I'm terrified of Emil! He's a freaking monster!"

"You never back down from monsters, Evie. Never."

In a daze, I rest my cheek against his sculpted chest. "Emil is the same as me, isn't he? A half-breed, right?"

"Yes, but I don't know what his range of abilities are...however, I didn't like what I saw a few hours ago."

"He can annihilate my soul, too, can't he? I could cease to be."

"That won't happen. I won't let it," Xavier promises.

I lift my cheek from him, looking up into his eyes. "How will you stop it? Emil has been waiting for me for a long time now, hasn't he? He knew I was coming back. It was preordained."

Xavier gives me a solemn nod. "I don't know how much he knows. We began by hiding you here," Xavier looks around my bedroom, "but some scouts found us once you became a teenager. Things got interesting after that."

"How come I never knew? How come no one trusted me enough to tell me?"

"Your father didn't want you burdened with it until you began your evolution into angel. He just wanted you safe. That's all. I was forbidden to tell you."

I step out of his arms. "You should've told me anyway! Emil has probably known who he is since he was reborn. *His* freaking parents probably told him everything from the beginning!"

"That doesn't give him the advantage. Your strength lies in your ability to love."

"You make me sound like a saint, which is a bad thing, because what I know from history is that they all die horribly."

"Not this time. I won't allow it. We need to find out how Simone died, Evie."

"Why?"

"Because therein lies the connection. You were specifically called upon—no one consulted me—even when I was a part of the last mission, too."

"Maybe Sheol requested my soul or something," I say with sarcasm. I see his eyes narrow. "What? You think they specifically named me for some reason?"

"You asked if you thought you were seeking revenge. Maybe it's not you who wants revenge."

"Emil wants another crack at me—wants to crush me?" I straighten my slouched shoulders as I look into his eyes, cobalt blue and bottle green. "What do I get for accepting this mission? Is this the price of my freedom? Annihilate Emil's soul, and then it's done? Do I get to walk away from Divine service? If I had to guess, that's what I was after. I'm so tired, Xavier. Deep-down-to-my-soul weary. I can see me risking everything to put an end to my eternity of servitude."

"You're a fighter; it's woven in every fiber of your being." Xavier's soft tone does something to me. I want to hide beneath it, wrap myself in it and rest.

"Maybe I'm a fighter because that's what you've made me—lifetimes of fighting for you. Was that the price we paid for being together? Did we have to agree to mission after mission just to see one another?" It's in his eyes. I'm right. I put both my hands to my face and cover my weary eyes for a moment. When I pull them away, I ask, "Did it get to be too much for me? Was the price too high to pay? Maybe I can't remember us because I wanted it that way. Did I decide to cut my heart out rather than to have it die slowly?" I feel like sobbing.

"No. You'd always fight for us," Xavier replies without a hint of doubt. "The answer lies in Simone—in her memories."

"You want me to go back there to him! Back to Lille with Emil!" I begin to pace again, biting my thumbnail anxiously.

"I want you to find out what happened," Xavier says in an even tone.

I point my finger at him. "No. You're asking me to relive what happened!"

"If it means defeating Emil in this lifetime then, yes, that's what I'm asking. I need to know the debt owed to iniquity."

"The debt to iniquity—to wickedness?" I murmur aloud.

"Emil's power is a concession—that's plain to me. I want to know why."

TUNK, TUNK, TUNK, loud creaking noises from the foundation of the house interrupts Xavier just as a wave of power surges into the room. A screech, the whine of straining pipes, echoes within the plaster walls. Magic surges heavy in the air; it saturates me in a deluge of fear. I draw some energy into me so that I can use it, but the feel of it repulses me. It's like the sweaty, overheated embrace from someone you hate. I expel it immediately. My flesh wants to crawl off me.

Xavier holds out his hand to me. "It's Emil. Let's go. I have a portal to your father."

I feel Emil everywhere in the air, a thorn in my side in a very literal way. I groan and grasp my side below my ribs as if I've been stabbed—or hooked. An invisible force yanks me forward. My feet slide across the floor, the tips of my toes curl under as I'm dragged. Xavier latches onto my waist from behind and tries to hold me back, but he lets go of me when it becomes apparent he'll snap me in two if he doesn't. I stop only when I'm pressed to the half-open window.

A lone figure is in the yard below. Strawberry-blond hair lifts in wisps in the crisp wind. His blue eyes engage mine, and he smiles a wicked grin. A heavy, gray coat that reminds me of the officer's dress uniform he owned a century ago covers his broad shoulders. Beneath his collar a dark, soft scarf is tied in a meticulously elegant knot; it brushes against his smooth cheek. The lines of matte buttons on either side of the wool coat are impossibly straight.

Emil smiles, his lazy eyes hood with pleasure. I exhale in a rush. He could be his own great, great grandson; he looks so much like his old self. Swiftly, he elevates off the frozen ground, not by the use of wings, but by an invisible force of power that I've only ever seen Brennus accomplish—or clones. It takes him just a moment to be inches from me, studying me like a scientist studies a germ under a microscope.

"Simone," he murmurs. The muffled resonance of his voice filters through the glass. The tone is so familiar. He causes a shiver of revulsion to run down my spine.

"Emil," I snarl, my lips taking the shape of hatred, "I'm not your Simone anymore!" I don't see anything but him, and as for feeling, there's nothing inside of me but pure, unmitigated rage. Punching my hand through the glass that separates us, I clutch a broken shard of it in my fist. Thrusting it forward, I use it to stab him in the neck.

CHAPTER 8
Divenire

A gush of red spurts from Emil's throat as the glass in my hand tears his flesh away. It feels like a knife cutting through watermelon rind as I drive it upward into his gaping mouth. Blood oozes from him. His eyes widen in shock, causing a grim smile to stretch my lips. It only lasts an instant before I'm ripped through the windowpane by Emil's power. Twinkling, broken pieces of glass shred my cheeks like razorblades.

I tumble through the air under Emil's power, smashing into a tree in the yard. Branches and bark cut into me before the trunk gives way and topples over. Instead of falling with it, Emil reels me back towards him as if I'm a fish caught on an invisible hook. Levitating in the air, he forces me to the space above the street. Opening his mouth wide, he pries the shard of glass out from beneath his tongue and tosses it aside. Spitting blood, he snarls and casts his arm back, the invisible hook inside me cuts deeper and I cry out in pain.

My wings spiral and beat in an attempt to break free of his magic. His arm casts again and I lurch to the side, slamming into an oak tree. The trunk splinters, sheering in half as wood and snow explode into the air. Teetering, the top of the tree falls over, smashing the parked car beneath it. The car's alarm goes off, shrill and deafening. Hovering above it, my hands go to my head, trying to hold it so that I'll somehow stop seeing double. Emil takes exception to the noise from the alarm. He magically lifts the car up off the street and tosses it into the Sansbury's' living room. The noise abruptly ends as the car catches fire and explodes, blowing the roof off their house.

That's when I notice the rooftops lining the street. They're covered with angels—*fallen angels*. Dark wings spread wide as every hierarchal type of fallen angel watches me struggle to break free from Emil. The door of my house opens. Divine angels pour into the yard with their wings outstretched in the golden glow of a waning sun. Xavier bursts forth from the window from which I was dragged. All the Fallen take flight, attacking him like vultures do a corpse. The divine Powers are quick to move into the fray, skewering Fallen to protect their Seraphim commander.

My heart feels like it's about to separate from my chest. I raise my hand throwing a white-hot beam of light at the Fallen who are nearest to Xavier. Orange flames and smoke curl the white feathers of the archangel on Xavier's back, turning them black. He cries out in agony as his flesh melts from him. My magical light lasers through the hatchet-wielding fallen Power about to cleave Xavier in two.

I lose my focus on them when Emil cracks an invisible whip of magic and embeds a second searing hook into my other side. I scream in pain, before gritting my teeth and focusing on the evil bastard once more. My hand wraps around his invisible energy as I try to yank it from me without success.

Emil shakes his head, acting as if he's concerned about me as I writhe in pain. "Now look what you've made me do. We've made a mess and I only wanted to reunite with you. I've missed you, Simone," he says with red spittle coming from his mouth. "I've missed hurting you. You shouldn't have run from me. You know how I hate to have to come and find you."

"Inconvenient?" I ask with a pant of pain, hoping the look in my eyes kills him. "How's this?" I growl. Pulling energy to me, I focus it all into a pulse of light that flows out of my hand. Intending to fry him with it, he merely lifts his palm, deflecting the intense heat of my magic, redirecting it into the Martindale's' two-story colonial. The house explodes into flames, melting a gaping hole in the aluminum siding.

"Simone, did you just try to murder me?" Emil smirks. "And here I thought you'd be happy to see me."

"You're sick."

"I remember the time when you couldn't take a breath without my permission."

"You enjoyed that."

"I enjoyed you."

I lower my head and beat my wings harder, no longer fighting his pull on me, but using his magical force to propel me right to him. I use my legs to coil around his waist. Driving my arm forward, blood spatters my face as I punch a hole through his chest and pull out his still-pumping heart. "Well then, how do you like me now?" I ask as his mouth opens in shock. His evil, hooded eyes meet mine as his body crumples. I unwind my legs from him and let his body fall to the street below with a sickening thud.

The throbbing pain in my abdomen eases as I pant, my wings beating to keep me in the air. Wildly, I look around at the street below. Mr. Kendrick, the retired postal worker who organizes our annual block parties, is on his front porch, staring at me with a look of horror on his face.

I hold up my hands to him, inadvertently displaying the waning heart in my fist. As blood drips from my wrist and elbow, I try to reassure him. "It's okay, Mr. Kendrick." Frozen for a moment, he just stares at me. The front of his pants darken as he wets himself. "I won't hurt you," I say, but I only scare him more. He stumbles back with a lurch, bumping into the yellow wood siding of his house before he pivots to his door. He rattles the black handle, his shaking hand like a club. When he manages to open it, he backs inside before slamming the door shut.

Numbly, I look down at Emil's body in the street. As I drop his dead heart on the ground, I look for signs of life in him, but he's still. A thousand different emotions assail me; the most prevalent among them are hope that he's dead and fear that he's not. All around me, the war between the angels has taken to the street.

They're tearing each other apart, hundreds of them, staining the snow red with their need to destroy one another.

Slowing the beat of my wings so that I land on the pavement, I stay well back from Emil's body. I glance over my shoulder, looking for Xavier; he's taking apart a fallen Seraph with his bare hands. The other divine angels are wreaking havoc on their enemies, too. I move to help Xavier, but I hesitate as Emil's corpse begins to change. His coat alters from a gray military trench to a short, black leather jacket. Emil's features shift as well. His hair turns from strawberry-blond to black, his skin tone darkens, his small, straight nose grows larger and becomes aquiline. Dark hair sprouts from his chin as his lips widen and lose their perfect symmetry.

My bloody hand comes up to cover my mouth as I rush closer to him. Crouching near, I pick up his cold, dead hand, and stare at the face of Owen Matthews—my date to the Delt formal in what feels like a lifetime ago. Tears of horror come to my eyes. His throat has been ripped open where I had stabbed Emil.

Mr. Kendrick's front door opens as Emil emerges with his hands shoved in the pockets of his gray trench coat. He strolls toward me with a sanguine smile on his lips. Chaos swirls around him as angels pounce on one another, slashing and cutting. Dappled brown feathers are being shred from a divine Power angel as a fallen archangel's fists tug on them while they wrestle in the snow. Emil ignores everyone, walking around flailing forms before stopping next to me. I rise to face him.

With a nod toward Owen, Emil assesses, "Your boyfriend. You killed him."

"Owen was never my boyfriend! He was just a random blind date!" I gnash my teeth, realizing what Emil says is true. I killed him. I tore Owen's heart out with my bare hand. Taking a deep breath, I smell the scent of urine on Emil. I realize what's happening. "You possessed him!" I accuse. "Mr. Kendrick—you're in his body—somehow. It's all an illusion."

Emil's smile is blasé. "They're so willing to let me in, Simone. They're weak," he replies with a casual shrug as he looks at

Owen. "All I had to do was promise your boyfriend here that I wouldn't hurt him if he let me in. It was really that simple. Humans are so willing to cooperate with us." He looks at me then. "They so rarely say no."

"And if they did say no, you'd kill them."

He shakes his head. "Not true. If they say no, then the laws of Paradise protect them. It's not like it was for you in Lille. When we reunited there during the war, I would've killed you had you defied me, just like I'd killed your aunt. You and I were both humans in that lifetime. Now, I can't touch a human unless they allow it." His head dips conspiratorially towards mine. "Fear is the best weapon. You see? They, the humans, have to agree before I can possess them, but it's not hard to convince them. Most people are willing to do anything out of fear—agree to anything—hurt someone else just to save themselves. The irony is that it is what truly damns them."

My mind reels. "Freddie—Alfred—he was an angel—a reaper—he killed my uncle—my *human* uncle!"

"Did he?" he asks with a smile. "That's not how I heard it. I heard that he convinced another human to slaughter your uncle while he watched. Otherwise, he'd have had to pay the consequences for his actions from both Sheol and Paradise. They'd never let him live after that. We just can't openly kill humans. It's not how this is done. It's a game of souls, Simone. Sheol doesn't like it when our angels give Paradise an uncontested soul, especially one that we've been after for several lifetimes. Given the right set of circumstances, your uncle could've been ours."

"He'd never be yours!" I retort, tasting bile.

"Everyone has a price, Simone. Everyone. Your uncle included. What's more, he could've been *your* price, wouldn't you agree?" Emil studies me. "I know you. You'd have done anything to save him...*anything.*"

What he says scares me, not because he's wrong, but because he's right. "I'm going to kill you," I promise.

Emil laughs with delight. "How?" he asks. "You're so much

weaker than me—always have been and still so very guileless. I do admire your iron resolve, however. It keeps me entertained in every lifetime I spend with you."

My eyes widen is surprise.

"What—" he smiles with delight, "you didn't know we've been together before? You don't remember us, do you? You don't remember me!"

"It was in Lille—"

His laughter causes me to fall silent. "Oh, you really *are* at a disadvantage, aren't you? Sheol must have negotiated it *all* from you! Everything! So...you remember nothing before Lille?" he asks me. He tries to tuck a piece of my hair behind my ear, but I evade his hand, stepping farther from him. "You've truly come here blind!"

"I know enough about you to know that you need to be destroyed at any cost."

"Any cost? Are you quite certain about that? You couldn't do it in our last lifetime, and I was merely a human then. Now I'm a god."

"You're a coward," I snarl. "You hide behind humans."

He's a mere breath away in a millisecond with his hand wrapped around my throat. He lifts me up to his eye level as my feet kick out wildly. "You have no idea what I've become. I'm going to kill everything you love, Simone, and I'm going to make you watch, helpless to prevent it. Then, I'm going to destroy you until there's no more you—just me."

I reach out to him and put my hands to his face, sending out all the energy I can gather into one, intense pulse. Mr. Kendrick's body is blown away from me as if I were a live grenade. Emil's essence separates from his human host into a black, smoky cloud. Mr. Kendrick lands on the icy pavement of the street and slides across it until he comes to rest in a snow bank.

The black cloud that is Emil collects and forms a gigantic, shadowy angel with sharp, pointy wings that tower above me. His skeletal mouth widens as he emits a horrible scream that sounds like a hundred thousand voices crying out at once. I cringe as my hair blows back from my face. His elongated, claw-like fingers cut a hole in the very air, tearing it open. It folds back to reveal an orange glow from the night skyline of a city on fire. Achingly elegant, gothic buildings rise up out of the darkness. Gargoyle-like creatures patrol the air with long, albino wings that swoop and cluster above the shrouded streets and the midnight river that runs crookedly through the ancient metropolis.

For a moment, the sight of it mesmerizes me; it's gruesomely lovely and soul crushingly frightening all at once. I'm aware of its scrutiny as well. It's as if a thousand eyes have turned towards me, hunting me. While the pungent scent of offal assails my nostrils, my heart contracts in a futile attempt to hide from it and the eyes watching me. I strain to get away from Emil's essence because this is worse than the 7-Eleven on the night Freddie tried to kill us. It's Sheol.

An invisible force yanks me toward the opening. Xavier gets between Emil and me. He wraps his arms around me, spreading wide his scarlet wings, shrouding me from evil. Xavier opens a compact in his hand. The world around me distorts, swirling in a kaleidoscope of shapes and colors as I whirl into the iridescent glow of his portal.

Reed

CHAPTER 9
Right Rode Away

REED

I rest my bound wings against the damp, brownstone wall at my back and listen to the sound of water lapping against rocks. I don't need to study the cell; I know every inch of my cage by memory. It's similar to the one they kept me in the last time I was at Dominion's château on the Gulf of St. Lawrence. Still, my eyes follow the mortared slabs of rock, reinforced with layers of metal stronger than steel. It's Trictofite, an oar mined from magma deep within the Earth, farther down than humans can dig and, unfortunately, the solid metal door is made of it as well.

My bare feet nearly freeze to the bedrock floor. I ignore their numbness as I gauge my position to be somewhere beneath the arena where the Powers had put Evie on trial and judged her. Anger over that thought warms me before I shiver; the last time I was here it was summer. Winter comes with a new set of hardships. My muscles are beginning to cramp from the frigid air. I bring my bound wrists closer to my chest as I draw my knees in. Closing my eyes, my mind moves through each hall that I'd cataloged while last in this stone prison. I study the intangible map as a means of doing something constructive and to repress the ache associated with the loss of butterflies—the loss of my proximity to Evie.

Centuries of control and ability to live in the shadow of

emotion collapsed within me today when Tau blew the boatswain. Within inches of ridding myself of Xavier from our lives forever, everything changed in that moment. Seeing Evie fall, pale and nearly lifeless, to the ground was like having the light cut out of my life. It had affected Xavier in the same way. We were both rendered powerless in that moment. It's apparent how much I need her; she's my air. She's what's keeping me alive. Without her, I'll suffocate.

I exhale, trying to compartmentalize my rage. I failed to kill Tau. Cole and Xavier pulled me off of him before I was done. I only managed to slit his throat open; I didn't go deep enough. He'll live. He'll heal.

In the minutes after he blew the boatswain and I attacked him, a swarm of Dominion Powers amassed to help the Seraphim. A dark hood was thrown over my head. My wings were tied along with my wrists and legs. I fought them to try to get to Evie, but I was overwhelmed and dragged off.

She was still breathing when I was beaten nearly senseless, shoved into a trunk of a vehicle, and driven off. I felt the attraction of butterflies even through the pain. I'm certain that she's alive; it's the only reason why I'm able to hold onto a semblance of calm. I'm clutching the invisible thread that binds me to her. *I won't let go, not for anything in this world.*

A soft, golden glow appears in the corner of my cell, dispelling the gloom. Russell takes shape as his head peeks through the wall. When he sees me, the light from Russell's illuminated clone pushes through the cold stone. His leg steps through next, followed by his arm and shoulder, and the rest of his tall frame. As he emerges, he takes a look around at the walls before his eyes return to me crouched on the floor. I don't bother to hide my bleak expression. It unnerves him; his clone runs his hand through his hair, mimicking his normal reaction to stress.

"You in a time out?" Russell asks with his slow, southern smile that attempts to hide the growing anxiety in his clone's eyes.

"It's more like a time in," I reply.

"They catch you jay walkin' again? I've told you to wait when the orange blinkin' hand—"

"I tried to kill Tau."

Russell's clone's playful grin evaporates in an instant. "How come you're not dead then?" he asks.

"They need me alive as leverage against Evie."

"Where are ya? We'll come get ya out."

"Dominion—the chateau, but you can't come here, Russell."

"Huh?" he asks without humor. "Where's Red? Is she here, too?"

My stomach clenches involuntarily. He would've sent a clone to her first. The fact that he's asking me means he failed to locate her. "No, she's not here—I can't feel her. You couldn't find her?"

"Naw," his clone's brows come together in confusion. "There's no connection. I tried to send her a bunch of clones, but none of 'em would move. It's like she's not here to find—I can't feel her anywhere either. Where did you last see her?"

"Xavier had her—the last I saw of her, she was at her childhood home—unconscious."

"You lost her to him? What's wrong with you? You were supposed to take him apart!" Russell's messenger glows brighter with raw emotion, as if it's fueling the clone.

"They have something, Russell," I reply.

"What? What've they got?" His clone comes nearer, squatting down in front of me so he can look into my eyes.

"What I'm going to tell you doesn't get relayed to anyone else. Not Zephyr, not Anya, no one. You understand?"

"No," he replies with a scowl. "What the *hell* are ya talkin' bout? We're a team here. We work together—"

"Not for this! This is too dangerous for them to know. The only reason I'm going to tell you this is because I think it will concern you as well."

"All right! You're freakin' me out! What is it?" Russell asks.

"They have a key to Sheol. It opens a doorway to Hell."

"Ffffaaaaaa—for what? Why would they need that?" Russell asks with a grim look.

I ignore Russell's questions. "She used it."

"WHAT? Evie's there—in HELL?"

"Shh," I look over Russell's clone's shoulder to the door before I glance back to him. "Evie took the key from Tau—she used it to open a doorway to Sheol. It tried to drag her into it, but Tau closed it before she could enter it."

"Why would she open it in the first place?"

I shake my head. "I don't think she knew what she was doing."

Russell growls. "What happened after she opened it?"

"Tau took the key back from her and closed the opening, but he nearly destroyed her doing it."

"Destroyed her how?"

"It was like a kill switch to her, Russell. It acted like a weapon that completely overpowered Evie."

"What does it look like—the key?"

"It's looks like a boatswain—a whistle that naval—"

Russell holds up his hand, "I know what that is—it's used to call out orders to sailors at sea. Different tone sequences mean different things like: weigh the anchor or time to eat—I've lived before, remember?"

"Tau has one that has a different purpose—one of the high-pitched sounds incapacitates your kind—half-angels. It's like a whistle that only your kind can hear—the frequency hurts you—or maybe it's the particular tone he used on her. She bled, Russell, from her eyes—her ears—her mouth—it came through her pores..."

"Why would he do that? He's her dad!"

"I don't know, but he did it. I tried to kill him for it—I failed."

"Which explains your new accommodations," Russell says without humor. "They beat the snot outta ya," he states, indicating the fading bruises that still haven't healed. "We'll have to come up with a plan to get you out."

"No," I say flatly.

Russell sighs heavily. "Whaddaya mean no?"

"I'll get myself out *after* I recover the whistle from Tau."

"And you're gonna do all that on your own?" Russell asks

skeptically. "You're gonna need help. Lookatcha, sittin' there all tied up and twisted. I can see your breath, so I know ya must be freezin'."

"I'm fine."

"You're not fine! We're comin' to get ya."

"You can't come here. Dominion wants you—wants to control you. They'll arrest Anya—they see her as a traitor. You have to protect her."

Russell's humanity rebels at the notion of leaving me here. "I'll make Anya stay behind—the Reapers will find her somewhere safe—"

I shake my head. "Tau can use that weapon on you with less remorse than on his daughter. He may just decide that he wants you gone and send your soul back to Paradise. In his mind, you're not supposed to be here. I can see it in his eyes when he looks at you—an extra man cluttering the board."

"That was until I busted into Brennus' lair and helped free his daughter. Tau promised me anythin' if I helped save her and I'm gonna collect: immunity for Anya."

The wind howls through the panes of the barred window above us. "I can't leave here without that whistle, Russell. He can't be allowed to use it against her again."

"Why do they even have somethin' like that? Were they afraid they weren't gonna be able to control her?"

I hesitate.

Russell snorts in derision. "And Tau used it on her? Just like that?" Russell asks in a hollow voice. "It doesn't make sense to me. I saw Tau's eyes when he knew his daughter was with Brennus. He was afraid for her—he was half insane with it. He'd never kill her; it'd destroy him. Trust me. I was a father—many times over. He'd die first before he'd let that happen."

"Then the weapon is not for her," I deduce.

"If it's not for her, then who is it for?" Russell asks. "They didn't plan on me. Evie changed the game plan by savin' me accordin' to Anya—I've always kind of known that since it happened."

"Brennus intimated to Evie that you're not the only one of your kind—there is another male of your species."

Russell's clone rises from his crouch and kicks the air in anger, his arms spreading wide. "We're relyin' on the undead freak's intel now? That *vampire* is like a hundred car pile-up waitin' to happen!"

"We can't deny that he has connections—his allies align with the Fallen. He knows what goes on in dark."

"It'd be nothin' to him to feed us false information!"

"Us, but not Evie," I reason. "It's in his best interest to keep her well out of the hands of the Fallen. She's his treasure; the only place his heart can beat is within hers."

"So this key thing—this weapon the divine Seraphim have isn't for Evie; it's for the fallen version of Evie?" I nod. His clone paces my cell, sometimes disappearing briefly into a cell wall before reappearing again. "Do they know who it is—the evil half-breed?" Russell's clone pauses and looks at me.

"No, or the army that Tau has amassed would be at war with him. They need Evie to draw him out. She's their lure. Bait. I think we've already met him Russell—at the house today."

Russell's clone loses some of its golden glow. "I have to get the girls outta Crestwood. Now."

"Zephyr should already have a new location."

"He does, it's—"

"Don't tell me—I shouldn't know where you are. Keep looking for Evie."

"What do I do when I find her?"

"She'll tell you what to do."

A smirk forms on Russell's lips despite everything. "You know her pretty well."

"I do," I nod.

"I should go then," he says with a reluctant look.

"You should."

"Alright then."

"Russell," I say, as his clone nears the wall.

He turns back and says, "Yeah?"

"How are you with knots?"

"I suck at 'em."

"How about magic?"

His eyebrows rise as he pushes out his bottom lip. "I'm better at that."

"You think you can break this angel hair knot tying my wings together?" I ask.

He frowns. "I never tried to use magic through a clone before."

"First time for everything." I rise from the floor, showing him my back so he can assess the problem.

"I'll have ya outta that in no time."

Despite everything, I smile. "I'm glad I didn't kill you."

Russell laughs. "Yeah? Me too."

Russell

CHAPTER 10
Past Is Present

RUSSELL

"We have to go!" I warn Zephyr the moment I allow my clone to evaporate and my consciousness to return to my body.

Zephyr stares back at me from his position on an overstuffed chair in the library.

"Did you find them?" Zephyr asks, his calm eyes scannin' me.

"I found Reed. He's screwed, like always. Dominion Powers have him at their château. He tried to kill Tau, which didn't work out so well for him."

"Have they harmed him?"

"I don't think he beat himself up, so I'd say they haven't been very hospitable."

"And Evie?" Zee asks with a grim look.

I shake my head, pretendin' not to be completely freaked out. "I don't know. She's not with him. Reed thinks she's still alive. She's an ass kicker; she'll find us when she can. Reed told me to stay away. He said he'd free himself and find us."

"They'll kill him," Anya says quietly.

"Huh?" I turn 'round to Anya's lithe body leanin' against the doorframe of the library. She pushes away from it and prowls in, her graceful steps makin' me lose my train of thought as I stare at her. Her dark wings move with her in a seductive, dangerous flutter, like she could chase down the devil without much trouble.

Her soft, full lips say, "Dominion. They'll kill Reed. If he harmed Tau in any way, it's a death sentence. We have to rescue him before he's shredded."

"He said not to come there."

"Of course he did," her lips spread in a cynical smile. "He's a Power; they think they never need anyone's help."

"Prostat Powers don't need to be rescued from other angels," Zephyr says gruffly.

Anya lifts her hand towards Zee, "See? We need to free him."

"Who's *we*?" I ask with a scowl. "You're not gettin' within a hundred miles of that place. Right now, you're public enemy number one to them."

Her perfect chin lifts as she smiles like I gave her a compliment. "I'll be fine. Xavier won't let them kill me."

My eyebrows slash together in a flare of jealousy. "Naw, *I* won't let them kill ya 'cuz you're not goin' there!"

"We have to get him back. He's not the one that was born to die."

"What's that supposed to mean?"

"Your girl won't last the year."

The wingback chair next to me makes a crackin' sound as my hand squeezes it too tightly. "You're my girl. I'm not gonna let anyone hurt ya."

She looks confused for a second. "I meant Evie," she says, uncertainly.

Her glance my way only feeds my desire for her. "You don't know the future, and Anya, you're my only girl," I state again unequivocally.

"Once maybe, but now..."

I lift my eyebrow. "What's that above your heart then?"

Her fingers glide unconsciously over the bindin' mark on her skin. "A mistake," she replies.

Her words make my heart contract painfully. It's a feelin' that I know comes from missin' a life that I've left behind—from missin' her. "You have to stay with me for now, Anya. That's non-negotiable."

"You don't even remember me."

"I may not remember everthin', but the crickets that I feel whenever you're 'round mean somethin'." My eyes shift to Zephyr who has been watchin' our exchange with fascination. He stands as I say, "We gotta move. This place is feelin' downright creepy, Zee."

He frowns. "What do you feel?"

"My flesh is crawlin'. It's like they're peekin' at us through the shadows, gatherin' in the crevices of this place. Whatever it is, it's here—under the bed, tryin' to get inside my head."

"It?"

"The evil that just kicked our asses out in the snow. It's back."

"Then I won't say aloud where we're going, should it be listening." His assurance that I'm right makes me uneasy. "Brownie, Buns..." he says in a tone that hardly rises at all.

Buns wobbles stiffly through the door of the library with Brownie not far behind. They're both twice their normal size because they're wearin' several layers of clothes, givin' them the appearance of bohemian Eskimos.

"Buns," Zephyr's tone is admonishin', "we discussed the need to travel light."

Buns gives him a petulant look. "Do you see me carrying luggage?"

"No."

"Then what's the problem?" Her chin juts out.

I clear my throat. Zephyr's sharp eyes pierce me. I shake my head, hopin' he picks up what I'm layin' down.

Zee turns back at Buns and murmurs, "You seem uncomfortable."

"I'm really hot," she admits with annoyance, "but what do you want me to do? I have to plan our wardrobes without even knowing what SEASON we're heading into because NO ONE has let me know where we're going!" She stabs her finger at Zephyr.

"You're good with surprises, Buns." His smile is placid.

She sniffs the air in derision and waddles forward like a golden-haired sumo wrestler. "I do like a good surprise," she reluctantly agrees.

"The portal is not activated to pull you through. You will need to shapeshift," Zephyr says, suppressin' a smile.

"That's something you could've pointed out to me an hour ago!" Buns sweeps her hands in front of her, indicatin' the pile of clothes layered on her. "Maybe I don't feel like becoming butterflies right now! Did you ever think of that?" Her hands find their way to where her hips might lie beneath the fabric.

Brownie gathers her hair away from her neck and fans her sweaty face with her other hand. "I can maybe manage moths—butterflies are a stretch."

"I'm okay with that if you can manage to change into them in the next few seconds because we've stayed here too long as it is." Zephyr holds out a delicate earthen vase. Crack lines in the gold and black enamel run through the angels depicted on its sides. He lifts the lid from it. The immensity of time and space swirls in a spiral within it; ready to devour us like a black hole does a star going supernova.

"None of us is going to look very good when we get wherever we're going in that portal," Buns pouts.

"I don't even care anymore," Brownie says irritably. "I just wanna go. There's something oppressive in the air we're breathing. It's starting to feel like two and two makes five around here." At that, Brownie bursts into a shimmerin' copper cloud of moths, shapeshiftin' to fit inside the portal. The clothes that she was wearin' fall to the floor, a discarded chrysalis of cotton, linen, and denim. One moth at a time, Brownie rains down into the vase that Zephyr holds open.

As Brownie slips away, Buns shivers despite her overheated skin. "Okay, sweetie," she gives Zephyr a half-smile. "I like you best when you're wearing nothing at all anyway." Zephyr's eyes get bluer just as Buns' iridescent skin glows golden and she closes her eyes. In a *poof*, like a smoky distraction in a magician's trick, Buns transforms herself into a kaleidoscope of golden-winged butterflies. The flock floats and ungulates, swimmin' in the air of the library. A landfill of coats, sweaters and pants collapse in the middle of the room at the loss of Buns' former shape.

"You're next," Zephyr says to Anya with a smile as he waits, holdin' the vase as the first few of Buns' velvety-winged thoraxes crawl into it.

The pit of my soul shakes in the next moment. The windows linin' the library shatter inward. Jagged shards of glass scatter golden butterflies, preventin' pieces of our Reaper angel from enterin' the portal. Hoards of fallen angels crawl into our sanctuary. Cold air infiltrates, too, turnin' my breath to wisps of white vapor. Powerful brown, white, and gray-colored wings unfurl from the backs of the evil angels. Their strong hands draw steely blades from jewel-encrusted sheaths.

Raisin' both my hands, I hit the enemies' first wave with magical white-hot beams of light. The flesh of evil Power angels burns from their bones, renderin' them to dust. Clouds of ash rise in the air. It doesn't stop the next wave. Hundreds of monstrous vulture-winged angels with brown and white feathers emerge from it.

From somewhere behind me, black-feathered arrows rip through the air. The arrowheads pass by my eyes, striking the foreheads of the fallen Power angels ahead of me. Anya ratchets four more arrows to the bow, firin' them off in one bow stroke. She sets four more with lightnin'-fast speed and strikes the eyes of her targets, fellin' them in less than an instant.

"Russell!" Zephyr calls to me. "Catch!" He throws the fragile portal vase with the force of a comet. The vase becomes a net, catchin' several golden butterflies within it as it tumbles through the air.

My reaction is ingrained. I shift into reverse. My feet move as my eyes follow the trajectory of the vase spiralin' through the air like a football. I stumble, runnin' into furniture in my path, but I never take my gaze from it. Spreading my wings, I leap into the air as the urn soars by my head. Its smooth surface slides over my fingertips. I fumble with the amphora shape, it tumbles from my left hand to my right and back again. I secure it in my grasp. Catching as many golden-winged creatures out of the air as I can,

I stuff 'em in the portal. They disappear in a swirl that mimics the Milky Way.

From the corner of my eye, I see Anya being forced backward toward one of the walls lined with bookcases. "Zee!" I roar. He glances at me. His back is covered with golden butterflies as he wields his broad sword with vicious intent. It flows through the onslaught of angels before him, stemmin' their tide and keepin' them in front of him so they can't crush any of the butterfly pieces of our Reaper. "Catch!" I yell.

I toss the portal into the air toward Zee. As it rockets to him, it swallows up several flutterin' butterflies in it's path. I only wait long enough for him to catch it in his raised fingers before my hands swing to the books on the shelf behind Anya's head. I cast a spell that has tomes flyin' off them, strikin' the snarlin' angels bearin' down on my girl. It only stops a few. A large Power with silver-gray wings manages to slip through them. Anya drops her bow at his approach because she's out of arrows. Drawin' out her bone-handled knife from her thigh holster, she grips it firmly in her fist. The towerin' angel swings his silvery sword, intent on cuttin' her in half. She ducks and it misses her by less than a millimeter. My fear for her safety is a steely blade cutting my belly in two.

Pure emotion ignites from me in the form of fire, causin' several whirlin' flames to dance forth in spinnin' orange tornadoes from my chest. Hot and angry, the first whirlin' fireball finds the silver-winged Power as he makes another pass at Anya. When the fire crashes into him, his body ignites, flames eatin' him until he's nothin' more than rollin', churnin' ashes.

While the other fallen angels surroundin' Anya meet a similar fate, I use my rage to push the more fallen angels back with an invisible protective field that I wind around Anya, Zee, and me. The Fallen are thrust from the room back outside. I seal the broken window frames with a spell. Zephyr drops his sword. He pulls the remainin' golden butterflies off his back and deposit them in the portal he still holds. "Thank you, Russell," he says as the last butterfly disappears inside the portal. "Anya, you're next." He tilts the portal in Anya's direction as an invitation to depart.

The air becomes thinner; it seems to wither. Energy shifts and flows away from me so fast it leaves me with tunnel vision. Closin' my eyes, I grit my teeth, tryin' to unrattle my brain. When I open them again, I stare into the eyes of the menace I had hoped to never see again in this or any other lifetime. I remember his eyes; they used to be the blackest of black, but now they're the bluest of blues. His hair is no longer the dark of midnight either, but a light blond with rust-colored highlights that makes him seem young and vibrant. But I know him; I've seen him in far too many lifetimes not to recognize him now.

My stomach tightens as I cringe. "Djet!" My eyes narrow to slits. "You. Royal. Psycho! What the fuuuaaaa—" My entire body is compelled forward, my feet draggin' across the floor until I slam up against the barrier I created to keep all the evil freaks back. "Bastard!" I groan as my hand goes to my bloody nose.

Djet smiles. "You remember me. Tell me, where is Zahra?"

I rub my nose. "You look a little different, but I remember you—you still have those lazy eyes, 'cept now they're blue," I say sullenly. I take in his new form. He has an angel shine to him, somethin' he never had before.

"You remember my eyes?"

"How could I forget 'em? They never looked away from mine when you had me burned alive. I'm still pissed about that!"

"You stole Zahra from me, Iah," Djet retorts as he moves closer to the barrier between us, comin' within inches of it. "She was everything to me then."

"She was your sister, ya sick psycho!"

"She was my half-sister in that lifetime, and she was perfection." He eyes the broken window in front of him, placin' his hand on the energy to test it. Energy bows out from it, I feel it crackle in the air between us, but it holds him back.

"Who is this?" Zephyr demands. He sets the fragile portal down on the small table next to the sofa.

Over my shoulder, I explain to Zee, "Remember when Evie cut

you with her knife when you were trainin' us and I told you that she was once a mistress to an Egyptian Pharaoh who taught her to spar with daggers?" I ask him.

"Yes," Zephyr growls.

"Meet Djet the incest-lovin'-royal-pain-in-my-ass who hunted us down and killed Evie and me for tryin' to be together."

Djet's ivory skin shines bright, far from a rottin' king wrapped in decayin' linens and sealed away in a stone coffin. I'd much prefer him buried in a tomb. "I have had many names," Djet says casually.

"So ya have. I probably know most of them, don't I?"

"As I know yours, *Nicolas*. Where have the Seraphim hidden Simone?"

I stiffen. "How do you know her as Simone?" I growl. "I don't remember you in our last lifetime."

"Who do you think murdered her? You want to know how I did it?" he baits me. I want to grab his knotted scarf from around his neck and choke him with it.

"I'm gonna rip your ugly head off!" I lose my mind and claw at my own magic to get to him, but Zephyr has his arms 'round me from behind, pullin' me back from the barrier. I point at him, "You touch her again and you're dead!"

"There is no saving her, Iah. You couldn't do it when she was Zahra or Simone, shall I go on?" he asks with a smug smile.

"My name is Russell now, not Iah, and I whooped your *ass* in most of our lifetimes—even when I was the girl! You think I don't know you? You think I don't remember them all?" I smile back. He looks like what I just said threw him off his game. *Was he expectin' me not to remember everythin'?*

"You get lucky," he says, but his smile is gone. "Your luck is played out. She made a deal. There is nothing left to chance. She's at my mercy...and she'll suffer." A vein pulses in his neck and the house creaks like he's squeezin' it in his fist.

I ignore the oppressive shift in the air. "You know what I remember the most about ya, Djet? You're a confident liar."

"Why would I lie when the truth is so much more devastating?

And why are you here? You weren't supposed to be. It wasn't what was agreed upon."

"I wasn't ready to leave," I shrug like his words don't affect me even though I feel a chill creepin' down my spine.

"I'm glad you decided to stay. She wouldn't agree to you as part of our deal—so nice of you to insert yourself into our game on your own. Your soul won't survive it," he promises.

"You're graceless, Djet. I get it now. It *finally* all makes sense to me. She came back for you, didn't she? She came to make you cease to be. I'd bet everythin' on it. She wants us to be free of you once and for all."

"She's here because I demanded that she be here and for no other reason!" he spits out with venom, losin' his cool. "She never gets to walk away from me."

"Yeah? Well ya gotta go through me first to get to her."

"How about if I go through her first?" he asks as his attention shifts to Anya. The barrier I erected bows inward toward us, visibly shimmerin' with a surge of power. Djet taps on it with his index finger: WHAM, WHAM, WHAM—the deafenin' sounds it makes shakes books from the shelves as figurines crash and shatter on the floor. I cover my ears to block it out.

With my heart beatin' in my throat, Djet walks right through my magic. An army of beefy-lookin' Power angels follow him in. They all look as if they could snatch the pitchfork from the devil. Zephyr advances toward Djet, but pauses when Anya gasps and starts to slide across the floor like she's bein' reeled in on an invisible hook. The Fallen advance on Zee and me at the same time. Anya skids over the dark threads in the Persian rug. Her black wings beat the air in hard thrusts in an attempt to stop her progression. By the look on her face, it's at the expense of pain.

Rage builds inside me. A howl sticks in my throat. I conjure barbed razor wire and use it like whips, lashing out at Djet. His evil bodyguards save him by steppin' in front of him. Hard metal wires twist like serpents around them, tearin' their skin to shreds as the fallin' angels try to dislodge from it.

I lurch toward Anya, tryin' to grab her and stop her from

being pulled into Djet's arms. My fingertips reach for her. Djet raises his hand in my direction, sending out a burst of magic. As I step onto the Persian rug, I sink down into it as if it's water. The carpet swallows me whole until I swim upward through the tangle of fabric. My arms flail as my head surfaces from the wool. The threads unravel, wrappin' 'round my arms and body in a spool of crimson and black.

With a roar, I flex hard, exudin' energy. I tear through the magic entwinin' me. Gettin' to my feet and breathin' hard, I'm ready to pull the arms off Djet and feed 'em to him. My stomach churns as I try to advance upon him, only to find that my feet have grown into the floor.

"Such a beautiful face," Djet murmurs, while rubbin' his fingers over Anya's cheek. She struggles to pull away from him, her face a mask of loathin'.

Fallen angels swarm us. Zephyr immediately cuts down the first wave of them with his drawn sword. Blood spatters the walls and ceilin' in deep rollin' patterns. I dislodge my feet from the floor and join him in dispatchin' the mob with my knives that I pull from the holsters on my thighs, but there are more angels than we can possibly handle. As I glace toward Zephyr, his skin is sliced open with a thousand different cuts. He resembles someone who has been thrown through the windshield of a car. I probably look the same, my forearms, face, and sides receivin' cut after cut from daggers and swords meant to torment, not kill. They're murderin' us slowly, deliberately, and for effect. I try to pull energy to me, but it has disappeared, leavin' me fightin' for air. A vicious stab to my abdomen drops me to my knees as my sword slips from my fingers.

One of the evil angels grabs me from behind by my blood-soaked hair while pressin' his dagger to my throat. Zephyr is next to me in a similar position, completely at the mercy of the Fallen and a gloatin' Djet. My eyes are forced to look into Djet's as he holds Anya in his arms with a dagger to her throat.

"We've been here before, have we not, Iah? And it's always about her—the one you call your soul mate. Aren't you tired of her, the little bitch? Where is she? Why are you here without her, protecting her like always? Help me find her—get rid of her. Tell me where she is—who is the Seraph with her?"

"Don't tell him anything, Russell," Anya growls.

"If he tells me, I'll kill you quickly. Otherwise, I'll give you to the angels here and you will die...slowly—all but you, Iah. I want to kill you in front of her. I want her to watch."

Hopelessness tightens my throat, as it had when he'd killed Evie when she was Zahra all those years ago. This time it will be Anya, *my* angel, who dies and it'll be forever—and she won't be comin' back.

"I don't—" I begin, but stop when I catch the sweet, cloyin' scent of—

The doors of the library swing open behind me. "Aww, whah's dis?" Brennus' smooth voice asks. "'Tis aingeals, Finn."

"'Tis." Finn agrees.

Brennus makes a rude sound, "and da other."

"Brennus," I hiss.

"Why are ye lettin' dem have da pretty dark-winged aingeal, da other?" he asks me conversationally, as he walks into my line of sight. He looks at the Power angel holdin' me hostage by my throat. His eyes shift to Djet and Anya. "Hallo, pretty aingeal," he says to Anya, "I've missed ye." Her eyes widen as her hands grip Djet's hand that holds the sharp dagger just below her chin. Brennus' eyes shift again to Zephyr. "And Genevieve's aingeal mentor! Zephyr, is it?" he asks. Zephyr doesn't answer him; he just stares back at Brennus with a blank expression.

"What are you doin' here?" I growl at Brennus.

He moves in front of me and bends down to my eye level, studyin' me. It's shockin' to see his black wings beyond the unbuttoned collar of his stark-white dress shirt. They're almost like an elegant accessory to complete his ensemble of tailored black trousers and expensive shoes. His meticulous well-kept black hair doesn't even move as he leans near me. Faerie writin' scrawls in intricate tattoos over Brennus' neck. Behind his ear, there's somethin' I'd never noticed there before; it's a glowin' tattoo on his not so pale flesh—one that looks like the battle axe I'd seen back at his castle.

"I came ta retrieve da portrait of me queen dat da Reapers stole from me castle," he nods toward his brother Finn on the other side of me. Finn demonstratively holds up a rolled up canvas; his iridescent green eyes twinkle like this is all very amusin'. "Nasty wee craiturs, dose Reaper aingeals—tink dey can reap everytin, but dat's moin—given ta me in trade by a Fallen one."

"Ahh, who are ya tryin' to kid? You killed Freddie and kept it."

"I did na say 'twas a good trade for him."

"You must be Brennus," Djet says behind him. Brennus' eyes narrow as he straightens to face Djet.

"If I must," Brennus says pleasantly enough, but his anger is recognizable to me. "And ye must be Emil." Fallen angels move in closer, surroundin' Djet, while their eyes focus on the back of the room by the doors. Behind me I hear *click, click, click, click, click, click*...hundreds of fangs engagin' at once.

"How do you know that name?" he asks Brennus.

"Ye're Emil. Yer last lifetime was in Lille, France was it na? About a century ago," he states, exudin' confidence. "And like a coward, ye enjoyed frightenin' wee lasses den." Judgin' by the look on Djet's face, I should start referrin' to him as Emil.

Emil goes rigid. He looks bitter as he assesses the threat in the room. "To whom have you been speaking? Casimir? Where is he? Do you have him?"

Humor enters Brennus' green eyes, turnin' them even lighter. "No one is talkin' ta Casimir. Genevieve's aingeal shredded him na long ago. Ahh, but ye do na know her as Genevieve, do ye? Ta ye, she's still Simone. Isn't dat right, Emil? She's still da weak lass ye tortured in da war."

"Tell me who killed my mentor!" Emil demands. He's torn up about it.

"Casimir? Was he yer mentor?" Brennus asks, toyin' with Emil. "Ye should tank da aingeal who did it. Casimir wanted

Genevieve for himself. He planned ta use her ta gain power in Sheol."

"He'd never betray me." Emil's anger is a tangible thing.

Brennus shrugs. "He did. Maybe ye're na dat important after all, Emil. Dey've probably been feeding ye dat nonsense since ye were born. Finn, whah's worse dan an evil aingeal?"

Finn grins. "A *spoiled* evil half-aingeal?"

Brennus grins as well. "Och, ye have ta luv me brudder; he's so cheeky. He was always da favourite."

Emil isn't amused. "You've kept Simone from me."

Brennus' expression becomes serious; his fangs engage, *click*. "She's Genevieve, and she's moin."

"You don't *know* her like I do. She's not worth it!"

"If dat were true, ye'd na be here. Ye burn for her."

"I'm here to make sure that there will be nothing left of her. What will it take for you to walk away?" Emil asks. "I could find your soul—release it back to you. You can be whole once more—"

Brennus laughs with derision. "Listen ta him try ta negotiate for me queen, Finn. 'Tis fair disgustin'."

"Or I could find your faerie soul in Sheol and make things a bit more difficult for him."

"He has been dere for a while. He can take care of himself," Brennus replies.

"Think what it would mean to have him back with you. You'd be more powerful—"

"I do na negotiate for whah's moin. Genevieve is moin," Brennus states with a deadly glint in his eye. "Let me tell ye whah's gonna happen here. We're gonna have a mill, and den whoever wins our fight—me or yous—will be da one left ta try ta win Genevieve for his own."

"I don't intend to win her. I intend to crush her. You've tasted her blood, haven't you?" Emil accuses. "You're infected with her."

"Her blood has awakened me ta whah I've been missing. I feel her heart beat inside me."

"She's a killer drug, isn't she? Enough is never quite enough. You'll always need more of her. I was once like you, pathetic,

Brennus. Lifetime after lifetime spent begging her to join me—the sun to my moon—the light to my dark."

"Grow old, did it? Or did she tire of ye? She did, didn't she?"

"I can kill you any time I want, Gancanagh!"

Brennus' eyes turn hunter; they stalk Emil. I look toward Emil, too. He has to feel the power in the room has long ago shifted to Brennus. Maybe Brennus is doin' somethin' to blind Emil from that fact, breakin' him down in a silent fashion. I don't know, but Emil appears oblivious to it. *I have to get Anya away from Emil before things turn apocalyptic.*

Brennus smiles. "Genevieve is never coming back ta ye, Emil—"

"Ahh, you're wrong. She can never truly leave me, Gancanagh."

"Why is dat? Why are ye in so many of her lifetimes?"

His face distorts with rage. "She's always in *my* lifetimes—she's always screwing them up! She's a thorn in my side! I'm going to enjoy smashing her face in until the only thing left of her is me."

"Has she been sent ta banjax all yer lifetimes?"

"He may be her soul mate—" Emil looks directly at me with disgust twistin' his lips, "—but he has always been the weaker of the two, just as my soul mate was the weaker of us. I made my soul mate fall with me...it was so simple. No fight in her—she blindly followed me into hell." Emil points his chin at me. "He's Simone's mate, but I'm Simone's complement—I made her stronger. I made her the perfect adversary. I'm the Yin to her Yang. She's the light that cannot exist without my darkness."

Goose bumps rise on my flesh and I suppress the urge to shiver. A part of me rebels at what he says. My hard-faced look is met by the coldness of his lazy stare. I stare back at him and wonder what's buried underneath those eyes.

From the other side of the room, Finn says, "I did na see dat coming, Brenn."

"Nor I," Brennus agrees. "If Emil here is ta be believed, den he's her evil da other."

Emil scowls. "She's not my soul mate! She follows me through eternity! We move through time in elliptical patterns—the two of us folding back on one another. She's always in my next life, trying to subdue me, trying to stop me from achieving any kind of power in this world. She's the bane of my existence! I'll enjoy watching her soul mate suffer before I annihilate him in front of my relentless, divine stalker." His lips turn sinister while his fingers tense on the shiny blood-red handle of the wing-shaped dagger in his grip. "But first, this thorn gets to watch me wipe this Throne from existence."

Brennus directs his magical power at me, strikin' me with the force of a movin' car. The shock of electricity surges through my bones. I lift my arm and point my hand at Anya, redirectin' some of the power to her as I cast a spell.

Emil's grip on his knife tightens before he swipes the serrated points of the wing-shaped dagger across Anya's neck. The expected gush of blood doesn't happen, instead, a grindin' sound of a blade being honed by a stone emits from Anya as tiny sparks fly from the surface of her throat. Emil lifts the blade away. There's nothin' more than a scratch on Anya. The relief I feel is short-lived. She's uncut, but she's also unable to breathe. Clutchin' her stony neck, Anya's eyes shutter in anguish.

Wall-shakin' crashes fracture every corner of the room. Gancanagh spill inside to clash with evil angels. I grasp the hand of the Power angel holdin' me hostage. His flesh turns to water and he plunges to the floor, becomin' just a puddle on the carpet. Liftin' both of my hands, I direct them towards Anya. Whisperin' a spell, I snatch her away from Emil just as Brennus pounces on him. She skids across the floor to me, landin' straight in my arms. She rests against my chest as my hands glide down her back, relievin' the enchantment I'd placed upon her. Her mouth gapes with a huge intake of breath as her throat opens enough to accept air.

Brennus lurches toward Emil, knockin' him into the air and across the room with a magical blast of energy. Emil smashes into the desk, flippin' over it. He comes to rest in the corner of the room. Instantly, he's on his feet again, strikin' Brennus with magic of his own. Brennus' skin melts. Thorns push out from his face, neck, and arms. Placing his hand to his cheek, Brennus' fingers glow with a green light, He reverses Emil's spell, eradicatin' the thorns.

To my left, Zee is covered in his own blood, stabbin' to death the evil, white-winged Archangel that had held him hostage. His wings look broken and I doubt he's able to fly right now. Zephyr notices us. He flips the portal urn off the table towards us. As the urn arcs in the air, I whisper to Anya, "Go now!"

"No! Not without you," she whispers in my ear. Grittin' my teeth, I decide not to give her the choice. My hands move up her spine, infusin' magic into her. She shimmers golden. Light pours from her body, as she becomes a fiery Phoenix.

The urn portal opens, I twist my finger like a corkscrew and the vase mimics the action; it spins like a top in front of us. Anya rises into the air, the embers of her Phoenix feathers sparkle down as her hawkish wings spread wide. She's can't resist the force that draws her to the portal. In a flash, she's sucked into it and is gone from my sight.

Relief washes over me that she's safe. I assess the fury surroundin' me. It's unclear just who's winnin' this fight. Pieces of undead Gancanagh lie next to pieces of very dead angels. Brennus and Emil are fightin' all 'round the room, throwin' magic at each other. Bursts of colorful light-energy explode, killin' angels and fellas as it's deflected. Debris and leafs of paper float down from above in wintery gales.

Emil disappears into thin air. He leaves behind a smoky vapor trail where he had been in front of Brennus only to reappear behind Brennus with the same smoky essence swirlin' 'round him. Emil's wicked grin is only there for a moment before Brennus elbows him in the mouth. Blood squirts into the air as his lip explodes. Brennus pivots and his green eyes glow in the growin' darkness surroundin' us.

The warm forearm of an angel wraps 'round my neck from behind me. I grasp it, and leanin' forward, I flip the rancid, brown-winged bugger over the top of me. When he's on the ground at my feet, I step on his neck, crushin' his larynx. Energy is freely flowin' to me once more. I use it to crush fallen angels near me.

Brennus backs nearer to me, struck by a whip-like current of energy from Emil. Black blood seeps from his left ear, coursing down over the glowin' tattoo of the axe I saw earlier. He stumbles to the left a step, his fingers comin' up to touch his ear. His other hand grips a chair as he tries to stay on his feet. The action draws Emil closer. Brennus whirls with his own whiplash of light, hittin' Emil with a lightnin' bolt. It singes the flesh from Emil's face. The lightning branches out to the evil angels near Emil, cookin' them alive.

Emil struggles for breath for a moment before he weakly raises his winged-dagger, holdin' it aloft. His lips move and I strain to hear what he's sayin'. It eludes me, but I feel no less damned by it. The blade glows red; he slashes the air with it, cuttin' the room open, like he's tearin' away the shroud of wrappin' paper. Another world beyond this one reveals itself. An intense reek hits me like a punch to the gut, and suddenly I understand what I'm seein'. We're exposed to the reekin' pit of Sheol.

Our library crumbles away. The panorama of a dark night sky surrounds us. Beneath it, a Gothic cityscape lies like the chalky outline of a murder victim. This place is like nothin' I've ever seen before. A blood red moon casts ripples of ruby light upon the river below as it twists a tangled spine for miles through the bones of the city. The beautifully gruesome buildings that line the pristine streets have an immense degree of detail. They have perfect symmetry; so perfect, in fact, that they look as if they're monuments to worship. The stone-white spires are gargoyle-infested. Rosette windows, like a thousand eyes, glow in multicolored splendor. Gazing upon them, they take note of me and they gaze back.

I detect movement in the darkness between the buildings. The limestone figures come alive and loft into the air. Scaly white wings beat against one another in their frenzy to reach us, a tangle of frantic bodies convergin'. I take a step back. The threshold of Hell follows me, encroachin' further into the library.

It's as if I'm the light within a lantern, peerin' out into the darkness beyond the dome of glass at the violent shapes of an army of evil moth men. My mind screams so loud it drowns out the frantic beat of my heart. *A spell! I need a spell!*

Wintry cold wind wafts into what's left of our fadin' world. With the reek of unbridled evil upon us, I pray to Heaven to escape. Golden light breaks from above, on the opposite side from where Sheol is emergin'. Before I can take it all in, Brennus unleashes a silver ball of energy from his hand. It zips 'round the perimeter of the room, Faerie dust fallin' from its path as it coats the walls with shiny gray light that runs down in tears. The lustrous ball spirals up to the ceilin'. When it reaches the top, it explodes in a shower of silver sparks.

I grab the vase just as Brennus' shimmerin' dust distorts everythin'. Seein' double, Hell fades, replaced by a black, white, and gray version of the library. The walls abandon their shape, bleedin' into one another, formin' indefinite lines and boundaries.

Before I can think, Brennus whirls on me with a look of frustration. "Whah were ye standin' around for? When Hell opens up, ye use yer powers ta close it." He motions to Finn to join him at his side. What's left of his army of Gancanagh gather nearer, checkin' their weapons and shakin' off the battle, but none make a move to harm Zee or me.

"You givin' me tips now?" I ask.

He stalks nearer, sayin', "Do na even breathe when I'm speakin', dat is da tip o' da day." He turns to his brother. "Finn, dey're attemptin' ta pull us back ta dem. Weave a stronger silver-linin' spell."

"What were those white creatures?" I blurt out, referrin' to the albino moth men who just came at us from Sheol.

"Motes," Brennus growls. "Dey consume fear. Stop feedin' dem! Dey could smell it on ye da moment our world was ripped open ta dem. Ye need ta learn ta control it if ye want ta become invisible ta dem."

"Why'd you save us from them?" I ask, indicatin' Zee and me with a gesture of my hand.

"I need ye ta speak to Genevieve—she's incapable of making a good decision lately—she only accepts me help when her circumstances are dire. I need ye ta convince her dat she needs me—dat we're allies."

I throw my head back and laugh. "You've been suckin' on Evie's blood again, haven't you? Are ya buzzin' or somethin'? 'Cuz you know me well enough to know we're not friends!"

"Have ye na assessed da situation?" Brennus asks in with a calculatin' look. "'Twas tousands of centuries o' *yer* past dat jus leaked out all over da room back dere." He points his thumb over his shoulder to the world just beyond this one.

In the backdrop of this new dimension, shadows from the ashen Motes creep 'round; their pensive movements stalkin' the magic of this realm, lookin' for a way in. The angels and Emil are there, too. Finn is holdin' up his hands with his eyes closed, murmurin' words that work to entwine silvery layers, creatin' thicker walls. I turn away from him to focus on Brennus.

"Have you forgotten the past few months? You tried to enslave all of us!" I remind him.

"'Twas before Genevieve changed me. I was different den."

I scoff. "You expect me to believe that after you just tried to possess her like a freakin' demon? You wouldn't hesitate to throw us all under the bus if it suited you!"

"I did na have ta save ye back dere. I could've jus left ye for Hell ta sort out, but Genevieve cares about ye. I do na want ta see her suffer."

The thought of bein' dragged to Sheol by the creatures I just saw makes my guts twist. "If that's true, then leave her alone!"

"'Tis impossible!" Brennus says with no small amount of disgust in his expression. "I'm incapable of leaving her alone! I'm always tinking of her! Hell is about ta rain down upon us all. I can na be more plain dan dat!"

I feel the need to refute what Emil said back there. "*I'm* her soul mate. I feel our connection!"

He sighs heavily. "I did na tink otherwise. Ye're Emil in reverse—da good ta his bad. Talk ta Genevieve—see whah she remembers," Brennus says in a quiet tone that I can't just brush off and ignore.

"I have to find her first. It's been a little harder than playin' Where's Waldo."

"Eh? Why is it dat I never quite know whah ye're saying?"

"Evie—I've been lookin' for her but I can't find her."

A suppressed smile twitches at the corners of Brennus' mouth. "I was jus wi' her—in her past—she has returned once again. It should prove ta be far easier for ye ta locate her now."

"I'm not even gonna ask you what you're talkin' 'bout," I say as I shake my head.

"Good. Da less ye speak, da better. Find her, and take dis." Brennus reaches down and pulls a dagger from a holster strapped to him beneath his pant leg. I recognize the knife; it's the one Evie had on her when she came to Zee's island—the one Brennus used to find her. He must have gotten it back from her bungalow before be blew the crap outta the island. "Yer blood on dat blade will summon me. 'Twill give me a way ta find ye when ye need me help."

"You think I'm gonna ever use that, Brennus?" I ask incredulously.

The dagger flies from Brennus' hand. Before I can move, it embeds in my side. I wince and look down at the hilt stickin' outta me. It's just a flesh wound, missin' my vital organs, but it still hurts like hell.

"I was na askin'. Ye'll use it so dat ye do na become a weapon dat Emil can wield against Genevieve. Either ye summon me for help wi' dat knife, or ye end yerself wi' it. I do na much care. Da choice is yers," Brennus replies.

Brennus waves his hand at me and I'm whirlin' away from the dimension the Gancanagh created as his magic shoves me into the vase portal.

Evie

CHAPTER 11
Stripped Down

EVIE

Xavier and I crash together onto a stone floor—me on top of him. My landing is probably gentler than his, but not by much because there's nothing soft about him. He sits up, reaching beyond my shoulder. I clutch his chest as he catches a spinning, silver compact out of the air. Snapping the portal closed, he holds it. Its shape resembles a snowflake, etched in silver filigree.

The shiny metal disk jumps in Xavier's palm. The lid dents from the inside out, lurching violently. Xavier's eyebrows slash together. He growls and crushes the portal until it's a silver pebble.

I let out a relieved breath. His eyes move to me, cataloging every scratch and bruise. He smoothes down my torn shirt. I hear a ragged sound—I'm breathing hard. My hair is in my eyes. He sweeps strands of it away and tucks them behind my ear. I stare at his colorful eyes. His thumb touches my bottom lip. I wince—it's sore.

"Are you hurt?" he asks.

I just stare are him. *I'm starting to hate that question.*

The firelight casts waves of light over one side of his face, leaving the other side in shadow. His eyes almost appear equal for a moment. "Do you have internal injuries—broken bones?"

Xavier's hands go to my sides where Emil had sunk his

magical hooks into me. I flinch. I'm tender. This is how a fish must feel when it's thrown back for being too small. "Illuminate room," Xavier says. Teardrops of crystals that comprise the beautiful chandeliers overhead switch on. The white light sparkles over the slate floors, showing thick, white rugs.

He lifts my shirt. We both see giant bruises on my abdomen. He lets it drop, and then leans his ear against my chest and listens. Slowly, he lifts his ear from me and the smile he gives me is beyond intimate. I'm sure the look goes back hundreds of thousands of years. "Nothing sounds off." His voice is a breathy sound.

I feel as though I can't hold my head up. I lean my forehead against his chest. He threads his fingers in my hair, holding me. I shift, resting my cheek against his chest so I can see his face. "I killed a human," I finally say numbly. "I tore his heart out. Owen —his name was Owen." My hands are still bloody from it. I whisper a magic spell. It cleans the blood from my skin, but not the memory of it.

Xavier's hand slips from my hair to my back. "I didn't see a human—"

"Emil possessed him. I thought he was Emil, but it was Emil inside of Owen."

"If Emil possessed him, then Owen allowed it."

"And I murdered Owen for it."

Xavier pauses, and then asks, "What do you think it'll be like leading an army, Evie?" My mind lurches back to the murderous street I just escaped—a street lined with fallen angels. I shudder. "It's what you said you want, isn't it? An army? You're going to make decisions that will *kill* angels, humans, and any other creature that chooses to join the fight. You've made your friends part of this—insisted they help you in a war they're wholly unprepared to battle."

"I didn't kno—"

"Don't tell me you didn't know." Xavier straightens. "I told you. Get used to this feeling—it won't go away. When one of them is killed—your *family*—it will be infinitely worse."

No longer in the mood to comfort me, he slips me off his lap and stands. He walks past a low glass table and blue silk-covered chairs, to an elegant doorway on the far wall. Pausing, he says over his shoulder, "This is your room. You'll be safe here." He leaves me alone, closing the double doors behind him.

With my head in my hands, I come apart. I pull my knees to my chest to hold myself together as I sob. Emil plans to kill everyone I've ever loved just to make me watch. I wipe my face on my sleeve and look around my ornate room—a bedroom. There aren't any windows, but that doesn't make it any less angel-chic. The walls are stone. Rounded archways and pillars make it look like a palace, but the walls aren't erected; they're carved out of rock. The air is thick—entombed. It's similar to what I experienced while in Brennus' underground lair in Houghton.

Cool colors of ice blue, chocolate brown, and white soften the look of the room in a decidedly feminine way. A bed juts out from against the wall. Its tall bedposts and massive headboard are caved from alabaster and piled high with white pillows. The white fur-like coverlet looks soft and inviting. Directly across from it, the stone fireplace cradles aspen logs. They crackle with flames in the grate. The scrolling stone supports beneath the mantel are positioned well above my head—I could probably stand in the fireplace with no problem.

I get to my feet, wrapping my arms around me for comfort. There are four sets of doors. I try one set and find they open to a closet filled with my-sized clothes. I frown. The Seraphim intend for me to be here for more than a few days. *Good luck with that*, I think. *I'm outta here as soon as I find the exit.*

The next door I open contains an opulent bathroom tiled in a multitude of blue-glass hues. I use the sink and wash up as best as I can. Wiping my face on the towel, I leave it on the immaculate countertop. I close that door and move on to a pair of wooden doors on the far wall opposite from where Xavier exited. When I open them, I'm surprised to find a thick, metal door behind them. It has a hatch-like round lever. Using both hands, I have to throw my back into opening it. The metal is frigid and whines as it scrapes against the metal catch. Shoving the door open, my hair whips around me as the coldest air I've ever felt in my life blows it back with enough force to take my breath away.

Stepping outside onto an ice-covered veranda, I look over the frozen railing at the sheer drop that goes on for miles. The veranda is carved out of the side of a mountain, which faces several other rock formations covered by ice and snow. Looking skyward, more balconies pepper the cliff face. The whole side of the mountain has been carved to resemble an ornate fortress. Other than this mountain fortress, nothing exists for as far as I can see. It's just barren snow-covered tundra and rock formations.

"I wouldn't advise going far in this weather, not without proper clothing and an experienced guide. The tundra is unforgiving on its best days," a voice from behind me says. Leonine features meet my stare when I turn.

Cherubim, I think as I look at the angel's face. His long, golden hair reaches to the top of his light blue wings. His eyes are that of a lion's, amber irises frame diamond-shaped pupils. He's wild. I take a step back from him, pressing against the frigid railing. He steps back from me, into my room. Lowering his chin, he almost looks tame. He extends his hand toward me. "Don't jump. Please."

"I can fly."

"The wind here is deceptive. It could slam you into the side of the cliff."

"How do I get out of here?" I ask, looking around at the bleak landscape.

"Where do you want to go?"

"Somewhere without angels."

"Does a place like that exist?"

I sigh. "How about somewhere with people?"

"Xavier wants you here."

"I don't care what he wants." I look the Cherub over again and have a nagging feeling. "Have we met? Do I know you?" The wind lifts my hair and blows it around, but I refuse to go back inside with him looming in the doorway.

"We've met—in a way. You were barely conscious the last time I saw you—Brennus was more than a little brutal to you in Houghton."

Images of Cherubim flying alongside Reed's car on the night Russell broke me out of Brennus' cave come back to me. "It was you—outside the car that night—as Russell drove. I thought I was hallucinating—"

"I had to speak to you that evening. I wanted to make sure you escaped. I wanted you to know..."

"You wanted me to know what?"

"I wanted you to know that we were proud of you."

"Who's we?"

"Heaven," he replies with a wary smile. Snow flurries around me. I quake from the cold. He sees it. "I don't want you to freeze to death. Do you mind coming back inside?" He motions with his hand for me to come in.

"What's your name?" I ask.

He says something in Angel.

"Err...in English?"

"Atwater." I move inside. He closes the metal door. I hurry across the room to the fireplace, extending my hands to it to warm them. "He's my responsibility, you know?" I look over my shoulder at him. He leans against the doorframe and studies me, toying with the hilt of a long broadsword strapped in a sheath at his waist.

"Who?" I ask in surprise as I turn toward him.

"Brennus." His eyes meet mine.

"What do you mean?"

"I was his guardian angel."

I stiffen. "When? When he was a faerie?"

Atwater nods. "When he still had his soul."

The ramifications of what he's saying strike me. My hands ball into fists. "You let Aodh get him!" I accuse.

"I did." There's regret in his eyes. It does nothing to alleviate my anger.

"Finn, too?" I ask. I don't care if he feels bad. He and Xavier should hang out. They both suck at their jobs.

"All of them," he affirms.

"Why?"

"I've already said too much," he replies. He moves to the door where he came in. "I'm glad to see that you're okay."

"He's not okay!" I snarl.

"I know," Atwater replies before he leaves my bedroom. I follow him. I want to know why he's here and what he's planning. It's about Brennus. That makes it about me, too. We're irreparably tied to one another by blood. By death. By love. By hate.

"Wait! Where're you going?" I enter the next room. "I need to talk to you!"

I stop short, almost colliding with Xavier who's covered by nothing more than a white towel around his hips. My face turns red. I crane my neck up to see his eyes. He blocks my way while he uses another towel to rub the water from the back of his neck. I quickly realize that this room is another bedroom, but decorated in masculine browns. Xavier's bedroom—attached to mine—like his and hers! I frown at him.

I duck around his outstretched wings, moving past him, out the door and into a circular corridor that's lined with clear glass pillars. They open into a rotunda—a hive-like arena. Angels of every type fly around in the middle of the open arena—the common space—moving from floor to floor without the need of elevators. No balustrades line the levels above or below, so either one uses one's wings to fly when stepping off the edge, or it will be a very long way down. The floors above us climb toward a glass-domed sky. Sunlight filters down into the center of the hive, sparkling off the blue glass-tiled floor about a mile or so below us. Atwater blends into the swarm of angels and disappears.

Xavier leans against the doorframe, watching me. I hitch my thumb in the direction Atwater disappeared. "Do you know him? He's Brennus' guardian angel."

Xavier nods. "He was, but the battle for that soul has been lost, hasn't it?"

"Has it? Has it really?" I cross my arms. "Why would he tell me that then? Why would he seek me out?"

"Maybe he feels responsible for what's been done to you by Brennus."

"I want to talk to him."

"I can arrange that, but later, after you've rested."

"I'd rather talk to him now."

"You're tired."

"I'm not."

"You were attacked by Emil twice today. You're cut up, bruised and beaten." I ignore him. Clutching a glass pillar, I look over the edge at the crazy hoards of angels.

This whole place has been hollowed out of the interior of a mountain. I have a feeling I'm not even seeing a fraction of it. Across the rotunda enormous glass sculptures of angels hold scepters and spears, guarding the threshold to an elaborately carved entryway. A narthex stretches out beyond the rotunda. More hallways on other levels burrow through the rock. The floor that is far below has a maze-like pattern. Xavier joins me at the edge. "It's a meditation labyrinth. When you walk it, you can feel the presence of God."

"So this is the army?" I ask, watching a few angels below walk the maze in circular patterns.

"This is some of our army—the ones that follow me. Your father has more."

"What does Tau plan to do? Will he bring Reed here? Will he attack Emil?" Xavier's eyes hood before he turns away and moves back into his room. I follow him and close the door behind us. Xavier rummages through his clothes in his closet. I cross my arms, watching him.

"You're safe here." Xavier says. "Why don't you go to your room and clean up—rest. Or we can eat, if you're hungry—"

"Why won't you answer my questions?" I retort. With his back to me, he drops his towel. My cheeks redden. "Xavier!" I turn my back to him. "It's not going to work. I'm not staying here—"

"There's nowhere for you to go, Evie. We're surrounded by

the harshest conditions on Earth."

"You can't keep me here."

"Actually, I can," Xavier says, as he walks past me into his room. Luckily, he has managed to dress himself in a long sleeved black thermal shirt. Long slits in the fabric allow for his red wings to be out. His black trousers are military in design. He goes to a side table and picks up a watch. Facing away from me, he straps it on his wrist.

"I don't want to be here with you."

Xavier is silent for a moment, long enough for me to regret saying that. I'm not looking to hurt him. I just want him to stop trying to control me. His tone is brittle as he says, "Should you attempt to leave, you won't like the consequences, Evie."

"But my friends are in danger!"

"They're in more danger when they're with you."

"I need to warn them!"

"I'll see what I can do to locate them. I'm not promising anything. They've proven to be uncooperative."

"They were helping me!"

"By keeping you from me? That's not helping you."

"You started it! You kicked them out of Brennus' castle."

"I said I'd see what I could do. End of discussion."

I growl in frustration, turning I go to my bedroom, which is only feet away. After I slam the double doors, I unleash my fury on the room. Energy leaks out of me. All the furniture in close proximity to me floats up off the ground. I exhale a calming breath and all of it drops back down with a loud *BANG*.

"Time to find Reed," I whisper to myself.

Climbing onto the bed, I sit on it cross-legged. I concentrate on slowing down my heartbeat, which is out of control. The room spins and whirls around me as I create a replica of myself—a clone. My consciousness inhabits her form, and I gaze around at the room; it's a rainbow of colors and shapes. I'm weary, making it hard to concentrate. Nothing in her vision is crisp, like I'm capable of seeing when I'm not tired. I take a deep breath and listen to the hive of activity all around me—angelic voices have a faraway drone. Giving in to its white noise, I become one with it. *Reed,* I think his name. I am pulled to the south. I let the energy inside of me go. My clone launches through the wall. She travels in a streak over ice-shrouded terrain. I lose perspective as she increases our speed—we spiral: white, snow-covered earth, blue sky, clouds, mountains, snow, ocean, blue sky, ice, growing darkness, stars, black water, falling through stone—cold, cold stone.

Dominion, I think as I pass familiar floors and artwork as I continue downward.

Several angels spot me as I descend through the fresco-painted ceiling of the chateau's lobby. Shouts and threats issue from the divine angels closest to me. It's sort of amusing to watch them stand helplessly by as I continue to descend through the stone floor.

All thoughts of other angels leave me for a moment when I feel butterflies riot inside my clone. *REED!* My clone slows and drops into a damp corridor outside a thick, metal door at the end of a shadowy hallway. Quickly searching the other end of the passageway, there are two angels posted at the entrance with their backs to me. They haven't noticed me yet, but they're the exceptions. On the levels above, there's a definite uproar of angels. The fact that they couldn't follow my clone through floors is causing chaos among them. They'll mobilize and they'll find a way to be all over me soon.

I follow the butterflies pulling me to a thick steel door. When I pass through it, I find Reed among the ocean of darkness and cold, salty air. He's dressed only in the blue jeans he had on when I last saw him. His hair is dirty and disheveled—matted in the back with what I'm guessing is his dried blood. Bare-chested, his fierce wings extend at the sight of me before him. His eyes drink me in. Reaching out to touch me—to take me into his arms—he hesitates, realizing that I exist in a clone of light energy, not flesh, sinew, and bone, like him.

"You're alive," he states, his voice is raw, like he somehow doubted it. His brow wrinkles in frustration at his inability to pull me to him. He gets as near to me as he can, inhaling the scent of me on my clone.

"What did they do to you?" I whisper.

"It doesn't matter."

I glance over my clone's shoulder at the door. "There're coming," I warn. I look back at him. "How do I free you?"

"Just stand there," he replies. "I'll take care of the rest." His eyes never leave the image of me before him. Shouting and clamoring sounds come to us through the heavy door in echoes, but still, he just stares at me.

"I have so much to tell you, Reed," I whisper.

His eyebrows pull together. "Where are you now?"

I shake my head. "I don't know. I'm somewhere in the Arctic—in a mountain—a hollowed-out fortress full of divine angels. There are probably thousands of them there.

"Who is with you?" he asks.

"Xavier. I think he's in charge. He expects me to stay there."

Reed nods, showing no emotion—I can't tell how he feels about that. "Stay with him. He'll protect you until I get there."

There's a big *BANG* against the door from the other side. It makes me turn and face it. Reed moves next to me. "There are a lot of them," I whisper. I want to grab his hand, but I can't.

"Good," he says with a reassuring smile. "I'll come for you soon—to the Arctic. I just have to do something first."

"What?' I ask with apprehension.

"I have to get the boatswain from your father."

"It's a key to Sheol. Why do you want it?"

"It's a weapon, Evie. It harms half-angels—it hurt you. It has different sound frequencies. Some sounds open doors and some sounds maim or kill. I have to retrieve it from Tau so that no one can use it against you." Scraping against the door causes me to shift from foot to foot in nervous anticipation. Reed is calm—ready for anything.

"There's something I have to tell you, Reed. There's another half-angel—an evil one. His name is Emil. He was in my last lifetime with me. He's—" *BANG* the bolt is thrown from the door.

Instead of finishing my thought, I whisper, "I love you."

"You *are* love, Evie."

The door swings open. Power angels swarm in. They run right through me, scattering my clone's light. I manage to reassemble the shimmering image of me in time to see Reed jump over several of them and fly through the cell's door. The door crashes closed behind him as he locks the other angels in the dungeon.

I can't help the smile that forms on my lips as I hurry to the cell's door and pass through it. Reed is on the other side, waiting for me. His perfect mouth leans nearer to my clone's lips. "I want so much to kiss you right now," he says. In this light, his face and body show the strain of his captivity. Although there are no marks on him, he has a hollow look about him that makes me feel even more contempt for his captors.

"If I thought for one second that I could hold my form, I'd have already kissed you, but I'm having a hard time keeping my consciousness in my clone."

"Are you hurt? Are they mistreating you?" he asks.

"No, it's not the divine angels. I'm just tired—so much has happened so fast."

While Reed casts a shadow on the wall, my form throws only light. "I was worried about you, Evie," he admits. "When I saw you fall, I thought for a moment that Tau killed you. I retaliated against your father—I nearly killed him."

"He doesn't look like you hurt him too badly," I whisper, my eyes going to the end of the hallway where Tau fills the archway; his red wings spread wide. He has no emotion except an expression of superiority on his face.

Tau doesn't approach Reed, but instead pulls his phone from his pocket and connects with a number on speed dial. Holding the phone to his ear, he says, "Evie's here. She sent a clone, Xavier." He listens for a moment before he adds, "Yes. Now." Pulling the phone away from his ear, he ends the call.

In the back of my mind, I hear a commotion. It's a build up of echoes—a slamming of a door—faraway, like the ocean in a shell—footsteps. I feel my upper arms seized, but Reed hasn't touched me. My clone fades, her light scattering sparks into the darkness of the hallway. My name reverberates off the brown stone walls surrounding us. "Do you hear that?" I ask Reed beside me.

"I hear nothing," he replies with a grim expression.

"It's Xavier." I draw my clone's light back to her in a desperate attempt to stay with Reed. Xavier's presence is all around me—his scent is time and distance—so vast I can't ever escape it.

A violent shake scatters my clone's light again in glowing embers like the stirring of a campfire in the middle of the night. Sparks dance away, up and out from me. I feel Xavier's touch. He becomes the wind lifting this body away.

"Xavier's in my room with me. He's trying to bring me back to him, Reed."

"I'll find you," Reed promises as his shoulders bend toward my clone. His need to protect me is written in his eyes. "Soon."

Looking away from Reed, towards Tau, I call to my father, "Don't hurt Reed."

Tau's voice is stern. "You're not in control here."

Something cold swabs my bicep. The scent of rubbing alcohol assails my nose. A dull pain sticks my arm. My head spins with dizziness; Reed and Xavier are before me as two different planes of reality merge at once. I become a dead star collapsing, compressing all my energy into an internal fire. The light within my clone bursts into a shower of sparks. My consciousness emerges from that reality, being torn away from Reed as I propel back into this one. I open my eyes and find my head cradled beneath Xavier's arm while he holds my limp body to him upon the bed's white blanket. The fire still crackles in the grate. It's quiet in my Arctic bedroom with just the soft sound of Xavier's heartbeat.

"What did you do?" I ask, grogginess overwhelming me.

"I had to bring you back," he whispers near my ear. "I gave you a mild sedative. You can rest now." His lips press to my forehead. When he pulls away, my cheek falls upon his shoulder.

I struggle against the darkness that is pulling me into it. "You shouldn't have drugged me. I'll fall asleep, Xavier."

"That's the plan," he says in a lulling voice.

"Brennus will be there...he'll be waiting for me," I manage to say in a thready tone. "He can find me...whenever I close...my...eyes..."

Through a half-lidded stare, I see Xavier's eyes open wider in growing understanding—panic. He grips my arms and presses his face nearer to mine. "How?"

"Blood. He has some of mine and he can use it...the dark red path that leads him to me." My eyes slip closed.

"Can he harm you in your dreams?" he asks with a wild shake when I don't immediately open my eyes.

I can only manage a squint. "He won't hurt me."

Xavier scoffs. "Didn't he just spend months trying to kill you?"

"We're...past that now."

"He's an evil killer, Evie!"

"Maybe he was evil—before, but now—"

"He's still evil! You did nothing that would change that."

"He's a weapon, like me—has been for a long time—just waiting to be wielded."

"You don't know what you're talking about!"

"Don't I?" I ask, feeling more relaxed than I have in months. "I'll be sure to ask him...what side he's on, but I already know the answer."

"Really? And what side is that, Evie?"

"Mine."

CHAPTER 12
Things I Shouldn't Know

In the darkness, my hand moves over the soft sheets beneath me. My breath exhales, a confession of life. With my cheek against the mattress, a golden glow falls upon the linens from over my shoulder. I frown. Slowly, I lift my head from the bed and rise up on my elbow. Brennus is stretched out next to me, his legs crossed. His black wings rest against a thick pillow. He plays with a golden orb of light in his hand in a distracted way, the light falls over his black leather jacket in such a way as to make it appear liquid, and then shadow.

"Where are we?" I ask while sitting up straighter. My hands smooth my rumpled hair. I'm light-headed, it's as if I've had too much to drink.

Brennus grins as he throws the ball of light into the air. Its golden glow hovers above us, dispelling the darkness in our immediate area, but beyond the orb, the absence of light seems to go on forever.

"Ye'll have ta tell me where we are. 'Tis yer dream."

"I don't know where I am." I still fear him, no matter whose side he's on.

"Where were ye when ye were drugged?"

My hands drop from my hair as I turn to stare at him. "How did you know?"

"Dere's nuting here." He waves his hand in the direction of the darkness. "Yer mind is so vivid—expressive. 'Tis unlike ye na ta have a tousand wee details. Ye see in light, na dark. Dis is da opposite of ye."

"It's scary how well you know me," I murmur.

"I am scary, never forget dat."

"Whenever I do, you remind me."

That gets another grin from him. "Show me where ye were as ye fell asleep—ye were in dis bed, I take it?" Brennus runs a hand over the white fur blanket.

"Why do you want to know?"

"Because I'm interested," he says with an unruffled mien. "I want ta know everyting about ye. Knowing where ye are is always a priority ta me. Dat should come as no surprise ta ye."

"Yes, you're a total stalker. The truth is that I don't know where I am," I confess. "All I know is that it's cold—" I'm cut off as Brennus' hand cups my cheek and his lips press to mine. His kiss is soft and sweet —so unlike his demanding personality. I fall silent, not responding, yet unable to pull away. Brennus' eyebrow lifts before he pulls away from me. His lips curl in a barely suppressed smile and his green eyes shine with inner fire.

I pull my jumbled thoughts together enough to murmur, "Don't kiss me."

"Technically, we're na even in da same room together."

"It feels real," I whisper.

"It does," he admits with a gleam in his eyes.

"So, don't do it."

"'Twas na a kiss so much as 'twas an attempt ta clear da fog from yer mind."

"It felt like a kiss—and what's so funny?" I ask at his growing smirk.

He raises both of his eyebrows. "Nuting," he replies, his smile spreading into a full-fledged grin. He glances around, causing me to do the same. The nothingness is being replaced by a watercolor of light. It bleeds from the ceiling downward, filling in the details and dimensions of my wintery bedroom. "I was jus tryin' ta get a clearer picture of dis place."

I grasp his hand; it's warm in mine. "You can't come here, Brennus. This place is crawling with angels."

His eyebrow arches in question. "Are ye worried about dem or me?"

"Neither. Both. Neither! "I shake my head in confusion, dropping his hand. Turning away from him, I rise from the bed and walk to the fireplace. Heat radiates from it just like a real fire. I face Brennus as he stands. "I didn't do what you asked."

Brennus frowns, "Dat's na surprisin'. Ye never do as ye're told—ye always need more tellin'. Ye'll have ta be more specific because I do na remember whah 'twas—"

"Emil's alive. He's here—in this time."

Understanding enters his eyes. "I know."

Confusion clouds mine. "You do?"

"I was jus wi' him—yer Emil."

"He's not my Emil!" I retort in an almost breathless denial.

"But he is—yers." Brennus extends his hand to me. "Take a walk wi' me." His head gestures toward the door. "We have much ta discuss."

I walk to his side, but I don't take his hand. "You were just with him?"

We move together, through the doorway. "Whose room is dis?" Brennus asks, his brow wrinkling.

"Xavier's." I watch him eye the enormous bed. "What?"

"He's guarding ye. Dey have ta go tru him ta get ta ye."

"Yeah," I agree as I continue through the room and to the door that leads to the rotunda outside it, "he's a bit possessive—kind of like all the men in my life."

"Ye tend ta bring dat out in us."

"Sure. Blame the victim."

He ignores me. "Except for Emil. I tink he jus wants ta end ye." The truth of Brennus' statement brings fear. I know the danger I'm in. Emil can tell tomorrow by where we've been. I have very few memories of him —only the ones from Lille.

We pause outside the doorway overlooking the center of the rotunda. We're across from the giant glass-cut angel statues on the other side of the track-like passageway. His proximity to me is intimate—unnerving —especially because it's just the two of us here. Brennus backs off the edge of the balcony. His strong wings beat the air as he hovers in front of me. "Has yer flying gotten any better?" he asks.

My wings arch out around me to half extension. "I can hold my own."

He studies the shapes my wings take before he gives me a cheeky grin and replies, "Ye can."

He turns away from me and flies upward, past several balconies and tunnels that lead away from the rotunda. I follow him up all the way to the peak of the glass dome. Sunlight is obscured by snow and ice, but there are enough scattered drifts in it to be able to see out.

The rim of the dome has silver filigree carved in the shape of angel wings. I hold onto the stone ledge that meets the silver edge, my wings keeping me aloft as I peer outside at the mountain peaks and snow beyond. There could be an ocean off in the distance, but it could also be refracted light of the bluest hue coming off the icy snow.

The air around me stirs from Brennus' wings as he poises beside me. "Da northern hemisphere—at da bottom of da world."

I give him a funny look. "How do you know we're not in the southern hemisphere?"

"I can tell da difference. Da magnetic pull stirs in a different direction from pole ta pole. In time, ye'll learn ta differentiate between dem."

"If you're so intuitive, why are you calling the northern hemisphere the bottom of the world?"

Brennus' eyebrows rise in challenge. "'Tis a matter of perspective, is it na? Change yer angle and everyting changes. 'Tis all in how ye look at a ting. Ye should try turning a map upside down once in awhile. Everyting looks different when ye do."

What he says makes sense. "You always surprise me, Brennus," I admit.

"Surprisin' ye has become a bit of an obsession of moin," he murmurs with a sexy smile. "Come. Let's see whah lies below." Brennus' green eyes dance as he retracts his black wings and free-falls through the hollow of the mountain. He's not looking at the approaching ground, but instead, he has his back to the floor as he stares up at me.

I face him as I follow him, pulling my wings in and feeling the thrill of speed while I fall away from the natural light. My hair flies back from my face, tangling behind me. Level after level rushes by in flight. I'm not weightless with Brennus just inches beneath me. It could be him pulling me down as much as gravity. To be alone with him in this place is a dream of falling with no ending—just he and I—out of sight.

As we near the ground, fear grows that he'll crash into it. From deep within me, I'm compelled to rescue him from impending doom. Before I can conjure a spell, however, one that will stop him from splattering all over the stone floor, my hair falls forward around my face. I'm caught in stasis for a moment, neither moving nor falling. I stare into his eyes, so close to mine, and I think for a moment that it might be okay if we never come down. Neither of us is here of our own free will—not really. We were both somehow forced to climb this hill, be these monsters, and our inevitable fall will probably destroy us both.

Brennus guides our landing, in one moment turning us from a horizontal position of falling to a vertical one where his feet touch the ground first. He draws me to him. My hands rest upon his shoulders as I slide down his chest. When my feet are firmly on the floor, I let him go, flushed by the intimate contact.

The sound of rushing water draws my attention away from Brennus. Water runs over the ice walls surrounding us. It drains through a grated edge, but some mist wets the stone tiles near it. A round labyrinth twists its way over the floor with a pattern tiled in shades of blues. Xavier had mentioned it to me earlier—it's a meditation maze. I've seen something similar to it in pictures of grand cathedrals, but it's different being near one; there's an innate sacredness to it that invades my senses.

"Would ye like ta try it?" Brennus asks. I nod and walk with him, following the obvious entranceway before us.

After we round the first bend in the maze, we follow the outer rim. The mist from the water walls wets my face. Lights fade in and out in intervals behind the water with tranquil effect. "You know something, don't you, Brennus? About Emil?" He glances at me. "You said earlier that Emil just wants to end me."

"Emil attacked yer boy-aingeal—at yer aingeal's house in Crestwood—he was looking for ye."

"Is he alive?"

"Emil?" Brennus asks.

"Russell."

"He survived."

"How? Emil nearly shredded me within the first few minutes of meeting him and he technically wasn't even fully there. He was inside a possessed human body."

Brennus pauses in the labyrinth. "Ye should be wi' me! I'll keep ye away from Emil. Did he harm ye?"

I stop walking as I face him with a shrug. "He didn't kill me."

"Dat's na whah I asked." I walk again in silence. Brennus catches up to me and keeps pace beside me. "When Finn and I found yer friends in Crestwood, Emil was already dere. He was planning ta execute da wee Throne and da Power—"

"Anya and Zephyr."

"Right, dem. He was going ta keep Russell alive until such a time as he could torture and kill him in front of ye."

"But Russell escaped?"

"Escape is maybe na da right word—more like he was rescued."

"You helped Russell?"

Brennus shrugs. "Finn and da fellas took exception ta da way Emil spoke about deir queen. Dey tought he needed ta be taken down off his high horse."

I put my hand on Brennus' arm, stopping and turning toward him. "No, Brennus. None of them do anything without your consent. It was you—you saved my friends."

Brennus tucks my arm in the crook of his elbow as he urges me to move alongside him again. "Do na tell anyone dat I helped, I have a reputation ta protect." My mind reels with the implications. "Whah happened wi' ye and Emil? When did he attack ye?"

"You have to tell me everything first—with Russell and Emil."

Brennus smiles at the shock on my face that I can't hide from him. "I had a wee chat with Emil—Djet. Do ye remember him by dat name?" he asks.

"No."

"May I touch yer cheek?" I stop walking and take a step away from him. He adds quickly, "'Tis only so I can show ye whah Russell remembers of yer lifetime wi' him in Egypt. 'Twill be easier ta do dat if I can give ye da memory rather dan explaining it all."

"How do you have Russell's memories?" My suspicion is clear.

"I stole dem from him while he was focused on Emil." I relent by moving closer to Brennus and facing him. The backs of his warm fingers brush a soft path down my cheek. When his hand drops away he takes my arm again, tucking it around his. We begin to walk the maze once more as transparent walls form around the curves of the maze—Brennus' magic is conjuring them. "Dese are Russell's memories from one of yer lifetimes together."

A golden-skinned Emil appears on the wall of the maze next to a slight, dark-haired girl that I know to be me. As we walk, the scene of my lifetime with Russell plays out. He was Iah then, and I, as Zahra, couldn't get enough of him. I witness our most intimate moments—our first meeting, our first kiss, the first time we made love in the secret alcove of Djet's Egyptian palace are all there—all the things I used to see —all the things I used to be in that lifetime—seen through Iah's eyes. My death—being burned alive—is gruesome, but it's not as if it's happening to me. It's not the same as when I was forced back into the memory with Emil in Lille. I'm not experiencing it—I don't feel the same pain, fear, or other raw emotions the way I had in France. This time, it's tolerable.

"So, Emil was Djet, too?"

"He was."

"Was he in every one of my lifetimes with me? Do you know?" My voice rises with sick desperation.

"Shh, hush now," Brennus soothes as he disengages his arm from mine. He wraps it around my shoulder, pulling me to his side. "'Tis difficult for ye ta hear dis, but 'tis yer past, na yer future." We round another bend in the floor. The transparent walls disappear by falling into the ground—no longer playing out the salacious aspects of my former lifetime

"Was he in all my lifetimes?" I ask again.

"I tink it's a distinct possibility..."

"Why do you think that? He's a monster."

"He is a monster. He convinced his soul mate ta fall wi' him, den he figured out a way ta take her soul apart." I stop where I am. I can't take another step forward. Brennus bends so that his lips are close to my ear, so close they brush the top of it, causing me to shiver. He whispers, "I tink he did it so dat ye'd be forced ta follow him in every one of his lifetimes. Ye'd have ta always be wi' him—ye always try ta stop him from doing evil. I tink he once believed dat he'd eventually win—dat ye'd lose yer soul ta him and be his forevermore. Now he knows. He understands dat ye'll never agree ta be a part o' him. Ye'll never be his partner, or his slave. So he wants revenge. He wants ta snuff ye out."

My mind is numb. "Why me—"

"Heaven does whah it wants. If ye want a confession or an apology from dem ye'll be waitin' for eternity. Emil fell. He was a part of da rebellion in Heaven. I tink dis is where yer turmoil began. Ye're a part of da aingeals' war now. We're in it...and we play ta win."

"There is no winning this, Brennus! We both just lose!"

"Na if we're together."

"You believe that?"

"I do. I can carry ye any distance dat I have ta. 'Tis different between us now—ye feel it, do ye na? Ye changed me and I'm in yer heart."

He's right. My heart is still intact...and I feel Brennus there.

"Listen to me, Brennus. You know I'm nothing but trouble. This war is eternal—"

"We'll all have ta choose a side soon. I'm only good when I'm wi' ye. Wi'out ye, I can na say for certain upon which side I'd fall."

I know he's right. He's different when we're together—still ruthless, but not to the same degree. With me around, he's capable of mercy. It makes me wonder what he was like before he lost his soul. "I met an angel here," I murmur.

"Oh, aye?" he says with a sarcastic smirk on his lips, making me aware of the ridiculousness of my statement. There are literally thousands of angels here. "Anyone in particular?"

"I knew him—this angel. I'd seen him before—after I'd escaped from your cave in Houghton. His name is Atwater. Do you know the name?"

Brennus straightens, hit by a wave of recognition. "He's here? In dis place?" I nod. "Did ye speak ta him?"

"Yes."

"Whah did he have ta say?" Brennus asks with his back now ramrod straight.

"When I first saw him in Houghton, after Russell came for me—I was delirious from the bites you gave me. Atwater told me then that you'd burn for me the way you've made the wans burn for you—that it was recompense. I'm bad Karma for you, Brennus."

"No, ye're na. He's knows ye're more dan dat. He knows dat I've been waiting for ye ta come for as long as Finn has been a Gancanagh. As long as he divided me family—and he best continue ta hide from me—should I find him again he'll know pain."

"You've been waiting for me?"

"I have. I've been waiting for me queen. Dere are tings we need ta do."

"What things? What are you talking about?"

"Whah else did Atwater tell ye?"

"He said he was your guardian angel."

Brennus' jaw hardens. "He's nuting ta me."

"He's something to you. What happened? He refused to help you...when Aodh took Finn?"

"Heaven does na help. Dey negotiate, Genevieve."

"What did you negotiate with Atwater, Brennus?" Secrets shadow his eyes. "What is it?"

"I was so young den—when I knew Atwater—immortal in youth, was I. When ye're dat young, ye never know whah ye're promisin'. I never wanted dis crown—ta be king. But ye do whah ye have ta do—even when it shakes ye ta da ground."

"What are you talking about, Brennus?" I whisper.

"Do ye remember when I told ye dat I saw me soul, Genevieve? Jus after ye changed me?"

"Yeah, it was when I tried to kill you."

He grins. "Och, had ye tried ta kill me, I'd be gone. Ye wanted me ta change, and change I did," Brennus says ruefully, and then he sobers. "I saw him again—me soul—after yer fire tore tru me."

"How?"

"Me soul was ripped away from Sheol. He tried ta reunite wi' me—become one once more, but I am still mostly undead, ye see?" I nod my head in understanding, and Brennus continues, "He gave me a message ta give ta ye."

"He did?" I ask, my eyes wide with surprise.

"He did," Brennus affirms with a nod. "He said ta say: 'Tell her I've been waiting for her. Tell her I'll know her by note.'"

"He'll know me by note? What does that mean?"

Brennus shakes his head. "I do na know. He took some of me memories wi' him ta Sheol. Finn speaks of tings in our past—sometimes I have no memory of dem. And now dat me soul and I are apart, I do na know whah he has experienced in Sheol. But I tink dat I made a deal wi' Heaven before all o' dis began."

"It's the same with me. Russell remembers so much more than I do. For some reason, you and I are not meant to know."

"Ye see. We're much da same," he murmurs as he grasps my hand and tugs me along beside him once more, leading the way through the labyrinth. Neither one of us speaks for a long time, lost as we are in our own thoughts as much as in the twisting path. We reach the center of the maze where it opens into a small circle. Upon the floor, a majestic, tiled tree is spread out, it's branches reaching in every direction, winding into the borders of the path from where we had just come and extending out to form other paths that were invisible to me when I'd been outside the circle.

Brennus looks around at the floor. "We are both on da same path, Genevieve, precisely where we need to be."

"Precisely the right path for what?" I ask breathlessly.

"For us," Brennus says as he bends, kissing me tenderly on my forehead.

Before he pulls away from me, his firm lips ease and become feather light. His presence wavers to transparency, a dark silhouette against the water falling over the walls surrounding us...and then he's gone.

∼

WAKING up from my all-encompassing dream with Brennus, I'm standing in the middle of the labyrinth. Xavier is in front of me. His mouth is white-lipped with anxiety. "Evie," he sighs my name while gathering me to him. With my cheek resting against his chest, I watch water flow down the ice wall. It disappears into the grates in the floor, just beyond the Power angels who have stopped everything to watch me. Brennus is gone. I must've come here in my sleep, following him wherever he led me. "I'll take you back to your room."

"Emil's my evil soul mate—" I pull away from Xavier's chest as I strain my neck to see his eyes, "and you knew—you've always known!"

Xavier stiffens. "He's not your soul mate, Evie. He's your inescapable."

"My what?"

"Your inescapable. You've sworn to protect the world from him. You fight him in every one of his lifetimes."

"Emil is my inescapable?"

"Yes, but this time, I have to find a way to not only annihilate his body, but also destroy his malicious soul so that he cannot return. I know that now. It will be my mission, Evie," Xavier answers, barely breathing. "I will eliminate him for you, and then we will be together for eternity."

Brennus

CHAPTER 13
Hear Da Wind Confess

BRENNUS

Me eyes open ta a high ceiling above; exposed stone beams hold up a barrel-vaulted ceiling, shedding its discolored, crumbling plaster. Light from several half-boarded-over windows dispels da shadows from da room. I bring me hand ta da bridge of me nose, pinching it in an attempt ta ease da ache dere. I feel as if I've slept in da arms of an aingeal, only ta awake in Hell. Me head spins around as me blood jumps tru me. I'm na accustomed ta dat—me blood flowing freely in me veins—liquid and on fire. Me heart does na pump it; it still lies dormant in me chest. Nevertheless, blood is circulating tru out me body now, making me stronger dan ever before. 'Tis just one of da ways I'm different since Genevieve changed me.

Rising upon me elbow, it sinks inta da soft mattress. One corner of da clean, linen sheet comes untucked; I ignore it. I wait until da pressure in my head eases, and den I drop me hand ta see Finn eyeing me from his poppy-colored, winged chair in a corner of da bedroom. Finn had located dis defunct seminary in a falling down part of Detroit—Genevieve's city.

"Any problems?" I ask Finn, wondering why he's here in me bedroom.

"Plenty, but none pressing," he replies, shooting out da white cuffs of his dress shirt from beneath his black suit jacket before smoothing his dark sleeve.

"How far are we wi' da move?"

He smiles. "We're better dan expected—'tis a sound location—easier ta keep hidden dan our place in Ireland." I nod. Da six-story Norman Gothic Revival building Finn found for us is spacious, constructed of brown ledge stone wi' smooth granite window sill courses. Me room is on the top floor of a turret of sorts wi' a pointed copper roof. Finn chose the location because it has several attached buildings in da same style. Dey encompass a few city blocks. At da same time, da structures afford us a great deal of privacy in dis abandoned neighborhood.

"Any complaints?" I ask.

"Truth be told, dere were a few," Finn says wi' a barely suppressed grin.

"Eh?" I respond with a raise of me eyebrow.

Finn's eyes twinkle. "Some o' da neighbors took offense ta da paleness of me flesh."

Both of me eyebrows rise now. "Whah did ye say ta dat?" I smirk despite me aching head.

Wi' a cheeky grin, he replies, "I told dem 'tis difficult ta get a tan when one's undead."

"How did dey take it?"

"Och, Brady ate dem before dey could respond. He was leppin' wi' da hunger."

I shake me head. "Anyting else?"

"I put Comgan in charge of da renovations. Da roof is sound, jus missing a wee bit o' da slate. In all, 'twas a grand structure at one time: now 'tis a skeleton whose flesh has been ravished by poverty. Dermot has layered spells over da location. I had Erskine aid him. No craitur should be able ta detect our presence here. Since we bought da property straight out, na even da humans will bother us."

I rub me eyes and nod. "Dat's good, Finn."

Finn studies me before he asks, "Do ye need anyting, Brenn? Is dere someting I can do for ye?"

"How long have I been gone?"

"Asleep?" He shrugs. "Na long—a few hours." He leans back in his seat. His calm, regal eyes miss nuting.

"Ye've been here da whole time?"

"I have." He nods as if he hasn't anyting better ta do. His black hair falls forward onto his brow.

"I can take care of meself, Finn," I mutter, trying ta clear me head.

"Even so."

"Ye plannin' ta guard me forever, brudder?" I ask.

"If need be."

"Ye worried one of da fellas will try ta kill me in me sleep?"

"Ye do smell delicious—very much like Genevieve at da moment—ye may want ta go wash off her scent before someone decides ta make ye his queen. And ta yer point, ye resemble such a peaceful craitur when ye're nappin'. 'Tis a wonder I do na end ye meself," he says with a grin. His green eyes, so reminiscent of our family's, glow wi' humor. Dere's na a bit o' malice in his voice, jus mirth. In truth, he'd protect me at his own peril, and I'd protect him at moin.

"Do ye plan ta be around whenever I close me eyes?"

"Ye sleep too deeply. Ye're like a wan," he says critically.

"Ye try sleepin' lightly after all of dese centuries wi'out—'tis no easy task."

"Ye're too auld, Brenn" he teases me.

"I might be at dat."

"Will ye speak of Genevieve or no? I've a care ta know how our queen fairs."

"She's grand."

"Is she now?"

"Da divine aingeals have her in a wintry, mountain enclave —'tis very Palladian—ye'd approve."

"So Emil hasn't taken her?"

"Na for da moment."

"Shall we go and collect her den?" Finn asks, but he seems in no hurry ta move from where he is.

"Dere's more ta it. Atwater is dere wi' her," I say. Finn's

demeanor changes as if I had told him dat a fella had touched his Molly. Quick as a *click*, he's on his feet by me side wi' a killer-shine is his eyes.

"Ye're sure 'twas him?"

"I did na see him wi' me own eyes. Genevieve told me he sought her out."

Finn's knuckles stand out on his fists, ready ta be bloodied. "Whah does da bugger want wi' Genevieve? Does he have a plan for her as well?"

"He's an aingeal. Dey all have plans, one way or da other," I say.

"Except dat Atwater's plans never come ta fruition."

"Do dey na? I seem ta recall dat we're both of us Gancanagh and Aodh is no longer in charge."

"Dat is da deal ye made wi' him—da one ta protect me. 'Twas na da deal I made wi' him. And he should never have led ye ta us! Ye'd never have found me on yer own and ye would have been better off!"

"I'd na be better off knowin' dat me brudder was at da mercy of a sadistic monster. I could na live like dat."

"So ye did na live! Ye became undead. 'Tis na whah Atwater promised!"

"How would I know da deal ye made wi' him if ye never speak o' it?"

"Ye were never ta be a part of it!"

"Again, Finn, a part of whah?"

"It does na matter. He lied ta me," Finn says bitterly.

"How did he lie?"

"He was supposed ta protect me family from Aodh and in exchange I'd..."

"Ye'd whah? Whah happened between ye two?"

"Ye want ta know whah happened? I lost me soul. Beyond dat, ye do na need ta know." An invisible serpent has wound itself around his neck in a strangle hold. He'll na say more. I know it well enough; we've had dis conversation a tousand times.

"Foin. Do na tell me. I'll jus say dis: Heaven knows all o' yer weakness—dey know jus whah will make ye do deir bidding. 'Tis after ye agree dat dey cut all da ropes from beneath ye and let ye fall."

"Sometimes ye have ta do bad ta do good—hide a wave in da tide," Finn says.

"Did ye mean ta fall den?"

"Did ye?" he counters.

I shrug. "Dere was no help for it."

"Ye say dat Atwater is wi' Genevieve?" He's lookin' right tru me now.

"He is."

"When do we go?" Finn asks wi' a new urgency.

"Whah is yer plan?"

He turns and walks ta da window, yanking away a board covering it. "I jus want ta have a chat wi' Atwater when we collect our queen, 'tis all." Cold air wafts inta da room. I rise from da bed and come ta stand next ta Finn. Outside, there are crumbling buildings painted a dull shade of gray tagged wi' neon-colored graffiti. Nuting stirs wi'out, save da fellas. Da humans who resided nearby have either been instructed ta leave after being touched or dey've become food.

"Whah do ye know about our souls?"

Finn shrugs. "Why would I know anyting about our souls? Dey're in Sheol."

'Tis true enough, whah Finn says, but I know me brudder; he keeps his own secrets. "I saw me soul once again, when Genevieve changed me."

Finn leans forward, his hands curl on the windowsill. "Why have ye na told me dis before?" He straightens and glares at me. "Did yer soul speak ta ye?"

"He did."

"Whah did he say?" Finn asks almost breathlessly.

"Whah deal did ye make wi' Atwater?"

Finn's jaw tenses. He glances out da window once more. "I can na tell ye."

I nod. "So dere was a deal—signed in blood."

"Whah did yer soul say?" Finn asks again.

"He had a message for me queen. He said to tell her dat he'd know her by note. Do ye know whah dat means?"

"I do na," he admits, but he can na hold back a smile as it spreads his lips.

"Why are ye smilin'?"

"Genevieve truly is da queen."

I grunt. "Did ye doubt it?"

He shakes his head no. "I was sure she was da one da moment she killed Keegan—in da caves—'twas as if time stood still and da life dat I'd known for so long was no more."

"She gave ye a purpose again."

He stares at me before he says, "She did. Ye felt it, too?"

"I did," I say wi' a perfunctory nod.

"I was na sure. I tought maybe ye jus fell in love wi' her."

"Is dere a difference?" I ask.

"Dere is—she's here ta do a job."

"Is she?" I ask wi' a lift of me brow.

"Ye know dat she is."

"And ye're here ta help her wi' dat?" I ask.

"I am here, let us leave it at dat."

"Whah will ye discuss wi' Atwater when ye see him?"

"Maybe I jus want ta catch up. Have a cupper wi' him."

"Ye do na drink tea," I point out. "Is it revenge ye're after?"

"And if 'twas, would ye begrudge me it?"

"I would na," I admit. "I'd help ye, ye know dat."

"I do." His nod is automatic.

"We have ta approach da aingeals carefully, Finn," I warn. "I do na know how dey'll react ta any attempts we make ta take Genevieve."

"Do ye tink dey'd harm her?" he asks wi' renewed anger in his eyes.

"Maybe. If dey still believe dat we'd change her, den aye."

He processes da information. "We will be more dan careful den."

"Good.

Russell

CHAPTER 14
Kiss Me So I Remember

RUSSELL

Crashin' onto a hardwood floor, the dagger embedded in my side rattles and digs deeper. I roll onto my back and grip it by the hilt, yankin' it from me. It makes a sickenin' suckin' sound as the muscles in my abdomen clench in pain. Openin' my palm, Brennus' dagger drops from it to land beside me with a loud clatter.

"ARRRRR," I shout between my teeth. "FFFAAAAAHHHHH—"

Anya looks down at me. She kneels beside me in an attempt to see my wound. I sit up straight, tryin' not to show her how my hands shake. My heart is a black sinkhole in my chest as thoughts of Emil and Sheol erode it further.

Anya tucks her long, black hair behind her ears, "Let me see," she demands. Her dark wings are retracted inside of her back. Someone has given her an oversized, red woolen jacket to wear, but because she was magically forced into the portal, she got to keep her own clothes too. Her hands are buried in the red sleeves. She's tiny without her wings—fragile and delicate. I find her fingers and hold them in my grasp. Her eyes shift to mine, lush as green fields. I want to sink into them, drift down her valleys—find my way back to her.

"I'm not dyin'. They didn't want to kill me just yet," I explain to reassure her. Anya leans her forehead against the middle of my chest, murmuring broken words in Angel. My hand comes up to rest against the back of her neck. Soft tears wet me. "Shh, it's gonna be okay. We're okay." I repeat those words like a mantra, wantin' her to believe them even when I don't.

She lifts her head from me. It's smeared with my blood from my chest. Her eyes shine like broken bottles in sunlight with unshed tears. She's determined to hold them back. Her fingers touch the edge of my jagged skin. A steady flow of blood seeps from it. There are many more slices, but that one is the newest. From over Anya's shoulder, Brownie hands Anya a kitchen towel. I suck in my breath as Anya uses the fabric to apply pressure to slow down the bleeding while I heal.

"What'd ya just say to me in Angel?" I ask Anya as I pant against the pain.

"I told you that you're a mess."

I laugh, and then wince as shootin' pain in my gut reminds me not to do that. "I wasn't always this bad. I keep wonderin' how I got here when just a couple of years ago I was cuttin' lawns for gas money." I try to smile.

"Now someone is cutting you." She frowns in concentration.

"I'll heal."

"This time," Anya murmurs. Over her shoulder to Brownie, she says, "Close the portal." Brownie moves to a table near me. She lifts a white pitcher and drops it on the floor. The painted blue porcelain shatters into a hundred pieces.

"It's closed," Brownie says. She looks like a child playing dress up in oversized men's clothing.

Relief floods through my veins as Buns runs into the room in a blur of speed. "What happened?" she demands. The bright white oversized tank top she wears is covered in splotches of blood, but it's obvious it's not her own blood. She's fully intact—no pieces of her were lost or left behind.

"Nothing! It's okay," Brownie assures her as she holds up her hand to stop her impending freak out. "I just killed the portal so all of Sheol can't follow us here."

Behind Buns, Zephyr limps into the room from a doorway that leads to a kitchen. The hollow part of my gut twists. His cuts aren't bleedin' now, but they're everywhere and have taken on the appearance of dents in an old rusted coffee can. Like me, he got to keep his clothes because he was magically shoved into the portal by Brennus and didn't have to shapeshift to get here, but everything he's wearing is cut up and gory.

I raise my chin to him in greeting. "You okay?" I inquire.

He frowns, like it's a dumb question. "I'm a Power," Zephyr replies.

"Right." I look 'round the room; it's a log cabin in that it's made of, but it's not rustic or lackin' in any amenities. Long glass doors and windows overlook a calm, frozen lake outside. The porch that wreaths 'round the back of the house would be great for sittin' and playin' an old guitar, singin' songs 'round the outdoor fireplace. They'd probably be blues songs, though. I don't think I'm capable of singin' anythin' but the blues now. "Whose house is this?"

"Mine," Zephyr says.

"Nice." I grimace as I get to my feet, holding the towel to my side. "That was kind of crazy back there," I add with my thumb over my shoulder.

Buns goes pale. "Sweetie, Zee said Emil opened Sheol."

I pull the towel away from my stab wound, probing my side gently to see that the edges have already closed over. "Yeah, I didn't know it'd be like that."

"Like what?" Brownie asks.

I shrug to cover for the fact that just thinkin' 'bout it makes all the hairs on my arms stand on end. "You know, like there is just a very thin veneer of our world between us and them—like wallpaper."

"You didn't know that?" Anya's green eyes fix on me. I shake my head mutely. "Where did you think Hell was?" Anya asks.

"I thought it was a lot farther away—you know, like literally somewhere down below, but it's not! It's just behind every gray day, every sunset—every friend turned enemy—"

"So is Heaven," Anya assures me. "It's there, too."

"Emil just tore away my blinders! He cut the air with a knife—it's not even a crappy metaphor—literally, a knife!" I begin to freak out inside and I can't calm down. Wiping my hand through my hair, I start to pace in front of the window.

"He has a key to Sheol," Buns says. She sits on the arm of the cream-colored sofa in the middle of the room, watchin' me. "That means there's a knife that opens Heaven, too."

I stop, turnin' to look at her. "How do you know that?" A shiver of fear runs crookedly through me.

"Sweetie, there's no Yin without Yang." She glances at Zephyr, "Who'd have it?"

Zephyr thinks for a moment. "That is an excellent question for Phaedrus. He is well-equipped to locate what's hidden."

"Why would you want a key to Heaven," I ask, and then pause when they all turn to look at me like I'm insane. I hold up my hand. "I mean, except for the obvious reasons!"

Zephyr answers, "Emil just opened a window to elicit help from Sheol. Because he acted first, we're entitled to do the same. Balance."

My frown turns ugly. "I know why I'm here—it's not about Evie, it's Emil. No way he gets to live. NO WAY!" I shake my head. "He doesn't get another lifetime. Can we destroy a soul? You're reapers." I wave my hand back and forth between Buns and Brownie. "Is there a way to end a soul so that it never gets to Sheol or Heaven? I want him to have zero chance of comin' back."

Brownie answers, "If Emil's knife is powerful enough to tear the fabric between our worlds, it could potentially dismember a soul."

I straighten my shoulders and stand to full height. "How do we find Phaedrus? I need that divine knife, if it exists. The last time I saw him he was with Tau in Ireland. Do you think he's still with him?"

"You said Tau is at Dominion's fortress in the Gulf of St. Lawrence?"

"Maybe. Do you think he'd be with Reed or with Evie?" I ask.

"It doesn't matter," Zephyr says quietly. "We don't need to know where Phaedrus is to get him here."

"We don't?" I ask in confusion.

"He's right." Brownie smiles at me for the first time.

"Okay, am I missin' somethin'?"

"All we have to do is ask for a miracle." Buns says.

I scowl. "Is that all—just a miracle? And how do we do that?"

"We pray," Anya says at my side.

"That's your plan?" I ask as I rub my forehead. "'Cuz I hate to point out the fact that I've been prayin' for us all along and we're still gettin' our asses kicked!"

"You've been doing a good job, Russell," Brownie says with a newfound grin. "We're all still alive."

I stare at Brownie like she has lost her flippin' mind, because she has. I don't tell her so though. "Okay, so we pray for a miracle and Phaedrus appears, like a genie outta the bottle?"

Buns shrugs as she holds out both her hands palms up. "With travel the way it is these days it might take him longer to get here. We may have to work on him, too—invoke Heaven to send him. He believes he should follow Tau's orders, but Heaven comes first. If Heaven deems that he help us, then he will."

I try not to give her my skeptical face, but dammit if it isn't hard not to. "Glad to know how this all works. So, do you think Heaven will be on our side because from this perspective we've been on our own for a while now."

"There are rules," Zephyr says. "Heaven is reluctant to disturb the balance or the scales tip in favor of Sheol."

"And nobody wants that," Buns agrees emphatically, as she point her finger at me.

"I don't know 'bout any of y'all, but I do my best prayin' before a meal—sometimes after. Do you think we can eat somethin'?"

Buns looks skeptical. "You might want to take a shower first. I have to go forage the island for food. This place is a seasonal resort—only a handful of humans remain on the island this time of year. We can go to the closed restaurants and see what they have in their freezers and pantries."

"Where are we?" I ask.

"We're in the Straits of Mackinaw."

"We're by the U. P. again?" I shudder. I don't want to be anywhere near the Upper Peninsula

"Yeah. Missed it?"

"Not really. No," I respond, "and just so you know for next time, I'm all for warm climates."

Buns hops down from the arm of the sofa. "Noted."

"I will go with you," Zephyr tells Buns.

"It's okay, Zee—"

"I. Will. Go. With. You."

"Ohh-kayyy," Buns states, holdin' up both her hands, like she wants to keep her head. "But there's nothing scarier than you on this island, Zee."

"Do not try to appease me," Zee replies.

Buns indicates that I follow her. Climbin' the stairs to a row a rooms above, she shows me to a bedroom that has an attached bathroom. "Brownie and I will scout for some clothes for you while we're out," she grimaces as she assesses my size before she turns to leave.

"Thanks," I call after her.

The shower is like a spa. With my hands braced against the tile wall, I lean my head down so water runs over my face. All the caked-on blood drains away from me as if the torture of the last few hours didn't exist. But it did. I have bruises inside me. No matter what I do to protect my friends or myself, we're vulnerable. There's no magic that'll stop what's gonna happen—whatever is meant to happen *will* happen. We're here for a purpose. I know what it is now and nothin' else seems very important. Emil has to be obliterated. Once he is, I'm truly free—one way or the other. Knowin' that is a type of freedom in itself—freedom from fear. I'll fight the fight, and then this will end. I want it to end.

Somethin' about that last thought shocks me. It's not that I want to die—that isn't it. I just want to be free to make my own decisions, to have my own existence separate from Emil's or Evie's—somethin' that's mine—somethin' beautiful.

I shut off the water and exit the shower. Findin' a towel on a shelf, I use it to dry off. Wrappin' it 'round my hips when I'm done, I move to the bedroom. The house is quiet. I pick up my bloody clothes from the floor where I'd thrown them and go in search of the washin' machine.

When I locate the laundry room, I stop in the doorway, takin' in the view of Anya in nothin' but a tight black cami and the sexiest pair of black underwear I've ever seen in my life. In truth, they're just normal underwear really, but they're coverin' her so they're enough to make my entire body flush. She has her head in the dryer next to the washin' machine. I have to readjust my towel before I clear my throat, "Urr hum."

Anya lifts her head fast and smacks it on the edge of the dryer. She stumbles back a step. "Uhh," she moans, putting her hand to the back of her head.

"Aww, I'm sorry! I didn't mean to scare you," I put out my hand as I move to her. Droppin' my clothes in front of the machine, I ease her hand away from her head so I can see if there's a bump growin' on her scalp. On impulse, I lean down and kiss her hair. "I think it's okay," I murmur. "What were you doin' with your head in the dryer?"

Anya turns in my arms to face me. A soft pink blush is colorin' her cheeks. "I was trying to make it go—I don't know how it works," she admits with a frustrated frown.

"You don't have to figure it out on your own. You just have to ask one of us and we'll help you." I smile down at her as I rest my hands on her upper arms.

She blinks at me for a second, like she's unsure of why I'm smilin'. Her lips turn down as she waves her hand in the air, disregardin' my comment. "Zephyr and the Reapers have gone for food, you were in the shower and I'm capable of dissecting a problem and finding a solution."

Turnin' away, she gathers up our clothes from the floor and shoves them in the dryer. She grasps the laundry detergent, twistin' off the cap with the aim of pourin' it into the dryer. "Whoa, whoa, whoa!" I pluck the bottle of detergent from her grasp. "You don't wanna do that."

Her eyebrow raises as she watches me pull the clothes back out. "This is a dryer," I nod toward the appliance in question with an easy smile. "You use it *after* you wash your stuff. This," I nod toward the front loader, "is a washin' machine—it cleans 'em." I dump our tangled pile into it. "You wanna use the cold cycle so the color doesn't fade." I turn her away from me to face the washer. With her back to my chest, I trap her between my arms. Liftin' her hand to the button, I slide my hand over hers, usin' her finger to press the settin' on the washer. The soft heat of her skin against mine is enough to make me ache inside.

My lips brush the top of her ear as I murmur, "You don't want to mix light clothes with dark—especially anythin' white with anythin' red 'cuz your whites will come out pink—and then people will laugh at you."

She leans back into me. "You sound as if you speak from experience." She turns her cheek to brush against mine.

"Let's just say my sisters inherited a few of my t-shirts when I was learnin' to do my own laundry." I release her hand and unscrew the cap from the detergent, placin' it in her grasp. "You'd usually just want a little detergent for a small load like this, but our clothes are sort of destroyed, so..." I pour out the soap, before slidin' open the dispenser drawer, allowin' her to pour the contents of the cap into it.

"Do you have anythin' else you want to put in there before we start it?" I ask. I close my eyes, breathin' in the perfume of her hair; it clouds my brain. I open them again as Anya turns 'round in my arms. Facin' me once more, her silky skin causes mine to vibrate at her touch. She lifts her hand and grasps the towel 'round my waist. With a gentle tug, she takes it from me, reachin' behind her and stuffin' it into the washer at her back. A smile plays upon her lips.

Standin' in front of her without a shred of clothing, I don't feel vulnerable—I'm powerful. I move so that we're a hair's breath away. Towerin' over her, her head only reaches my chin. I'm not fooled though; she's delicate, but she's ferocious—a warrior. She has the cunnin' to turn me inside out. "You forgot this," I murmur, reachin' for the hem of her cami. I ease it over her head; her long, hair falls through it, black silk against her flawless skin. I toss her cami behind her into the washer.

My finger traces her shoulder, before windin' down her. She bites her bottom lip. I run my thumb over it, rescuin' it from her cruel mouth. I want to feel it pout against mine. She traps my thumb with her mouth, sucking it in, doin' things to it that makes my knees weak.

My other hand trails leisurely down her to her abdomen; her muscles contract. Desire is a railroad spike through me. Her shallow breathin' is air for my soul. I catch hold of the edge of her black underwear, hookin' my thumb through the side of it. The lace is warm liquid against my fingertips. I continue down, tuggin' the thin scrap of material away from her.

A *snap* draws my attention upward; her midnight wings spread wide from her back. My heart thunders in my chest as her wings serrate to black arrow points. They shine with iridescent fire in tones of purple, blue, and green.

The crickets inside me remind me every second just what desire is. They're ready to consume everythin' in their path. I grasp her 'round the waist. She leans against me. The impact of her skin against mine fills me with insatiable hunger. The low, passionate sound that breathes from her has the muscles low in my abdomen contractin'. My wings punch from my back, spreadin' out, responding to hers. When she sees them, she smiles —they must be talkin' to her—tellin' her things that I haven't said.

Extractin' my thumb from between her lips, I cup her cheek. My neck bends as my mouth hovers near her ear. "What did my wings say to you," I whisper, before brushin' my lips to the place just beneath her earlobe.

"Something I didn't know," Anya murmurs.

"What?"

Her half-lidded gaze seduces me. Easing closer, her lips flirt with mine, hoverin' just above. "You missed me." The vibration of her silky voice drives me crazy with a rough-edged need to possess her.

I nip her bottom lip, suckin' it into my mouth before lettin' it go. "I—"

"Shh, your mouth never tells the truth. You should let your body speak for you."

My heart clenches tight. "I'm not lyin' when I say I need you."

"I need you as well."

"And I'm not lyin' when I say I love you."

"Show me."

Reed

CHAPTER 15
The World Keeps Spinning

REED

I have a gut-wrenching reaction to Evie evaporating into the night. The need to smash something is nearly overwhelming. Clenching my muscles is the only outward sign I allow. In truth, I can't control that, no matter how much I try. It's a physical reaction to the loss of her—the loss of butterflies between us. Tau observes me from the other end of the stone corridor. He is the epitome of control. I slip my belt from the loops of my jeans and wind the supple leather around one of my fists. The buckle I hold between my flattened fingers.

"I can't seem to keep you two apart," Tau says.

"I know." I wait for him to make a move.

"Will you walk with me?" Tau gestures with his arm extended to the adjacent hallway. I assess the Power angels amassing near Tau. They make no move to attack me. "I promise you that you will be unharmed." I straighten from my defensive posture. Powers line the corridors at measured widths, strategic in their formations. At the smallest signal from Tau, they'll crash in on me.

Tau sees the direction of my stare. He speaks to the soldiers closest to him, dismissing them. Their reluctance to leave him is obvious, but they obey his order, departing with vicious stares in my direction. Alone in the corridor with Tau and a handful of

Powers, I unwrap the leather from my hand. I thread it back around my waist. With measured steps, I walk to Evie's father. Face to face with him, he looks me in the eyes. His are so much like Evie's, gray with a hint of blue. "It's this way to the reception hall. We can speak on the way." He starts down the corridor. "Do you need anything?"

I walk beside him. "No."

"No? Would you like a change of clothes?" He indicates my bare chest and dirt-streaked jeans.

"I'm capable of clothing myself."

"Still," Tau replies. He gestures to a Power behind us, calling him over, ordering clothes and food for me to be brought to the reception hall.

We turn a corner. Phaedrus is just ahead of us, waiting. His caramel-colored, owl-shaped wings are resting behind him in a nonthreatening posture. He joins us, walking beside Tau, matching his steps. I don't acknowledge the Virtue angel. I'm aware that Evie believes Phaedrus betrayed us by siding with the Seraphim. I know Phaedrus was only attempting to keep her safe from Brennus by letting me die. I cannot fault him for it. It was a sound decision at the time. He couldn't have known that I was not permanently lost to the Gancanagh. Even if he had known, I still cannot fault him. He has done me a service for which I can never repay him. He performed the ceremony that bound my life to Evie's. *I'm in his debt,* I think, as I touch the mark of Evie's wings on my chest

Tau notices my hand on my heart. "I may have miscalculated your role in this mission, Reed. There are circumstances at play here that suggests you were chosen for this." His words surprise me, but I don't show it.

"Circumstances?" I ask. I drop my hand from my heart.

"The extra sensory gift you possess—your ability to influence humans—it's a mystery to me. I'd like to know how you've used it."

"I'm not inclined to explain," I reply. Phaedrus is quiet, but his presence speaks volumes. He's here to help facilitate something between Tau and me.

"Your ability to influence humans eliminates free will. Without it, humans cannot be judged for their actions. They'd more than likely go unpunished for any wrongdoing, if you were to order them to sin."

"I don't use my influence in that way."

"Never? You know the rules we have with humans? We're not to interfere in their lives."

"I know."

"Ever break the rules?"

I shrug, noncommittal, but my mind searches for instances. *I have used my talent a few times recently with Russell*, I think, but I don't say it aloud. A thought pushes its way to the periphery of my mind. I glimpse a girl on a stone floor...I lose the thought. It evaporates and I can't seem to call it back. We climb stairs leading up to the main level.

Tau reads my silence as reluctance to answer his question. He presses on. "You attract Evie to you."

"It's a mutual attraction," I reply.

"And you'll do anything to stay together."

"That surprises you?"

"You're a Power. You're designed to follow my orders, but you would've killed me had Xavier and Cole not stopped you." There's respect and admiration in his demeanor.

"I wouldn't have hesitated. I've promised to protect Evie with my life. You were threatening her life." We reach the next floor.

"She wanted to end the fight between you and Xavier."

"And killing her was your best solution?" I cannot hide the anger in my tone, however much I wish I could.

"I didn't use a killing tone when I blew the boatswain. It was meant to subdue her, nothing more, and thereby get your attention and that of Xavier. I did not anticipate the damage it would do to her. It was not supposed to be that way, but it did demonstrate something to me. Now I see that she's ready to die rather than lose either of you. I also understand that you're both here for a purpose. I cannot allow either of you to cease to be now without fulfilling your destinies."

"So you had me thrown in a cell here and separated from my *aspire*."

"No. I've just recovered from getting my throat cut, and then I was gathering information before I freed you. Evie just got to you first."

Traversing a short hallway, we enter a reception area of the Chateau. Its floor is ancient marble. The ceiling is painted with scenes of angels at war. Gilded mirrors and furniture serve as elegant accouterments to our negotiations. "You believe you know my destiny?" I ask.

"Evie chose her champion. It's you." He stops at a sitting area in the middle of the room.

I face him, standing in front of a chair, but neither of us takes a seat. "You know this, how?"

"The ring on your finger," he indicates it with a flick of his hand. "I thought at first that it was a random act of misguidedness on her part. It belonged to Jim, her uncle. She loved Jim more than anyone—her surrogate father. The ring was divinely made, given to him in a covert way to protect him from magic and evil. He was human; it was necessary. When I learned that she gave it to you, I believed she was attempting to transfer her love for Jim onto you."

"What made you change your mind about that?"

"Phaedrus," Tau says, indicating the Virtue angel standing nearby, silently watching our exchange. His black eyes are missing nothing. "He convinced me otherwise. He explained some of the pieces of information to me that I've been missing. You work alone—a Prostat Power. You've occasionally made strategic partnerships over the millennia—bands of hunter-killers. Anytime you come across evil, you don't hesitate to annihilate it, or at the very least, send it running back to Sheol. You prefer to work alone. Why is that?"

"Killing is personal." A Power angel appears with clothes in his outstretched arms. I ignore him. Tau indicates that he can leave the clothes on the table near us. After the Power does so,

Tau waves him away with a small gesture.

"Yes, every angel has his or her own style. You prefer to make death quick; you don't linger over prey—most times, they never see it coming. One doesn't usually find that type of killing in a group of Power angels. Groups of Powers tend to be more vicious. They want to judge—berate—exact vengeance."

"Avenge God."

"Avenge," he agrees. "And Zephyr? Does he avenge?"

"He's more like me. We do our jobs—stalk and kill. We're efficient. We work together when it's warranted."

"And you have a bond." It's a statement. I neither agree nor disagree. I don't know how he'll use the information, so answering would be unwise. In this instance, Tau understands me better than I'd like. "Zephyr is your closest ally. He probably saved your life more than once, and you, his. You've both grown close. I daresay it's a bond of brotherhood."

Again I don't answer.

"It's rare, a bond like that," Tau continues. "We're not made for such emotions—angels. But it's different when one is around Evie, isn't it? She changes us. We can't help but feel everything."

"Do you find a bond of brotherhood a weakness?"

"It could be," he replies. "All emotional attachments are costly in their own way. It can sometimes blind one to the truth."

"You speak as if you have some experience."

"I've experienced it, only my bond of brotherhood is with Xavier. We grew close while taking care of Evie."

"Has that relationship blinded you?"

"Perhaps. You didn't kill Evie when you discovered her in your territory. By your very admission, you kill swiftly and decisively."

"I kill fallen angels. She's not one of them."

"You kill a myriad of evil."

"She's not evil."

"How many Power angels would've hesitated to find that out?"

I shrug. I know it's not many. "You're making a point. I'm just not clear what it is."

Phaedrus retracts his wings and sits down. He looks expectantly at Tau. Tau gets the message. He retracts his blood-colored wings and sits as well in a high-backed chair. He offers me a seat with a gesture of his hand. I retract my wings, sinking into a similar chair. Tau continues, "I know Evie's history with Xavier. I know she's aware that he's our most resourceful fighter; he's extremely well-suited to be her champion."

I want to kill him where he sits. "You're saying that because he wasn't here, she chose me in his absence?"

Tau holds up his palm. "No. I'm not saying that, but it could be true. What I'm suggesting is that she chose you before all this began."

"You mean before she ever came here to this mission—she chose me as champion prior to this lifetime?" I clarify.

"It's a theory."

"Why would she do that? We didn't know one another."

"There could be several reasons for her to do so. The simplest one I can think of is she didn't want to allow for the chance that she'd lose Xavier."

It's a logical theory, but that possibility has my stomach clenching again as if he has struck a blow there. "What makes you think this?"

"The attraction between you both is divinely made. You have to find out why she chose you as her champion."

Champion, I think. *Is that all I'm meant to be to her?* "You want to know 'why me'?"

"It could be that she chose you for your skill set. You nearly killed me. That's no easy feat." Tau rubs his neck where I'd slashed it. "But if there were another reason..." He stares at me as he contemplates the question, and then he asks, "Did you know her before this lifetime? Had you ever had the occasion to meet her? She would've looked different. She may not have been female."

"It's possible."

"I'd say it's probable."

"I'm her *aspire*. I only need to know where her enemy is so that I may eliminate the threat to her life."

"You met her enemy—in Crestwood. We believe we know the evil that attacked you. His name is Emil. He didn't kill Evie then, not because he couldn't, but because he needs something from her."

"What does he need?"

"We don't know. What we do know is he couldn't kill you. The magic wouldn't touch you. We believe it's because of the ring you wear."

"Can this ring protect Evie if I give it to her?" I try to tug the ring from my finger. It won't move; it's as if it is bonded to my flesh and bone.

"We attempted to cut it from you while you were unconscious. The Power who touched it ascended. Do you know why?"

"Heaven wants my help."

"Yes. You're not just Evie's champion; you're Heaven's champion as well."

"What do you know about the target?" I ask, leaning forward to hear every word he utters.

"He's Evie's inescapable and he's more powerful than we ever imagined."

"Do you know why he's here?"

"It's unclear, but I believe he's here to confront Evie. The boatswain was given to us to protect—the key to Sheol. I didn't anticipate that Evie had been preprogramed to use it. She's meant to go there; for what purpose, I can only speculate."

The thought of Evie in Sheol is a knife in my heart. "Heaven has been playing chess while you've been playing checkers, Tau."

"Isn't that always the way? We only ever get to know a piece of the puzzle—we're left to discover how it fits. That way, no one can be forced to divulge the plan to Sheol."

"What do you expect from me?"

"Evie needs to find a way to remember her past. We'd like you to convince her to try."

"I want the boatswain."

"I cannot give it to you. I am sworn to deliver it to an angel."

"Who?"

"He's Cherubim and goes by the name of Atwater."

"Do you know him?"

"No. I have been searching for him for a long time. Xavier has just located him. He arrived unannounced at our mountain enclave, looking for Evie."

"Has he spoken of the boatswain? Does he know about it?"

"He has requested an audience with me. I suspect that it is to obtain the whistle."

"Will you meet him?"

"I leave within the hour. We are to meet this evening."

"You're aware it's a weapon against half-angels? It can be used to harm your daughter. Are you eager to give that away when you don't know how he'll use it?"

"No. I'm not eager to relinquish it to him, especially now that I've seen what it can do. I didn't know the extent of its power. I was told it would subdue, not that it had the potential to kill."

"It's also a key."

"It is and I don't believe Evie made the conscious choice to use the whistle to unlock the gateway to Sheol. She was conditioned to do it. The moment she touched it, she was no longer in control of the consequences of her actions or even aware of them. Once the gateway opened, it attempted to pull her into it."

"Do you believe it wise to give the boatswain to an angel you don't know?"

"I have to trust in Heaven to know what's right."

"What's right for them or what is right for Evie? It's not always the same thing. They don't always coincide."

"No, you're correct, they don't. I said I have to give Atwater the key. I never said you had to let him keep it. He's at the same base as Evie. Will you come with me to deliver it?"

"What would you like me to do once you deliver the boatswain?"

"Whatever comes to mind," Tau murmurs, touching his throat lightly.

"When do we leave?" I ask.

Phaedrus rises from his chair. "I must leave you both here," Phaedrus says absently as his soft, fuzzy wings unfold from him.

"What is it?" Tau asks.

"I've just been given a mission." His black owlish eyes grow even darker. "It would seem I have to depart at once."

"Do you know your assignment?" Tau asks, standing as well.

"We've met. It's Reed's friends: the half-Seraph, the Power, the Throne, and the two Reapers."

I lurch to my feet. "Are they in danger?"

"They're in no immediate danger. They want my help to locate something for them."

I frown. "What do they want?"

"They want a weapon capable of destroying a soul."

"Is there such a weapon in existence?" Tau asks.

"Heaven says there is. Heaven says they're looking for a Faerie weapon—one that sings."

Evie

CHAPTER 16
The World Below Zero

EVIE

A beefy Power angel with beige-colored wings brings me a delicate plate of seasoned cod. Xavier and I sit alone at our table in a posh dining room beneath low-hanging crystal chandeliers. Around us, Power angels savor the exquisite cuisine, casting covert glances at Xavier and me. I would've preferred to eat alone in my room, but Xavier insisted that I show myself here. He wants the other angels to grow accustomed to my presence—to my supremacy inherited through my Seraphim blood.

My skin feels paper-thin as Xavier's hand comes within a breath of it. He picks up his wine glass, watching me, expecting me to suddenly recognize him for more than the human he has always been to me in this lifetime. I also remember him now as a British soldier from another lifetime—the life I don't want to remember. In that time, he'd dangled the carrot of freedom before Simone—a desperate girl and she'd agreed to help him in exchange for her life. The biggest problem I have with that is I'm not entirely sure how it worked out for her. Not well, I'd imagine, because she died—I died. *I'm Simone...or I was.*

I scan the room for the diamond-shaped pupils and blue wings of the Cherub angel I'd seen when I first arrived. Atwater. I need to speak to him. If he knew Brennus before his fall, then I want to know why he's still hanging around the Gancanagh and hasn't tried to kill them. The Gancanagh lair in Houghton is not something that angels would normally let slide. Atwater knew I was a prisoner there, and yet, he'd done nothing to help me escape them. He had only come to me after Russell had freed me.

"You're quiet." Xavier lifts his glass to his lips and stares at me over the rim. His blond hair is dark under the dim light of the chandelier.

"Why would Atwater be following the Gancanagh?"

"I don't know. He must have his reasons."

"Do you know where he is?"

"Not at the moment."

"But you can find him, right?"

"I can."

"Find him for me."

"Okay." Xavier leans back in his seat, toying with his glass. "What are you going to do for me in exchange?"

"What do you want?"

"Cooperation."

"Am I fighting you?"

"No. You're biding your time, waiting for Reed to rescue you."

"He's my aspire. You're keeping us apart."

"I'm allowed to protect you from everything that can harm you now. I could never do that in your previous lifetimes as a human. This is a much better position to be in. I don't have to watch you die and do nothing."

"Reed won't hurt me."

"He'll destroy you."

"Why do you say that?"

"He doesn't know who you are. He doesn't understand you."

"He understands me fine."

"His only goal is to protect you."

"Why is that so wrong?"

"You're here to change things, Evie. It's not about you, it's about what you've become—a half-angel. There has never been your like in all of history. You're changing the world. You're the wave that will crush our enemies."

"Why must I be a crusher? Why can't I be a uniter?"

"You fight evil. It's what you do. It's why you've always been chosen. Do you think Emil deserves to live?"

"No." I mutter. He has a point. Emil cannot be allowed to live.

Xavier's lips twitch in a suppressed smile. "You've always been an excellent crusher. You crushed Kimberly Cline. I distinctly remember you making her cry," he teases me.

I make a face. "She told everyone that she was going to get you to break up with me junior year."

"Yes, and you told people I said that she had bad breath."

"She did have bad breath."

"True, but I never said that."

"You thought it. Anyway, you did end up breaking up with me senior year." *Why does that still hurt so much? It makes no sense.*

Xavier sees it. I can hide nothing from him. He sets down his wine glass. "I didn't want to hurt you, but I had to put some distance between us."

"It's fine—"

"No. Let me finish!" he growls.

I look at him. "Go on."

"You were…such a temptation for me. We weren't engaging in just kissing anymore, like we had been sophomore year. I was supposed to be protecting you, but I was becoming your direst threat. You were so fragile. I couldn't touch you without hurting you, not the way I was feeling about you. I wanted you. You had been the love of my life for centuries."

"I thought there was something wrong with me," I admit.

"There *was* something wrong with you! You had the body of a sixteen-year-old girl and the ancient soul of my love. There was clearly something wrong with that."

"Your body looked about the same age as mine."

"Looks are so deceiving, aren't they, Evie?"

"They are. With a look, you made me believe you found me repulsive. I thought you didn't want me at all."

"You held all the power and you didn't even know it. And so what if I *had* been a stupid boy and not an angel and I had thought that? It would mean that *I* was a fool, not you! But you know now what I am and that I love you—have *always* loved you. I wanted you then, but it's nothing compared to how much I want you now."

"It's too late," I whisper.

"It's never too late. Not for us! Not for where we've been."

"Where have we been, Xavier? I want to understand. I do. I need you to stop talking in riddles and explain where we've been. What do you remember about our last lifetime together?"

"I pushed you too hard and it all fell apart," he says in a quiet tone.

"What do you mean?"

"I should have gotten you out of France earlier. I could've, you know? I could've saved you from him—from Emil—but you were such an ace! You had the potential to end him before he harmed anyone else. You just needed to find yourself in Simone. So I left you in the game, but I left you too long."

The air around me is suddenly haunted by Emil's scent—it's the fragrance of his hair tonic. It's scent memory from Simone's lifetime. I put down my fork and pick up my wine glass, taking a sip to allow the taste of the red to expunge the odor of my tormentor.

"Why would you do that to me, if you loved me?" My hand shakes, causing my wine to weep rosy tears on the inside of the glass. I set it down.

"I sometimes expect perfection from you. You rarely give me anything less than it."

"But this time I was less than perfect?"

"I...don't know. I can't remember my last hours there. I know I was supposed to meet you at the bridge. I know I was there early. I remember checking my watch, waiting."

"What would've happened at the bridge had everything gone to plan?"

"You would've reported Emil's new location to the allies. They would've had the information and I would've seen you safely away. The goal was to undermine Emil. Human soldiers would've hunted him down for his war crimes. I would've followed you at a safe distance for the rest of your life, watching over you."

"Why were you allowed to interfere with my life at all? I thought angels couldn't do that."

"I was your *guardian* angel. I alone was allowed to interfere in your life. I could manipulate you in order to help you achieve the goal of your mission, which was to subdue and put an end to Emil in that lifetime."

"So I was your pawn."

"It wasn't like that. You mostly lead me."

"But I never made it to the bridge?" I ask.

He shakes his head. "I truly don't know."

"Maybe this is bliss, Xavier."

"What do you mean?"

"Why would I want to remember any of this? Just the imagined smell of Emil makes me want to vomit." I look in his mismatched eyes. "Maybe the kindest thing you can do for me is to allow me to forget."

"I'm never kind, Evie. Do you think for one moment Emil will go away? He's here to kill you, of that I have no doubt."

"I know he is. He's always here to kill me, isn't he?"

"He is."

Out of the corner of my eye, a flash of blue catches my attention. Atwater sees me staring at him from my seat. He motions with his chin for me to follow him. Turning, he disappears through an archway at the back of the dining room. "Excuse me for a moment, Xavier."

Xavier stands when I do. I make my way across the beautiful rug to the archway. It leads to a long hallway. At the end, Atwater waits just long enough for me to see him. He darts away. I bolt down the corridor. At the other end of it, there is a shear drop of several stories. I spread my wings and dive into the air, following the trajectory of the blue wings in front of me. I land at the bottom next to Atwater. He doesn't look at me, but takes huge strides across the marble floor. Moonlight shines through gigantic windows carved from the side of the mountain. It's almost perpetual night here this time of year. A beautiful set of silver doors lead outside. A large cloakroom is situated next to the doorway. Atwater goes to it. He runs his hand over several long coats and parkas in all shapes and sizes, finally choosing a white parka with long slits in the back of it. He holds it out to me, waiting patiently for me to put it on. My wings fit through the slits in it. He walks around me and zips it from the back so that only my feathers are exposed. I take care of the zipper in the front. Reaching his hand up to a shelf, he selects a white ushanka from it and squashes it onto my head. I don't say a word; I just whisk away my hair from my eyes. He grabs a heavy white parka for himself that matches mine. Tossing me some white gloves, he walks out of the coatroom. I hurry after him, pulling my gloves on as I go. He thrusts open the door and my angel vision adjusts to the darkness outside. He walks out into the middle of a lovely courtyard. Ice sculptures of fierce warrior angels are the only figures near enough to overhear us. Still, Atwater takes me by the elbow and leads me away from the doors.

"Your father is on his way here. He should arrive shortly."

"Tau is coming here?"

"Yes. Some of his army comes with him. He brings Reed as well."

"How do you know this?"

"Heaven told me."

"Why is Tau coming here?"

"I asked him to come."

"For what purpose?"

"To deliver the boatswain to me. He was ordered to keep it safe until it was needed. When the time came, he was to give it to me."

"Why do you need it?"

"I'm to either give it to you or I'm to use it on you."

"What?"

"If you are not worthy to be the champion of Heaven, I'm to use it on you. If you prove yourself to be worthy, I'm to give it to you."

"How do I prove myself worthy?" I ask.

"You already have."

"How?"

"You survived the Gancanagh."

"That proves I'm Heaven's champion?" I feel disoriented by what he just said. *Is he insane? Is he evil? Is he a lunatic?*

"No. The fact that you're their queen proves that you're Heaven's champion."

"I don't understand."

"No, but you will. When your father arrives with Reed, I need you to get Reed alone."

"How?"

"You're a resourceful being. I'm sure you will find a way. Tell Reed to come here to this statue." He holds out his hand to the ferocious ice angel holding a sword aloft, ready to smite us at any moment. "Inside the ice shield will be the boatswain. I want him to have it. He plans to kill me for it, but that's unnecessary. I want everyone who knows about it to believe I still have it. It will be safer for you if they do."

"What do you want him to do with it?" I ask.

"I want him to take it and to leave here with you."

"How?"

"Find a way. Once you get somewhere safe, I want him to call out these tones on it," he says, before whistling a soft tune that is hauntingly familiar. "Can you remember it?"

"You want him to kill me?" I ask.

He scowls. "If I wanted you dead, I'd do it myself!" His catlike eyes narrow to slits. "There are several different tones. At its worst, the boatswain will only subdue you—separate your soul from your angelic body. It cannot destroy your soul. What I want is for you to use a tone that will make you remember our deal—Emil has negated part of the contract by speaking of that night."

"Our deal?" I ask. "That night?"

"If you keep repeating me I will smite you. I need you to go somewhere safe with Reed and only with Reed. I need you to remember our deal. Then I need you to lead your army into battle.

The gates of Sheol are wide open. Demons are pouring in as we speak."

"Whoa, wait! The gates of Sheol are open?"

"Emil has cut through the fabric of this world and opened hell to it. The Gancanagh have attempted to close it, but it has not held."

"Where?"

"Where you once resided—in your little college town."

"Crestwood?"

"Yes. Emil tried to capture your soul mate there. The Gancanagh saved him."

"Which army am I to lead into battle? Tau's or Xavier's?" I ask.

"Not their armies, your army! You're the queen of the Gancanagh. You rule beside their king. You must lead them into battle. It is the only way to defeat Emil. We must have them all: Tau's army, Xavier's army, and your army. And Reed must be at your side. You must unite them all."

"What happens if I fail?"

"Then you cease to be and everyone you love falls prey to your inescapable."

"What about my soul mate?"

"You need but ask him and he will move a mountain for you. Do you understand what I'm telling you? We don't have much time!"

"Can you give me the tune you want Reed to use one more time?" I beg, feeling completely desperate.

Atwater whistles it for me again. When he finishes, he asks, "Do you have it now?"

I nod, overwhelmed by all he's said. He straightens then, turning toward the silver doors. "We should not be seen together. Wait a bit before you return inside." Atwater leaves then without a backward glance.

I wander around, covering up the tracks that had led to the ice figure of the avenging angel before making new tracks to other ice statues in the courtyard. Something stirs in my abdomen. It tugs me toward the silver doors. I have a sharp intake of breath. *Reed!* I think as I touch my hand to my belly. Forgetting the tracks on the ground, I round the last sculpture. I pause when I see Xavier's dark shape in the light of the doorway. As I near him, I notice he's without a coat and his skin is turning rosy from the chill. "What are you doing out here, Evie?" he asks.

Snow falls around me, trapping us in a shaken snow globe scene at the top of the world. "How did you know I was out here?"

"You never returned to the table. I have angels looking for you. I saw Atwater. He said he saw you, but wouldn't tell me where because he said you wanted to be alone. I noticed his nose was red from the cold. Did you speak to him?"

"Yes. I wanted to talk to him about Brennus, but he was in a hurry to get away from me. I think he's the one who wants to be alone."

Xavier nods, distractedly. "Your father has arrived," he says with a guarded look. His breath curls away from him like smoke.

"Oh?" I ask. "You look upset about that."

"I would like you to go to your room until I come to get you."

"I'd like to speak to my father."

"And you will. I want to speak to him first."

"Why? Is something wrong?" I ask.

"He plans to give the boatswain to Atwater."

"And you believe that's a bad move?"

"I do. I saw what it did to you. I'm never letting that happen again. I'll destroy it before I see it in another angel's hand."

The wind is so cold that I can believe that we're living at the edge of the world here. I shiver. "Do you think Heaven has a plan, Xavier?"

"I know they do."

"Do you trust them?"

"The end game is all that matters to them. How they get there is what matters to me."

"Maybe the courage is in letting go, Xavier."

"If only I could," he murmurs, "but I can't." He takes the hat from my head. My hair falls and frames my face. His hand finds its way to the nape of my neck. His fingers thread through my hair. He leans down and whispers in my ear, "Reed is here. Tau insists that he remain alive for now; so do not make me kill him. Go to your room and wait for me." He kisses my cheek and lets me go.

I walk through the door he holds open for me. Tens of thousands of angels reside here ready to do whatever Xavier tells them. It would only take them minutes to kill Reed. I shrug out of my white coat and hand it to Xavier. He gives it to a Power who has come to attend us. It occurs to me that I'm a lethal woman. I could kill them all. I glance at Xavier. I don't want to hurt him. I love him, even if he acts jealous and arrogant. And we need his cooperation and his army in order to defeat Emil. I'll have to be smart and use my head instead of force—or, in this case, magic and genetics.

Xavier looks away from me. He begins speaking in Angel to the Power by his side. I don't know what he's saying exactly, but I can guess it something like, "She's to go directly to our suite. Follow her and report to me if she leaves or has any visitors." I frown at them, but they ignore me.

I turn away from them. I take a few steps and lift off into the air, flying in the direction of my room. When I'm out of their view for a moment, I duck behind a massive column. Creating a clone, I release her to continue on in the direction of my room. I whisper a hasty spell to make myself invisible. My Power bodyguard passes me, following my clone. Hopefully she can make it to my room and through the door before he gets there, or my ruse won't work for very long. I peek around the column and see Xavier flying in the opposite direction. I follow him, avoiding angels who nearly collide with me. I may be invisible, but I'm solid, so if they bump into me, they're going to realize something is wrong.

I almost lose Xavier in a crowd, but I manage to locate him near the entrance of a tunnel. It really doesn't matter anymore though, because butterflies are careening inside of me, begging me to follow them to Reed. Xavier turns down a corridor that has images of Heaven carved into the very walls. When he enters the room at he end of it, I have to cover my mouth and hold my breath to keep from gasping. It's a huge round room carved from the gray rock of the mountain. An X-shaped cutout bisects the floor and ceiling in a crisscross pattern. As I look up, the cutout goes clear up for several stories to the moonlight and stars far above my head. When I look down over the cutouts in the floor, the drop goes on so far I cannot see its end for the darkness below. White recessed lighting glows almost blue, causing everything to have a soft, ethereal glow.

Tau stands on the other side of the abyss with Reed. They're both dressed in black long-sleeved shirts and black utilitarian trousers. They look like human assassins without their wings out, but still very much like they're ready to kill something. Tau's attention is on Xavier, with his hands behind his back and chin up, he has perfect military form. Reed has a similar stance, but his eyes are not on Xavier, he's looking at the door behind us. *He feels me. He's waiting for me to come through the door.*

Xavier flies over the abyss in front of him, speaking to Tau in Angel. Reed doesn't look at them. He keeps watching the door. An argument quickly breaks out between Xavier and Tau. I've rarely seen either of them in anything but full agreement with one another. The last time they argued in front of me was in high school and it was about me—about the amount of time Xavier had been spending with me and not with his friends. It was the time Tau had walked in on us in Xavier's room and we were doing a little more than just talking, of course, he was Drew then. I don't know what they're fighting about now, but I can guess it's about me again.

As quietly as possible, I fly over the cavern in the floor. Nearing Reed, I watch his pupils dilate when he picks up my scent. His nostrils flare. He doesn't move an inch otherwise. I circle behind him. My first touch is to his sides as I slip my arms between his arms and wrap them around his waist. He stops breathing for just a second, but it is a testament to his control that he doesn't flinch. I press my cheek to his back for a moment as I hug him and breathe him in. The riot of butterflies inside of me is chaos. I want to tear his shirt from him and feel his skin against mine.

I distinctly hear Xavier say the name "Atwater" during his Angel tirade. Tau is calmer than Xavier, but not by much. Xavier turns away from Tau. He strides to the hole in the floor, leaping over it to the other side without even having to fly. Tau calls to him, saying something more. I splay my invisible hands over Reed's chest, holding him as I hide behind him at the same time. Xavier leaves the same way he came in. Tau follows him, jumping the huge X in the floor. He says something over his shoulder to Reed before he leaves the room as well.

"Are they gone?" I whisper.

"They're gone," Reed turns in my arms and wraps his around my invisible body. I let go of my spell and watch his mouth curve in a beautiful smile when he sees me. He leans down and kisses me hungrily.

"Where did they go?" I ask him between kisses, my hands skimming over his firm biceps. "How much time do we have?"

"Not much." Reed relents and lifts his lips from me. "Tau told me to wait here. Xavier went to bludgeon Atwater and let him know that he will never allow Atwater to have the boatswain here, in Heaven, or in Hell. Tau went to make sure Xavier doesn't kill Atwater."

"But Tau still wants you to kill Atwater?"

Reed's eyebrows pull together. "How did you know that?" I hold onto Reed's wrists and feel something beneath his shirt. My grasp shifts to just one wrist, while moving his sleeve up, exposing a leather wrist holster. Clasped inside the holster is a spade-shaped blade. I move my hand to his other wrist and find another one.

"Atwater told me Tau wants you to murder him for the boatswain." I pull his sleeves back into place. "You don't have to kill the Cherub. He's going to give the boatswain to you. Heaven wants us to have it. He's going to make Tau give it to him, and then he's going to leave it in the shield of the ice angel in the courtyard. It's the one that has it's arm aloft and looks like it's about to smite something."

"And once I retrieve it?"

"Find me and we'll leave."

"How?"

"I haven't figured that out yet, but it has to be just you and me. Atwater wants you to use the whistle. There's a special tone he made me learn."

"A tone?"

"It will make me remember some kind of deal I made."

Reed grips my upper arms. "I'll bring it to you." He kisses me again and it feels as if I'm living on the edge of a blade with him, sharp with painful longing.

The door handle rattles. I let out a little squeak before I whisper another hasty spell. I think for a second that Tau sees me as he pauses at the door and gazes at Reed's back. Reed has resumed his military posture, but he's unable to turn around right away and face Tau because of what I've done to him with my kisses. I look up at Reed's eyes. I know he can't see me anymore. I place my hand on his heart, right where I know my wings to be branded. It's beating furiously in his chest. With a small smile, he winks at me.

I let go of him. I wait until Tau jumps the cavern in the room. I time it so that I land on the other side just as he touches down. Behind me, Tau murmurs something I recognize in Angel to Reed, "Be ready." I'm almost to the door when Xavier comes through it with Atwater trailing him. I skitter to the side out of their path. They're all speaking Angel now. As they pass me, I creep to the door. Behind me, Atwater and Xavier join Tau and Reed on the other side of the room. Tau lifts his arms and pulls a chain from around his neck, attached to it is the boatswain. He hands the whistle to Atwater. The moment that it is in his palm, Reed's wings unfold out from his back. He rushes Atwater and tackles him, falling with him into the hole in the middle of the room.

Xavier growls. His red wings extend as he dives into the cavern to follow them. In the chaos I bolt through the door and out into the corridor. I have to find a portal. It doesn't matter where it leads as long as I find one in the next few minutes.

Navigating unfamiliar hallways, it takes me awhile to figure out where I am, but I eventually find the aisle that leads back to my room. Flying through the door to Xavier's room, I land and quickly open bureau drawers and dresser drawers. I almost scream when I notice the Power angel, who must be guarding the door to my room, get up from a chair. His deep voice asks, "How did you—" He looks at the door to my room. Going to it, his gray wings spread wide as he scans my bedroom for me, but my clone has long since evaporated into the air. He closes the door and turns to look at me.

I shrug. "I won't tell Xavier if you don't." He scowls. Hurrying past me, he leaves the room in a rush. "Tattletale," I mutter.

The time for a delicate search is over. I go to Xavier's bookshelves and pluck books off one by one, flipping through their pages and dropping them on the floor. Vases are searched, the laptop is opened, rugs are shaken out, bed is looked under, and the mattress too—sheets stripped. Nothing. On my hands and knees, I blow a strand of my hair out of my face. I get up and run to the closet. Clothes fly off hangers as I shove them aside to look inside shoes, open sock drawers—toss out underwear. Nothing.

Outside this suite of rooms, angelic voices are beginning to rise. Powers are flying around like they're mobilizing for something. I pop my head outside the closet to listen. Panic makes my hands shake. *I have to find a portal!* The room looks like a typhoon hit it when as I return to it. Slumping down on the bed, I look up at the ceiling, trying to think. What I know about Xavier is he is used to hiding in plain sight. He blends in as human. I glance over at the bedside table. His headphones are attached to his digital music player. *Who uses one of those when you can stream music on your phone?* I know he prefers vinyl. We used to listen to records in his room for hours. Picking up his on-ear headphones I switch the power on to the music player. My hand that holds the headphones distorts. Instead of playing music, the small phone-like player tries to suck me into it. *A portal!* I have no idea where it leads, but it's somewhere other than here, so I'll have to take my chances.

Now, I have to find Reed. I still feel him faintly, the butterflies inside me pointing me in the direction of my room. He's somewhat nearby. I hold onto the portal as I move to my room. The tug comes from the door that leads outside onto the icy mountainside balcony. I sprint to it, opening the heavy metal door. It whines in protest from the cold. Stepping out onto the porch, I see nothing at first but darkness and the drift of snowflakes. The butterflies become more intense until, out of the darkness, the shape of my angel takes form. He lands beside me on the stone balcony. His exposed skin is red from cold and he's quivering from the chill. I wrap my arms around him, hugging him to me. "Did you get the boatswain?" I ask.

"I have it here." He pulls it from beneath his black shirt. It's a good thing that his shirt has a detachable panel in the back made for angel wings because without it, he'd be a shirtless popsicle by now.

I waste no more time. "This is a portal. I have no idea where it goes." I rise up on my tiptoes to put the headphones on him.

Reed stays my hand. "You go first. I'll follow right after you."

"Okay." I shift direction and place the earphones on my ears. Using my thumb, I flip on the music. My body contorts and I'm extracted from the cold world around me and thrust into darkness.

CHAPTER 17
Fascination Street

I know where I am the moment I spill out of a record player portal onto the exquisite parquet floor. It's Xavier's home in Grosse Pointe. I've been here thousands of times. I know my way around it—can navigate every inch of its five stories. It's almost like being home.

The well-used record player spins on a turntable in the loft room at the top of the massive house. Xavier and I used to sit for hours here after school, listening to music on it. I never once suspected that it was anything other than a benign way to play music. He never once told me what else it could do. Nor did I ever question why he always let it spin, even when the music wasn't playing. I thought it had been funny, the way he'd set up a little purple-haired troll in the center of it, letting it travel around in circles. He'd ended up giving me that troll. It was in my room for a long time until the Gancanagh took it. A familiar feeling of angst nearly overwhelms me for a moment.

My hands are still freezing. I rub them together and watch for Reed to come through the portal. He is way more elegant than me when he arrives. He lands on his feet. He turns around, removing the needle from the record player, stopping it from spinning. He closes the lid, locking the portal from our side. I get to my feet. "No one can follow us here, can they?" I ask.

"No—at least not through this portal," Reed replies. He turns and faces me, catching me as I throw myself into his arms. My knees weaken as my lips yield to his. His hand touches my hair. "Are you alright?"

"Yes. You?"

"I'm fine."

"What happened with Atwater?"

"We fell to the bottom of the cavern. He gave me the boatswain, told me not to tell the Seraphim that I had it or they would attempt to kill me like they had him. He said there's a reason they aren't being told the plan—I would know what it is soon. He said he'd find us later. He wished me 'Godspeed'. Then, he disappeared into a portal of his own. I narrowly avoided Xavier and found you."

"It would be nice if any of this made sense." I turn away from him, looking around me. The room is exactly the same as I remember it. High ceilings, soft overstuffed chairs, and an inlaid wood floor with a map of the constellations set into it. A few fat couches lounge in front of shelf upon shelf of the most exquisite books I've ever read. Xavier has a larger, more formal library on the first floor. This smaller one on the fifth floor, however, has always been my favorite. I would often choose a book, and then walk out onto the rooftop patio and read it in the sunshine, or under the moon by twinkle lights and lit wall sconces.

Nothing has changed. Xavier must have had some kind of service maintaining his residence; automatically paying the bills or something, because he was gone for months and it is still immaculate. "Do you want me to tell you the notes for the boatswain?" I ask Reed.

He nods, lifting the chain and boatswain from his neck. It catches the light and glimmers. I shiver, unable to shake the dread it elicits in me. I have no desire to be transported to the past—I'm afraid of what I'll see and feel there. I don't want to remember another moment with Emil. I also don't want a gateway to Sheol to open up and drag me into it. The boatswain is bad news. I wouldn't mind destroying it right now by squeezing it into a small paperweight.

"We can't destroy it yet, love," Reed says, as if reading my mind.

"It's a really satisfying fantasy, though."

"Yes, it is. I've indulged in it several times myself already."

I hum the tune for him. He listens intently, and then flawlessly hums it back to me.

"That's it," I say breathlessly. I walk to the dormer window. My fingertips skim over the cool metal of Xavier's telescope mounted on a tripod. The brass shines as if it were polished just yesterday. I lean over, draw my eye near the eyepiece, and close the other one. Before anything comes into focus, I already know what I'll see. It's a view of the water—Lake St. Clair in all its frozen splendor. Freighters with red and black hulls crash through the ice on their way to and from the Detroit River.

I straighten and glance over at Reed. He's staring at a picture of Xavier and me. Xavier is kissing me under the mistletoe at Cole's girlfriend, Kirsten's, Winter Wonderland party. Reed lifts the framed photo and turns it over face down on the table. "Where are we?"

"Grosse Pointe. It's next to Detroit. I lived a few miles that way," I use my thumb to gesture over my shoulder. It's like night and day, huh?" I ask. "The haves and the have nots, so close to one another and yet worlds away."

"You went to the wealthier school?" Reed asks. "One in Grosse Pointe?"

"My test scores were off the charts. It turns out I have an angel brain." I give him a doleful look. "My scores allowed me to be bused to this school district. It was a hard transition, though. My only friend was Molly for a long time. She was in the same situation as I. She had amazing scores as well—teachers used to ask us if it was in the water where we lived or something."

"Was it?" Reed asks with a small smile.

"Umm, no. There was stuff in the water where I lived, but I think it was lead."

"So you went to a nicer school."

"I wouldn't say it was 'nicer'. Nicer implies kindness."

"People weren't kind."

"Some were. Some thought we were trash being brought in—they felt we tainted the gene pool of their hallowed halls."

"Who would think that?"

"You'd be surprised at how much money matters to some people. They claim it doesn't, but the minute they find out you don't have any, is the minute you become undesirable—a parasite."

"Those aren't people you want in your life anyway. It's okay to let them weed themselves out early."

"Where were you when I was growing up, Reed?"

"Waiting for you," he replies, as if it is the only explanation. "So, you and Molly traversed the class line to come to this school district?"

"You could say that. We crossed the line between Detroit and Grosse Pointe for sure. We both had more intelligence than most kids, but not enough money to keep up with them."

"And then you met Xavier?" Reed asks.

I nod. "He was in a lot of my classes. He transferred in from a school in Germany. His mom was from a wealthy family there, but they both spoke perfect English. She and his father were not together in the traditional sense, at least, that's what he told me. They were still married, but they hadn't lived together in years. It turns out that he really doesn't even have parents, does he?"

"No, not the way you're thinking. He was born of fire."

"Rebecca, his fake mom here, wasn't around much. She was always on her way somewhere, traveling. But I liked her when she was here. She was really kind to me."

"Was she a Reaper?"

I shrug. "I don't know. Maybe? It would fit her personality. I never even suspected that she could be anything other than human."

"Are you sure?" he asks.

"Wait, what?"

"You may have suspected she was an angel. You may have even found out, but they wouldn't allow you to know it for long." Reed picks up the white knight from the marble chessboard, toying with it in his hand. "You remember Torun?"

"Yes," I whisper.

"A lot of things there were completely destroyed by angels. Even in a blizzard, people saw what was happening in their city."

"You erased their memories?" I ask.

"Not me. I was with you. A host of Cherubim most likely performed the task, putting things back together and making things right once more. The underground bar probably looks the same today as it did before Valentine's friends crashed through it to pluck you from it."

I think about all the things I may have witnessed but cannot possibly remember. I have a key to all of it now. It's in Reed's hand. I'm just not certain I have the courage it takes to face my past.

"You spent a lot of your time here before coming to Crestwood?" Reed asks. He picks up another framed picture of Xavier and me. It's from Homecoming our sophomore year.

"Yeah. I spent a lot of time here, mostly as Xavier's friend. We were friends before we were anything else."

"Just like in Heaven?"

"I don't know. I can't remember that part of it," I admit. "Do you need me to hum the notes again?"

Reed shakes his head. "I know it. Do you trust Atwater?"

"Not completely, but what choice do we have? I need to know what happened so I can figure out how to kill Emil. He holds all the cards. I want some of my own."

"I'll be with you. I'm always with you. Are you ready?" he asks.

"I'm ready," I whisper. I look at the pictures that line the table next to us. They're all of Xavier and me. Reed places the boatswain between his lips. The first note sounds like a scream. It raises goose bumps on my flesh. The world around me fades. The next few notes break apart the room, opening it up to pure sky. The final note from the whistles makes the sky collapse in on me. I'm lost in darkness. I fall. The only sound I hear is Reed's strong heartbeat, until it is replaced by beautiful, mournful sounds from

Iniquity

a solitary piano as gunshots ring out in the air.

CHAPTER 18
Debt To Iniquity

The smooth ivory-colored piano keys beneath my fingertips are cool to the touch. Forlorn notes float in the air while I play Cannon in D for the monster standing behind me. Emil's ever-present, oppressive shadow looms nearer, darkening the keys. The scent of his flowery shaving soap is enough to make me physically ill. With it, I smell the acrid odor of smoky gunpowder in the air. Terrifying rapports of guns and bullet shell casings rain onto the floor above us. They taper off as I come closer to the end of the song until the only sound is the achingly beautiful fade of the final note. Then...stillness. The silence is even more frightening then the noise.

My mind is buzzing with thoughts of Xavier. He should be somewhere close. I'm supposed to meet him by the bridge. My scattered thoughts and prayers hurtle through my mind, making me flinch as Emil's fingertips brush my hair away from my nape. He bends and presses his lips there. I don't move, but my pulse races with fear and loathing.

Emil lifts his lips and sits beside me on the piano bench with his back to the keys, facing me. "You play so beautifully, just like an angel, Simone."

"Do you believe in angels, Emil?" I ask. I can't even remember formulating the question, but it's out of my mouth before I can stop it.

"Of course. I have one beside me."

"I mean real angels." I shouldn't be speaking. It will upset him.

"Do you?"

"No."

"Why not."

"If there were angels, you wouldn't exist." The truth I never meant to say.

"The world needs me to rid it of its imperfections."

"Who are you to judge anyone?"

"I'm the one with all the power."

His hand rests against my skin, rubbing my cheek. He moves his hand downward. My fingertips touch the fabric of his trousers. I glide them up the length of his thigh, watching his pupils grow larger until my fingernails bump against the supple leather of the holster of his sidearm. Emil's hand cups my breast. A soft gasp whispers from me before I swallow back the bile in my mouth. I skim my hand over smooth leather, feeling the transition from warm hide to cool metal. My heart hammers in my chest.

Emil reaches to the back of my dress. He deftly slips the ivory top button of my collar through the eyelet. I feel sick. Our eyes are locked on one another's. I touch the handle of his gun. The second button on my dress springs free of its eyelet. I ease my arm back, heavy gunmetal slithers against leather. With my shaking thumb, I push the safety off. Finding the trigger with one finger, I use my other hand to pull back the toggle of the pistol. It slides back into place.

Emil's hands have stilled, recognizing the sound of me arming his Luger. "Do you intend to shoot—" I push the barrel against his ribs. The trigger clicks as I pull it, but nothing happens. It doesn't fire. My eyes leave his as I fumble with the toggle once more. It's in the up position, indicating that there are no bullets in the magazine. I cock the toggle anyway and try to fire the pistol. Again, nothing happens, except that the toggle springs back to the up position once more. I lift my eyes to Emil's. He's amused.

"We're running low on ammunition. I gave my cartridges to Axel so he could dispose of the staff. I am, as you see, out of bullets." I can't seem to swallow. I stare into his cold, blue eyes. "I thought you loved me, Simone."

"I don't," I hear myself whisper. "I hate you."

"Isn't that the same thing?"

"No. Not even close."

The violent crack of his backhand across my cheek sends me toppling from the bench. Landing hard on the floor, I pull my heels up to me so that I have a better chance of rising fast. His Luger flies from my hand, spinning to a halt underneath a table.

"Pity," Emil says. "I love you. You're dear to me."

My palm cups my throbbing cheek as I look up at him. "You love to torture me. It isn't the same thing."

He rises from the bench, towering over me. "It is to me." He lifts his cane from against the side of the piano. The silver wolf head shines in the light from the window. "You've grown rebellious. Why is that? It's as if something has given you hope. Is that it? Do you hope, Simone? Do you believe you will be liberated by my enemies?"

I don't answer. I'm afraid that he'll see the truth on my face though. I did hope. I placed my hope in a British soldier who has abandoned me. I rise to my feet with my hand on the nearby table. Backing away from him, he watches me move. My clumsy hand stumbles over the table, knocking over the kerosene lamp, breaking the top of it off. Emil's eyes go to the growing stain of liquid as it pours out. I retreat from it, my feet walking backward toward the doors to the hallway. Emil goes to the table, catching up the broken bottom of the lamp. He looks in my direction. Flicking his hand at me, the oil from the lamp soaks the front of my dress, splashing onto my face and arms. I close my eyes, trying to avoid getting it in them. Blurrily, I try to wipe it from my face with the back of my sleeve.

"Do you hope, Simone? Do you pray to be rescued? Do you wish for someone to take you from me, now that we are in retreat? Do you believe that I will ever let you go?" He sets the broken lamp back on the table. A matchbox rests next to his hand. Running his fingers over it, he snatches it up. Blood drains from my face as he opens it and withdraws a matchstick. With trembling knees, I force my feet to move.

Driven by terror of the madman behind me, I stumble into a chair, toppling it over. I put my hands out, trying to feel my way across the room while my red-rimmed eyes burn with tears. Managing to find the doors, I fling them wide. The hallway is quiet. Empty. My hands go to the plaster wall and follow it to the kitchen. The scraping sound of a dragged foot follows me as I cross the stone floor. I fumble for the latch of the back door, finding it I fling it open. Leaning heavily on the railing, I descend the stone steps that lead to the cobbled drive.

The hazy shapes of soldiers crowd around at the end of the drive, loading the rest of their belongings into trucks in preparation of the evacuation. I avoid them, switching direction toward the carriage house. The wooden sliding door looms ahead. I hear Emil following me. In desperation, I throw all of my weight into the task of rolling the wooden door open on its glide. A diagonal sliver of light cuts the darkness inside. The space has been cleaned out. There are only a few bales of straw in the loft above. The cobblestone ground is dank beneath my feet. A blackbird flies onto the beam of the high ceiling. Rushing in, I roll the door closed. I try to throw the bolt, but Emil opens the door from without. He calls to his men outside, telling the soldiers to go on to the next location without him—he'll catch up with them. Truck engines rev and softly fade as his men depart.

I pant in fear, but stand my ground. There's no point in retreating further. There's nowhere left to go. Emil slides the door closed behind us. Light from a window near the gables is plenty to see by, but Emil strikes a match anyway. He opens the glass of the wall sconce and touches the fire to it. It flames to life.

He looks down his nose at me, as if I'm some sort of insect he has to dispose of before I infest the world. His lower lip pushes up, curving his mouth down. "Simone, I'm very disappointed in you. You not only tried to kill me, you ran from me."

"You're not disappointed. You're offended. You believe I should love you."

"You should love me!" he snarls. "I've labored to mold and shape you into the perfect woman. You should thank me!"

"I should kill you," I don't even try to keep the venom from my voice.

"You haven't the strength to kill me. I own you."

"There's a whole world inside me that you'll never touch!"

Emil walks in a slow circle, casing me. I want to remain unaffected by it, but my knees weaken and my hands tremble. I'm nauseated by fear as my bravado erodes. Emil swipes his cane though the air, it makes a terrifying whistle. I flinch. I know what it will feel like when it finally falls on me. Brutal. "Ahh, so you do still fear me." He stops in front of me so I can see his smug smile. "Now I want you to beg me."

I don't have to ask him what for, I know he means my life. My whole body begins to shake. "Plea—"

Emil's fist connects with my upper lip, pushing it into my teeth. My soft flesh explodes. Blood drips between my front teeth. The metallic taste stains my tongue. My head lurches to the side. I crash onto the ground, bouncing off the uneven brick. Emil stands over me. "Get up. I didn't hit you hard." But he did and he knows he did. He uses his cane, landing blows on my back and legs. "Get. Up."

I blink. Tears seep from my eyes. More blows strike me, tearing my soul away with my flesh. I can't stop the pain. My breath rattles in my chest. My ribs ache. It feels as though they're pressing into my lungs. I manage to push myself up to my knees. The rough brick cuts them. A part of me wonders why I'm bothering to move. The distressing answer is I want to live, but I doubt this time that I will. He's always been in control of his vicious nature, but his control is slipping. He's giving in to the darkness inside him and it'll only stop when I'm in pieces.

His cane hits my arms that I lift to protect my head and face. The bones in my hand shatter. I realize vaguely that I'm screaming until he punches me in the stomach. A whoosh of air goes out of my mouth. I land flat on my back, looking up at him hovering above me. All sound is muffled. Emil is saying something. He leans near me and shakes my shoulders. His face looms in front of mine. I squint at him. My eyelids are swelling. Blood oozes into them from open cuts on my brow. Sound crashes back in.

"You're pregnant?" Emil demands with a desperate look in his eyes. He touches the ground beside me, lifting his palm; it's covered with my blood. "Tell me!" He shakes me again. "Are you pregnant with my child?"

A gush of blood pours from me, wetting my thighs as my abdomen contracts violently. I moan. "My child," I croak. "Never yours."

Emil swears in anger. "Why didn't you tell me? This is entirely your fault! I wouldn't have struck you there if I had known." He touches my forehead with his bloody palm, pushing back my hair from it. "You cannot leave me, Simone." The room grows darker. I lose focus on his face. He shakes me again until my teeth rattle. "Why didn't you tell me you were carrying my baby?" He's afraid. I'm slipping away from him.

"Never your baby. Just mine." I look over his shoulder. Sparkling embers of golden light, like glowing dust, falls through the crack of the open door. Amid the light, a charcoal-colored feather blows toward me. It gently falls against my swollen cheek. My cloudy eyes become clear. Dark, widespread wings show on either side of Emil as he kneels over me. A large hand encircles Emil's neck, cutting off his breath. Emil jerks away from me, lofting into the air, held up by an angel. I blink. The angel strangles my enemy with one hand as his flapping gray wings beat the air.

Emil's face turns blue. His hands claw and slap the angel's fist, trying to pry it from his throat. Strawberry-blond hair waves disheveled and messy on his forehead. A mask of agony contorts his face as his legs kick the air. The dark-haired angel has a look of vengeance. He bares his teeth, closing his fist harder, crushing Emil's spine. Emil's arms drop and his legs no longer flail. The angel says something to Emil, it sounds like music. His wings continue to move as his other hand reaches up and twists Emil's head at an unnatural angle, breaking Emil's neck. Then the beautiful creature rips Emil's head clean off his shoulders, spraying blood on the floor and walls. He lets go of Emil's body. It crashes to the floor in a tangled heap. My abuser's blood mixes with mine in a pool on the ground.

Still hovering in the air, the angel turns in my direction. I look into his green eyes, the color of a field in summer. "You feel no pain," the angel says to me in English. His deep voice echoes in my mind. All pain evaporates from me, floating away as if it had never been, but I can't move. I'm broken.

The angel's wings rustle. He lands near me, but his wings still flutter—restless air fans me. Reaching down, the angel picks me up, extracting me from the cold cobblestone floor. My cheek rests against his bared chest, leaving streaks of red on his perfect skin. I hear the powerful beat of his heart. Mine slows, making me pant for air. He flies us upward, landing on the loft. Gently, he lays me in the straw. His hands move over me, checking my injuries. I know it should be painful, but it isn't.

A growl turns his expression dark. His perfect mouth twists in anger as one of his hands touches my ribs. I feel him move the shard of bone, pulling it in a way that he shouldn't be able to if it weren't broken. There's a sucking sound as he moves it.

I can't breathe! My eyes go wide in distress. Quickly, he moves my rib back. Whatever hole he'd opened by shifting the bone from my lung fills once more. The angel gathers me to him. He sits and leans against the dusty wall with me in his lap. I look up at the exposed rafters of the carriage house. His hand goes to my forehead, moving my blood-soaked hair from my eyes. I cough hard. Blood spills onto my lips.

His deep voice vibrates through his chest, "Do you need to say goodbye to anyone?"

My voice is thready as I ask, "I'm dying?"

"Yes. I cannot save you."

I think of Nicolas—his beautiful brown eyes, boyish grin—so kind and so perfect. Being in my husband's arms was what I wanted for my life once, but that's so far away now. Is he still alive somewhere out there?

I hope I never see Nicolas again, I think. A tear falls from beneath my lashes.

He'd never understand that I'm not the same person with whom he fell in love. I'm not her anymore. I've done things that he can't ever know about—things he could never forgive. I'd never be able to look him in the eyes again. I'm broken. I think of Xavier...my British officer. He'd needed me to stay here—to gain information to sabotage my enemy's evacuation of weapons. In exchange, he said he'd help me escape when the time was right. Will he ever find out what happened to me?

"No," I gasp. "There's no one." I'm cold. My lips tremble.

"There will be no pain where you're going," the angel murmurs. He strokes my hair.

"Where am I going?"

"Home."

"You sound sad..." I cough again and taste more blood. "Why are you sad?"

"I wish I was going with you."

"You want to go home?"

"More than anything."

"Then come with me."

"I'm not allowed back unless I'm called. After what I just did, I will never go home again."

"You did something wrong?"

"I've broken the law."

"How?"

"I hunt evil. This place has drawn my prey near to it. The one I sought to destroy was helping the human I ended down there." He moves his chin in Emil's direction. "I'd been waiting for the fallen one to return. Byzantyne is never far away from his charge."

"Byzantyne..." I say the name that feels familiar to my tongue. With effort, I extend my cool fingers and rest them against the angel's cheek. Startled by the contact, his head moves back from me. After a moment though, he leans into my palm, lifting his hand to cover mine and hold it in place. Our eyes connect.

"I'm never to interfere with humans," he whispers, like a confession. "I saw what Byzantyne's human was doing to you and I should have walked away. But I couldn't! Not this time! He shouldn't get to live after what he did to you. He needed to die. My only regret is that it hadn't been more painful for him."

"Emil was bad," I whisper, trying to calm him.

"To his core," the angel agrees. "The only angels coming for his soul will be from Sheol."

"They'll come for me, too?"

The angel shakes his head. "No. Not you."

I feel a flood of relief at his absolute surety that I will be spared that fate. "What's urr name..." I slur.

"Shh ..." He tries to soothe me; his fingers thread through mine. My hand leaves his face as he holds it.

"Your name?" I insist in a raspy voice.

"Reed."

"Reed." The sound of his name is a benediction.

A tremendous rumble of thunder roars around us, shaking the carriage house. Dust falls from the rafters even after the angry sound fades.

"What's happening?" I ask, fear bright in my eyes.
"I've made Paradise angry. They'll be coming for me."
"Why?"
"I killed a human."
"He was killing me. You protected me."
"And I'd do it again."
"What's going to happen to you?"
"I'll be executed."
"What? But, you're good!"
"Am I? I really don't know anymore. I think I've been here too long."
"Why would you do this for me? Why would you try to save me?"
"I wanted it all to end…I wanted to go home to Paradise, but it never happened. And I saw you…and I watched you…and I knew—we're the same, you and I. We're both caught in the wheel and it just spins."

Another violent crack of thunder rumbles around us, shaking the foundation of the carriage house. I shudder at the sound right before a high-powered beam of light comes through the ceiling and strikes me where I lay in Reed's arms. It's so bright, but it has no heat. My eyes roll back in my head…and I know. I have clarity, and with it savage fear blankets me. I can never beat Emil the way things are. I'll be destined to be his slave in every future lifetime. I exist only to fight him, but he has all the weapons save one—love.

I can stop fighting Emil anytime. I can give up and remain in Paradise. But, if I don't live another lifetime and defeat Emil, I'll never be with Xavier again. If I don't come back, there is no purpose in having a guardian angel. He will be taken from me. This is the price to be with my Angel—horrific death over and over and over… The light ends. Everything is darker in its absence, especially the knowledge that it left behind.

I glance at Reed. This Power angel has attempted to save me, even at his own peril. He would change my destiny, just because he couldn't tolerate one more moment of Emil hurting me. Divine angels will be here soon with only vengeance to impart to Reed. He won't survive it. He's broken the law by saving me! Sheol will have its revenge on him for what he's done to Emil. He will never see Paradise again. He'll cease to be!

I unthread my fingers from Reed's. Gripping his wing, my hand curls around a silky, gray feather. I tear it from him, clutching it in my fist. "I'll come back for you, Reed. I'll meet you in my next life. I swear it. Wait for me! I won't let them hurt you!"

Reed caresses my swollen cheek and murmurs, "You can't save me."

"I will save you," I promise him. "You will go home one day!"

Angels ride in on the storm swirling outside. Entering from above, they crash through the ceiling, the windows, and the door. A swarm of them hover in the air in the center of the room. Black wings of Thrones and bold blue wings of Cherubim flail around us. Reed eases me off of his lap and settles me beside him against the rough wood planks of the wall. The moment he lets go of me, two Cherubim with lion-like features swoop down upon him and tear Reed away into the air. He's flown into the center of the carriage house. He goes willingly, accepting his fate. A Cherub with golden hair emerges from the crowd.

The cat-like eyes of the Cherub stare at Reed as he speaks in Angel, "Are you responsible for the death of this human?" He indicates Emil's broken body on the cobbled stone beneath them.

"I am," Reed admits.

"You have violated Angel law."

"I have."

"The penalty of that is death. This is not unknown to you."

"I understand the consequences of my actions."

"Why would you surrender your life so foolishly?"

"Was it foolish to intervene? I don't see it anymore." His eyes hold centuries of weariness. "I'm divine. It's my duty to fight Sheol...and they're winning. You need only step outside to know that. Innocence is slaughtered in the most horrific ways imaginable."

"You cannot change the laws!"

"Why not? What are they for if they don't protect the innocent?"

"All you have done is create a debt to iniquity!"

"That's not all I've done. I gave Simone a few lasts breaths of peace in this world."

"Why would you do that? She was dying anyway! She was going home."

"I've watched her as I've stalked my prey—Byzantyne—his evil guardian angel." Reed gestures toward Emil's lifeless body. "She's worth saving. This world needs her. My only regret is that I failed! I'm too late."

"Why would you keep her here? Why would you change her destiny?"

Reed hesitates. He looks in my direction. His jaw sets. "I...needed her here."

"You needed...you love the soul?" The Cherub asks incredulously. "You wanted her to stay with you!"

"Love? What do I know of love? I'm merely a Power, isn't that right?" Reed asks. His eyebrows draw together. "But I'd gladly give up my life to save her an instant of pain. So you tell me, what is that?"

"Not your job."

"It should be."

"A payment to Sheol must be rendered for this divine breech of Angel law. You will pay the debt when the Thermopylae delegates arrive. We will end you in front of them." Reed is stoic, accepting his fate and facing death as if it were a foregone conclusion. Divine angels swarm him, preparing to tear him apart the moment the order is given. He glances in my direction once more. Our eyes lock on one another's.

I raise Reed's crushed, gray feather into the air. With my dying breath, I utter a single word in Angel, "Champion."

CHAPTER 19
Champion

My spirit lifts from my body. I gaze back at the beaten shell of a crushed young woman, lifeless upon a bed of straw. Reed's feather is still clutched in her gnarled fingers. Surprise shows on some of the angel faces at my ability to liberate myself from my body so quickly without the assistance of a Reaper.

The air grows denser with the swirl of a storm and the heaviness of unspent electricity. Crackling thunder cuts the air outside. A black booted figure emerges from the darkness. Steam rises off the rain-sodden head of the Seraph. I cannot smell him, but if the wrinkled noses of the divine angels are any indication, then he must reek. Even so, he's brutally handsome with his slicked-back black hair and dark brown eyes. Bare-chested, his crimson wings rest behind him in a casual mien, as if he hadn't just walked into a nest of killers who'd be only too happy to end him in the most painful way possible. He extracts a handkerchief from the pocket of his trousers. I recognize his attire as being part of a British officer's uniform — similar to what Xavier wears. I try to stifle the need to ask him where he procured the uniform.

Wiping beads of water from his face, Byzantyne peers up at me. He shakes the water from his wings as he lofts into the air. "Simone," he says as he approaches me. "You look divine." His smile is rueful.

I feel the need to shiver, even though I don't possess a body at the moment. "Byzantyne, forgot your umbrella?"

"I was in a hurry. I wasn't expecting this summons. Something went awry, did it?"

"Depends on how you look at it."

"This is, indeed, interesting timing. I just left Xavier. He isn't faring well, I fear. I daresay he won't be joining you. Ever."

"You know what I remember the most about all of my afterlives, Byzantyne?" I ask.

"That I nearly always win?"

"That you enjoy lying to me."

"I would never lie to you. I have only the utmost respect for you. I always tell you that one day I will possess your soul."

"Why am I so important to you?"

"Because you're important to Xavier…or at least you were. Sorry he couldn't meet you at your rendezvous at the bridge. He was otherwise engaged."

Fear makes my glowing light pulse in thumping beats. I try to control it. The light from me strobes Byzantyne's face, making his features more pronounced, and then deeply shadowed. "I never made it to the bridge."

"I can see that," Byzantyne replies. He turns in circles, assessing the holy host of angels before him.

"Xavier had become more and more predictable the longer he stayed with you. He allowed us to kill your soul mate right away in this round. It wasn't even fun for us. Casimir just let the chlorine gas take Nicolas. You should've seen it though, Simone—Nicolas clutching your picture as he struggled to take his last breath. In that way, it was an exquisite death."

I try to ignore the gruesome images that evokes. "I know Xavier is alive. I would feel it if he weren't."

"Would you? I wonder how long it will take me to inspire such loyalty in you when you become mine."

"I'll never be yours."

"That sounds like a challenge." Without looking away from me, Byzantyne barks out, "Why has no one released my property from his meat sack?" he indicates Emil's dead body on the ground.

A Throne responds, "That's not our concern. It can rot in there for all we care."

Byzantyne's eyelids hood, and then he gazes at me. "It's a little embarrassing that you can transition so easily, Simone, and Emil cannot. But," he sighs, "Emil makes up for his shortcomings in sheer brutality, wouldn't you agree?" He's playing with me. He's in a cheerful mood, as if he has a horrible secret that he just can't wait for me to find out. I feel like I'm melting. What if what he said about Xavier is true?

Byzantyne directs his attention at the divine angels. "Which one of you has stolen this life from Sheol?" he demands.

"I am responsible for sending your killer home early," Reed replies without emotion.

"A Power has gone rogue! What has this world come to when you cannot trust a divine Power to play by the rules?" Byzantyne shrugs. "Alfred!"

A very slight Reaper angel slips in from the darkness outside. He's maybe the scrawniest angel I've ever seen. Condescending laughter comes from the divine angels when they see him slink in with rounded shoulders, clearly terrified to be there. Byzantyne gives him a haughty look. "Transition the soul from his prison."

Alfred's translucent dragonfly wings buzz in agitation. He runs a hand through his wet, blond hair. Rainwater drips from his pale, pointed chin. He moves to Emil. Wielding his scythe with the flair of a Samurai, he cuts through Emil's aura to split it wide open. Most souls, when they emerge from their bodies, are luminous, the brighter the light, the more vibrant the soul. There's an absence of illumination from Emil as he claws his way from his corpse. He's a black hole devouring radiance.

Humiliation and rage ravage Emil's features. He turns these emotions on Alfred. "WHERE WERE YOU? I HAVE BEEN DEAD FOR HOURS!" This is a blatant exaggeration. It has been less than one hour. In the old days, it could take days of languishing in rotting flesh before being emancipated. It speaks to his Sheol status that an hour now seems an eternity to him. He must be very important to them—especially high on the evil food chain.

Alfred doesn't cower from Emil. His vindictive glare and pinched mouth promise retaliation. The Reaper raises his scythe, spinning it around with deadly precision. "Alfred," Byzantyne's contempt for the Reaper is in his tone. "Do not threaten my protégé." Alfred's head tilts forward with involuntary submission, but his blue eyes still stare unblinking at Emil.

Emil shifts his blind animal fury to me. "You were mine! I had you this time! You would've fallen! It was inevitable!" I don't find this a bit amusing, but I force a smile as I extend a luminous limb, turning my arm over in front of me to assess its shine.

"I don't think that's quite true. I seem to be lighting up the room."

"You will dim when I play with you in Sheol," Emil rages.

"If I ever fell from grace, I don't believe Byzantyne would allow you near me. I'd replace you as his favorite." I force another smile. "Maybe you shouldn't try so hard to make me fall."

"Maybe you shouldn't try so hard to stop me. Byzantyne is much more powerful than Xavier."

"Xavier will crush him one day and you'll be left all alone to fend for yourself in Sheol." My words elicit fear in Emil; it comes off of him as black smoke. My attention draws away from him as someone comes through the door below us.

Two figures emerge from the shadows: one is a Cherub and the other is a Seraph. The Cherub's blond hair plasters to his head. Rainwater and a thick cake of mud soak his British uniform trousers. Robin-egg blue wings spread wide behind him. In his arms is the nearly lifeless body of my guardian angel. Xavier is a mess; cut up and broken, blood pours from a multitude of wounds. The blue-winged angel takes a few steps nearer and nearly collapses. Other Cherubim are upon them, lifting Xavier from him and laying my wounded angel on the ground where they work to save his life. I want to go to him, but I find that I'm unable to move. Fear has me rooted were I am. He cannot die. Not Xavier. Not like this!

"You were saying, Simone?" Emil chuckles. The coldness of his soul reaches out to me, trying to pull some of the heat of my being to him. "I don't think Byzantyne is too worried about Xavier ever defeating him."

Byzantyne isn't paying any attention to either of us. He's flying toward Reed in the center of the room. The evil Seraph stops right in front of the Power angel, wearing the most ferocious snarl that I've ever seen from him. "I will eviscerate you, Power! You have robbed me of the one thing that has meant anything to me!" Normally, he's unemotional except for an occasional look of disdain. This uncharacteristic display of feeling has me reeling.

Reed tilts his head to the side, studying Byzantyne. "You didn't get to finish your kill." Reed gestures to where Xavier lies writhing in agony, his beautiful red wings nearly shredded from him. "You were called away—called here. You couldn't linger over the Seraph like you wanted—and a quick death was out of the question for him, not after the length of time you've been stalking one another. You wanted a sweeter revenge for your prey. You thought you'd be able to come back for him—after you took care of whatever you were being summoned to do."

Byzantyne's face turns a startling shade of red. "This is your fault!" Spittle from his mouth flies in every direction as he shouts and points his finger at Reed. "You brought me here!"

Reed is calm. "You couldn't ignore the summons. You had to come because I killed the malevolent soul you were charged with protecting when you weren't looking. How does that make you feel...having your prey snatched away from you at the last possible moment?" Reed taunts.

"You will know! I will make you feel every second of torment that I can wring from you!" I've never seen Byzantyne so angry in all of my lifetimes. The realization dawns on me that Reed has done more than just spare me pain, he has inadvertently saved Xavier's life, too.

"You won't." I try to control my fear so that no one sees it. "You won't hurt him."

Byzantyne swings around, pinning me where I am with a horrible sneer. "Will I not?" How do you propose to stop me? It's a debt and I intend to exact more than just a pound of flesh!" To the angels holding Reed, he says, "You can leave him to me. I plan to take my time making him cease to be."

"You can't kill him." Serenity eludes me, so I pretend to be calm.

Byzantyne's hand forms a claw. With his back to me, unwilling as he is to look away from Reed, he pushes his claw out in my direction. "Do not think to interfere, Simone. There's nothing you can do. His fate is sealed!"

I glance at Reed. He's watching me. He shakes his head almost unperceptively, warning me not to speak. I ignore him. Instead, my eyes return to look at the back of Byzantyne's head. I call out in Angel, "CHAMPION!"

Byzantyne, who has been bent toward Reed, slowly straightens. I can't see his expression until he looks over his shoulder at me. He's stunned. The entire room quiets. "What did you say?" he growls.

"I challenge you for this angel's life. I will be his champion."

A laugh of disbelief escapes from Byzantyne. "You challenge me? For this." He waves his hand in front of Reed with a scornful look.

"No!" Reed's jaw clenches as he throws a ferocious look in my direction.

"Yes," I reply simply.

"You. Challenge. Me?" Byzantyne asks as he turns toward me and stabs his chest with his finger. His exquisite Seraphim wings become almost heart-shaped for a moment.

"That's right," I affirm.

Byzantyne's mood changes, he titters as if he's heard the best joke of his life, but cannot believe it. He flies toward me. Reed wrenches his arms, attempting to free himself from the Cherubim holding him. They won't let him go. Right before Byzantyne gets to me, the Cherub who brought Xavier in inserts himself between us. His blue feathers, spattered with mud, move to keep him in stasis in the air. He blocks my view of Byzantyne. Byzantyne growls at him. "I have negotiations with this soul!" he warns the Cherub.

"I will mediate the terms," the Cherub replies. I peek at Byzantyne from behind the angel.

"And who are you?" Byzantyne looks down his nose at the blue-winged angel.

"My name is Atwater."

"Move aside, Atwater. You interfere."

Atwater holds his ground. His wingspan widens to keep Byzantyne from seeing me. "There are no promises made from Paradise without me to mediate them. You either exact your vengeance on the Power or you allow me to agree to terms on behalf of Heaven. There are no other options. Choose."

"You would not last a moment in Sheol," Byzantyne snarls.

"We're not in Sheol," Atwater replies.

"Let us discuss terms then. We can bury you in the weeds later."

"Excellent choice," Atwater says. He moves so that he's beside me.

His blue wings flap effortlessly, keeping him beside me as if we were standing on the ground.

Byzantyne has managed to squelch all emotion now. He's every inch the horrifying, unfeeling monster that I remember from my past deaths. He's always nearby when I'm killed—waiting, hoping that this time I'll be his. Face to face with this ancient Seraph, I begin to doubt my every decision. What I've done hits me like a slow-moving bullet. I try to hide my growing terror at the cunning gleam in Byzantyne's brown eyes as they devour me. He's warming to the idea of having me at his mercy. He'll enjoy this much more than destroying an anonymous Power angel. If there was ever a time to attack, it's now. I have to set my trap just right. I need him to agree to every point I make. He needs to believe I'm caught up in his web.

"So you're offering your soul for his life?" Byzantyne's low, menacing voice jolts me out of my thoughts. He indicates Reed with a gesture over his shoulder.

My eyes lift to Reed's green ones. He struggles to get loose from the Cherubim. "Do not do this! I am prepared to die!" Reed orders. His regal charcoal-colored wings flail with effort. He is maybe the most beautiful angel I've ever seen. Elegant and passionate in a way that Power angels almost never are. They're normally robotic precision. Ready to do their duty—obsessed with killing—anxious to destroy anything they deem evil—drone-like, but not this one. He's a knight.

My attention turns back to Byzantyne. "Yes, I'll champion this angel."

"You believe you'll win!" Byzantyne's eyes glisten with hunger. "Still so naïve, even after all of this time. You can't possibly defeat me!" His enormous chest puffs as he hits his fist against it. The sound is a drumbeat.

I raise my glowing chin. "Then you don't mind if I ask for whatever I want should I win?"

His eyebrows lower, settling at an arrogant angle. "Not at all. I'll enjoy hearing what would make you do this, aside from ridiculous naiveté, I might add."

"Well, then...first, when I win, Reed will ascend to Paradise. He gets to go home."

Byzantyne's eyes widen. He looks back at Reed. He did not see that coming. "I can only erase his debt. I cannot give you his ascension," Byzantyne replies.

"No, you can't, but he can." I look at Atwater next to me.

"It will be done," Atwater agrees immediately—maybe too quickly. I would step on his foot if I had a body and we weren't hovering above the ground. I try not to look at Atwater. His easy response will make Byzantyne counter.

Byzantine peers at me thoughtfully. "But if you lose, the Power ceases to be."

I want to dispute this, but it will only make the wicked Seraph dig in harder for it. Byzantyne looks baffled by my first point. I need to keep him unbalanced.

"Second, I don't ever want to have to return here to fight Emil." I gesture toward him, watching his handsomely ugly face twist with rage once more. "He never gets to come back for any more lifetimes. He has to stay buried in Sheol."

"She can't do that!" Emil lurches forward.

Byzantyne holds up his palm and stops Emil in midair with the gesture. "CEASE!" he orders. Emil slinks back, but his eyes betray his venom.

Byzantyne returns his attention to me. "You don't enjoy meeting your inescapable in every lifetime? You could surrender—accept no other missions."

"I cannot ask another soul to endure his cruelty in my stead."

"Always the little fixer, aren't you? You would deny him a chance at redemption?" Byzantyne's lips twist into a wicked grin at the very thought of Emil attempting to gain redemption.

"If it means saving future souls who would fall because of his influence, then yes, I would."

"Isn't that heresy, Simone? Aren't you all worthy of redemption?"

"Are we?" I ask, knowing he doesn't think so. I am giving him something he wants. I hope he doesn't see through it.

"There is one small problem in your plan. You're challenging me. I cannot kill a human. If I did, I would find myself in the same situation as that Power over there. How would I fight against you?"

"That Power over there has a name. It's Reed."

"I don't care what his name is. How do we solve our conundrum?"

"What if I'm not human when I return?"

Byzantyne laughs with derision. "What else could you be? You're a soul!"

"If I had a different body—not human? Would that work for you?" I'd be holding my breath if I had a body.

"In theory, yes, but what other body could a soul inhabit—"

"Angel."

Byzantyne appears to have stopped breathing. "What you suggest is..."

"...Is what you've always wanted—to be an angel with a soul. To prove to everyone that angels are worthy of redemption—more so than humans."

He can hardly contain his glee. He attempts to hide it though. "Still, even with an angelic body, your soul would not die, it would fall to me."

"If I lose and you kill my body, then my soul is Sheol's, but I won't lose."

"I want your soul mate as well"

"No!" I nearly shout it. "You never get him! He goes free!"

"But you're together. He's part of you."

I can't let Nicolas suffer for eternity. If I lose my soul to Sheol, I want him to be free. "I will see that our soul mate connection is severed."

"You would give up your soul mate? For a Power?" This makes no sense to him. I have to keep him unbalanced.

"I'll do it to see you cease to be—to banish Emil to Sheol for eternity. It will give my soul mate peace like he has never known in any lifetime."

"You think your soul mate is too good for all of this?"

I want to wipe the smirk off his face. "My soul mate is the best part of us. I'll pay the cost of this, not Nicolas."

"Does he know that you've fallen in love with your guardian angel? It's why you force him into mission after mission—so you can be near Xavier," Byzantyne taunts.

I cringe at how well he knows me. "I accept mission after mission to fight my inescapable. You play Emil whenever you can because you know I'll agree to face him. It's you who is obsessed with me."

"Oh, I am obsessed, Simone. I would love to have you all to myself and violate you in every possible way."

He means every word. "You know nothing of love, Byzantyne, and that's how I'll beat you."

"You'll beat me with love? That sounds salacious. I'm so looking forward to it. Now let me tell you what I demand in exchange. I cannot have you return as a more powerful being and have you unmatched by us. That hardly seems fair to have the strength of an angel with the latitude given to a soul. It's gluttonous of you, Simone. Unless..." his scheming gaze falls on Emil, "I'm allowed a champion of my own."

I close my eyes briefly. "You need a champion? That's a little cowardly of you. Are you afraid of me?"

"Afraid? No. I merely seek to maintain a balance, and because I don't have a soul, I will require a soul to act in my stead. I choose your inescapable, Emil. He will return here as a half-angel. He'll dance circles around the pieces of your broken heart."

Emil, who kills for fun, can't believe his good fortune. He knows what this could mean. He'll be one of the most powerful beings in the universe. He'll believe himself God-like, even though he cannot even imagine how miniscule he really is.

Emil sizes me up once more, his depraved soul growing darker. "I accept," he says without hesitation.

"Does Heaven agree?" Byzantyne lifts his eyebrow to Atwater and waits for him to respond.

Atwater pauses for a moment. His eyes become white, losing any indication that he has irises as they disappear. His body trembles as if enduring a shock from some outside force. It only takes a moment for his eyes to become normal once more. He stops shaking. "Heaven accepts."

"I still feel as if Simone is getting the better part of this bargain."

"What is it that you want?"

"I want you blind. You have something planned. I don't know what it is, but you came into this lifetime hoping for this outcome. Didn't you?"

"You know I can hardly predict what will happen when I enter a new life. There are too many variables to ever know the outcome of a life."

"It's not so hard when you know the players."

"But I never know the setup, do I?"

"Don't you? Still. I want you to go into this next lifetime with no prior knowledge of these negotiations. You don't get to know who you are or why you're here. And whoever is sent to protect you from us will be blind to the goal of the mission as well." Byzantyne looks down at Xavier on the ground. My guardian angel is unconscious, having succumbed to the pain of having his wings readjusted. "He doesn't get to know your mission either."

"We don't have to know the goal of the mission or that it involves you and Emil when I return here. It'll be the only logical choice though, given Emil is my inescapable and you're his handler. What other reason would I have to come back here?"

"As you say," Byzantyne accepts my logic. "You will be born into this next life as a human, so you will know nothing of Heaven or your inescapable. You'll follow the biological progression of an angel with an angelic body. You won't have angelic strength until you begin to evolve. When that time comes, if you make it that far and begin your evolution into angel, you will lose Xavier and whoever else is protecting you. They must ascend. You'll be left on your own. No one else is to be told of your arrival on earth or your purpose here."

"Someone has to know."

"Atwater can know—Heaven can know, but they can't tell you or the players in our game."

"Xavier will never agree to leave me."

"Then Heaven will have to force him back. He doesn't get to stay with you."

It's as if he has punched me in the stomach. I want to curl into a ball and hide. What he is proposing is sure disaster for me. I try to imagine it. I'll be a new being alone in the world, weak and transitioning into angel with no protection. I scrutinize the warrior angels surrounding us. They're not what one would term as open-minded. I glance at Reed. His clever eyes see the torment of my decision. Restrained from me, his face is a mask of agony, watching me struggle through this. "What would you do if you met an angel with a soul, Reed?" I ask as if we're the only two beings in the room.

He doesn't smile, but there's a tender quality in the look that passes from him to me. "If it were anyone else, Simone, I don't know. But, because it will be you, I'd have a better chance at harming starlight. I would protect you. You can trust me."

Byzantyne barks with laughter. "A Power with the eloquence of a poet! Do you believe him, Simone? He's programmed to murder anything that could be seen as unnatural. It's innate in him. He'd be made blind as well. He wouldn't remember any of this the moment he leaves here." Smug humor resonates from the Seraph.

Reed strains against the Cherubim holding him. Their blue feathers rustle and thrust, trying to maintain control and subdue him. It takes four of them to hold him back from Byzantyne. His voice hardens, "You believe you know me? You think I'd slaughter innocence—that I am a mindless drone? Give her to me to guard when you drive away her guardians. If you're right, I'll shatter her heart for you, and then you'll win before it even starts," Reed challenges. "But if you're wrong, you'll only have an infinitesimal Power with which to contend.

Byzantyne's eyebrows twist like threads above his brown eyes, arching as Reed uses the Seraph's boastful words against him. "Oh, this is interesting! Should I give you to the Power, Simone? He has been stalking me for months now. It was fortunate for me that you've been a dazzling distraction for him. I may not have known he was near if it were not for his penchant to watch you. He hovered around you as if he'd never seen a female before in his miserable life. Will love triumph, Simone, as you so desperately want to believe? Will you stake your eternity on his love for you?"

Reed's green eyes pierce me. "I will not fail you, Simone."

The deep, mesmerizing quality of his voice slices through my fear and I reply, "I will stake my eternity on it."

Byzantyne, looks from me to Reed in disbelief. I hardly spare the Seraph a glance because I'm entangled in the radiant smile on my knight angel's lips. The dark-haired demon hums with superiority." You'll blow into this Power's life, a dead leaf on and autumn breeze. He'll tear you down and bathe in your blood within the first hour of your meeting."

"Why are you afraid then, Byzantyne?" I ask.

"I fear nothing." He wants me to believe he's already won.

"You should fear us," Reed mocks him. "We'll slay the demon you keep on a leash." The divine Power turns a menacing grin on Emil. Emil flinches, more smoky essence curling off of him. Reed looks back at Byzantyne once more, "And then we'll come for you, wherever you are. You can hide in fire and we'll find you."

"You will lose," Byzantyne replies, the muscles in his face tightening as he attempts to be unemotional.

"Then you won't mind if I add one more thing if I win?" I interrupt.

"Name it," Byzantyne croons condescendingly.

I turn to address Atwater instead of Byzantyne, because this has to be granted by Heaven. "I want a love of my own choosing." I force myself not to look in Xavier's direction.

Byzantyne laughs with derision, as if I've asked for the most inane thing imaginable. "So this is truly all about Xavier after all. You would sever the ties to your soul mate and challenge me just to be with him? Such fealty and loyalty to an angel who watches you get butchered in every lifetime you live—and for him no less. He orchestrates your demise. You do know this, don't you? If it's to his advantage for you to die in order for him to defeat me, he does not hesitate to use it. No matter what price you have to endure. You are his pawn. And, yet, you love him still. Love is blind."

"We both know the risks going into every life."

"Yes, but do you know how easy it would be to get you out of some of the torture he allows you to suffer? He's ruthless when it comes to you. He absolutely does not care what happens to you."

"He's doing his job."

"Always at your expense," Byzantyne gives me a fake look of pity. "I only tell you this because I would not do that to you. If you were mine, I would cherish you." There is some truth to what he says. It's in the yearning in his eyes as he looks at me. He does want me, maybe even more than I ever imagined. But he wouldn't cherish me. He wouldn't even know how.

Atwater replies to me, "It will be done. You will have a love of your own choosing."

Emil careens forward suddenly. "I want something as well," Emil growls like a petulant child.

"Ah, it always wants something," Byzantyne shoots Emil a look of censure.

"As your champion, when I win, I want Simone to cease to be. She doesn't get to survive in Sheol as your favored pet. I want the ability to erase her soul from existence."

Byzantyne scowls at him. "You cannot annihilate a soul. It is imposs—"

Atwater's eyes become milky white once more. When his fit of shaking ends, he faces Emil and says, "Heaven accepts your terms with one stipulation."

"Which is?' Emil asks.

"There must be a balance. If you are given the ability to destroy her soul, than she will have the ability to end yours as well."

Before Byzantyne has a chance to interfere, Emil replies, "As champion, I accept all the terms." And just like that, the game is on.

"You set this up!" Byzantyne turns on me accusingly, narrowing his eyes at me. "This is what you wanted all along. What did you ask Heaven for in exchange for agreeing to attempt to erase Emil from existence?"

"Love."

"For Xavier?" Byzantyne asks in rage. I'm being snatched out of his grasp. Either way, if I lose or if I win, he doesn't get me. That fact isn't sitting well with him. He looks as if he's ready to drag me off to Sheol himself.

"What other reason could there be?" I ask.

Atwater gets between Byzantyne and me once more. "It is done. The terms are set. We will each return to our sides and negotiate the finer points of the agreement—time and place, arsenals, abilities—"

"I know the rules." Byzantyne fumes, trying to rein in his emotions. "Alfred."

Alfred jumps, startled at being addressed. His iridescent dragonfly wings buzz loudly. "Reap this traitor! Get him out of my sight!"

Alfred turns a wicked grin on Emil. With his golden scythe, he whirls it through the air, cutting a slash in the very fabric of this world. A small hole rends and gapes. Using his booted foot, Alfred kicks Emil, knocking him through the hole where Emil disappears from sight. He seals the gap back up using the same scythe.

Byzantyne notices the look of pleasure in Alfred's shiny eyes. "Reapers are such worthless maggots. Soon, when every last soul falls to us, there will be no use for them." he says with a look of disdain. "You will wait for me outside, Alfred."

Alfred ducks his head. His shoulders round as he slinks off to the door amid growls from the other angels in the room. He slips out into the darkness and downpour. I almost feel sorry for him for having to deal with such a maniacal leader…almost.

"I want all of theses angels' memories erased, Atwater," Byzantyne orders. "They will not remember what occurred here."

"So let it be," Atwater says. He raises his arms. An invisible force begins to retract the Thrones and Cherubim upward, through the holes in the ceiling out and into the night sky. It only takes moments for Xavier to disappear into the air. When Atwater lowers his arms, the only angels still with Atwater, Byzantyne, and me are the ones holding Reed.

Byzantyne's eyes fall on Reed. He wants to tear the Power angel apart. The feeling is definitely mutual because Reed studies Byzantyne as if he's finding out all of his weaknesses. Reed said he was hunting Byzantyne for a while. Once a Power has selected a target, he almost never wavers from it. If he were to let Byzantyne go, it would be a failed mission. By the looks of Reed, I'd say he's never failed in his entire life.

Byzantyne's expression grows more and more intolerant the longer Reed stares at him. "Why is this Power still here?" he asks Atwater. "Blind his memory and return him to the hole from which he crawled."

"You aren't in charge here, Byzantyne," I reply. His eyes narrow at me. He's not used to waiting for vengeance. He exacts pain from whomever he wants whenever he wants. I look past Byzantyne to the angels holding Reed. "It's done. You have to let him go." Atwater nods in agreement to what I've just said. The angels turn Reed loose. As they do, Heaven draws the Cherubim soldiers from the carriage house, ascending them into the sky.

Freed, Reed flies between the scary monster and me. "You can go now," Reed orders, dismissing Byzantyne. "You will have your chance at her in her next lifetime…except there, I won't be restrained."

"I will bury you in blood," Byzantyne replies. He growls at Atwater, "You are the only divine one here who will remember these events! You may never speak of them. Am I clear?"

"It will be done," Atwater agrees, "...unless..."

"Unless?"

"Unless one of you speaks of it first."

"Be clear, Atwater! Byzantyne's eyes are so narrow he's squinting.

Atwater shrugs. "We can't be held to the agreement if someone from your side were to say something that would jog a memory in Simone. If no one speaks of this night from your side, then Simone won't know, but the moment any of you say anything about what has occurred here..." He shrugs again.

"So a boast from Emil should be sufficient enough to allow you out of the stipulation in his contract with you."

"It is rather unfortunate for you, given his arrogant nature," Atwater replies.

Byzantyne turns his anger on me, pointing his finger. "You will beg me in your next life to save you from Emil."

"I always beg...in every life. I'll pray this time will be different."

"Still so naïve." He shakes his head in disgust. "Until we meet again, Simone." Byzantyne folds in his crimson wings. He falls to the stone floor below, landing on his feet as if it were nothing at all. Without a backward glance, he strides toward the door. His booted feet make almost no sound as he slips outside and vanishes into the night.

Atwater's gaze travels from Reed to me. "I will give you a moment to say goodbye, after which I have to send Reed out into the night without any memory of this." Atwater retracts his wings and falls to the floor below. He leaves the carriage house.

I shift my eyes to Reed, knowing that we don't have much time left together. I'll be called home to Heaven soon. Strategy and the details of my mission will be undertaken and debated by high-ranking Seraphim. They'll work out angles of pursuit and arsenals in which to endow me for survival. Upon my return here, my memory of this event will be erased. I need to discover a way to survive him when we meet again.

"Do you—did you find me attractive?" I ask. "My former body—Simone?" Reed just stares at me, clearly reluctant to answer. "I'm not looking for compliments." My words come out in a rush. "I need to know what about me made you want to help me so that I can try to replicate it in my next life."

"I did—" he closes his eyes as he misspeaks, "—I do—" he opens them, "—find you attractive." I could lose myself in his green eyes.

"Me too. I'm attracted to you, too." I'm so glad I don't have a body. If I did, I'd be blushing.

"I promise you, if you're anything like you are now, I'll want to help you."

"You like what I looked like?"

"It's more than that. I'm attracted to your radiance...not just your beauty, it's you." He places his hand over his heart. "It's as if there is an invisible string wound around my heart and you control its beat—with a look—with a gesture. I feel the mark of you here." His finger traces his skin above his heart. "But there's nothing there."

"The sensation is more like butterflies for me."

"Oh, I have those, too," he admits. "They threaten to consume me."

"What should I do when we meet?"

"Just be you. I'll be unable to resist you."

I stare at him. "Be...me?"

"It's rare for me to notice humans anymore. I go out of my way not to see them, but I couldn't help seeing you. You smile and I feel as if I'm living on the edge of Paradise. There is no one like you, Simone. You are unique. I will always notice you."

Atwater returns from outside, his blond hair soaked again with rain. He calls to us above him. "A Reaper has arrived outside, her name is Suni. She's here to help Simone ascend. It's time for you to leave, Reed."

Reed nods and folds in his dark wings. He drops to the stone floor below, landing on his feet. I have the most peculiar feeling. It's as if I'm losing my heart as he walks away toward Atwater. I call to him, "Why does it suddenly feel like the end of the world, Reed?" I fight the urge to go with him.

He pauses. He turns back to me, his smile radiant. "It's not the end. It's just the beginning, Simone. It's the beginning of us."

CHAPTER 20
Until The End Of Time

I open my eyes to Reed's breathtaking green ones. My head is in his lap. He stokes my long hair, smoothing it away from my brow, just as he'd done for me when I was Simone. He exhales in relief when he sees me focus on his face. "Love, you've come back to me," he whispers. Leaning down, his lips skim mine. Primitive hunger awakens inside me. I return his kisses, drawn in by the soft glide of his bottom lip. All too soon, he straightens to look at me. Touching my cheek with the back of his hand, he caresses it lovingly.

I stare at him, unable to speak. My eyes blur and cloud with tears that I can't see past as my bottom lip quivers. He's a virtual stranger to me in terms of the hollowness of time we've spent together. I hardly know him at all. He barely knows me, and yet, he's become such an essential part of me. An all-consuming ache squeezes my heart, contorting it with indescribable anguish. No matter what I do now, I'll lose Reed. If we fail to kill Emil and Byzantyne, we cease to be. If we manage by some stunning twist of fate to beat all the odds and accomplish our missions, we lose one another. Reed will be called back to Paradise as part of the deal I made. I don't know what will happen to me, but I know Heaven. I know they'll never take me out of the fray here while I live. I knew that going in. Once I accepted my role as an archetype being, there was no going home until my angelic body dies and my soul ascends. I am their pawn for life here.

Covering my eyes with my hand, I feel the burn of tears in them. I thought I could save this stranger who, on a whim, had rescued me from Emil. But I didn't know—I didn't see that I would come to love him so desperately—would need him more than I've ever needed anyone or anything.

I sit up, tears falling onto my cheeks. Crawling onto Reeds lap, I wrap myself around him, burying my face in the hollow between his shoulder and his throat. I choke back a sob. He wipes a tear from the edge of my jaw. "Shh…Evie, it's okay. Tell me what happened. What did you find out?"

I shake my head. My throat burns with unshed tears. I kiss his neck then trail my lips along his jaw. Claiming his mouth, I recklessly stroke his tongue with mine. A groan of desire emits from him. Reed's arms encircle me. He rubs his strong hands up my back touching the soft material of my sweater. His palms slip beneath the fabric to set fire to my skin. He guides my top over my head. I lift my arms from him only long enough to help, and then my hands are on his arms, pulling his shirt off over his head. I toss it away, uncaring where it falls. Running my palms over his shoulders, my urgent fingers warm from the contours of his skin. I move them up to his nape and splay my fingers in his hair. Reed's nose grazes my neck. It has an incendiary effect, scorching my angelic flesh with wild sensation. My fingers tighten in his hair. I lean into his kisses, my senses raw. "I love you," I whisper. "I always will."

Reed rises from the floor with me in his arms. My legs wrap around his waist. He holds me, his hands cupping my bottom as his wings unleash from his back in a *whoosh*. Mimicking the extension of his feathers, mine unfurl and spread out, a red sunset against the dark night of his wings. I cling tighter to him, knowing that one day soon he'll be taken from me. "I am yours, Evie— yours and no other's until the end of time." His powerful wings slice through the air. He flies forward until my back is forced against the wall. Far from being hurt by the impact, pleasure rushes through me at the contact against my wings.

His chest presses against mine. Raising one hand to my wing, his fingers curl in my feathers, a fragmenting ache of desire surges inside me. His cheek grazes mine. My body reacts, becoming dewy at my savage need to be possessed by him. He tears a red feather from me. Holding it between his fingers, he runs the silky tip over the flesh of my throat. A soft moan slips from me, making me suck in my bottom lip. Trailing the plume lower over my curves, my skin quivers from his relentless torture.

"Reed," I breathe his name. The feather floats from his hand. His arm around my waist lifts me from the wall as he pops open the top button of my jeans. His hand slides over my bottom, pushing the denim and lace from me. I lean into him, finding his earlobe. I nip it between my teeth before sucking on it. His body tenses. His sharp intake of breath is followed by a desperate groan. He starts speaking to me in Angel, "It's impossible sometimes not to touch you."

"I need you to touch me, Reed. I need you to never let me go," I whisper in Angel as I undo his belt. I suffer the loss of his skin against mine for a moment as he leans back so he can see my eyes.

"You spoke Angel." His mouth curls into a heart-stopping smile.

My blood hums in my veins. I hunger with a potent ache for him. "I gave you a stolen heart, Reed," I confess in Angel.

Reed loses his smile as his body stills. "Stolen?"

My eyes grow shiny again with unshed tears. "I'd given my heart to someone else before you. How could I know you'd be everything to me, Reed?"

"You're my air, Evie. Without you, I drown in breathless sky." He peels the rest of our clothing from us; his lips find mine once more. Dissolving into feverish intoxication, I vaguely realize that Byzantyne may have been right about something. Reed may truly be the one to shatter my heart and destroy me forever.

~

I DON'T WANT to move. I don't want to tell him what I saw. We'd found one of the guest rooms on the fourth floor. We managed to destroy most of it. Only one lamp is left unbroken, but the lampshade is askew. Reed leisurely strokes my hair, waiting for me to work up the courage to explain everything to him. I don't know how. There are no right words. Words are feeble. My mind works franticly, trying to figure out a way to win and still keep Reed. If I kill Emil, I lose Reed. If I don't kill Emil, Emil kills me—I'm dead and I lose Reed. It's a catch-22. And then there is Xavier, and all of the dangerous feelings that now radiate through me for him.

I squeeze my eyes shut and rub my aching forehead. An unwanted tear slips down my cheek. Hastily, I scrub it away with the back of my hand. "It's that bad?" Reed asks.

"Yeah, it's that bad," I murmur.

"Can you talk about it?"

"No."

"Can you show me?" I move my cheek over his chest so I can see his eyes better. He raises his eyebrows. "Can you send me a clone of you? One that contains the memory of what happened in your past?"

I look away from him for a moment, thinking. Sitting up, I face him, pulling the sheet with me. "Okay. I'll try." Concentrating, I begin by remembering playing the piano as Simone with Emil behind me while Emil's men were murdering the staff. I try to incorporate every detail up to the point where Suni, the Reaper, helped me to ascend from my life as Simone. The room spins. Light glows from me as I appear to be cut in half. A radiant image of me launches out of my body. Without far to travel, she enters Reed in a split second, disappearing inside of him. He glows for a moment as he absorbs the memory I sent to him. My emotions ravish him. He grimaces, unaccustomed to the intensity of my raw humanity. Or maybe it's what he's seeing that makes him flinch.

"You're my champion," he assesses. This strong, virile Power doesn't know what to make of that.

"As you are my champion," I reply.

"I thought..." his voice is hollow, "...I convinced myself after we met in Crestwood that we were meant to be—that you're the love of my life. I couldn't have been more right—" he laughs self-effacingly, "—and I couldn't have been more wrong. You are the love of my life. I'm just not the love of yours."

"Reed," my voice breaks.

The look he gives me is one of despair. "Do you remember him?"

"Xavier?" I ask. He nods. I can't look in his eyes, so I look up at the ceiling. "There's so much time…when I think back…I can't see a time or a memory without him in it."

"You're still in love with him and I'm still in love with you."

"I came here to find you, Reed—"

"I found you. I didn't slaughter you because I love you."

"When we finish this, you'll get to go home to—"

"Then we finish it." He turns away from me, shifting me off of his lap. He swings his legs to the edge of the bed. Rising from the mattress, he walks from the bedroom.

"Wait!" I drag the rumpled sheet with me as I scramble off the bed and follow him. I pull my wings inside me so the sheet fits snug.

"You don't have to say anything. I know how it is." He's already up the stairs and in the library room at the top of the house.

Rushing through the doorway, I find him buttoning his black pants. He picks up his shirt off the floor and retracts his wings into his back. "Then you know I don't want to finish this!"

"Why not?" he asks, all business now. He's acting like the Reed I first met at Crestwood and it's scaring me. "It's what you asked for, right? We kill your inescapable and his wicked guardian and you and Xavier are together for eternity."

"That's not what I want!"

Reed balls up his shirt. "No? Did I miss something?" His handsome mouth twists with anger. "I thought you made it all clear in your negotiations."

"It's what *Simone* wanted! It's not what *I* want! I'm not *her* anymore."

"I'm sorry," he says cuttingly, "if you're not Simone, then who are you?"

"I'm me, Reed!" I put my palm to my chest and pat it. "I'm Evie! I'm not just a soul anymore! I have this angel body!" I hold up my hand, letting him see the angel shine of it. "I have fire inside of me." Opening my hand palm up, I ignite a ball of fire in it. "Simone is only a small piece of me! She may still love Xavier, but Evie—me—I love you, you stupid angel!" I let the fire go out in my hand. "You have no idea what losing you will do to me, do you?" I turn away from him.

His voice is rough as he says, "I'm not stupid. I'm stubborn and I'm not going anywhere without you."

My shoulders round. "You won't have a choice. It's part of the bargain. You ascend if we win. Period."

"Not *if* we win—*when* we win." I feel Reed's arms wrap around my waist from behind. "And you don't know for sure what will happen when we do." His voice resonates through me like sex.

"I do know," I whisper, leaning back against him. I may be a new being, but I'm also ancient and I know how things work.

"Heaven could allow you to ascend with me."

"Reed, they'll never allow me to come with you."

Reed places his hand on my chin, turning me in his arms to face him. "You're my *aspire*. I'm not leaving here without you. We'll end Emil and Byzantyne, and then they'll have no reason to keep you here."

"If we win, I'm here until something kills me," I murmur. "You know it as well as I do." He knows I'm right. I've traded places with him. He knows Heaven will never call me back as long as I live and can fight for them.

"You asked for a love of your own choosing. You could choose me." *Could I choose him? Could I deny him Heaven? It's the only thing he had ever wanted before he found Simone broken on the floor of the carriage house.*

My hand reaches out and touches his cheek. "I do choose you. You're everything to me. It's your wings that are branded into my flesh, Reed," I say, tugging the sheet lower, exposing the binding mark of his wings above my heart. "I chose you."

"There is no heaven without you, Evie. I cannot say it any plainer than that."

"So we fight?"

"We fight and we win."

And then we say goodbye, I think, because I know it's true and my heart bleeds because of it, but aloud I say, "We win."

Reed leans down near my ear, "This *is* the beginning of us. I won't give up. Not ever." He nuzzles my earlobe. The seductive feel of his body pressing to mine is almost more than I can take. He loosens the sheet around me. His fingertips trace my skin, but his hand stills as a golden light bursts into the room in the form of Russell.

The clone of my soul mate slows when he nears us. His brown eyes, although made of light, shoot daggers at us. "Seriously, Red? I've been worried 'bout you since you left Crestwood and now I find you two goin' at it." He throws a disgusted look at Reed. "What happened to 'Wait for Evie, she'll contact you'? Meanwhile, you two are gettin' freaky and I'm a mess 'cuz I can't find either of y'all. So thanks! Thanks a lot for that!"

"I'm sorry, Russell—"

"You should be!" he retorts.

"Did Phaedrus locate you?" Reed asks, holding me at his side.

"Yeah," Russell replies, "he told me he saw you. He said Tau wants peace with you. Is that true?"

"Peace is a subjective term. He wanted me to kill Atwater and retrieve the boatswain we discussed…peacefully."

"Did you do it?" Russell asks, looking troubled.

"No. I didn't kill Atwater. He slipped into a portal." Reed leaves out the part about us having the whistle that opens Sheol. I shoot Reed a sidelong look. He acknowledges my question, answering me with a squeeze to my upper arm that says 'don't tell him'. I know that Atwater told me not to tell anyone except Reed about us having the boatswain, but this is Russell—my soul mate. I trust him with everything. Still, I don't speak of it. Russell

Iniquity

doesn't seem to notice our omission.

"Good," he says with a look of relief, "I'm glad you didn't kill him. Anya told me Atwater is my guardian angel. I have to find him. He has a *ton* of explaining to do." I search my mind and I know it's true. Atwater is Russell's guardian angel, but he hasn't always been. Russell used to be guarded by a Cherub name Tulie, but Byzantyne stabbed her to death only a few lifetimes ago. Russell wasn't the same after losing Tulie. He loved her. My soul mate doesn't notice my complete shock as he continues on. "Okay, what I'm 'bout to say is gonna sound really stupid comin' from me, especially given our history with the Gancanagh, but I need y'all to hear me out—"

Reed holds up his hand, palm out. "We need to parley with Brennus because he has a Faerie weapon that will annihilate Evie's inescapable's soul. Without that weapon, we can't kill Emil."

Russell's clone blinks—his image straightens up to a taller height. "That's freaky, Reed. You're freaking me out."

"Russell may not know him as Emil, Reed," I explain. "They never met in Simone's lifetime. Russell, Emil is Ronan...Ionia...Tasha...Zanzibar—"

"Djet," Russell whispers our enemy's name. "You remember."

"I do, Iah." For a few moments, my lifetimes with my soul mate spread out in a tapestry before me. I am nearly crushed by the weight of it. In human form, Russell was always the one I wanted. Nothing and no one came between us. When I died and my soul detached from my human form, things were different. I remember everything—I was in love with my angel in Heaven, Xavier. I would do anything for my Seraph guardian, even forget him over and over and die for my angel a thousand times, and then a hundred thousand more, just for a few moments together with him in Paradise when it was allowed—when Russell still lived on Earth and I was in Heaven. I shake my head. *There are so many broken pieces of me.*

Russell's clone comes closer to me, his light falling on my face. "I have a dagger that Brennus gave me. If I cut myself with it, it will bring Brennus to me. I can't use it though. I won't use it. I can't allow the Gancanagh to get close to Anya or the Reapers again. We need to meet up. You have to go with me to talk to Brennus. He'll listen to you. He'll do anythin' for you."

"Of course he will. I'm his queen." Both Reed and Russell frown. "I *am* his queen. I have to lead his army into battle against Emil. Brennus will give me whatever I ask for, but even if he doesn't, I could take it from him just as easily."

"How?" Russell asks.

"Russell, we're the most powerful beings on Earth. We don't even need a reason to take what we want."

"Ah, so now you remember that you're an ass kicker?"

"I can't believe I ever forgot. You don't have to come, you know? I can deal with the Gancanagh on my own."

"I wouldn't miss this for the world, Evie," Russell replies.

"Okay, where are you now? I will find out where the Gancanagh have set up their new lair, and then I'll meet you and we'll go there together."

Russell's clone smiles. "I'll come here. It's not terribly far from where I am now. I'll see you in a few hours." Russell looks at Reed. "You're in, right?'

"I'm in." Reed nods. "Tell Zephyr to keep our Reapers away from Crestwood."

"Why?"

"Before he slipped away from me, Atwater told me the hole Emil created between our worlds has ruptured. Evil souls and demons are escaping through it into Crestwood. Sheol's souls will possess any humans who will let them. The demons will rampage. It will be a thousand fold worse than the angels in the 7-Eleven ever were. Reapers will be drawn there, feeling the need to reap souls. The sheer numbers of the evil dead will overwhelm them. They'll be slaughtered. Tell them to get the word out to other Reapers."

"We have to close that door," Russell says urgently.

"We do. We need our armies in place first, or we don't stand a chance. It's a trap, Russell. Emil set it. He most likely has his angel army just on the other side of the gate, waiting for us to come to close it. When we do, he plans to meet us and butcher anyone who gets between him and Evie."

Russell's clone shivers. "He told me he wants to kill her last. He wants her to watch us all die first."

"Yes, he wants to kill us, for sure, but he wants more than that."

"What do you mean?"

"His mentor, Byzantyne, is obsessed with possessing Evie. To him, she is the wildest, most beautiful butterfly that he's never quite gotten for his own. She makes Emil look like a moth in comparison. Emil doesn't like being anyone's moth. Her inescapable arranged a deal wherein Byzantyne never gets Evie's soul, but that won't be quite enough for him."

"How do you know that?' Russell asks.

"I know it because he would've killed me right away the first moment we met at Crestwood. His plan was to kill me first, but he found he couldn't because of this." Reed holds up his ring that I gave him. "It ruined his plan and allowed us to escape. He followed Evie and me, but I was taken to Dominion and Evie escaped once more with Xavier. Emil went back for you, Russell, but the Gancanagh saved you. Now his plan is to draw out our reapers as bait. He'll try to capture or kill them. He wants us to return to Crestwood—back to him. It's a simple plan, really."

"So what does Emil do with Evie if he gets her?"

"He exacts revenge upon her and Byzantyne. It's a good plan."

"How do you know all this?"

"I remember him. I hunted Byzantyne and I watched them both linger around Simone. It was obsession."

"Obsession. Are you talkin' about them, or 'bout you?" Russell asks.

Reed's smile doesn't reach his eyes. "I was referring to all of us."

"Wait. You mean, you knew Evie when she was Simone?"

"I was there when she died. I will explain it all to you when I see you."

"Russell, Reed and I aren't safe here. Xavier will know I used his portal. He knows it leads here. You have to meet us somewhere else. We need to leave here as soon as possible. He's probably on his way here now."

"Where will y'all be?"

"Go to Detroit. I'll think of a place in the city where we can meet, and then I'll contact you. Hurry, Russell, Sheol is open and there isn't much time."

"Hurry, she says," Russell's clone mutters sarcastically, "like I didn't just catch her making out with her aspire in the middle of a situation." His clone disappears into the air.

"I need to find Brennus."

Reed nods. "You may want your clothes for that."

"I think that's wise." I pick up my clothes from the floor and put them on. Reed shrugs into his shirt. "It's best if we leave now. We can find somewhere private for you to track Brennus."

He's right. Xavier's mountain fortress is far away, but not if Xavier finds a portal in the vicinity of this house. He can be here at anytime. "We need to move."

"What kind of car did Xavier drive?" Reed asks with a grin.

"C'mon, I'll show you his garage."

I take Reed to the underground stable of chrome and steel horses. When I turn on the light, I see what I now know is part of an angel arsenal—endless rows of motorcycles, cars, and SUVs polished to a high shine. "Which one do you like?" Reed asks. I walk down the row of SUVs. "The white one."

Reed chuckles at my total disregard for the makes and models of the luxury vehicles. "The white one it is." He opens the passenger door for me. I climb in. He's sitting in the driver's seat in a fraction of a second. I smile at him. He shows me a chip in the palm of his hand. "What is that?" I ask.

He closes his hand and crushes the chip. Dust falls from it when he opens it again.

"I disabled the tracking device and anti-theft protocols." The keyless fob is in the console. Reed opens the fob and disables more components. He starts the car, glancing over at me. "I'll find us a safe place to meet Russell while you find Gancanagh."

I exhale and close my eyes. As Reed uses the car elevator to take the SUV from the basement to the driveway, I concentrate on creating a clone. Reed drives the car onto the street. My shimmering image floats through the roof of the SUV, up through the leafless branches of oak trees and into the night sky.

Brennus

CHAPTER 21
Fate Calls

BRENNUS

I close da door ta me room. Having jus left Finn ta manage da fallout of whah we learned from our parley wi' da trolls, I rub me face wearily. I despise da weakness associated wi' needing ta sleep. Da only consolation I have in it is dat I can search for Genevieve in me dreams. I miss her more dan I care ta admit, even ta meself. I need her more dan I need anyting in dis miserable world.

I've had ta abandon her dis long because circumstances dictated it. Dere's unrest everywhere. Craiturs are mobilizing. We have a very small window of opportunity ta persuade dem ta our side—ta join me queen's army. I could've used Declan on dis front. He was adept at finding da angle dat gains compliance. I miss da counsel of me captain o' da guard. Beside Finn, he was like a brudder ta me.

I go ta me bedside table. Tugging da small vial from da chain I wear around me neck, I lift it over me head. I set da vial of Genevieve's blood down next ta da lamp. Dere is na much left in da small bottle. I will need ta ration it until I can get more or until she sees reason and joins me in dis fight. She is so stubborn. It's da Seraphim in her.

I lie down on me bed, propping me head on a couple of white pillows. I reach over, intent on unstopping da vial of Genevieve's blood when I pause. A commotion stirs from da hall beneath me room. Electricity surges tru me body as a radiant image of Genevieve enters me room. I set da vial back on da table, watching as she moves gracefully ta da edge of me bed. She hovers near da footboard before she climbs up on da mattress and crawls seductively ta me side. She lies down, looking up at da ceilin'.

For a moment I tink dat I'm already dreamin', but den she turns her head and faces me, saying, "So, dis is a crap room ye're livin' in."

A bark of laughter peels from me as da bed shakes wi' me mirth at her attempt ta sound like a fella. "'Tis, Genevieve. Now do ye see da lengths I will go ta in order ta protect ye?"

"Is that why you chose this place?" She gazes around. Her eyes linger on da vial of her blood on da bedside table.

Me voice is gentle as I say, "It's where ye're from, is it na?"

"It is, but as it turns out, I'm from a lot of places."

"Yer guardian angel was right about dis place. 'Tis a foin city in which ta hide from angels. Dey do na seem ta like it here."

Her tragic sadness dat so attracts me ta her is in her eyes when she turns ta look at me. I suck in me breath, wanting ta be da one ta save her from her sorrow. "I'm coming to pay you a visit. I should be here in a few hours."

"Is dat so?"

"'Tis," she replies, trying to hide her sorrow in humor.

"Ta whah do I owe da honor?" I have ta catch me breath and resist da impulse ta try ta reach for her across da bed. She's in phantom form.

"We need to parley. You have something I need."

"Whah have I dat ye need?"

"I'll tell you when I arrive."

"A hint, perhaps?" I wheedle.

"I don't think so."

"Why na?"

"You always want something in return. You rarely give me anything I really want without my having to bargain for it."

"Dat's jus good business."

"This is more than business."

"I know. 'Tis flesh, bone, and soul. Ye're welcome ta whahever I have ta give. I've information ta impart ta ye as well."

She looks skeptical. "A little hint?" she asks. Her eyes are so dangerous. Dey make me want ta open me veins ta her—ta bleed for her.

"Sheol is a rising tide dat is flooding our shores wi' unwanted guests. Evil souls are inhabiting da earth in unprecedented numbers. Da less dan divine craiturs of dis world are choosing deir sides. We're negotiating wi' da trolls. Dey can be swayed ta our side."

"We have to rise above the flood soon, Brenn. What are you doing to manage the tide?"

"Me magic is na holding against Sheol—even wi' Finn and da other fellas' help. Da ground dere shakes wi' fury. All is at stake now. I need me queen by me side when worlds collide."

"Fate calls," she murmurs.

"Dere is someting else."

"What?"

"Da fact dat ye saw Atwater troubles me. He can na be trusted. Whahever deal ye make wi' him, he'll fail ye."

"He wants me to join your army—to lead it by your side. He acts as if he has made a promise to you—that he owes you something. He believes we cannot prevail without the Gancanagh in this fight."

I blink. I was na expecting dat. "He leads well wi' little lies. Like a blind man, I have followed him before. I would na have ye make da same mistakes as me."

"Maybe he's been playing a larger game than either of us realizes, Brennus."

"Dat's da problem wi' Heaven. Ta dem, dis is all a game, Genevieve."

"It's a fragile thing—this life."

"'Tis even more precarious in undeath," I say wi' a quirk of me eyebrow.

"Get some sleep, Brenn. You look tired." She reaches a glowing hand out ta me, touching me cheek. I feel da heat of her soul in da hollowness of me body. It eases da ache in me for a moment. "I will see you soon."

Her clone rises from me bed and travels tru da wall, out onta da city street. Shadows creep in on me wi'out her light ta keep dem at bay, and I'm forced to obey whahever spell 'twas dat she placed upon me. I close me eyes and I drift off ta sleep, dreaming of her.

Evie

CHAPTER 22
Fade Into You

EVIE

I don't return my consciousness to my body after leaving Brennus. Instead I think of a golden-haired Seraph with one eye the color of sky and the other the color of clover. My clone moves through the night, retracing the path I'd just taken. I'm a blowing feather, floating downward, into the house that I left a short time ago—Xavier's house.

I go through it, passing from room to room, each one more destroyed than the last. My light illuminates the night as I float back outside, onto the rooftop patio. I find Xavier, his shoulders rounded as he grips the railing overlooking the water. His hands have bent the metal. Snow falls around us. He's shirtless, his crimson-colored wings shifting in the frigid air. He must be cold.

"You should go inside. It's freezing out here."

He whips around, facing me. The savage pain etched upon his face is almost more than I can bear. "Where are you?"

"Not far from here."

"Show me where you are and I will come get you."

"I can't."

"Why not?"

"Please go inside," I beg. I hate seeing him like this. He's an open wound.

He takes a few steps nearer to the image of me. "Not until you tell me where you are." His warm breath clashes with cold night, causing white wispy vapor to curl away from him.

"I need you, Xavier. I'm dead if you don't help me."

His face stiffens as he attempts to rein in his emotions. "Tell me what's happened."

"I know about that night—the night I was suppose to meet you at the bridge. I never made it there."

"You have the boatswain." He inhales as if he can take his first deep breath in a long time.

"I do," I say in Angel. I know I'm not supposed to tell him, but I have to in order to make him understand.

"You remember Simone? You remember us?" he asks in Angel. His handsome face is hopeful.

I close my clone's eyes in concentration, breaking off a small fragment of her. I open her eyes again as I thrust the glowing shard of my energy into him. It pierces his heart like a dagger, disappearing inside his chest. He glows brighter for a moment. His face is one of shock until the memory plays out to the end. The light dissipates from him and he sags a little, unharmed, but trying to make sense of all he saw in my memory. When he looks at me again, the hopeless ache that was in his eyes is gone and reckless joy replaces it.

"You told me you made a deal for us, but you couldn't tell me anything else." He would hold me in his arms now if he could. His hands open, and then close tight. "I will destroy your inescapable and Byzantyne. Your soldier will ascend, and then it's you and me together for eternity.

"Reed is my aspire." My voice is as haunting as my clone body.

"Only until he ascends. Once that happens, his binding mark will strip from your skin and you'll be released from your obligations to him. You'll be his champion no more. You can choose your love."

"I'm in love with him, Xavier."

"You love me."

"I do love you—"

"It's always been us, Evie, even when you were tied to your soul mate. No one knows you like I know you."

"I remember, but I'm different now. I'm not the being with whom you fell in love."

"I know exactly who you are! I've protected you in this lifetime, too, until your contract with Byzantyne made it impossible for me to remain. I love you. I will finish this for you, and when I do, Reed will ascend. He'll vanish from your life. All that will be left is us."

I ache inside my real body, the one that is with Reed. "Until then, you have to respect that he's my aspire," I say through my clone.

He doesn't like what he sees—my sorrow. "Where are you?" he asks again.

"I'm on my way to gather my army."

He frowns. "Your army is where we were—in the mountain."

"No, that's your army, Xavier. My army is the Gancanagh and any other being who would follow me."

"The Gancanagh are evil!"

"This is about redemption."

"Whose redemption?"

"Theirs—mine. They deserve a chance to change and we need them to fight for us."

"And you would give them redemption?"

"I would, but it's not up to me."

"No, it's not. Only Heaven can decide their fate."

"These are the flames by which they will burn then—or not. If they must die, then let this prove them worthy of forgiveness."

He paces in front of me. "The gates of Sheol are open, Evie."

"I am aware of that." He stops to look at me, surprised by my calm, in-control demeanor. "You have to return to Tau and convince my father to meet us with his army in Crestwood. We have to join our forces in order to defeat the Fallen."

"You're asking divine angels to fight alongside undead demons? They will never agree to such an arrangement."

"Then you have to make them agree. You have to lead them."

"Your father—"

"He'll listen to you if you explain it to him. Tell Tau that Emil is waiting for me there. The more time that passes, the more humans Emil will corrupt to fight for him. He hides just behind the gates. He has a plan to draw us in. He will attack us with an army of fallen. The boatswain wasn't meant to open the gates of Sheol, it was meant to close them. And when that happens the sound of its music will separate Emil's soul from his angelic body, just like it almost did to me the moment we used it before. Once Emil's soul has divided from his body, we have to use the weapon Heaven has hidden for us in order to destroy his soul. His soul has to be annihilated or the contract is not fulfilled."

"Tau said that Phaedrus is working with your soul mate to secure such a weapon—"

"We'll find it. I promise."

"The thought of you at the mercy of the Gancanagh is more than I can take, Evie."

"I won't be at their mercy, Xavier. They'll be at mine."

"How do I get in contact with you?" he asks.

"I'll contact you. Convince my father, Xavier. My life depends upon it. I will see you in Crestwood." I let go of my clone and she evaporates into the air.

~

I RETURN TO MYSELF, waking up from my clone. Opening my eyes, I look through the windshield of Xavier's car. Red neon light blinks the word "Opa" on and off from a sign, turning my skin rosy, and then pale. I straighten in the passenger seat of the SUV. Soft Greek music plays from somewhere out on the street. I glance over to the driver's side of the parked car. Reed is there, watching me. He squeezes my hand clasped in his. "Hey," I murmur, trying to smile but finding it too difficult to manage right now. "Brennus is here—in Detroit—not far from where we are now."

Reed's eyes narrow in confusion. "How did he know we were here?"

"He didn't. He's here because it's my hometown. He associates it with me."

"Your hand is cold," he says, rubbing warmth back into it. "Would you like to get something to eat while we wait for Russell? I need to find a phone so I can contact him."

"I can send a clone to—"

"Let's conserve your energy for more important battles, Evie. I'll call him instead." He's out of the car and opening my door in an instant. With his hand on the small of my back, he leads me into an upscale Greek restaurant. We find a dimly lit table by the window. I look around at the dark wood walls and gas-lit wall sconces that give an old world feel to the place. A beautiful waitress appears to take our order. She becomes chatty when she sees Reed. I take the menu that Reed hands to me while she hovers by him with suggestions, pointing out her favorite dishes. After we order, Reed asks her if he can use a phone. I'm sure they never normally allow anyone to use their phone, but because it's Reed and he has the face of an angel, she automatically agrees. He doesn't even have to convince her with his persuasive voice. As she leads him to the back, she can't help staring at him.

She returns before Reed with our water. I have the urge to stab her with my fork, but I'm better at controlling those impulses now. Instead, I take a sip of my drink, gazing through a picture window at the falling snow. "They're close," Reed says as he slips into the seat beside me. He leans to me, kissing my cheek and nuzzling my neck.

"They?" I ask. "It's not just Russell?"

"I don't think he could leave any of our family behind if he put a spell on them to make them stay."

"Zee?"

"All of them." Guilt, denial, and fear crash in on me. I want them anywhere but here. My aspire reads my mind. "It's not your choice to make. It's theirs. You're not responsible for what evil does." I know that he's right. Everyone involved has to decide the role they want in this. It's a war and it's here.

"You're right," I murmur. Our food arrives. As we eat, I savor the exquisite torture of phantom touches from Reed's nearness. I pretend that this is our life—that we're just a normal couple having dinner together. I pretend that we don't have dire consequences of an impossible contract between us.

I can't help asking myself questions. *What if it was the two of us forever? Could I hold onto this much happiness? Could anyone?* My pulse races even now with him next to me. I swear that my body is made for his. *Could I be content with someone else now?* I know the answer is no. He has ruined me for anyone else.

When we finish eating, Reed's expression becomes serious. He looks off through the window at the street outside. It's getting really late. The staff is looking at us with an expectant air. They want us to leave so they can. Reed rises from the table and pays the bill in cash. He walks to where the staff has collected. With his persuasive voice, he says, "All of your guests are gone. You're free to lock up now and carry on with your evening." His voice whispers and hisses in my head. I want to itch my brain, but I'm unable to through my skull. Luckily, the sensation passes quickly.

The staff collects their coats in a drone-like stupor, before filing out of the restaurant. Reed trails the last one to the door. "You'll remember tomorrow that you put your key in the mailbox after you closed tonight," Reed says with an echoing voice, taking the key from him. The man walks away in a daze. Reed closes the door behind him and locks it, leaving the key in it. He goes to the bar. Selecting a bottle of wine and two glasses, he beckons me over.

I walk to the bar and slide onto a barstool. He pours me a drink. Taking the glass of wine Reed offers me, I touch the rim of mine to his. "To us," I murmur.

"To always," he replies.

I take a deep sip. He crouches behind the bar. A stereo system comes on with the muffled hum of electricity. Haunting music pipes through the speakers, defying gravity, floating through the room on a current of air. A soft guitar and mandolin with a bass instrument and violins weave in and out of one another at a slow tempo. Before I realize what he's doing, Reed has moved the tables aside and is in front of me, holding his hand out. "Dance with me."

I set down my glass on the bar. My hand closes in his. He lifts me off the barstool. My body presses and slides down his until my feet touch the floor. My heart beats faster. I'm in his arms. My head rests against his chest. Fire meets fire. He moves to the languid beat of the music. We're really not dancing, not the way he's capable of dancing. This is more like holding one another beneath the moonlight coming through the picture window. I only move when Reed moves, fading into him as if two becomes one. It feels as if he soaks into my skin and there is no way to tell where he ends and I begin.

"Did I thank you for everything you gave me?" I ask Reed in a whisper.

"Every day."

"There was so much in this world that could hurt me and you kept it from me. If this doesn't work out for us—" my chin begins to tremble.

"Shh...it will." He holds me tighter.

"If it doesn't, I'll meet you on the other side. Okay?" I press my face to his chest, holding back my tears. I know it's ridiculous, what I just said. There is no other side for us if we lose. We just end.

Reed plays along. "It's a date," he whispers into my hair. We sway together long after the music ends.

There's a loud rap on the door. Reed's forehead rests against mine. He whispers, I love you, Evie." His hand still lingers on my hip, like he can't let me go. I look over his shoulder. Russell is on the other side of the glass. His tawny hair is covered with a Detroit Tigers knit cap. Russell nods his head toward the doorknob. He's holding Anya's hand. White, new snow clings to her ebony hair and her long, black eyelashes. Lion-shaped earmuffs cover her ears. Reed lets go of me to unlock the door. I glance through the picture window. Buns and Brownie close the car doors of the Golden Goose, Buns' semi-luxury gold-tone car from the nineteen eighties. Zephyr is on the street, checking out the area with his hunter eyes, trying to calculate the danger surrounding us.

Russell allows Anya to enter ahead of him. Reed reaches out and hugs her. Russell's low growl makes him sound like a wolf resides in his heart. Reed smiles despite the warning. "I get it," he says to Russell. He lets go of Anya. He extends his hand to Russell. Russell takes it without hesitation.

"It's instinct, Reed, and given our history, can you blame me?" Russell asks.

I walk to Anya and hug her, "How are you?" I ask.

"I'm well. We've managed to evade divine and fallen angels all the way here. Everyone is looking for us, but we have excellent karma."

"Yes, you do," I agree.

Buns squeezes past Russell and Reed to get inside. "And we have the Goose!" Buns exclaims, referring to her car. "No one messes with the Goose!" She runs to us, tackle-hugging Anya and me. Brownie slips in to join our circle, squeezing us fiercely. When we break apart, I have to wipe away tears.

Zephyr walks through the door. Looking at Reed, he says, "When Russell told me you said we couldn't miss you—to just look for wings, I was skeptical." He gestures outside to the glowing neon sign of a white-winged Pegasus.

"It seemed a fitting place to meet," Reed replies.

Zephyr turns to me and hugs me. "I missed you," he says simply.

"I missed you, too." I rest my head on his shoulder. I let go of him. "I heard you ran into some trouble with my inescapable."

"I will kill him for you."

"We have to locate the weapon we need first."

"That is why I brought Phaedrus with me," Zephyr replies.

He steps aside so that I can see Phaedrus in the doorway. I don't smile, but walk to him and hug the black-eyed angel. "Thank you for coming, Phaedrus."

Phaedrus wraps his arms around me. "You're welcome. Do you know where the Gancanagh are?" His body is burning up.

He's like holding an electric blanket that is turned up high.

I let him go and nod. "Yes. They're only a few miles from here—in an old seminary."

"I can visualize the place in my mind. It's very hot in here, isn't it?" Phaedrus asks. He unwraps the plaid scarf from his neck and takes off his coat. It must be extremely warm for him here because we're so close to the Gancanagh base. Phaedrus locates his targets by following heat signatures. The closer he gets to something he's looking for, the hotter he feels. It's a relief to me that my instincts were right—Brennus has the weapon I need.

"Let me get you some water." I go to the bar and retrieve a glass for him. On my way back I almost drop it. Another angel stands in the doorway. It's Preben. His silver-blond hair is covered with snow. The Power angel shakes the flakes from his head and smiles at me, before looking at Zephyr and saying, "The rooftops are clear. We weren't followed."

"Preben, how did you find us?" I ask.

"Zephyr called me. I've been running reconnaissance on Dominion for us. I was coming up with a plan to free you, Reed, but you freed yourself."

"I had a little help," Reed replies, glancing at me.

"Hey! I helped, too." Russell teases. "Those knots did not untie themselves."

"I owe you," Reed replies to Russell.

"You do."

Buns strips off her coat and tosses it over the back of a chair. Going to the bar, she starts lining up flutes. "We're celebrating!"

"What are we celebrating?" I ask, handing Phaedrus a glass of water. Turning, I go to help her. She passes me a bottle of champagne. Taking another from a refrigerator under the bar, she pops the cork without even breaking a nail.

"Family," she replies, pouring the sparkling liquid into tall stemware.

I pop the cork on my bottle and fill glasses. Russell and Anya take off their coats. Preben casts a glance at Brownie. She looks pale. He helps her remove her coat. Setting it aside, he places his arm around the small of her back; she leans on him as he guides her to the bar. My eyes open wide. "What's wrong with Brownie?" I ask.

Buns looks over at her best friend. "Nothing is wrong with her, she's perfectly healthy. She just really needs this right now."

"Why?" I ask. I hand Brownie a full glass of champagne when she leans against the bar.

"She's more sensitive than me," Buns explains. "She feels souls more acutely."

Brownie doesn't wait for the toast. She drinks it down and holds her glass out for more. "I feel all of the souls who need to be reaped. They're screaming out to me to help them."

My hand goes to my forehead. "It's that bad in Detroit?" I ask, completely shocked.

Buns shakes her head. "No, sweetie, the souls are in Crestwood. We can feel them from here."

"What is it like?" I ask. It occurs to me that I should know the answer to this. I remember Heaven. I've met more Reapers than I can count, but I never interacted with them to any great degree. I'm ashamed to admit that, even to myself. I was different than I am now. I had bought into the angel caste system to a certain degree. I accepted the way things have always been, instead of how they should be.

Brownie looks at Buns before she says, "It doesn't hurt at all if I go right away to a reap and do my job, but when I try to resist, my pain increases the longer I wait."

"Maybe it's a little like being in labor?" Buns looks at Brownie for confirmation.

Brownie raises her shoulders. "I wouldn't know about childbirth, but if it is, I'm not ever signing up for that."

Buns winces and bends forward, clearly in pain as well, but trying hard to hide it. I touch her back, asking, "How do I help you?"

"You can't. I need to reap," she pants.

"Has it ever been this bad, Buns?"

"No. Whatever's happening there, in Crestwood, feels like the end of the world. It's like nothing I've ever felt before."

I hand Buns a glass of champagne. Zephyr walks behind me and pulls a bottle of vodka from the shelf. "They might do better with this."

He starts to pour out some shots. I blanch. Without thinking, I place my hands on Buns' shoulders. I whisper a spell, asking her pain to come to me. It does. Like lightning strikes, her pain climbs up my arms in jagged, yellow bolts. I redirect the sizzling snarling pain. Removing my hands from her, I clasp them on the neck of the champagne bottle, stuffing the glowing bolts of white-hot pain down the throat of the bottle. I shove the cork back into it. Pain shakes and flashes inside its emerald cage in a raging tempest.

Buns stands up straight. "Sweetie, you're like a redheaded witchdoctor!"

"Are you okay?" I ask.

"I'm much better!"

Brownie groans. "Do me next!"

"Zee, hand me that other empty bottle," I order. When he does, I repeat the same spell I used on Buns. Yellow lightning strikes climb from Brownie up my arms. I channel them into the container, and then cork that one, too. Anya gets close to the first bottle. Tapping her finger on it, she stirs up sparking chaos inside.

"Thank you, Evie!" Brownie stands up on the rung of her barstool and reaches over the counter. She liberates the shot from Zephyr's hand. Without really tasting it, she swallows the vodka and sets the glass on the bar.

"It didn't work?" I ask.

Brownie dabs her mouth with a bar napkin. "Oh no, it worked. I just really like vodka."

I look over and see Russell watching me. He raises his eyebrow in question, asking me silently what else I can do and what else I know. I pick up two flutes of champagne and walk toward him. Behind me, Zephyr tries to remove the cham-pain bottles from the bar, but Buns stops him. "What are you doing with my pain?"

"Getting rid of it," Zephyr replies.

"Don't take my pain. I have plans for it."

"You have plans for your pain?"

"Yes."

Zephyr's cunning grin matches hers. "Tell me of these plans."

I hand Russell a glass. He taps the rim of it to mine before sipping from it. "I never figured you for a Tigers fan."

He makes a funny face. I point to the navy-colored knit cap on his head. He tugs it from his tawny hair, using his fingers to comb it. "Oh, this," he holds up the hat, "was Buns' idea. She got 'em for us when we stopped for gas."

"How was that?" He looks confused, so I add, "Stopping at a gas station convenience store?" Of course I'm referring to our aversion to going into one since our brush with death at the hands of Alfred.

He shrugs. "There are worse things than fallen angels, so I just try not to think about it. And I like my hat." He puts it back on.

"It's not too late, you know?"

"Too late for what?"

"You can still take Anya and go somewhere—I have all the money you'd ever need—you can be happy."

He shakes his head. "I'm in this fight, Red. I can't be happy livin' with your ghost, knowin' I could've helped you and I didn't."

"That's just it, Russell. You won't have to live with my ghost either way."

His brown eyes see right through me. "That's not what I meant, and anyway, I always liked your ghost. It would be a shame not to see it around once in a while, so I have to finish this with you so I can start over fresh, like you intended." There is no bitterness in his words, just honesty.

"If all goes well, you won't have to fight Emil ever again."

"If all goes well, you get to live, 'cuz I gotta tell you, Red, I don't think eternity will be half as interestin' without my best friend in it. Or him," Russell tips his glass in Reed's direction. "I kinda like him and I never thought I'd ever say that."

"I kind of like him, too."

"Then figure out a way for us to win this, like I know you can."

"I don't know if I can this time." I feel crushed by the weight of my own words.

Reed moves away from the bar. "Balance," Reed murmurs when he comes to stand beside me.

"Hmm," I ask, raising my eyebrow at him.

"Something just occurred to me—about balance."

"What about it?"

"We have a key that opens Sheol." Russell leans in closer, listening to our exchange.

I nod and say, "I think we need to use it to close Sheol. I think that's its purpose."

"Maybe," Reed says, noncommittal. "It could also be a way in to Sheol to get to Byzantyne, should he try to hide from us, but that's not what concerns me at the moment."

"What worries you, Reed?" I touch his arm; he wraps it around my waist holding me to his side.

"If we have something that opens Sheol, then it stands to reason that Emil has a key that opens Paradise."

"Why would he have that?" Russell asks, his body tense.

"The Fallen want to get back into Paradise," Reed answers. "If we needed the key to get into Sheol, they'd only relent if they could have one to Paradise."

"Why would we need to get into Sheol?" Russell asks.

"I don't know, but the fact that we have the means is telling. And if I'm right, then Sheol already knows we have this boatswain."

"What boatswain?" Zephyr asks as he joins us. We have everyone's full attention now.

"I think we all need to tell our stories of how we got here." A hush falls over the room. I have everyone's attention. "I want to tell you a story about Simone and Reed, and I want to tell you about how we will unite our three armies."

Zephyr's ice blue killer stare is focused on me. "Yes. I have been patient long enough. I need to know it all, the strategic points, positions, and players in the conflict so that I can force them to submit to me."

Something about that makes me smile, even as I try hard to hide it. "We can all sit at this table and I'll fill you in." Choosing a seat at a round table, I start at the beginning with a girl who loved her soul mate and her Seraph. I tell them the tale of a Power who would save a dying girl, and gradually come to where we are now. Along the way, each member of my family fills me in on things I missed. When we come to the end of our pasts, the only thing left to discuss is our future.

"What is our next move?" Zephyr asks. I lean back in my chair. "When the sun comes up, we meet Brennus, find the magical Faerie weapon, and collect our undead army for war.

CHAPTER 23
The Queen Of Hearts

The sun rises, shining light through the restaurant window. I didn't sleep, but it doesn't matter. I'm not tired. My body is changing, becoming more and more angelic as time goes on. After our discussion last night, everyone found his or her own places to sit and talk. Reed and I gravitated to a corner near the back. We're sharing the same side of a large booth. His back is to the wall and I'm propped against his chest. He strokes my hair, occasionally wrapping it around his finger.

"We should probably go," I whisper to Reed. His arm around my waist tightens. Pressing his lips to my hair, he shows no sign of letting me go.

"Just a few more minutes." The deep resonance of his voice rumbles through me. I relent, easing my head back against his chest. We both know that once we leave here, it's the end of us. My lips take an ugly shape as I try to come to terms with that fact. I'm not going to cry, though. I don't want that to be what he remembers about our time here.

Phaedrus opens the front door and walks outside without his coat on, into the falling snow. He sits in the snow bank by the street, scrubbing his face with icy handfuls of it. Zephyr walks over to us with his eyes on the window. "We have to go before Phaedrus melts."

I make a sound that's halfway between a laugh and a sob. "Okay," I agree. Reed says nothing. Zephyr nods and walks away, rousing the others to action as he goes. I lift my head from Reed's chest and scoot to the end of the bench seat. Standing, I look back at my angel. I've only seen that look on his face one time before, it was when he knew Simone was dying and there was nothing he could do to save her—to save me. I try to smile, but I can't. I hold out my hand to him. He takes it in his and presses it to his lips. He says in Angel, "I'll fight for you and with you until my last breath." It's a vow he has made to me before, just days ago in Crestwood.

I speak in Angel, "Whatever comes we face it together—as one."

"As one," he agrees. He gets to his feet. With his hand in mine, I lead the way to the door. I don't have a coat and neither does Reed, but it's a short dash to Xavier's SUV still parked outside. Reed holds the door open for me and I climb into the vehicle. He turns it on. Russell opens the door of a black SUV for Anya before he goes to collect Phaedrus from the snowdrift. He pauses at my window. I open it. "I got the Heat Miser," he says, indicating Phaedrus with the point of his chin. "Do you know where to go?"

"Yes, you can follow us if Phaedrus lets you."

"Okay. I'll tell Buns to follow me."

Zephyr, Preben, Buns, and Brownie get into the Golden Goose. Russell runs back to them, relaying the message, and then he gets into his black vehicle.

Reed pulls away from the curb. We resemble a small funeral procession as I direct Reed to drive to the shadier part of town. Passing rows of abandoned houses and buildings, we're getting close. I know it because there's no one on the streets for a couple of blocks. Then, I feel them. The coldness I associated with the Gancanagh when I first met them no longer exists for me. Since Brennus bit me, the awareness is more of a familiar tingle raising the hair on the back of my neck. Fellas watch us move closer to the seminary they inhabit. I don't see them, but I know they're there. That means they're either under orders not to approach me, or they are afraid of me. Either way suits me just fine at the moment. I don't plan to cajole them into fighting for me. I plan to lead from a position of power.

Reed pulls up and parks in the circular drive in front of the defunct seminary. He turns off the car. The view of the building from the passenger side window is gorgeous. The structure is old and gothic—something out of a fairytale. The fellas have been working hard to return it to its former glory. Snow has been cleared away from the cobblestone walk and the grand staircase in front. Intricate wrought-iron handrails lead up to heavy wooden doors. One of the doors opens. Brennus emerges from the shadowy foyer. He looks every inch a king in a dark suit and an exquisite black coat. Finn follows him. He's similarly attired, a slightly paler version of his older brother. As they walk toward our car, wind stirs their black hair, causing it to fall and play on their foreheads.

When Brennus reaches us, he opens my door for me. Extending his gloved hand, he says, "Welcome home," and waits for me to take it. I place my hand in his and allow him to help me. As soon as I'm out of the car, I let go of him. Standing beside Brennus and Finn in the cold, I wait for Reed to join us. Snow floats in the gray, overcast sky, making everything appear magical. Brennus takes off his coat and drapes it around my shoulders. The heavy fabric is warm from his body heat, which surprises me a little. He's different, physically anyway.

Reed approaches us. Brennus hardly gives Reed a second look as he says, "We have a truce until dis is over, aingeal."

"The moment that it is, you should worry," Reed replies. He stands beside me. I look over at him and try to reassure him with a smile that falls flat.

Russell and Anya join us on the walkway. Russell doesn't look happy to be here. He stands rigidly in front of Anya, ready to defend her at any hint of trouble. Anya reaches out and touches his side. Russell wraps his arm around her shoulder, pulling her beside him. Brennus' sea foam-colored eyes rest on Russell. "Da other, I see dat ye've recovered from yer wounds. Ye and yer aingeal look grand."

"It didn't take me long to heal after I pulled your knife from my belly. But I guess I gotta thank you for savin' us."

"Consider it a debt paid for healing me queen." He looks past Russell and Anya to Buns and Brownie. "Ah, da Reapers have arrived—and more Powers—yer entourage is growing, mo chroí." He smiles at me, indicating Zephyr and Preben, but then his eyes darken and his eyebrows clash together. Without warning, his fangs engage with a *click*. Stepping in front of me, he growls, "Someting is wrong." His back is to me. Finn gets in front of me as well, ready to defend me from whatever Brennus senses. I can't see around the wall of Faerie.

Reed remains relaxed beside me. He takes my hand in his, trying not to laugh. "What you sense is Phaedrus. He's a Virtue. He came with us to help us locate something."

Brennus relaxes, turning to look at Reed. "Ye couldn't have mentioned dat before I sensed da Virtue?"

It suddenly occurs to me that Virtue angels are invisible to most beings. It's only because I'm part angel that I can see him. "Wait. You can't see Phaedrus?" I ask.

Brennus retracts his fangs. "I can na see him, but I can feel him. At da moment, da Virtue is radiating enough heat to burn da place down."

Phaedrus strips off his shirt, exposing his skin to the icy air. He wraps his shirt in his hands. "He's right. I need to get inside and locate the item we came here to collect."

"Can you hear him?" I ask.

"No," Brennus replies.

"You can't even see his clothes?" I press on, still hung up on the notion.

"Na if he's touching dem. He has a magic of his own," Brennus replies. He makes a gesture with his arm, "Shall we go in and find whah ye've come here ta collect? I do na tink I can bear da suspense much longer." He leads the way to the doors. He's beside me after I enter the foyer. The inside is breathtaking. It's so much crisper though through my own eyes than through the eyes of my clone.

This is the cathedral part of the seminary. Intricately crafted wooden pews flank a long marble floor. The aisle leads to an apse. Instead of an altar there are two enormous thrones. I face Phaedrus. "Where are you being pulled?" I ask.

He walks up the aisle. "This way," he replies over his shoulder. His owlish wings eject from his back and unfurl. I follow him. His wings stretch out wide as he approaches the apse and stands under the colorful light from the stained-glass window. He takes flight, soaring around the carved stone images of saints recessed into the walls. He lingers near the back wall. "It's somewhere..." He lands back on his feet. He drops to one knee, feeling the marble floor. His deft fingers search for a crease.

Brennus clears his throat. Is dere someting wrong?" he asks me.

"What's beneath the apse?" I ask.

"Dat would be me archive. Would ye like ta see it?"

Phaedrus scrapes the floor with his fingernails. "Tell him yes."

"Yes," I relay to Brennus. The Gancanagh king waves his gloved hand in a graceful gesture. The floor beneath Phaedrus moves. The Virtue flies upward as a passage in the floor unfolds to reveal a set of descending stairs.

"You do love your tunnels," I murmur.

"Dat is someting da religious clergy and I have in common. Maybe na da only ting." Phaedrus does not ask for an invitation to the world below. He lands in front of the stairs and descends. We follow him down into an elaborate round stone chamber connected to several hallways that lead away from it in a sunburst pattern. Thousands of magical Faerie weapons line the walls of this room. Gleaming glass cases, like coffins, display shiny metal daggers, swords, and axes. They're masterpieces that have forgotten how to sing. In the center of the circular room, I recognize Brennus' Faerie armor; it holds the long battle-axe that he gave to me. I walk to the armor and touch it. It feels cold and lonely—the most extraordinary things usually are. It's the consequence of being timeless.

Finn is beside me. On my other side, Phaedrus passes his hands over the armor next to Brennus' armor. I grasp the etched silver and gold shaft of the battle-axe Brennus made so long ago. The metal vibrates and comes to life. Its music whispers to me a concerto of hope.

"This." Phaedrus sighs with relief as sweat falls from his brow. He holds a battle hammer that has two faces. One side is a hammerhead; the other is sharper and sickle-shaped. The Virtue extends the weapon for me to take. My eyes widen in surprise. It's Finn's. I glance at him. His pale-green eyes connect with mine and I know. It's always been Finn. He's here for a purpose and his brother wouldn't let him fall alone. Brennus came to help him.

I touch the sculptured silver; it's like the living dead. It has been waiting forever for me to be born—for me to come for them both. As my fingers move over it, the weapon begins to sing. It's not the elegant song of Brennus' weapon. No, this one has a beat meant for crushing. Finn's eyes squeeze closed when he hears its music. He drops down to one knee in front of me, bowing his head. "Me queen," he says in a reverent voice. "I am yours to command."

"Finn." I rest his battle hammer against his ancient armor. Placing my hand on Finn's shoulder, the heavy fabric feels wet from melted snow. He looks up at me and I gesture for him to stand.

He does. Getting to his feet, he says, "I made dis for ye—many, many years ago, Genevieve, before ye were ever born."

"Why?"

"Dere once was a young Faerie prince from a powerful family—he was a de Graham. At da time, dere were Faeries aplenty in da world and everyone knew da name. One day, an aingeal appeared ta dis prince. Da Cherub told da lad a tale of epic adventure. He said dis prince would face a terrible demon and fall to him. He told da lad he would suffer for his sacrifice, but in return, da demon would be slayed and his family would have peace. So dis prince agreed ta meet dis terrible demon, Aodh. He agreed ta sacrifice his life and da light of his soul for his family. Da aingeal told him dat one day a queen would come and she would rescue him from da horror of Sheol. Do ye know who dat lad was?"

"You."

"Me. Da aingeal's name was Atwater."

"Atwater? Brennus' guardian angel?"

"Da very same."

"Why you?" I ask. "Why not Brennus?"

"Why me? Because I can make a wicked weapon, Genevieve. But, ye're wrong about one ting. 'Tis Brennus, too. Atwater lied ta me. He told me dat me family would be safe. But dat didn't happen. Instead, he recruited me brudder as well for dis mission."

"How long have you waited for me?" I whisper in anguish.

"Too long," Finn replies.

I look from Finn to Brennus. There is sorrow in the king of the Gancanagh's eyes. I gaze at the battle hammer next to me. "Do you know what it can do?" I ask, running my hand over the metal again. It sings some more. I lift my hand and the melody stops.

"It can kill anyting ye swing it at," Finn replies. "Anyting."

Brennus comes closer to us. Finn growls a warning at him. Brennus stops. He's stunned by the aggressive response from his brother. "Finn?"

"Ye'll na interfere wi' her mission. I'll na allow it," Finn responds, his body rigid, ready to strike at anyone who gets too close to me.

"'Tis na me intention ta interfere, Finn," Brennus replies. "I'm here ta help as well. I want her ta live more dan anyone."

"Evie," Reed says softly, extending his hand to me in a nonthreatening way, indicating that I should move to him. He wants to extract me from in between them. Finn turns his attention to Reed and narrows his eyes, assessing his threat level. Finn growls at my aspire, apparently finding something amiss in Reed as well.

"Finn," I say, touching his arm. "It's okay. We're all here for the same purpose."

"I'm na all here," he says, and the torturous depths in his eyes make my heart squeeze and ache for him. "Ye've come ta fix dat." A shiver runs through me to my marrow.

"What do you mean?"

"Me light—ye're here ta free it."

"Your light? I'm sorry—I don't—"

"Me light is me soul. Whah was inside me was me light—most o' whah was good and whah made me special—'tis Faerie. It has been gone ever since Aodh made me Gancanagh. I've been waitin' for me queen ta arrive ta free me from dis and make me whole once more."

"How do I do that, Finn?" I whisper, desperate for information.

"I do na know, but I know ye will na fail me."

"How long have you known I was your queen?"

"I dared ta hope 'twas ye when Brennus touched ye at da library—dat night in Houghton. Ye did na lose ta us—ye did na become jus another wan. But 'twas when ye destroyed Keegan in da mines dat I truly began ta *believe* 'twas ye. I tought den dat if yer soul separated from ye, 'twould travel ta Sheol and free us."

"Why didn't you tell me all of this before?"

"I could na. Someting has always kept me from speaking of it —a magical force like da one we created wi' yer contract. But 'tis gone now. I do na know how or why, but 'tis no longer a slipknot around me throat."

Brennus speaks to Finn, "Atwater told me da only way ye'd survive, Finn, was if I went after ye. Ye'd already been made Gancanagh, but I didn't know it. I went ta meet Aodh and yer whole crew had already been changed inta undead craiturs.

"I remember. I know whah ye did for me. Ye're still me king, brudder," Finn says, "but Genevieve is me queen. She's da one I fight for now. She's here ta dig up me soul and reunite it wi' me bones."

I look from Finn to Brennus. "We need to prepare for battle. We have to mobilize the fellas and get them to Crestwood—"

"'Tis done," Finn says. "Most of our army is near dere already. We have a few hundred or so fellas here ta protect ye until we depart. Ye need ta prepare for da battle now. I've armor dat I made for ye." I look at the medieval Faerie armor beside me. He catches me and smiles for the first time, "'Tis na like dat armor. Da armor I created for ye looks modern and will chafe ye less. His eyes travel over my entourage. "I have armor for all of ye and modern weapons charmed by our best spell crafters."

"Thank you, Finn," I murmur.

Brennus approaches me slowly, saying, "We stand little chance against all of da aingeals. We can fight da fallen or da divine, but we can na hold out against both of dem."

"We won't have to, Brennus. We'll fight Emil. Xavier and my father will bring their armies to help us."

"Eh? Divine aingeals do na fight wi' Gancanagh," Brennus says in disbelief.

"They do now," I reply.

"Emil will be hard ta kill, mo chroí. His brand of savagery is someting I've na seen in a long time. Do ye know whah he did when he found out da location of his soul mate on Earth in dis lifetime?" Brennus asks.

I pale, shaking my head. "No." I glance at Russell to see that he's listening. Russell's mouth forms a grim line.

"When Emil was only fifteen, he went ta her home a few cities away. He knew who she was and whah she was because unlike ye, he had total recall of all of his previous lifetimes. His soul mate was still a little girl—only eleven. He found her and he butchered her. She was da other's inescapable," he gestures toward Russell, "but she does na exist anymore. Neither of ye will ever see her again in any lifetime. Emil used da weapon dat is meant ta kill ye, mo chroí, ta annihilate her soul as well as her angelic body."

"Why would he do that?" I whisper.

"He does na want anyone ta be as powerful as him."

I feel like I can't breathe. Finn notices. He gestures to the hallway that leads from this room, "If you come dis way, I will get ye and yer friends outfitted wi' whah ye'll need ta face whah lies ahead."

I nod. Finn picks up the battle hammer and ushers me to the adjacent corridor. We enter a room that has state-of-the-art weaponry and lightweight modern armor. "Dese weapons," Finn says, spreading his arm wide, "have all been charmed. Da body armor has been enchanted ta repel other magic, but I do na know how 'twill fare against Emil. He's exceptional when it comes ta conjuring energy. Ye have ta be spry and avoid his spells as much as possible."

He rests the weapon in his hand against the wall as he opens a glass case that contains ebony body armor. Lifting it out of the case, he holds the shapely combat uniform up to me. The breastplate is a hard shell, the surface of which appears black until I touch it. When my skin meets it, scrolling Faerie writing illuminates it in silver and gold light, showing the protective magic layered into it. Finn presses it into my arms. "Dere's a room," he points to one of the several silver doors to my right.

"I have to pee," I blurt out. I do. I'm so afraid that it has made finding a bathroom a dire necessity.

"Dat is why we'll win, mo chroí," Brennus says behind me, "because ye're still so human."

Am I still human? I don't know. All I know is I'm terrified and I need a few seconds to myself.

Finn takes pity on me. "Ye can do dat in da room I jus showed ye as well. Dis part of da seminary was an underground bathhouse. Dere's a shower and grooming—"

I avoid everyone's eyes and don't wait for Finn to finish explaining it all to me. I hurry to the room with the silver door and close it behind me. Setting down my armor on a red velvet-covered bench near a three-way mirror, I locate a private attached bathroom and use it. There's an enclosed shower in the bathroom as well. Turning the water on, I strip off my clothes and wait only long enough for the water to become somewhat warm before entering it.

As I shower, my mind wants to detach from all of this, so that fear goes away and I can be numb. But I know I can't escape it. This is happening. There's no way I can stop it, or go back and change it, or issue a do-over. I have to face it. I turn off the water. Finding a clean robe on a hook, I dry off. A small vanity has everything I need. I towel dry my hair. Locating a comb, I use it to untangle snarls. I gather it into a ponytail at the crown of my head and secure it with a hair tie from the pocket of my discarded jeans.

When I go back into the room to collect the armor, I pause. Reed is leaning against the door with his arms crossed over his chest. He already has his black Faerie armor on. His hair is wet from a shower. He straightens as I approach the bench near the mirror. "Would you like some help with your armor?" he asks.

"Yes. Thank you," I murmur, looking at his reflection in the mirror.

He walks to me. Picking up the armor, he opens the back of it. You should start off with your wings out."

I nod. Untying my robe, I let it slip from my shoulders, and then my arms. I catch it and lay it over the bench. Reed's eyes focus on me. My skin flushes in response. My wings release from me; they spread out in a fiery display of red. He catches himself staring and looks down at the armor in his hands. He stretches the back section of it apart and holds it out to me so that I can step into it. I place my hand on his shoulder for balance, before stepping into the footwear and greaves. As I do, they become liquid and form to the contours of my feet and legs, only to harden when they take the shape of me. Threading my arms into the sleeves, the armor grows over my shoulder. It knits together in the back, smoothing and enclosing me in a black casing that shines with scrolled Faerie writing over the breastplate. For a few moments, the light is bright and ethereal. It fades. I still see the writing, but it has dulled to a deep shade of gray, appearing etched into the armor.

"You can retract your wings or redeploy them at any time. The armor will adjust."

"I could've used this when I first got my wings," I reply with a small smile.

"I hope it didn't bother you too much. I tried to make the transition as smooth for you as possible—"

"You were perfect." I kiss him. "You *are* perfect." He holds me and it becomes like fire inside of me, relieving my fear.

"He takes my hand in his and leads me back out to the weapons room. Buns and Brownie are outfitted with Faerie armor. The Reapers have military-style backpacks that they're loading with arms. The menagerie of death is spread out on top of a glass case in front of the angels. Gancanagh soldiers hover around them, attracted by their angelic auras. The undead pretend to be focused on inserting weapons into similar packs, but their fangs all but hang out of their mouths. My eyes go to their gloved hands. The new added feature to their uniform attests to a new code. Once the battle begins, I'm sure they'll shed them so that they can be more effective killers when they meet the fallen, but for now it's a much-needed precaution.

One undead faerie, standing next to Buns, is particularly interested in the flashing cham-pain bottle Buns has set on the glass case in front of her. He reaches out and taps his finger on the glass. The bottle reacts violently, vibrating and flashing with rage.

"Oh, sweetie," Buns warns the undead killer with a wicked smile, "don't touch that. That's pure pain."

Russell has opted to keep his Detroit hat on. It looks amazing with his assassin Faerie armor. He stands with Anya, choosing their weapons carefully. Anya holds an automatic faerie-charmed rifle up to her shoulder. Russell adjusts her form and points out its features while his hand slips to her bottom. She doesn't seem to mind his hand being there.

Preben and Zephyr are going old school. They're more interested in the swords, daggers, and the charmed throwing stars that boomerang. Brennus draws my attention. He's watching me. He has Finn's hammer in his grasp. I let go of Reed's hand. "Have you chosen your weapons, yet?" I ask.

"No."

"Go get what you need. I'll join you and Zephyr in a moment. I want to talk to Brennus."

"Alright," he says. I cross the room to where Brennus stands with Finn. "This is going to be awkward to carry." I gesture to the huge battle hammer.

"Ye need na worry. All ye have ta do is talk ta it and 'twill obey ye."

I must have a skeptical look on my face because he sighs. "Here." He puts the shaft of the weapon in my hand. "Give it a command."

The battle hammer sings and vibrates at my touch. "Urr...can you stop singing?" I ask. Finn's killer weapon silences. I look over at Brennus and smile.

"Dat will come in handy if ye need ta surprise yer opponent. Tell it ye need it ta be small so dat ye can carry it wi'out killin' someone accidentally."

"Umm...be small." The weapon shrinks to pickaxe-sized.

"Now tell it dat ye need it ta cling ta ye and ta stay put. Da best place ta carry it is over yer left shoulder because ye're right handed." He moves behind me.

I speak to the hammer. "Hang on to me until I need you."

I reach over my shoulder and place it under my left wing. It rests against my back. When I let go of the handle, it doesn't succumb to gravity. It grips me. I hardly notice it because it feels like it weighs nothing at all.

"Now grasp da hilt and tink of a command when ye do, but do na say it aloud," Brennus orders.

I do. I reach for the handle, finding it, I think, *Let go and grow.* The hammer lets go of me and as I swing it back in front of me, it has become full-sized once more.

"Now, wield it like da fellas taught ye when ye lived wi' us in Ireland," Brennus orders. I do, whipping the long-handled axe-hammer through the air like a bo staff warrior. "Ye're lethal," Brennus says proudly.

I've caught the attention of every single being in the room. Everyone has gathered their weapons and has them in packs on their backs. Finn comes close to me. "If ye're ready, we'll go and join yer army now. I have charmed da revolving door jus dere." Finn motions to the round turnstile door. "All we need ta do is make da trip."

"I'm ready." But I'm not, so I have to fake it. If any of the Gancanagh senses weakness or fear, I'm dead before it even begins.

Zephyr and Reed join me, taking up positions on the other side of me. "You are ready, Zephyr says, giving me a nod of approval. "You are the second best fighter that I've ever seen."

"Who's the first?" I ask.

He blinks. "Me," he states, as if I should've known that.

I try to suppress my grin, saying, "You are, Zee." Buns and Brownie elbow their way next to me, linking their arms with mine, they escort me toward the revolving doors.

"Let's go beat the Fallen," Brownie says, as if we're going to a field hockey game and facing the Kappas.

"I will set them up for you," Buns advises, talking strategy, "and you can knock them back to Sheol. They'll fall like dominos."

"When it gets bad, Buns, run," I warn her. "I need you here when this is all over."

The fellas move to the revolving door. They enter it so fast it blurs and whirls.

"We know what to do, sweetie." Buns lets go of me and enters the portal.

It's Brownie's turn next. "See you on the other side," she says. She disappears in a swirl of copper-colored butterfly wings.

Reed places his hand in mine and whispers in my ear, "As one?"

I squeeze his hand and reply, "Always," before we disappear together into the whirling dervish of the portal.

CHAPTER 24
Red Sky

It's a wild Matterhorn ride to the other side of the portal. Arriving on the snow-covered grounds of Crestwood, I manage to land on my feet with Reed's help. Distant lightning sends thunderclaps rolling in, threatening the already darkening skies. Cold air blows my hair, but my armor keeps me warm. The campus is the same, except it's not. Not really. My head leans to one side. Now there are undead faeries everywhere, hanging off the bronze statues of the founders and pretending to do lewd acts to them.

"Most of da fellas are disciplined," Brennus mutters behind me. "Dere are only a few left who do na know how ta conduct demselves. I will kill dem later should dey survive." I let go of Reed's hand and stop to face Brennus. He's so close to me that I'm looking at the center of his massive, black armor-clad chest. His ebony wings only add to his height as I look up at his face. He's always gorgeous in a tailored suit, but his combat attire is even more impressive. Whereas his suits are elegant, this shows just how powerfully built he is. My cheeks redden and I hope it can be attributed to the cold wind.

Whatever I was going to say to him eludes me now. I look away from my dark, handsome king, catching sight of the irreverent fellas hanging on the statues once more. I raise my hand to them. Casting a spell, the gyrating Gancanagh soldiers are knocked off the pedestals and into the snow. I raise my eyebrow to Brennus. "I've taken care of the problem. They've learned their lesson. Now you don't have to kill them."

"Ye still know little of how tings work." Brennus sighs. "Showin' no mercy is how ye lead."

"Power and mercy are two different things, Brennus." I want to change the subject to more pressing matters. "Are there any signs of divine angels?" I ask, holding my breath.

"Na yet," Brennus admits. His beautiful lips turn down. I feel almost devastated by what he says. *What if they don't come? What if Xavier and Tau were made to abandon me again?* Brennus reads my look. "Dey're na as fleet as a Faerie army, Genevieve. Dey can na charm dere way here."

"You think that's it? That they're just more cumbersome than Faeries?" I can't hide the hopeful lilt in my voice.

"Ye know me. I do na trust divine aingeals ta join our side in dis fight."

We've been transported to the area in front of Central Hall. It's dark inside the building, as if no one is there. "Where are all the students and staff?" I ask. At this time of day, there would normally be a lively crowd walking to and from classes.

"It's winter break," Reed says beside me. I didn't know that. Time means almost nothing to me now. The goings-on of normal people's lives means even less. "Some have not made it home, though." Reed points to human figures standing across the street on the frozen sidewalk in front of Calhoun, one of the men's dormitories. They're not acting like humans. They aren't panicking or trying to run away from undead faeries that have invaded their campus. Nor do they display the devotion on their faces that wans exhibit when fellas have touched them. No. They stand erect with their arms at their sides, watching us with sinister expressions.

I shiver. "Who are they?" I ask. One of them is female. She stares at me as if she'd like to stab me in the face. Her clothing is pristine. She's dressed just like anyone would be for the cold weather in a warm coat, scarf, mittens, and a hat. Her makeup is flawless. The way she tied her scarf is in fashion.

"They're possessed souls, Evie. I think you called the first one you ever saw a 'shadow man'. They're spies of Sheol now. They will report your arrival if we allow them to live."

I would never know she had a demon in her if I was merely human. They hide well. "If you kill them, their souls will crossover to Sheol. Fallen angels will know I'm here all the same."

"Yes," Reed admits, "but these possessed wouldn't be able to join the true fighting when it begins if we slay them now."

"Can they be saved?" There has been so much bloodshed and collateral damage already. I don't want anyone else to feel what I felt when I lost my uncle. How many will suffer when their sons and daughters don't ever come home?

"Normally, I would say no, but I've seen too much lately to the contrary to ever make that bold of a statement again. But, that said, I'll kill them now if you don't."

"But what if they can be saved?"

"Kill dem," Brennus gestures to two of the Gancanagh who have been following him. Without hesitation, both of the undead soldiers sprint across the snow-covered lawn and across the street, cutting down the shadow people with hatchets.

"Why did you do that?" I demand. My hands are in fists at my sides and my jaw is rigid.

"Let me show ye someting," Brennus replies. He takes me by the elbow none too gently, and leads me over the crest of a small hill. On the other side of it, human carcasses and the dead bodies of divine Reapers turn the snow red with blood. There was a massacre here of epic proportions. Brennus takes me by the shoulders and growls in my face, "Dat is whah da Fallen and deir demons do. Ye show no mercy, mo chroí. No. Mercy! Anyting else and ye have dis outcome." He sweeps his arms wide, indicating the carnage once more.

Brownie and Buns are beside me. The shock quickly gives way to grieving as they see their kind amid the casualties. I know it would've been them too if they had remained here, or if Zephyr had allowed them to come back here when they wanted to return. Emil would've slaughtered my friends. As it is, he has slaughtered enough to make what I've come to do to him and anyone who helps him more than justified.

"Where do I meet Emil?" I ask.

"Da gate of Sheol at da aingeal's estate—where he cut da world asunder."

"Then we should go there now and finish this."

Brennus lets go of my elbow. He strides away from me toward Finn, an undeniable general, barking out, "Right lads! We've waited lifetimes for dis day ta come! Up now and get 'em boys! Yer queen demands it!"

Finn calls out orders of his own, directing his commanders to mobilize for the short trek to the end of the world. I straighten my shoulders. If nothing else, all this ends today. Something about that gives me the confidence I need to face what's ahead. There is no going on to my next life. This one is it. I have to make it count.

Reed, Zephyr, Russell, Preben, Anya, Brennus, Brownie, and Buns gather around me. I know the way to Reed's house by heart, literally. I take to the sky, flying away from campus. Legions of Gancanagh, more than I could have ever fathom, strike out on foot in blurring speed. They have no trouble keeping up with us as we set the pace. I know the element of surprise is not with us. Emil knows we're here. He can probably smell the Gancanagh from miles away. I'm curious to know if he's surprised by whom has decided to join me—or that I let them join me. I pray he has no idea what it means.

Landing on the lawn that runs up to Reed's house, trenches have been dug into the frozen terrain for protection. Inside the maze of trenches, Gancanagh mix with baldheaded creatures that have hairy ears and enormous lumpy bodies. I touch down near one such creature and have to almost cover my hand over my nose at his odor. "Eion told ye Trolls smell like arse, did he na?" Brennus asks next to me. He pulls his battle-axe from his back. The hilt grows to full extension. The king uses the end of it to nudge the troll intent on touching my hair away from me. "Dat's close enough, baldy. Go find yer regime and prepare for battle," Brennus warns him, showing his fangs in a hiss when it looks as if the troll would protest. The lumpy creature shuffles off into the growing crowd of unwashed bodies behind us. "And brush yer teeth once in awhile," he calls over his shoulder in irritation.

My attention returns to the house ahead of us. It was an English manor that resembles a modernized hunting lodge. Now, it has taken on a very sinister mien. The ground around it is fuzzy, resembling the haze of the terrain in the desert. Seeing my bedroom window, I wonder if Emil has slept in our bed, or rolled around in my sheets. If we survive, we'll have to burn the place down and rebuild. I glance at Reed by my side. He's poised for battle. "We need a protective shield, Brennus. Will you help me make one?" I ask.

"I will gather energy and push it inta ye." He does, pouring copious amounts of shimmering energy into me. My insides singe from it. I use it to weave an intricate spell of protection around my army. Brennus tests it with his own magic. When it not only holds, but also spits his energy back at him so that he has to jump out of its way, he says, "It'll do."

The front door of the house opens up. Emil emerges from it with his hands raised in surrender. A hush falls over the crowd of us watching him. Before I can say the word, "Wait," a hundred or more beings open fire on him. Emil is riddled with bullets, arrows, throwing stars, and a menagerie of other projectiles. He's reduced to a bloody pile of flesh in the driveway.

Zephyr, who hasn't moved, comments on the fact that Anya was one of the first to unload her entire magazine on Emil. "Thrones," he says to Russell, "need vengeance. Good luck with that."

Russell replies, "She got him good, though."

Whatever Zee was going to say fades from his lips as another Emil emerges from the house with his hands up. I cringe. Behind this Emil, a slew of Emils run from the house. They move over the snow, stumbling and getting up to trudge through the drifts.

Russell says, "Remember the paintball fight on the beach, Red? It's like the Delt Wars. He's throwing Freshmen at us." My soul mate is right. It's just on an entirely different scale.

Reed clarifies, "He's trying to deplete our ammunition and

demoralize us by making us kill his victims." I choke back the sour flavor in my mouth.

"Nobody fire!" I order. The victims with Emil's face keep coming. They swarm into the yard with his strawberry-blond hair and his lazy eyes. I want to smash all of their faces in. They trip and stumble toward us. That's when I realize that some of them are wearing vests covered with incendiary devices.

"Evie," Reed says while he looks over the edge of the trench.

"I know! I see them!"

"Can you amplify my voice?" Reed asks, his eyes never leaving the fake Emils as they struggle to get to our trenches.

"I think so. I have to come up with a spell—"

"Do it!" he replies urgently, his assassin's eyes honing in on a fake Emil running across the frozen water of the small pond only yards away.

I whisper a spell over Reed, nodding my head for him to speak. My Power angel looks in the direction of the possessed human wearing Emil's face. He calls out, "Stop!" My head vibrates with the resonance of his persuasive voice. It echoes and reverberates in my mind causing my brain to rebel as if it were being scrubbed by steel wool. I hold my head in my hands, looking through my splayed fingers. The possessed soul halts only a yard or so from us. "Go find your master. He's waiting for you to embrace him."

The soul doesn't waver for a moment. He turns around and stumbles back across the frozen water. Reed repeats his order. It amplifies over the mass amount of evil souls coming at us. They turn, fighting one another to claw their way back into the door of the house to get to their master. Hissing sounds, like the spray of fire from a flame-thrower, and then *BOOM!* The house explodes shaking the ground and throwing debris up in the air for miles. Fire and smoke billows up. I straighten, feeling a cautious sense of elation bubble up in me.

My angel grasps my wrist and says through clenched teeth, "Get down!" I have just a second to comply before he pulls me to him and covers me with his body. I catch a glimpse past his shoulder of magical flames traveling at us over the mall in front of where the house used to be. The flames pass over the trenches, moaning. Everything that was in its path is ash in a millisecond. My magic shield is wiped out.

Reed shifts off of me. He leans against the frozen dirt wall and uses the blade of a sword to reflect the area above us. The house is completely gone. It's reduced to ashes that float around us like snow. In its place is a gigantic gaping hole to another world—a hellscape I only glimpsed once before. I peek over the edge of the trench. It's as if our world is a solemn, ethereal landscape painting that's been torn to reveal a dark, sinister masterpiece with blood-red skies underneath. It's something out of a Bosch nightmare. I cover my mouth as the reek of Sheol hits us all at once. I have to choke back my gag. It is so bad it makes the Trolls smell like perfume.

In the Sheol sky, legion upon legion of fallen angels fly. There's every type of fallen angel, from Seraphim to Reaper, swirling around in the putrid air. Even with their ability to fly, some angels ride upon the backs of enormous dragons whose scales shine like embers. Dark-winged bulls with polished black horns and hooves ferry other evil angels on their backs. Some Fallen have harnessed teams of powder-white mothmen to carry them in gilded chariots across the sky. Vulgar creature mashups of man and beast hurtle toward the open doorway to our world.

Finding Emil among the fallen angels is impossible. They darken the sky like locusts. The sheer numbers I'm seeing of my enemy is horrifyingly bigger than what I could ever imagine. But they're not just angels and demons. Evil souls numbering in the hundreds of thousands are being set free from Sheol. They're spirits—bodiless evil entities—until they find a human host here to possess and inhabit. Once that happens, they'll be powerful with the ability to maim and kill. We're outnumbered at least a thousand to one in this fight. My little army doesn't stand a chance against the malevolence coming for us.

"We have to close Sheol," I whisper to Reed. "If you give me the boatswain, then I'll do it automatically—I think—I hope—this hole will collapse before they get here!" I hold out my hand to him for the whistle.

His hand moves to where the whistle lies beneath his armor. He covers it, making no move to give it to me. "If I do, you could get trapped on the other side and slaughtered by them."

Russell crawls over to where Reed and I crouch in the trench. "We need to pool our energy, Red, and come up with a spell to kill the apocalypse of evil that's about to crash in on us." He calls out to Brennus and Finn who are giving orders to the fellas to prepare to leave the trenches and storm the field. "Hey! Brothers Grim! Do you mind helpin' us out with some magic?"

Brennus scowls at him, but moves closer to us. Finn has never been more than a few yards from me, always protecting my back from Gancanagh and Trolls behind us. It's a very precarious position to be in. My army could turn on me at any time if they feel they have a better chance of coming out of this alive. And right now, I kind of wouldn't blame them.

Brennus crouches down in front of me. "I'm going ta give ye energy, mo chroí. Ye have to accept it as yer due. Channel it inside ye and hold on ta it. Do na hurl it away in a spell. Make it part of ye." Brennus holds out his hands. He channels his energy into me. It's painful and pleasurable; I hate the duality of it. Finn joins him. His energy is contrary to his brothers'. Whereas Brennus' energy is power and dominance, Finn's is playful and effervescent. Russell puts out his hands to me. I feel his energy flow inside my body and it's like the feeling I get when I hear my favorite song. When they all drop their hands, I stretch my arms out to the sides because I cannot seem to hold them down. I'm not anchored to the ground. I levitate in the air, defying gravity. Without the use of my wings, I lift out of the trench. Reed is by my side, flying next to me. My movement out of the trench signals my army into action. The hoard of mythical creatures behind me catapults out of the trenches, running over the torched ground toward the invading evil.

Now I know how Emil creates such devastating magic. He's basically doping off of other beings' energy like I just did.

Knowing this, I whisper a magic spell to conjure fire. Aiming it at Sheol, I ratchet up the pain when I control the flames like an extension of myself instead of a cannon ball let loose. White-hot light burns through the clouds, connecting with the swarms of beasts on the other side of the divide. Clear paths of red sky ripples through the vile creatures. Angelic figures catch fire and fall in flames to Hell's terrain.

Fallen angels pour over the divide because I can't stop them all. Flying low to the ground, Sheol's angels hatchet Gancanagh, severing heads from bodies. Automatic weapons fire rings in the air. Bombs explode falling angel carcasses from the air in a color array of magic. I switch my tactic. Instead of burning the skies, I try to narrow the gap. This will force them to enter our world in a smaller, more manageable way that will enable us to cut them down easier the moment they cross over the divide between worlds.

Whispering a spell, I pull my arms together; the sky knits and seals in a section, closing a small part of Sheol. I'm making headway, cutting off a procession of mothmen driven chariots and blocking them from entering. They pull up, reaching the edge of the world that has become too tight to get through.

A sigh escapes me at my small victory, but it's short-lived. My magic is only a bandage on the wound. It unravels and opens again. A golden armor-clad angel with bright red Seraphim wings flies along the divide, scoring his dagger over the fabric between our worlds. It rends and frays growing larger than it was before.

I recognize the angel. It's Emil. My heart pounds; I had almost no hope of finding him among the damned, yet, there he is. I glance beside me. Reed hovers in the sky to my right. His dark wings beat with a graceful rhythm. His attention is on the masses of Fallen engaging in battle around us. I've been so focused on my spells; I hadn't questioned their proximity to me. Now I see I'm at the center of the conflict. Reed swoops in front of me, slicing off the arm of an angel who would've tackled me from above. The carnage falls to the ground where Gancanagh are tearing apart possessed souls.

Buns is just a small distance from me, her golden butterfly wings flying her in zigzag patterns. She clutches the neck of the cham-pain bottle. Using it like a bat, she smashes it into an angel, yelling, "Take my pain!" The brutal Power cramps up, yellow lightning bolts of suffering charging through him as he falls from the sky. At her side, Zephyr stabs his sword through the belly of an albino mothman, its mouth opens wide like a dying fish, showing rows of pointy rotten teeth.

It's not enough, though. The pathway into our world from Sheol is widening with every slice Emil makes with his soul shredder. Soon, there won't be just a hole; Sheol will be the horizon. I need to get to Emil to stop him. I try to catch Reed's attention, but as I do, I hear a scream that nearly stops my heart. Glancing over my shoulder, I see Buns' golden wing fold in. Blood sprays from her chest and mouth as she's impaled on the end of a spear of a dark-haired fallen Seraph. My response is automatic. I reach over my left shoulder and grasp the handle of my battle hammer. Wielding it like a shot putter, I let it fly. The silver hammer tumbles through the air. The flat side of it connects with the depraved Seraph, knocking his head clear off his shoulders, casting it down to the ground below. The angel's body goes limp and chases his head to the ground. I whisper the command, "Come back to me." The hammer twists and returns, striking my palm.

Zephyr catches Buns in his arms, refusing to let her fall. His face is one of devastation as he yanks the spear from her chest, letting the blood-covered metal shaft drop from his fist. Zee's hand smoothes her hair back from her forehead, smearing red in her flaxen strands. Before I can move, Russell flies up to them and hovers in the air, his red wings beating behind him. He holds out his hand and uses a spell to encase Buns, Zephyr, and himself in a bubble. It's like the kind of bubble little children blow with soap and plastic sticks in their back yards, only his bubble is huge. Fallen beat on the curve of the bubble, trying to get to them. The wall bows in, but it doesn't pop; the spell holds. Russell's hand begins to glow with golden light. He presses it to Buns' wound while he punches his other fist through the wall of the bubble. Again, it doesn't pop, but closes in around his wrist. He palms the froglike face of a Sheol demon. The grotesque flying frogman's chest breaks open and orange-colored blood projects out of him to cover the side of the iridescent bubble with evil frogman guts. Buns' arms flail as the wound in her chest closes.

I feel numb with fear. I glance at Reed, he's a windstorm blowing through straw men, scattering and killing everything that gets close to me. A knicker beside me jolts me out of my shock. My waist is seized and I swing up behind Brennus on the back of a black-winged horse. My hair streams behind me as Brennus drives the steed forward, aiming at the expanding red sky and the evil freak who's cutting my world to pieces. Holding onto Brennus' waist and looking behind me, Finn is right there on the back of another winged-horse whose nostrils breathe fire with each powerful stride and flap of its beautiful feathered wings. I wonder where they got the mythical creatures, but because the equines seems real enough, I'm going to go with them being from Hell.

"Clear a path for us, mo chroí!" Brennus orders over his shoulder.

I lift my hands. I'm a matchstick poised to strike. I spark, lighting the fuse inside me, becoming an arsonist, destroying fallen angels and demons without mercy. Emil notices the commotion that I'm making with my magic. He pauses from his task of ripping the world in two. Focusing his full attention on us, his lips move. "My inescapable lover," I hear Emil whisper in my mind, "how shall I enslave you this time?"

He aims his magic at us, thrusting energy. The army of fallen in the path between Emil and me become crumbling sand sculptures slowly falling apart. Brennus tries to block the spell with his own magic, but it keeps coming, crawling over him and turning his forearm crispy. He urges the black winged-horse aside, soaring away from the beam that will kill us. Emil lifts his hand once more, his golden armor gleaming, even in the lack of light. Aiming his palm at us, he's unable to throw his magic because Reed appears in front of him. Emil shifts his diabolical magic to Reed, plying him with heinous energy. Reed's ring takes the brunt of the curse Emil would cast upon him.

With the spade blades notched between Reed's fingers, he slashes Emil in the throat, cutting an X pattern in his flesh and watching his blood spurt from his body. Emil reels back, his blood flowing down the front of his golden armor. He reaches for the first being he sees. A Cherub falls into his clutches. Emil's hands glow golden. The gaping slits in his throat closes in seconds, appearing on the neck of the Cherub in his grasp. Emil takes a huge, ragged breath in; his eyes wild and wide with the need for air. Reed presses forward, cutting through bodies of evil creatures that get in his way. My inescapable is in full retreat, flying across the divide, back into the underworld. Reed doesn't stop at the threshold, but follows him into Sheol. His ring glows blue, the jewel in the center glows with its own fire

The other demons Emil has left behind press into our realm, engaging in the battle without any sign of retreat. "REED," I scream. I dismount the winged-horse. "REED!" I soar after him, veering into the mass of fallen, swinging my hammer and knocking the life out of everything in my way.

Reed tugs on the chain around his neck that holds the whistle. It emerges from underneath his armor. Placing it to his lips, he steps over the threshold of our world into Sheol. The second he does, blue light from his ring closes in around him and he disappears, becoming invisible. I hear rather than see him blow the whistle. Atwater must have taught him the notes to use to close our worlds when he gave the boatswain to him. The sound is muffled. It doesn't affect me the way it had when I was next to it. This time, I hardly feel it at all.

The sky around us begins to change. The fabric of our world, the one of gray skies and dark clouds closes in, making the red sky behind it shrink. I panic knowing Reed is on the other side closing the gateway to Sheol. He plans to try to kill Byzantyne and Emil on his own. It's not a bad plan. If he can make Emil's Seraph mentor cease to be and slay Emil's angelic body, only Emil's soul would survive. *Wouldn't it?* But Emil would be trapped in Sheol. It could work! It would allow Reed and me to remain together, but it's still a horrible plan for one reason: he intends to do it without me.

Trumpets sound. Startled, I turn, scanning the clouds behind me. Divine winged warriors careen through the air in rows like paper angels strung up in the sky. Weapons gleam from sunbursts that cut through the clouds. Some divine angels are attired in black armor with red Xs on the front of it. Others wear red armor with black Ts across the chest and abdomen. They engage in the fighting. The roar of their war cries echoes in the air.

Even though the gateway is closing, it doesn't mean the battle is any less excruciatingly real. There are hundreds of thousands of fallen and divine angels clawing at one another everywhere I look. I turn and keep moving toward Sheol, slicing through anything that gets in my way. Brennus and Finn are by my side, cutting and slashing demons to get us to the entrance of Sheol. "Do ye intend ta go dere den?" Brennus shouts, while beating back a bald skeletal beast that is in a very serious stage of decomposition.

"Yes," I reply, not looking at him, but using the long handle of my battle hammer like a bo staff to beat away anything that gets near me. I reach the threshold to Sheol. It's closing in fast.

"Den I go wi' ye," Brennus says, raising his chin as if he expects an argument from me. On the contrary, I think it's a solid plan having someone with me to help. It might just be the best plan he's ever had in his undead life.

"Okay," I agree. Finn takes a position on my left side, protecting me from being assaulted by flocks of bat-winged reconnoîtres with taffy puller-shaped mouths.

Struggling through the misshapen mess of violent creatures, we make it to the edge of Sheol. I fly over it to the other side. My hammer glows an eerie blue. Finn calls out, "Genevieve! It works!"

"What works?" I ask, but something strange is happening. Evil creatures are now avoiding me, careening around me as if I repulse them.

"Da weapon I made for ye repels demons and makes ye invisible ta dem when ye're in deir realm. Dey feel pain when dey get close ta it—it stings dem with da power it emits."

He's right. Sheol's finest are giving me such a wide berth that they're even avoiding Brennus and Finn because they're near me. "This is the best gift ever, Finn," I breathe. "How come your magic works on angels, Finn?" I ask.

"It only works like dis when ye're in Sheol. It will na work dis way on Earth. Sheol has different energy." Then I notice that, although it works on the lesser demons, the sting does not seem to extend to angels. They don't see me, but they're not shying away from me either.

Finn tries to come nearer to me, but he's brought up short on the threshold to Sheol. He tries again, but it looks as if he is walking into a wall each time. Brennus scowls. He attempts to cross the threshold as well, but it prevents him from passing, just like Finn. He growls in anger.

"I can na go wi' ye!" Brennus' voice is thick with frustration. "I'm mostly undead. I ca na pass over da threshold. It rejects me."

"Why does it do that?" I ask, as my heart sinks.

"Me soul is dere," he admits. "Dis realm keeps me out so dat I can na rescue me soul. I'd hoped dat because me body is different now, 'twould let me in."

"I have to go." I do. If I don't leave now, I may lose my courage and cross back into our world. I have to find Reed. I have to help him end this. I turn away from them.

"Genevieve, wait! Are ye still here?" Brennus asks.

"Yes," I answer, hesitating.

"Remember whah me soul said. He'll know ye by note!"

"Okay. I'll remember," I reply. "And, Brennus?"

"Whah?"

"I will find your soul and return him to you."

He looks as if I just broke his heart into a million pieces. "Jus come back. Dat is all I want."

Lifting my hammer as a light in the darkness, I turn away from

Brennus and Finn and face a ghoulish city in the distance. The spires of the buildings appear to dance amid the fiery sky. I fly toward them in search of my angel and the one being who, for me, has always been inescapable.

CHAPTER 25
Surrender

Following the butterflies in my belly to search for Reed, I come to an elegant stone bridge. I've been taking a break from flying, choosing to run instead so I can rest my wings. I hesitate on the path. The bridge spans the twisting red river and is covered in a fine layer of ash that floats everywhere here. The stone road over it has the perfection of glass. Every brick is set at exactly the precise height. On the other side, in the distance, towering spires and graceful domes raise up to stab the scarlet sky. My hammer glows brighter, tugging me toward the bridge. *I know you want to cross the water;* I talk to it in my mind. *But I don't need a bridge to do it. I can fly.*

It tugs me harder toward the bridge. I stumble forward. *You indicated earlier that I should go to the city to find Emil. The city is that way. If I fly across the river, it's a more direct route.* It tugs me again in the direction of the bridge. *Okay...* I trudge on cautiously.

I'm not alone here. The harrowing creatures around me are real. They're not ghostly or made of light, like souls are when they emerged from Sheol to Earth. Here, they're one hundred percent solid—flesh, bone, sinew, scales, claws, and teeth. Because of the weapon I carry and the fact that I'm camouflaged with invisibility, they all avoid my path. Whenever they get too close, they veer away, feeling the sting of the aura my hammer gives off. They're also avoiding the bridge ahead, choosing to wade into the blood-red water rather than take the beautiful stone path. That means something.

Continuing on toward the bridge and the river, I pass a naked man with a robin's head. He pecks at the abdomen of a frogman, eating his entrails. I have to swallow back the bile in my mouth. It's not even just the sight of them that turns my blood to ice, it's the shrill sounds they make. Some bray like goats or snort like swine. It makes my flesh run with goose bumps.

I feel another tug urging me forward, but this one is a different kind. This one comes from my abdomen. Butterflies. Scanning the area, I don't see Reed; he's still invisible to me in this realm while he wears his ring, but he has to be extremely close. I would call out to him, but I think that would make me too stupid to live.

Cinders fall from the sky, blown by the malodorous breeze. I hear a giggle near the bridge and have to quell the urge to crouch down. I know I'm invisible, but the creatures here are terrifying and my instinct to run from them is powerful.

Creeping forward, I find a little girl of five or six years old frolicking on the bridge. She has an enormous head that's twice as big as it should be to be in proportion with her torso and legs. Skipping from side to side on the bridge, she leans over the parapet, her pigtails falling toward the red flow. A ripple of chilling giggles emits from her at the writhing corpse-like creatures dangling from hooks on its keystones. I recoil from the scene and almost scream when someone grasps my hand. Reed pulls me down in a crouch near the abutment of the bridge, hugging me. "Werree," he whispers in my ear, pointing to the little girl-monster.

Now that our skin is in contact, I can see him. I throw my arms around him as best I can, considering I have a huge weapon in my grasp. "Reed," I whisper.

"You're so reckless!" Reed says, kissing me like he might die if he doesn't. "Why did you come? You were supposed to stay with the army." His lips tangle with mine again. His arms around me are almost unbearably tight.

"I'm your champion," I murmur. I pull back to look into his lovely green eyes. "Stop trying to leave me out of this."

He touches his forehead to mine. "I never wanted you to see this place. I wanted to show you Paradise."

I cup his cheek with my hand. "I've been there. When we're done here, Reed, paradise will be wherever you are."

Reed pulls away from my embrace, but he slips his hand in mine once more. Leaning near my ear, his voice is low, "I've been tracking Emil. He's going to that city ahead of us."

"That's what my hammer says, too."

"Is your hammer speaking to you?" Reed asks in surprise.

"Yes. It's so much like Finn, Reed. It's him in weapon form."

"We should go." He gets out of his crouch, taking the stairs from the abutment up to the bridge and entering from the side. The little skipping demon doesn't even notice us when we're right beside her. I realize that her head is from some other kind of being because it has black eyes the size of saucers. I shiver. I swing my hammer at its head. It knocks the Werree's real shadowy body out of this scarecrow carcass. The lifeless Werree falls over the side of the bridge.

Reed glances at the pile of doughy flesh hanging on the stone parapet. "Nice one," he whispers, squeezing my hand.

I stop, pulling Reed back to me. His gaze follows mine. On the other side of the bridge, Brennus' soul stands in front of several scary-looking Faeries. His eyes are milk-white, as if a film covers them; I can just make out the green of his irises underneath. White wings rise out of his back and spike at sharp points. His skin is pallid and drawn, especially under his eyes, but his body is solid, like he toils with it daily. The ragged tunic-style clothes he's wearing are from another realm and possibly another time, too. In his hands, he clutches a battle-axe similar to the one the king of the Gancanagh possesses on Earth, except this one glows with Faerie script the color of thistle.

Beside Brennus' soul is the soul of his brother. My weapon tugs my arm, wanting to lead me to the fallen Finn. Behind the two brothers are the souls of other Faeries that I recognize. My heart breaks when I see Declan's soul. He's somewhat like his Gancanagh counterpart, a little older than the rest of them, but just as handsome, except now he has white wings—he never had those as a Gancanagh. I realize he's not the Declan I know. He has never met me. He has no idea who I am, nor does the fair-haired Lachlan. I know him as the one who likes to play cards and teach me spells and who is best friends with Faolan, the dark-haired Faerie standing next to him. I went to Lachlan's funeral on the cliffs. I watched his body burn.

A sinister growl comes from Brennus' soul. It makes my eyes shift back to him. He see's me. I know he sees me, I can feel it like a wolf howling inside my heart. All of their cataract-covered eyes home in on me. I look behind us; Eion's soul is there with more fella souls. We killed most of their Gancanagh counterparts on Zee's island and in Torun. *Stupid Faerie weapon! I'm not invisible to them! It works on Gancanagh, but not Faerie souls!*

Brennus' soul swings his battle-axe menacingly. It arches in lethal patterns, slicing the air with unbelievable speed and deadly thrusts. I want to whimper.

"Keep his attention, Evie. I'll cut them down from behind and we'll escape to the city."

I don't let my eyes leave Brennus' soul as I scowl. "No!" I whisper-shout. "He just doesn't know who I am. I have to free him from here. It's a promise I made."

"The only promises we keep are the ones to destroy Byzantyne and Emil!" Reed retorts.

Brennus' soul springs toward us. He swings his battle-axe so hard it creates wind that blows my hair back. I leap upward into the air to avoid his counter move. Reed flies with me, not letting go of my hand.

We land on the wall of the bridge. "Brennus," I plead, "it's me! It's Genevieve. Your queen—" Brennus' soul nearly takes my head off as his battle-axe comes within millimeters of my neck.

Reed takes to the air once more, hauling me with him. His charcoal-colored wings beating hard, flying toward the nightmarish city. The evil Faeries follow us, careening in and out of other malicious beings that get in their way. The weapon in my hand would like to go back to them, but Reed is so much faster than our pursuers. We fly over the river; bodies float in its current. Tortured souls are driven by pig-headed creatures to construct gorgeous, ornate structures on the outskirts of the city.

Reed flies us to the rooftop of a building that would make the Notre Dame Cathedral in Paris look quaint. He lands on the eave, holding his finger to his lips he walks with me, checking out the space to make sure nothing is sharing it with us. Finding nothing, he takes a deep breath, asking, "Did they hurt you? Did he cut you?" he holds me to him, gently rubbing my back. Ash falls around us like snow. I shake my head. "No. They didn't hurt me. They didn't use magic." I whisper to my hammer, *Be small. Hang on to me.* Reaching over my left shoulder I place the small hammer on my back beneath my wing.

Reed sighs in relief, but then his eyes narrow, "Why didn't they use magic?" he asks.

I shrug. "I don't know. They just didn't."

"Faeries always use magic. It's their thing."

"Maybe they thought it wouldn't work on us because we're angels?"

"Maybe. I've heard rumors..."

"What rumors?"

"I've heard that inside Sheol, not everything will work like it does on the surface of Earth. It's mostly speculation; divine angels rarely have the opportunity to gain first-hand knowledge of this place. I've seen interrogations—torture. None of it was concrete for me until this moment."

"This is all new to you?"

"Well, yes. Is it new to you?"

"Yeah," I say it like that's an understatement.

"When you promised earlier that we'd find a new city and make it our own, I'd like to go on record as passing on this one."

An unexpected giggle tumbles from me. How he can make me laugh in this place at this moment is beyond my comprehension. "Not even a summer home?" I ask.

A *bang* rips between us, making me flinch. As I do, a net drops over Reed's body, pinning him underneath it and making him visible by his silhouette. The rope is shiny and perfect, which makes me think its made of angel hair. I'm forced to let go of Reed's hand when the souls of Lachlan, Faolan, and Declan tackle him. Another bang and I'm harpooned with a net as well; it wraps around my legs and arms, and goes all the way up to my shoulders. I fight against it, but it's strong—angel hair.

Finn's soul puts a knee in my back and twines rope around my wings through the large holes in the mesh. My hands and legs are bound with more rope. He unwraps me from the snare, but the other cords secure me as his prisoner. He hauls me up from the shingles of the rooftop. Slipping a knife to my throat, he pulls the hammer from my back. It goes to him as if it missed him. I become visible to all the demons of this place. Brennus' soul moves out of the shadows, his white staring eyes are on me, but there is no recognition—no hint that he knows me. I move my fingers, whispering a quick spell to break through the binding, but it doesn't work. I try again with a fire spell. Again nothing.

"Brennus," I say in a tortured voice. "I know why you're here. I've come to take you home. Please. Listen to me."

He comes to stand a hair's breadth away. His hand wrenches my chin up, his fingers bruising my flesh. Behind him, the other fellas have drawn their knives, preparing to stab Reed to death. Brennus' soul leans his face down to mine. We're almost nose-to-nose. He growls deep in his throat. My heart beats furiously. "I'm here to free you from Sheol—I have to kill Emil and Byzantyne—you said you'd know me by note! What does that mean?"

Another faerie creeps from the shadows. His voice is sexy and deep when he says something in a Faerie dialect that I understand, although I don't know why. I think for a moment and I realize he said, "She is the one. Secure them. We deliver them to Byzantyne tonight." Brennus' soul lifts his head, complying with the other faerie's orders like a good little drone.

"You must be Aodh," I say in Faerie, watching the souls of Lachlan and Declan drag Reed from the ground, tying the net around him tighter. I can't see his face; he's just a lump in the net.

"I am. And who might ye be?" Aodh's soul asks. He comes

into the half-light. He's strikingly handsome. His long black hair is pulled back from his face and tied behind his head. He has a strong jaw and a sharp chin, and his skin is smooth and pristine. His eyes glow with green fire. White faerie wings arch upward, forming sharp points above his head. I want to throat punch him. Something shifts in me. I become the hunter, picking out all of his weaknesses.

"Brennus sends his love," I say with a smile. Aodh's soul lunges toward me and hits me in the face. It doesn't really hurt. He's not that strong and I'm an angel. I laugh because I know it will enrage him. "Take me to Byzantyne. I dare you. I'll slaughter all of you."

"And ye'll bathe in me blood," he says in a bored tone.

"No." I wrinkle my nose. "Why would I do that? What's wrong with you and your disgusting sense of hygiene?"

He doesn't know how to take that, so he ignores me. "We have found Emil's aingeal. Move dem. I want dis handled before darkness. Dis will earn me a new station in a higher city instead of dis hole we've been livin' in." Brennus' soul takes me in his arms. It's so familiar that I have a hard time remembering this is not the Brennus I know. This one has been in this nightmare for so long he may never remember anything else. I need to keep that in mind —to differentiate the Brennus I know from this Other Brennus.

The white wings of Other Brennus push downward, lifting us off the rooftop. The souls of Declan and Lachlan each take a side of Reed's net, lofting into the red haze of sky with him. We fly between buildings that are a mishmash of styles. It appears that each has tried to outdo the other with ornate embellishment.

We approach a fantastical piece of architecture at the end of the city, near the red river. It hurts my stomach to look at it because it is everything I know about Emil. The building is Rococo, which means it's supremely ornate. Made of stone, the structure soars into the red sky much higher than a stone building should, given its weight. On the façade over hanging the doors, is mounted Emil's enormous carved face, also done in Rococo-style. It's his hooded eyes staring blankly out for ten stories or more

Iniquity

while a twisting, snake-like tongue crawls from his mouth. There are two smaller statues embedded on either side of Emil's face. They're identical, naked likenesses of Simone holding long metal pikes with heads of angels impaled upon them. One angel head is clearly Reed; the other one is that of Xavier.

We enter through the door below Emil's vile stone head. It's cavernous inside. Elegantly dressed angels mill around on plush furniture, sipping sparkling liquid from beautiful glasses. Everywhere I look there's a statue of my inescapable or some carved tribute to him from a past lifetime. Our presence causes a stir—feathers ruffle, high-pitched guffaws pierce the air. The faeries souls don't stop here, but merely cross the room to another one.

The next room we enter is asymmetrical, and heavily laden with ornamental carvings. Chandeliers hang low from the high ceiling. Brennus has to walk around them like trees. This is a type of throne room. There's a balcony above our heads that Emil must use to look down on the peasants. Emil emerges from it. He has shed his golden armor. He stands at the railing attired in black dress slacks, but his chest is bare and he has on a black, silk robe that is open. He doesn't bother to tie it now as he leans his forearms on the railing and looks down at us.

"Simone," he breathes the name, like it's the most exquisite thing he's ever heard. "You've finally come to visit me—after all this time. What do you think of my home?"

"I think it's an ugly shrine to you."

Emil laughs. "That isn't a very nice thing to say, Simone. And if there's one thing about you that I know, it's that you always try to be nice."

"I'm not Simone anymore, Emil."

"Yes, you are. You're still Simone and I'm still Emil and I still own you." He leaps over the railing, falling a story to us. He lands on his feet. Shedding his robe, he unfurls his crimson Seraphim wings. They spread out around him, majestic and primal at the same time. He would be so beautiful to me if I didn't know him, but I do. I know him almost as well as I know myself. He is evil incarnate. He is pretty pain.

Aodh's soul interrupts Emil. "We have delivered her to you intact. We would have our reward."

"DO NOT SPEAK!" Emil's face twists in anger. He doesn't look at Aodh's soul. He only has eyes for me. "Cut her legs free." Other Brennus complies with his order. My legs are unbound. "Have you brought Reed with you? Is that the divine Power, wiggling like a fish in a net?"

I try to distract him from my angel. "What's that around your neck, Emil?"

The evil half Seraph looks down at his necklace, touching the shiny metal whistle that hangs from the chain. "It's a boatswain. I'm sure you recognize it. I believe you have one too, but mine unlocks a much better place than yours will. I have the key to Heaven, my inescapable. I just need to clean up anything on Earth that could threaten our flank before we storm Paradise. That was the reason I invaded Earth today. I started a war. Once the earthbound divine and the Gancanagh are annihilated, there will be few left who will interfere with us as we advance to Paradise and take back our rightful place."

Emil approaches me with a vulture stare. He puts his hand on Other Brennus' shoulder, pushing him away from me. The faerie soul moves back, complying with Emil's will. Emil embraces me, pressing his face to my hair and inhaling my scent. "Ah," he says at last, "I have missed you. I keep telling myself that you're the thorn in my side and I'd like to smash your head in, and that's true, but it's also true that when you're at my mercy, like this, I feel as though I cannot live without you."

"That's because you're a psycho," I reply. "You started a war, and then you ran back here to hide like a coward while other beings fight it for you."

"I see that you have forgotten just how bad your life can be when you anger me, Simone." He puts his arm around my shoulders, leading me across the marble floor to a set of doors below his balcony. Behind us, all of the faeries follow along, bringing Reed with them. Emil opens the door and we enter a darkened room. Soft light from wall sconces make the room feel ritualistic.

A huge slab, altar-like table resides in the center of the room, but it's partly blocked by a Seraph who has his back to us. I shudder. I don't need to see his dark brown eyes to recognize Byzantyne. His wings spread wide as he bends over the altar. I watch his arm pull back, as if he's wrenching something away. I catch sight of what it is when he moves to the side a little. He has just sawed the wing off of another angel. Fear clenches my stomach and I retch. Byzantyne rests the severed wing on the ground, leaning it against the side of the altar. I turn my head and vomit, unable to stop my violent reaction.

Byzantyne turns and faces me at the sound. His hands are red from blood and gore. He steps aside for me to see his victim on the table. My heart turns black and dies in my chest. It's Xavier. My knees weaken, and if it were not for Emil's arm around me, I'd crumble to the floor. "Simone," Byzantyne's smile is crushing. "There you are. You're late. I've already started. I couldn't wait. I know you'll forgive me my impatience. I've waited so long for this moment."

Emil tries to bring me closer to the altar, but I resist him, fighting to stay away. I can't see this. I'll go mad if I see this. *Xavier!*

"There, there, Simone. This is what you need. You have to see this to remember who we are. You need to know that I am your master and you will never be anything but my slave."

Emil drags me to the altar. I shut my eyes, unwilling to look upon the carnage that is Xavier. A hand presses to my forehead, pinning me to Emil's chest. "Look at him, Simone. Look at him, or I kill Reed now!" I open my eyes. I have seen torture before—have experienced it myself in many, many lifetimes. All of that past experience still leaves me unprepared for this. Byzantyne has stripped off the skin from half of Xavier's face and body. My guardian angel is still alive, but it can't be long before shock and trauma render him unable to survive. Xavier's eyes open, he stares at me as if he's seeing a vision before him. There is no fear on his face, only acceptance. "He was willing to die for you," Emil taunts. "He came here to save you only you weren't here, were you? He's always too late. He never helped you much before and now he has failed you again."

The faerie souls move in closer, wanting to see the torture of a Seraph. Other Brennus stands next to me, his white eyes are almost unblinking. Byzantyne lifts another saw in his hand. I flinch and a moan escapes me as I tremble with wracking shakes. Emil lets go of my forehead. I turn my head, trying to think of a way to drown out the sound of the saw. I begin to hum; I don't even know what the tune is until another soft voice joins mine. The humming comes from Other Brennus. It's the melody that his battle-axe sings to me whenever I touch it. Other Brennus' eyes are on me and they're no longer white, but iridescent green with flecks of black in them. I turn my head, seeing Other Finn on my left side. His milky eyes stare straight ahead. In my mind, I think, *Sing your song softly to Finn.*

The hammer in Finn's soul's hand begins to sing at a whispery volume. His eyes change suddenly to bright green. He blinks, and then his eyes connect with mine. "Help me," I mouth the words.

Other Finn looks beyond me to his brother. Other Brennus slips the soul slayer dagger from the sheath on Emil's belt. The two faerie souls stare at one another, until Other Brennus signals his brother with a nod. In unison, they both attack Emil, stabbing and beating him with vicious thrusts. Emil crashes to the floor behind me, his body being quickly transformed into a bloody pulp. Emil's soul rises up from his decapitated angelic body. Other Brennus growls at it. Raising the dagger that was made to kill me, Other Brennus stabs it into Emil's soul. His lazy eyes register agony as his image turns black and explodes in a swirl of ebony smoke. Other Finn faces me, looking at me for his next order. The ropes that bind me fall away as Other Brennus uses Emil's soul slayer to slice through them.

"Kill him," I order, pointing at Byzantyne. The faerie brothers turn their attention to the barbaric Seraph.

Byzantyne has a stricken look on his face. He stumbles back

from the altar, dropping the bone saw. His mouth opens in shock as he sees the mess that was Emil on the ground at my feet. I look away from him to Other Lachlan. I hum Lachlan's song. The faerie soul's eyes turn blue and he blinks, as if he's waking up from a nightmare. I change my tune to Faolan's song. Faolan's soul becomes lucid.

"Set down the net and free the angel inside it," I order the souls of Faolan and Lachlan. They cut the netting off Reed. He springs free of the snare. Pulling the ring from his finger, he becomes visible once more. He drops the ring on the floor as he extracts his spade blades from his wrist holsters.

Reed comes to me, checking quickly to see if I'm okay. Then he crouches down and examines Emil's dead corpse for a moment. When he rises again, he pulls the chain of the boatswain from beneath his armor. He lifts it over his head, transferring it to me. The key to Sheol settles around my neck.

"Why are you giving this to me," I try to take it off.

Reed stays my hand, covering it with his own.

"The faerie souls annihilated Emil's soul, love," Reed replies. "You'll need a way out of here no matter what happens."

"Reed," I say his name in shock.

He lets go of my hand. "I will always love you, Evie. Always." He presses his lips to my forehead, and then he turns and joins Other Brennus and Other Finn in stalking Byzantine. The cornered wicked Seraph pulls a dagger from a sheath attached to his waist, while adopting a defensive crouch. Every time the faerie souls try to get near him, Byzantyne strikes out, nearly decapitating them. Reed moves in. He's so fast that Byzantyne hardly knows he's been cut before he's sliced open again. Reed is killing him slowly and by degrees. His black armor is covered with the arterial spray of Byzantyne's blood.

Aodh's soul sees what's happening and tries to leave, but the souls of Lachlan and Faolan are on him, seizing his arms and binding them with rope. Tearing off his shirt, Faolan's soul stuffs it in Aodh's mouth so no one will hear him scream.

Xavier moans in agony. The sight of his blood running in

rivers off the sides of the altar makes me blanch. I go to him, my hand hesitating above his flesh, not knowing where I can put it that will not cause him excruciating pain. I find his hand and hold it. Lifting his fingers to my lips I kiss them while tears roll down my cheeks. "I'm sorry, Xavier," I whisper.

He opens his mismatched eyes and looks at me. "Now," his feeble voice whispers, "you know how I feel every time I watch you suffer—every time I watch you die." The agony in my chest won't subside. I feel as though I can't breathe.

"I have the advantage here," I reply, wiping my nose with my sleeve, "because I can do something about it. I can take your pain from you."

"Do not, Evie," Xavier groans, his pain nearly unbearable.

"I can't let you die, Xavier."

"You have to," he growls.

"No, I don't." I lay my hand on his chest, urging it to turn golden so that I can take away his pain. Seconds pass and nothing happens. Xavier's breath becomes thready. He sounds as if he's dying. Panic makes me press my palm to him in a different place on his chest, concentrating on taking his wounds into me, but the light that would do it doesn't glow. My ability to heal is gone, or it just doesn't work in this horrible place. I clench my fists again, trying to make it work, but nothing happens. I can't take his wounds from him. I choke. Fresh, hot tears rush to my eyes. "I SURRENDER! DO YOU HEAR ME?" I yell. I look upward. "I surrender! I give up my stipulation in the contract! I forfeit my choice! Do you hear me? Please take Xavier back to Paradise! Don't let him die! *Please!*" My face reddens and my eyes burn. I lay my forehead on Xavier's chest and I cry my heart out.

The music of Angelic voices echoes around me, calling Xavier's name. Opening my eyes, I don't see them, but I feel Xavier's chest fall. I lift my head from my crossed arms. He has become paper-thin, flickering with bursts of light. I lift my arms from his chest. He loses his features as they become dark. A galaxy of stars replaces them. The stars turn shadowy; it shrinks in size until it is just a pinpoint of light, and then Xavier is gone.

Among the blood and guts on the table, I find his ring—the one with the shield and sword on it. I pick it up and slip it into the knife holster on the side of my combat armor. Tilting my face upward, I strain to get the words, "Thank you," past the constriction in my throat.

A scream of pain jolts me from my thoughts. Byzantyne falls to his knees, at least I think he's Byzantyne. The wicked angel is slick with blood and so cut up that he's unrecognizable, except for his hair and what is left of his wings. His head slumps forward on his chest. Reed walks behind him grasping Byzantyne's head by the ear, he wraps his forearm around the evil Seraph's forehead and jerks it to the side, breaking his neck and crushing in his skull.

Reed straightens and looks at me with sorrow in his green eyes. "I can hear them, Evie. They're calling me."

Tears spring to my eyes again. I hear them too, the whispering voices of a multitude of angels. "Then you have to go," I whisper, because I know he can't fight the call of Heaven.

"You could choose me, Evie. You can choose me as your love," he says desperately, looking up at the ceiling as if something is there.

"I do choose you, Reed. I will always choose you as my love." The most beautiful smile I have ever seen passes over his lips.

Reed's body begins to flicker as if he's a piece of film on a screen that isn't threaded properly. His smile fades. "Say it again, Evie."

I take a step closer, saying to him, "I choose you, Reed. You are my love."

Reed's body flashes with light, fading more and more each time. "No!" Reed cries. He becomes flat—two-dimensional. His features fade so that he is no more than a silhouette filled with stars that transforms to just a shadow, fading until he's gone in a pinpoint of light.

"Reed!" I sob. I don't move for a moment. I can't move. Something shines on the floor beside me. I go to it. Crouching down, I pick up Reed's ring and ball it in my fist. The faerie souls come to stand before me, waiting for me to give them an order.

They're all awake now, having freed one another from the curse that was on them. When I still don't move, Other Finn approaches me. He crouches down to my eye level and touches my wing reverently. I glance at him. He extends my battle hammer to me. "Dis belongs ta me queen." He speaks in Faerie to the weapon, it become small once more. He reaches out and puts it on my back. It clings there, singing its melody, trying in its own way to cheer me. I look down at the floor again, lost in sorrow—*tristitiae*.

Other Brennus comes to stand in front of me. He crouches down so that we're face to face. His hand lifts to my cheek; he runs the back of his fingers over it, wiping away my tears. "Ye're me queen. Tell me whah ye need and I will do it for ye."

I lift my eyes to his. "I want to go home," I whisper.

"Show me da way," he replies.

I touch the boatswain around my neck. Putting it to my lips, I play the tones that I used the first time I touched it. In front of us, a doorway to Earth opens up. Other Brennus picks me up off my feet, holding me in his arms as he straightens to full height. Dazzling sunlight shines in on us. The faerie souls shield their eyes from it, unaccustomed to the glare. Other Brennus doesn't flinch, he faces it as if it was an answer to a prayer and carries me into the daylight on the other side.

CHAPTER 26
The Battlefield

Other Brennus strides out of Sheol with me in his arms. Crossing the threshold into my world, he becomes a ghostly soul without substance. No longer able to hold me up, I drop through his arms, landing on the frozen ground that once had snow, but now is charred with only a few grassy areas to cover the mud. Brennus' soul spirits away from me, as if he's an overfilled balloon that's untied and let go. He disappears through a crowd of monsters still fighting on the battlefield where I'd left them. I watch him go, a shiny light in the growing darkness. The ground beneath me shakes from a tremendous explosion. My ears ring at the noise it makes. Dirt rains on me. Screams of anger and anguish fill the air as pieces of angels fall from the sky.

Finn's soul enters Earth's realm, crossing the threshold from Sheol. The same thing happens to him. He loses his Sheol body and his ghost snaps away into the crowd. I rise from the ground, numb and disoriented. I walk without thought of destination. "I'm wi' ye, aingeal," a voice says next to me. I glance beside me, but don't stop walking. It's Declan, but not the Declan I know. He's not Gancanagh; he's Faerie. He pats my wing, his eyes surveying the buzzing swarm of killers surrounding us. "Dey've given me a second chance—a new body—'tis like me old one—da one I had before Aodh..." he doesn't finish.

"Who has given you a second chance?" I ask.

"Heaven," Declan replies, "and ye. I will na fail ye, me queen."

Declan snatches up a discarded sword next to a dead angel. A troll runs toward me with his arms raised above his head. The blade of his hatchet is poised to cleave me in two. I stare at the bald creature, numb, wondering what it will feel like to be cut down by him. Declan raises his sword to block the hatchet, but the troll bursts into flames from an elf dart thrown at him by Eion. Faolan and Lachlan run on ahead of me, blocking clashing demons from getting too close.

"I hate trolls," Eion grumbles beside me, while scanning the sky to make sure nothing is targeting me from above, "dey smell like arse."

My sense of déjà vu is not helping with my sense of unreality. I keep walking, but everything is a violent blur. Ogres clash with angels and Werree pick through the abandoned flesh of corpses. More faeries join us, spreading out around me: Goban, Alastar, Cavan, Eibhear, Torin, Lonan, and Ninian. I stumble when Keegan moves beside me. He has a dagger. The blade reflects the color of his red hair right before he plunges it into the skull of the fallen angel who tries to reach me in the center of their circle.

"Keegan," his name falls from my lips. He was the first being I ever killed. I slaughtered his Gancanagh counterpart in the copper mines in Houghton when I had to fight him. Keegan yanks his dagger from the angel's forehead as the Power crashes to the ground. He glances at me, concern in his eyes. "Me queen, are ye well? Do ye need me ta carry ye?" My world spins. I'm dizzy. My hand rests on his shoulder. His arm goes around my back, supporting me.

"You're alive," I breathe. I touch his face as tears well up and spill down my cheeks. "I didn't want to kill you. I didn't…"

"Ye did na kill me. Aodh did. Ye saved me from Sheol." I nod my head stroking his face. I can hardly breathe. "We have ta go. We have ta get ye ta safety."

I nod again, too overwhelmed to be able to speak. A series of explosions rock the ground. Keegan and I are both knocked sideways. My fingers trip over the silky softness of my feathers. The acrid smell of smoke is all around me as my head lies against the grassy ground. Above me, angels are flying, moving chaotically.

Fire rains across the dusky skyline, turning what is left of the blue filament to red and orange as giant rockets burst and riot. The explosions make the ground tremble. There is a pain in my belly; fear twists it. A shrill roar causes all the hairs on my body to stand up at once. I've never heard its like and I dread seeing what is capable of making such a sound.

As I sit up, my head throbs painfully. Using my trembling hands, I rest my head in them, hoping that the world will stop spinning. From the corner of my eye, I see an armored-clad Power angel flying low to the ground near me. His forward trajectory switches in the sky as a hulking Seraph broadsides him. They rapidly lose altitude, plummeting towards me.

When the warring angels tumble to the ground only a few feet away, my hands go up to cover my head and I brace myself for their impact. Rather than being crushed by them, I'm scooped up and thrown over someone's shoulder. My cheek rests against his strong, blood-colored wing. Yelling in Angel echoes in the air as carnage from the war waging around me litters the ground.

From my position, I see my faeries rise from the ground as well. They chase after us, hacking at attacking beasts that try to stop them from getting to me. There's a small clearing where divine angels stand guard. We land there and the Seraph puts me on my feet. I straighten, noticing the red armor of my father's army. I'm disappointed to see gray eyes instead of brown and auburn hair instead of tawny. Tau waits for me to speak, scanning me with critical eyes. I glance down at myself. My black armor is covered with mud and blood. My hair is caked with dirt and tangled in knots. I must look like hell.

"Do you have the boatswain?" Tau asks in a voice one would use when speaking to a frightened child.

"Yes," I answer blankly.

"Can you do something for us?" he asks. The feathers of his red wings are stirred by the wind

"Who's us?"

"All the divine angels fighting on this battlefield right now."

"What do you want me to do?"

"Will you close the gateway to Sheol? The Fallen are retreating into it. We'd like to cut off their escape." I look away from him. He's right, the path to Sheol is still open and monsters are fleeing into it. Tugging the boatswain from beneath my armor, I put it to my lips, piping out the key that will lock it down. Tau moves a short distance away to get a better view. The fabric of our world knits together, closing off the way in to Sheol.

I stare at Tau. His hands are braced behind his back as he watches the carnage from this clearing on a hill. He looks like a general surveying his troops. For him, this might be what it's all about, what it has always been about—finding ways to draw Fallen out of Sheol—setting dangerous traps by using enticing bait to lure them. Maybe all this ever was about is the war of Heaven and Sheol.

Or maybe it isn't. "I found Xavier."

Tau stops breathing for a moment, but he doesn't turn to look at me. "Is he dead?"

"No. He ascended. You will see him again when you return."

"What happened?"

I can't even begin to explain it to him. I don't think I'll be able to ever speak of it. "He'll tell you."

"And Reed?" Tau asks. His name, said aloud, is a knife wound in my heart.

"He ascended, too."

"Then your contract with Heaven and Sheol is fulfilled?" When Tau sees the look of confusion on my face, he adds, "Xavier told me the deal you made."

"Byzantyne ceases to be…Emil has been annihilated—body and soul."

"You are extraordinary, Evie," Tau says, his eyes shining with pride.

"No. I'm just done," I reply in a thready voice, "with all of it."

"There is no done. Not while we're at war with Sheol."

I don't argue with him. There's no point. He has his views on my life and I have mine. Only time will tell who is right. Instead, I move away from him toward the line of angels who are protecting us from the fray. Tau calls after me, "You haven't asked me about your friends." I halt and am unable to move forward even though I need to leave. *I won't survive it if one of them was killed.* I glance over my shoulder at him, my eyebrow rising.

"They ascended."

My knees become weak. My first reaction is relief, but I need to clarify, "All of them?"

"All of them."

"Buns and Brownie?"

"Yes. The Reapers were taken by Heaven right after you left for Sheol, and from what I understand, they were not happy about it."

"Zephyr?"

"The Power stayed for some of the battle, but he was pulled home when he was injured—" Tau holds up his hands when he sees my eyebrows take the shape of concern, "—nothing that cannot be mended. He went with Preben, who is also your friend, yes?"

I nod. "And Russell?" I whisper his name.

"He wanted to stay—he wanted to wait for you. He said he knew you'd be back and he was going to wait by where the door had been until you got back, but Anya was injured and when she ascended, he went with her."

"Did he say anything else?" I ask.

"There wasn't time."

"Of course," I murmur absently. I look away from him. There's an argument brewing just down the hill between divine angels and my faeries who have collected there. They're demanding the return of their queen.

"You have a job to do," Tau says. "It's why you didn't ascend."

"A job?" I don't really care what *they* want me to do.

"You saved the faeries. You can save more."

"How can I do that?"

"You can do that by helping Brennus."

"I'm not following you."

"He has a mission. He has created thousands of Gancanagh throughout the years. He now has a chance to save them—to give them a second chance. He'll need your help to do it."

"Why do you think I can help?"

"You could be a team. You and he could use the boatswain to find faerie souls in Sheol, rescue them, and reunite them with their Gancanagh counterparts on Earth."

"What if they're evil?" I ask.

"You would watch them, if they continue to disappoint once they return from Sheol, you would send their souls back."

"Revoke their green cards?"

"You could start with Molly," Tau says offhandedly.

An excruciating ache squeezes my heart at the thought of my childhood friend. "You know what Brennus says about Heaven?" I ask.

"No, what does he say?"

"He says Heaven knows all your secrets. They know exactly the right buttons to push to get us to do what they want."

"I've been told that he possesses an uncanny sense of intuition. So you'll do it—for Molly?"

"I'll do it." My voice is a whisper on the wind.

"Mo chroí," Brennus calls from behind me. The sharp points of his white wings meet my gaze as I turn to find him moving toward me from down the hill. His black hair falls onto his brow, over skin that's flawless—a normal hue, turning rosy from the crisp air. The black armor he wears is streaked with mud and blood. He's no longer Gancanagh; his soul has merged with his body and he's Faerie once more.

I've never felt so lost. I stumble toward him. Falling into the shelter of his arms, I hide my face against his chest, trying to blot out the violence around me. His heartbeat is fast and strong, and wrapped in the sound of it, I feel safer. "Help me, please," I manage to say. Holding onto him with weak fingers, my knees buckle beneath me.

He picks me up. "I will, mo chroí. I'll protect ye wi' me life." He turns us away from Tau and takes me down the hill to the faeries waiting for us.

Finn is at our side. His soul has merged with his Gancanagh body. He's no longer undead; he has become a faerie once more. His white wings spread wide when he looks upon me. "Ye did it, Genevieve. Ye saved us." The respect in his look just about breaks me. He goes down on his knee, bowing his head. All of the faeries except Brennus who holds me follow his action, getting on their knees. "We pledge our lives ta ye, me queen, for now and forever."

When he rises, I can hardly see him through my tears. Brennus notices my distress. "I'll take ye home now, if I may?" he asks.

I nod my head, unable to speak. Brennus gives a perfunctory nod, looking beyond me to Finn. "I'll meet ye dere, brother." Finn steps back from us. Brennus whispers a spell. A soft glow emits from us. The battered skyline with its smoke-filled night fades from view, gradually replaced by an elegant bedroom. It's just the two of us. I hear movement in other parts of the building—the faeries are arriving home, but we're alone on this floor.

He sets me on my feet. "Finn worked on yer room for ye. If ye do na like it, we can change it."

The room is bright and timeless with a lovely bed all in white and two soft chairs that face a fireplace. Brennus waves his hand and the pile of logs in it catches fire. There's a row of windows that show the fading light. Snow piles in waves on the windowsills. A full-length mirror nestles in the corner of the room. Brennus goes to a beautiful armoire. Finding a set of cotton pajamas, the kind I like, he brings it to the bed and lays it on the gorgeous coverlet.

"Do you know what they want us to do?" I ask.

He nods. "Atwater found me, jus after I transitioned back ta Faerie. He explained da path of redemption ta me."

"Are you going to do it?"

"'Tis a chance for me ta right all dat I've done wrong, Genevieve. I'll take it and be grateful. Will ye join me in it?" he asks.

"I will," I murmur. "Do you...do you remember me?"

"I tink I remember everyting—whah happened while I was Gancanagh and whah happened ta me soul while I was in Sheol."

"Is that good or bad?" I ask.

"Both. Ye need ta rest now. Can I help ye wi' yer armor?" I nod, presenting my back to him. He brushes my hair from my nape, causing goose bumps to rise on my flesh. Magic glows from his hand as he runs his finger down the spine of my armor. It opens, revealing my skin beneath.

I shy away. Facing him, I say, "Thank you. I can manage the rest."

He nods, my awkwardness making him smile. "As ye wish. Dere is a shower tru dere." He indicates a door attached to the room. "'Tis a lot like Ireland."

"It is," I agree. I know he means the room, but I mean it all.

"Me room is next ta yers. We share dis wall," he indicates the wall behind my headboard. "If ye need me, ye jus need ta call for me."

"Thank you," I murmur, holding the front of my armor. He nods. Without a word, he crosses the room to the door and leaves me alone. I walk to the bathroom. Peeling the black armor from me, clods of dirt fall off of it, scattering mud on the white tiles and bathmats. I leave it in a heap on the floor. I don't cry when the water hits me. I'm too numb to think. Standing for what must be an hour under the shower, I let it keep the thoughts of Hell and loss from me. When the water starts to get cold, I shut it off. Finding a towel, I move back to the bedroom. The pajamas on the bed are perfect. I dry off quickly, and don them.

Sitting at the small vanity, I brush my hair. My hand stills with my brush in mid-stroke. I gaze at my reflection in the mirror. The low neckline of my cami-style top reveals my skin over my heart. Reed's charcoal-colored wings are gone. My binding mark has been stripped from my flesh, leaving behind no indication that it ever happened—that Reed ever loved me. I set down the brush and rise from the vanity. Crawling into the enormous bed, I curl up in a ball and I grieve.

CHAPTER 27
Da Faeries

I wake up after only a few hours of sleep. My eyes are swollen from crying. At first, I don't know where I am. Everything is dark. Everything is unfamiliar. I dare not breathe. Then I remember where I am and why. Overwhelming fear and sorrow crashes in on me. Cold desperation makes it feel as if the earth is shaking, but I realize it's just me trembling in my bed. I pull the blanket up to my chin.

"Do ye need anyting?" Brennus' voice comes from the chair by the fireplace. He has pulled his wings into him, so he looks like the Brennus I know. I didn't think I could be more scared than I was a second ago, but I was wrong.

I sit up in bed and reach for the lamp next to it. A soft glow illuminates the room. It shines on his skin, showing the vibrant color of his handsome face. He is extremely beautiful as a faerie, even more attractive than when he was a Gancanagh. I turn the light off again. Somehow the dark feels safer. I can see Brennus just fine with my angel vision and I know he can see me too. "Why are you here?" My voice sounds like someone else's.

"Ye were screamin'. I tought ye needed me, but when I came in here, I found ye asleep."

My dreams have turned against me. I'd had a nightmare of angels tearing the skin from Xavier—I couldn't find Reed. He was gone—he *is* gone. "There's nothing you can do."

"In a very real way ye died yesterday. Ye'll never be da same.

Do na try ta be."

He's right. The life that I knew, the one I wanted, was slaughtered in Sheol. Emil may be dead, but he's still inescapable. I'll carry him around inside of me forever. The pain in my chest is unbearable and it only grows.

"What do I do?" I ask. Anguish is the bitterest poison beneath my skin.

"Ye go on from here. Ye learn from da past, but ye try na ta live in it. 'Tis gone and ye can change none of it."

My heart aches. The thread that Reed held has unraveled me. I panic. Without Reed, I'm vulnerable to the darkness. He always kept me from thinking of all the creatures that would like nothing better than to bring me to my knees. My teeth chatter. I'm chilled to the marrow of my bones.

Brennus comes to me. He sits upon the bed, taking me into his arms. "Hush now, mo chroí. Lay yer head here." He lets me rest my cheek on his chest. "Ye're in shock."

"I'm so lost," I whisper. I have no guard to put up. I'm defenseless.

"Ye will find yer way. I will help ye. Ye will never be alone. I promise ye." His deep voice speaks in some language long forgotten. I know it. I don't know how I know it, but I do. It calms me. The backs of his fingers are golden upon my cheek. "We'll heal our scars one day and be who we are." He enchants me. I close my eyes. In my dreams I run and scream with peals of laughter. Brennus dances with me through fields of green, under the fairest sun.

~

THE FIRST FEW weeks after our return from Sheol are a blur. I have days where I cannot get out of bed, even when I don't sleep. I squander those days. I count the cracks in the ceiling, listening to whispered notes of a piano played by one of the faeries somewhere in the house. In many ways I'm very much in the company of strangers. The faeries who were killed and had no

Gancanagh bodies to return to, like Declan and Eion, do not remember their time on Earth as undead creatures. They only remember Sheol and their lives as faeries before Aodh. Brennus and Finn remember it all.

Nightmares plague me, but I don't sleep very long, so my torture becomes less and less. I focus on creating a routine. I try to do all the things that will break me out of the enslavement of sorrow. The one thing I find that helps most is work. The job I've come here to do, hunting down Gancanagh and freeing their faerie souls from Sheol, becomes my new obsession, something to live for.

Time passes quickly with so much to do. I rise every morning and dress in black leggings and a black t-shirt, which will easily allow me to slip into combat armor later if needed. I wrestle my long hair into a ponytail at the crown of my head and jog downstairs to have breakfast with the fellas. I know they're technically no longer "fellas," but I can't stop myself from thinking of them that way. In the kitchen, I take a seat beside Finn who has set a place for me. I smile at him; it's automatic. He smiles back, chewing his pancakes. He hands me a dossier of our next client. I scan the file as I pour syrup on my pancakes. "Ohh... Bruno's bio reads like a terrorist's resume. Do you think he can be saved?"

Finn shrugs. "He's a demon, but I try na ta judge. Most o' da vilest Gancanagh I know weep at da sight of ye, but others dat I tink will be easy conversions end up makin' us send deir souls back ta Sheol."

I nod, knowing exactly what he means. "Is there any news on the other?" I ask. It's a delicate subject; one I usually don't broach this early in the morning.

Finn stiffens. "Dere has been no sign o' her. I may have taught Molly too well. I should've been less comprehensive on how ta avoid Brennus and da fellas."

"We'll find her. She has to agree to everything before we can hunt for her soul in Sheol."

"A contract must be made wi' her. I know da rules."

"Sorry," I murmur, "I know you do."

Brennus walks into the kitchen. He selects an orange from the giant bowl of them on the stone island. Tossing it in the air, he catches it. Walking behind my chair, his hand rests on my shoulder. He squeezes it. I tip my face up at him and smile. "Good morning," I say.

He leans down and kisses my cheek. "Good morning," he replies.

He looks over at the file in front of me. "Bruno Sarcasey?" He frowns. "Is he yer client today, mo chroí?"

"He is up to bat." I say, looking at my plate. I butter my toast.

"I should take dis one." Brennus picks up Bruno's dossier.

"Drop it, faerie. He's moin." I smirk, using his accent to humor him and ease his anxiety. He worries too much about me. If anyone should be worried, it should be me. I listen to him in the next room every night while he tries to sleep. He has terrible nightmares, too. Whenever I go to him, he's drenched in sweat and pawing at the air, fighting unseen demons. He tries to hide it during the day, but he's tortured, just like the rest of us. "Anyway, don't you have that thing with Atwater?"

"Whah ting?"

"That thing…the meeting?"

"Oh, dat." He gives an irritated shrug. "I can put dat off. He hasn't even said why he wants ta see me."

"Then you should seriously take the meeting. If he didn't say, it's bad."

"'Tis always bad. He's an aingeal," he replies.

"I resemble that comment." I feign outrage.

He waves his hand dismissively. "Ye're na one of dem. Ye're one o' us. Da queen."

I smile and rise from my chair, taking my empty plate. I slip the file from his grasp. "You're forgiven. Eat your orange. I'm going to go give Bruno a look see." I walk toward the sink.

"Ye're takin' da fellas wi' ye, are ye na?"

"I am not. I'm just going to get eyes on him. I won't approach him yet."

"Dat was na a request," Brennus says scornfully. "Ye do na go anywhere wi'out protection."

I rinse my plate, before sliding it in the dishwasher. "Keegan," I say, speaking to the redheaded faerie near Brennus. "What are you doing in an hour?"

"I'm going wi' ye ta get eyes on Bruno."

"Happy?" I ask Brennus.

"Na even close."

I sigh. "Declan, Lachlan, and Faolan, can you come with me in an hour?"

"Aye," they all say in unison, while continuing to eat.

I give Brennus a there-you-go gesture. "Happy now?"

"Trilled," he says with a sarcastic smile.

∼

BRUNO, it turns out, is a wan-loving playboy with poor business practices and a really scary sense of style. From our position in the abandoned building across the street from his warehouse, I have an unfettered view of our target and his over-sized lapels.

"He's an arms dealer," I murmur.

"He is," Declan growls. "He recently sold me a chillax charm dat jus about blew me face off. I say we end him on principle."

"Why were you buying a chillax charm from him?" I ask.

"Never ye mind," Declan replies. "Have ye seen enough yet? I have some personal tings I want ta take care of today."

"What things?"

"Personal. Tings," Declan replies. "I agreed ta stay longer wi' ye while da other fellas followed Bruno's connection ta da freight yards. Ye could say tanks."

"Tanks. I guess I've seen enough." I pack up my stuff, shoving it in my backpack. My battle hammer sings when I touch it, it makes me smile. "Shh, little brudder!" I say to it before closing the bag. "I know what will make you happy, Deck. We could stop and get those paczki you like in Poletown."

"Da ones wi' da butter cream?" he asks.

"Uh-huh and coffee." Now that Declan eats real food, we have so much more in common.

"'Tis on da way ta one of me errands."

"Oh," I ask, "what do you have to do?" We walk through the dilapidated building to the windows on the other side. We jump five stories to the ground, landing on our feet.

"I have ta pick up me lucky shirt from da cleaners."

I wrinkle my nose. "That's why we have to leave."

"Genevieve, I have a date."

"Shut. Yer. Gob!" I get into his nineteen-seventies black Cadillac. The white leather of the seat squeaks as I slide over and close the door. I open the window because it's grown hot in the sun. It's been a warm spring. "Who is she? He?"

"She. And ye do na know her."

"When do I get to meet her?"

"I will let ye know."

"Please do!" I smile. I catch Declan smiling, too.

He drives through town to the dry cleaner. I get out with him and say, "I'll meet you at the paczki place. I'll get a dozen of the kind you like."

"Get two. Eion will eat a dozen by himself." I nod and walk in the direction of the bakery. I cross the street and jog down the sidewalk. I'm almost to the corner when someone grabs me by the throat and drags me into the alley.

Bruno lifts me off the ground and bashes me into the side of the building. I wince as pieces of the brick wall crumbles to the pavement. "Who are ye?" he snarls. He has one of his Gancanagh crew with him. The thug is rummaging through my bag.

"You don't want to do that," I mutter to the undead faerie with the eyebrow piercings holding my bag.

"Whah have we here?" piercings asks with avarice in his tone.

"That's little brudder, and he hates it when undead faeries mess with him."

Something stirs in my belly. It feels like butterflies. My eyes widen. Bruno punches me hard in the stomach. The air in my lungs is forced from me. I gasp. Without speaking, I give my hammer a command, *Fly to me, little brudder.* My weapon is in my hand in less than an instant. Swinging it at Bruno's head, I crack his skull and knock him sideways. I gaze down at him sprawled on the ground, holding his head. "If you would just listen to me for a moment, I will explain *why* I'm here and *why* you want me here. I have a proposition for—" Before I can finish, there's a blur of charcoal-colored wings. Bruno and his piercing associate are nearly torn in half and their bodies thrown into a dumpster at the end of the alley. Reed drops a lighter into it. It ignites into flames.

Reed is in front of me in an instant, cupping my cheek. "Are you hurt?" he asks. He checks me for wounds. "Did they hurt you?" His angelic face frowns in concentration. I'm speechless, unable to move. All I can do is shake my head no. He picks up my bag from the ground and hands it to me. I hold it for about a second, and then drop it. Reed frowns. "I know I'm technically not supposed to kill your clients unless they show definite intent to murder you, but he hit you, so to me that's intent."

I find my voice. "What are you doing here?" I don't sound like me.

"What do you mean?" he frowns. "I'm guarding you."

I blink. "Why?"

"It's my job."

"You're job?"

"You don't know?" he stares at me, his face becoming hopeful all of a sudden.

I shake my head. "Know what?"

"You don't know that I'm your guardian angel?" he asks. Little brudder drops from my hand, falling with a clank on the concrete.

My eyes fill up with tears. "Did Xavier die?" I try to hold back my sob.

Reed puts his hands on my shoulders and says softly, "No. He's alive. He has been reassigned. I won the position."

"You won it?"

"I had to fight for it, but in the end, the job was awarded to me. Nobody told you?" he asks.

"No," I whisper.

"So that's why you haven't come to see me?" His beautiful lips begin to turn up in the corners

"Come to see you? How long have you been here?" I choke.

"Months, Evie. I've been here months, just like you."

"Who knew?" Anger flourishes inside me.

"Atwater."

"Why wouldn't he tell me?"

"I don't know."

"Why didn't you come see me?"

"There are new rules for being your guardian angel, Evie. I'm not allowed to interfere with your life unless you seek me out or you are threatened. You didn't seek me out."

"I didn't know you were here."

"So…you still love mm—" I lean forward, covering his lips with mine. I meant it to be gentle, but he reacts almost violently, threading his fingers in my hair and kissing me as if there will never be enough of me for him. He holds me to him, dragging me with him midway down the alley. He pushes in a locked steel door as if it were made of paper. Kissing me as he guides me inside, I vaguely realize it's some kind of bike repair shop by the old tires hanging on hooks on the wall. Judging by the dust in here, I don't think anyone has gotten her bike fixed in awhile.

Reed pushes me against a large workbench. Our lips remain together as he lifts me up on the edge of it while I strip away my jacket. The intensity of desire his hands elicit when he touches my skin is agony and ecstasy. I shudder with need for him, as his kisses tease me with paradise. He peels my shirt from me. I lift his over his head.

My feathers dust the workbench when they unleash from my back. He groans as his hand cups my jaw. He covers my parted lips with his. Trailing kisses down my neck, he pauses when his lips come to my heart. It no longer has his mark on it. He rubs his thumb over the place where it had been. "I grieve that I no longer carry your wings on me," Reed says. His eyes reflect hollowness. "But not seeing mine on you is agony to me." My heart responds to his words, bludgeoning the walls of my chest trying to get to him. "You're mine, no matter if you have my symbol on your skin or not," he growls, possessively. The primitive way in which my body quivers is telling. There is no need for words between us now. He shows me how fiercely he missed me with every feverish touch of his body against mine.

∽

REED BRINGS my shirt to me. Reaching out to take it, I pause when his other hand touches my necklace. Reed's warm fingers lift it from my skin. Dangling like charms from it are his ring, the boatswain, and Xavier's ring.

"You have my ring."

I unlock the clasp and take his ring from the chain. "I kept it safe for you, hoping that one day I could give it back to you." He slips it on his finger while I close the clasp of my necklace. I retract my wings before slipping my shirt down over the key to Sheol to hide it from sight.

"You have Xavier's ring as well," Reed says. "Do you hope to one day give it back to him?"

The tension in his voice makes me look at him. "I don't know," I say breathlessly. "I only know that I couldn't leave it in Sheol."

Reed twists his ring as if he's lost in thought. "Do you want to come over to my house? I want to show you something."

"You have a house?"

"It's not actually mine. It's more of a headquarters at the moment."

"Where?"

"I'll show you."

"Oh, so it's a surprise?" I ask.

"It is."

His talk of home makes me remember my home and the fact that I was supposed to be there over an hour ago! "I have to go, Reed!" I say with my eyes growing wide. "They'll be worried about me. I'm usually never late. Oh no! Declan! I forgot about

Declan!" I try to pull my jacket on, but the sleeves are inside out. I shake my arm until I can get it into the sleeve. Rushing over to Reed, I go up on tiptoes and kiss him quickly on the lips. "Do you know where I live?"

"Of course," he answers, beginning to frown.

"Pick me up there in an hour." I hurry to the door.

"Evie, wait!"

I press my back against the door, opening it. "I have to tell them that I'm okay. They're very protective of me."

"I'll take you there." Reed follows me.

"I have to talk to him alone, Reed." I reply. "He won't understand."

"Brennus?"

"Yes."

"I'll make him understand." The threat in his tone is implicit.

"That's exactly what I don't want."

I enter the alley. Declan is leaning against the brick wall, holding my bag in one hand and my battle hammer in the other. He straightens; he's been waiting for me. I cringe, knowing what he must have heard. He gives me my things with a stoic look. "I tink ye dropped dese."

"Thank you," I mutter, accepting my bag from him. I place my battle hammer in it and close it.

Declan glances at Reed. "Aingeal, I did na know ye were back."

"That seems to be a theme here," Reed replies with irritation.

Declan's attention shifts to me. "I guarantee Brennus did na know either, Genevieve."

"I'm going to find out exactly who knew what and when." I move down the alley. Declan matches my stride. "I'll see you later, Reed."

"One hour, Evie," Reed replies.

I stop and look over my shoulder at him. "I'll be waiting."

Declan leads me to his car. We get in and he wheels it around and drives in the direction of our home. "I'm sorry if I scared you, Declan. I never made it to the shop."

"I found Bruno in da dumpster. I take it he's a 'no' for redemption." He raises his eyebrow.

"Reed's my guardian angel," I blurt out.

Declan looks straight ahead at the road. "Dat's a little awkward."

"Atwater knew."

"Atwater always knows. He's older dan dirt—older dan da sky by two."

"I'm sorry that I messed up your date."

He smiles like it's the least of his worries. "I'm beginning ta tink dat me lucky shirt is na so lucky," he says and despite everything, I laugh. "I can reschedule it. Maybe 'tis insane of me ta want ta go on a date a tall."

"No, it's not insane. It's necessary. What's the point of having a life if you don't live."

"Ye're a wise queen." He pulls up to the walkway that leads into the part of the estate where I reside.

I go inside. The first fella I see is Eion. He's chewing a piece of apple while he sits in the den cleaning weapons. He's constantly eating since his return from Sheol. "Do you know where Brennus is?" I ask, watching him swab the barrel of a gun. He swallows, and then blows into the barrel, expelling lint out of the bottom of it.

"He's in his office wi' Atwater. They've been arguing for hours. Ye do na want ta go in there."

"That's exactly where I want to go," I reply. I walk in the direction of Brennus' office.

"Call me if ye need me," Eion shouts. "I've sworn ta protect ye, na dem."

Finn is leaning against the doorframe to Brennus' office with his arms crossed. He frowns when he sees me, as if the situation just got worse. "Ye do na want ta go in there, Genevieve."

"Yes I do," I reply with relative calm. I open the door. It's dark inside the room. The curtains have been drawn and the lights are low. Atwater is leaning against the windowsill with his arms crossed. I look for Brennus behind his desk, but the chair is empty. Instead, I find him in the far corner of the room. He's in a black leather chair sitting beneath the dim glow of a floor lamp. In his hand is a glass filled with an amber liquid.

"Yer aingeal has returned, mo chroí," Brennus announces. Ice rattles in his glass as he takes a sip.

"You didn't know?" I ask.

Brennus laughs scornfully. "No. How could I know when Heaven is so good at keepin' secrets?"

"You knew, though," I say, looking at Atwater. His lionlike features are more pronounced in shadow.

He turns his diamond-shaped irises to look at me. "I did."

"And you didn't think that it was important to tell me that my aspire has returned to me as my guardian angel?"

Atwater shrugs. "He's no longer your aspire."

I take exception to that. "He is. He's branded on my heart and I can feel him there, even if you cannot see his mark. Why would you do that to me? Why would you keep him from me?"

"It was important that you be here without any distractions. You needed to become a unit—to bond with one another. You were doing that." He gestures to Brennus and me.

"You're against this. You're against Reed returning as my guardian angel." I ask Atwater.

His blue wings flutter. "It's a setback."

"A setback?" I ask incredulously.

"You have a destiny, Evie."

"And I'm fulfilling it. It's my life. You don't get to dictate all of the aspects of it."

"You cannot see the big picture."

"You're keeping something from me. What is it?" They both remain silent. I put up my hands. "Fine. I'm moving out. I'm going to live with my aspire."

"Please take some time to consider—"

Turning, I leave the room. I go to my bedroom and pack some things in my bag. Brennus joins me. He watches me move about the room, collecting items that I'll need. His silence is awful. I have to break it. "I love him."

He sighs wearily. "Ye love him, ye love me, ye love dem—ye love us all."

I rub my forehead in frustration. "Reed started all of this. He's the reason we're here now."

"He's na da reason we're here now. Ye have no idea where ye come from, do ye?"

"I have a pretty good idea. I have a rather long memory now."

"I'm talking about da time before yer memories began—before a Russell or a Xavier ever existed."

"What are you saying?" I ask, fear erupting in the core of my being.

"One day I'll be able ta show ye whah I'm talkin' about. One day ye'll need no tellin'."

"I have to go."

"Den ye have ta go. But ye come back. Ye live here wi' us when he's away. We protect ye as da Keeper of Da Key of Sheol and our queen."

"Okay." I try to move past him.

He puts out his hand and holds my elbow. "Ye still have a job ta do."

"And I'll do it," I assure him. "We're a team, you, me, and the fellas. I will hold up my end of it."

"And I'll hold up moin, mo chroí. I promise ye."

CHAPTER 28
I Am The Messenger

Reed is waiting for me in a shiny red SUV when I emerge from the old church portion of the seminary. Getting out of the driver's seat, he opens my door for me when I reach the end of the walkway. "Hello," he says, leaning down and kissing me. It's more than a quick peck.

"Hi," I say breathlessly, my heart beating faster just because I'm near him. He takes the bag in my hand from me. I climb into the seat. He closes my door. He's in his seat in a millisecond, starting the car.

"Do you have everything you need?" he asks.

As he pulls away from the curb, he studies the rearview mirror. "We're being followed," he says softly. At least three cars of fellas trail us.

"I'm sorry," I sigh the words. "You expected that though, right?'

"I did."

"I'm their queen, Reed. They've sworn to protect me."

"I know. I will try to be okay with it."

"Thank you. So where are we going?"

"Tau gave me his home to stay in for as long as we need it." I know the place he's talking about. It's one of the biggest mansions in Grosse Pointe on Lake Shore Drive, right on the water.

"Is he there?" I ask.

"No. He's currently in Paradise with your mother."

"Is he happy?"

"He is."

I'm silent for the rest of the ride, thinking about my father. I wish things could have been different, but maybe, when I see him again, they will be. Reed drives through an open wrought-iron gateway into a circular drive. He parks in front of the graceful French Normandy style façade I know fairly well from hanging out with Xavier in high school. The house is built from limestone and the roof is covered with slate. The copper accents have a verdigris patina that compliments the limestone.

Reed turns off the car. He gets out and comes around to open my door for me. Taking his hand, he leads me into the house through the stone-carved frame surrounding the front door. We walk beneath the enormous chandelier in the foyer, crossing the room to the impressive formal living room that overlooks Lake St. Clair. The room has exquisite glass windows on one wall. The other walls are paneled in the finest carved wood, housing recessed bookshelves. The furniture is impeccable. He takes both of my hands in his and looks into my eyes.

"Evie, I know that our hasty binding ceremony was not what you ever expected would happen when you risked everything to find me in Dominion. I have thought since then that we should renew our commitment under less dire circumstances. Now that we are no longer bound to one another, we have the unique opportunity to do everything exactly the way you'd like to do them. I love you. I will always love you. Will you commit to me again? Will you bind your life with mine?

My eyes cloud with tears. "Yes, of course I'll bind to you, Reed." He exhales deeply. Picking me up off of my feet, he swings me around before setting me down. He kisses me with heart-stopping sweetness, teasing my lips and making me hunger for more.

I have something I need to show you," he says. He puts his hand to his neck, tugging a chain from beneath his collar. Attached to the chain there is a golden charm in the form of a boatswain. I recognize it at once. It's the whistle Emil wore in

Sheol. "Just as you're the keeper of the key of Sheol, Evie, I protect the one to Paradise."

"You took Emil's key—in Sheol." I say in awe. I reach up and touch the charm that shines with an ethereal light.

"Just before I gave you your key when we were in Sheol, I took Emil's off of his corpse. I couldn't leave it there. I thought I would return it to Earth with us, but I ascended with it instead."

"So, you can open a door to Paradise with this whenever you want to?"

"I could, in theory, but there are strict rules regarding how or when I can use it."

"Which are?" I ask.

"I'm not allowed to tell you."

"Of course not."

"But," Reed grins, "this job comes with some perks." He tugs me with him as he walks backwards so he can still face me. I follow him.

"What perks?" I ask. "A 401K?"

"No."

"A retirement plan?"

"Nope." He brushes up against a huge door. Twisting the handle, he throws it open. Inside the brightly lit room that is similar to the one we just came from, Buns and Brownie are arguing about who has the best destination getaway idea for my binding ceremony. Zephyr is killing Russell at chess. Anya is snuggling a gray kitten in her lap. And Preben is arguing with Phaedrus over what, exactly, a miracle entails.

"The best perk of the job," Reed says, "is that I get to have a team to help me protect the key." I stare inside the room, unable to move right away.

Buns and Brownie notice us. They squeal while bouncing up from the elegant sofas they were lounging on. Crossing the room, Brownie leaps at me and hugs me in a death grip. Sparing Reed less than a glance, Buns throws her arms around Brownie and me. "You finally decided to visit us, Sweetie! I'm so happy! I missed you!"

"Me too" Brownie agrees. "Buns has been so hard to live with since you've been busy."

"I was," Buns admits. "I was super hard to live with, but that's about to change now that you're finally here!"

The Reapers let me go, passing me off to Russell who picks me up and gives me a hug. I rest my head on his shoulder, trying not to cry. It doesn't work, a few tears sneak out of the corners of my eyes. Buns takes Reed by the hand and pulls him inside the room, shutting the door behind them and leaving us alone.

Russell finally lets me go. When I'm back on my feet, he shoves his hands in his pockets. "So, Detroit, huh?" he says with a grimace. "You couldn't have picked a warmer climate? You know it makes it hard to come back to Earth, knowin' I might freeze to death when winter rolls around again."

"You came back," I whisper, wiping away tears with the sleeve of my shirt.

Russell reaches out and tenderly wipes a tear away with his thumb. "Yeah, I sort of had to, I missed my best friend. Nothin' is the same without you."

"Anya didn't mind coming back?" I ask.

"Anya has to do a rotation on Earth as karmic retribution for disobeyin' Heaven when she escaped Paradise to be with me—blah, blah blah." He swipes his hand through his tawny hair. "I didn't have to come with her, but Reed was offerin' us this key job and it was a way to be together *and* see you. I mean, I've had worse jobs, right?"

"Oh, for sure," I agree with a tear-streaked smile. "There's that time you were a messenger—"

"Do *not* bring that up!" He laughs. "Anyway, what would I do in Heaven when everyone is here? I'd be bored, Evie. After the lives we've lived, I don't think I could hang there for more than a decade before I'd need to get back into the game. And we don't have inescapables anymore. No more Emil to ruin our lives."

"Your inescapable is gone too."

"Good riddance," he says harshly, not at all unhappy that his evil counterpart has been destroyed.

"I don't even know what it will be like not to have Emil around."

"You still have to deal with demons all the time."

"Yeah, but at least I know what they are now and I'm not at their mercy anymore."

"Aren't you?" he asks with a sad expression.

"No. I'm not. The faeries I've been living with aren't demons anymore."

"But you have to rescue souls from Sheol. That's a dangerous job."

"I can handle it."

"If anyone can, it's you," Russell says. "Anyway, I know Reed's glad he's here. He *hated* Paradise. For a guy who once pined for it, he couldn't wait to get back here."

"He's been in the game too long."

"So have you."

"I am the game."

Russell smiles ruefully. "Truer words were never spoken, Red. I think he also missed you too much. So, when are you movin' in?"

I'm spared from answering that question when Zephyr throws open the door. He picks me up and hugs me. "What is Sheol like? Reed would not tell me. He said that I had to ask you."

"I'll tell you everything you want to know," I promise.

He sets me on my feet. His ice blue eyes search mine. "Is there any way you'd consider taking me with you on a redemption run to Sheol to rescue souls?"

"Umm, I don't know. I don't see why not."

"Excellent," he replies with a wicked gleam in his eyes.

Reed takes my hand and leads me into the room. I settle on the sofa next to him. Leaning against his chest, he wraps his arm around my shoulder, teasing strands of my hair between his fingers. Buns, Brownie, Anya and I discuss all the things Reed and I can do for our binding ceremony. Buns get Phaedrus to agree to perform the rites again. We spend hours chatting. I listen to their stories of Paradise.

"Do you want to see the rest of the house?" Reed asks. I nod enthusiastically.

Getting up from the sofa, he takes my hand. He gives me a tour of the house. Much of it I recognize from high school, but he leads me upstairs to a room I've never been in. It's the master suite. The far wall is made entirely of windows. Two doors lead out to a grand stone porch overlooking the water. "Please tell me this is our room." I grin. He closes the door behind us.

"This is our room," he says. He walks to me and takes me in his arms and together we make it our own.

～

Living with Reed is effortless. He fills a void in me. I've been given a second chance at love. I appreciate it so much more than I did before; I take nothing for granted. My obligations, however, have not gone away. I am still the queen to my faeries. There are things that I have to do that I can't discuss with Reed. He has his own secrets that he's not allowed to share with me as well, secrets of his key and its gate to Paradise. Because we have mutual respect for one another, we're able to get past it and accept the things we cannot change.

I glance at my watch again, and then gently move Reed's arm from my shoulder. As silently as possible, I get up from my seat and I try to creep out of the dark home-theater room so that I don't disturb the angels as they watch a movie. Reed follows me to the door. I slip out into the hall. Reed murmurs, "You have to leave now?"

"Brennus is coming to pick me up. We have a strategy meeting." I gesture with my thumb over my shoulder. "He should be here any minute."

"What's your meeting about?" Reed asks as he follows me up the stairs and into the foyer.

"I can't talk about it," I say awkwardly. "I'll be back in the morning, though. We can have breakfast together." I gather a light jacket from the closet and my bag, which contains my battle hammer in it.

"You'll be gone all night?"

"I'll stay at the seminary tonight," I say with a cajoling smile. "We plan to get back late and there's always that transition from Sheol to Earth that I go through. It's better if I just stay with the fellas until I'm over it." He knows what I'm talking about. It's hard for me to relate to anyone or anything upon my initial return from Sheol. There's always a period of adjustment, but I'm working through it. I see concern in his eyes. "It will be okay."

"I know you will," he says, but I know he'll worry about me until I return tomorrow. He can't guard me when I'm in Sheol and it bothers him.

The doorbell rings. "I love you," I say, pulling on my jacket. I give him a quick kiss goodbye, and turn away to get the door, but Reed hauls me back to him.

"He can wait," Reed murmurs and he leans down and kisses me until I'm breathless and wanting more.

The doorbell rings again. "I have to go," I whisper.

"I love you, Evie," Reed says against my lips.

"I know." I smile at him and go to the door. Opening it, I grin at Brennus. "Hi."

"Ye look grand, Genevieve," Brennus says. "Are ye ready?"

"Yes," I say, and then hesitate. "Wait. I forgot! I bought the fellas some paczki. They're in the kitchen. Can you wait while I get them?"

"I'll wait for ye," Brennus replies.

"Come in for a second." I hold open the door. He steps into the foyer.

Seeing Reed, he nods his head in a stiff greeting, "Aingeal."

"Faerie," Reed replies.

I rush to the kitchen and retrieve the boxes of paczki. When I near the foyer, I pause and listen.

"How long do ye tink dis arrangement of ours will last?" Brennus asks.

"As long as it takes for her to realize that you're still evil."

"She knows I'm na. But I do worry about ye, aingeal. Ye have a much more dangerous job dan we do. Ye guard da key ta Paradise. Dere are many who would give anyting ta possess such a priceless commodity as dat."

"I have a team in place, just as you have."

"Ye'll need more dan a few aingeals. Na many demons are aching ta get inta Sheol, like dey are Paradise."

"I control two armies—Tau's and Xavier's."

"Ye'll need dem. Ye put Genevieve in danger jus by her being around ye and dat key."

"I'll protect her. She's agreed to be my aspire again."

"Have I ever told ye da story of da Faerie queen, Reed?"

"I'm not sure, Brennus. You've told me a lot of stories."

"Did ye know dat once upon a time, dere was a faerie queen? She was da heart of her realm until one day when an aingeal came ta her world from Paradise. He warned her dat her world was destined ta be destroyed—dat a time would come when da Faerie realm would be overrun by its enemies and dere would be no peace.

Da queen, caring only for da welfare of her subjects, begged da aingeal for mercy for dem. Da aingeal relented, tellin' her dere was only one way for her subjects ta be reborn after its destruction. Da aingeal told her dat if she agreed ta be human, she could one day save da human world from da evil dat is jus a thin veneer away. She listened ta him when he said she would face terrible danger and suffer greatly, but one day, a Faerie king would return from da grave ta save her. He said dat once da queen was finished wi' her mission ta help da humans, she would again be da queen of da faeries and da savior of her race. Have ye heard of dis tale, Reed?"

"No, I haven't heard that bit of fiction."

"Och, maybe ye should look inta it."

"Maybe it's a story for another day."

"I hope ta tell da whole ting ta ye soon, aingeal."

I rush back into the foyer. Giving Reed a quick kiss on the cheek, I turn to Brennus. "I'm ready," I murmur.

"So am I, mo chroí."

Acknowledgements

God, all things are possible through You. Thank you for Your infinite blessings and for allowing me to do what I love: write.

To my readers and bloggers: Thank you! The outpouring of love that I receive from all of you is incredible. Your generosity toward me is humbling. You make me want to write a thousand books.

Gloria Lutz, your unwavering support and unconditional love are a guiding light in my life.

Tom Bartol, you're my best friend. I cannot imagine my world without you in it. I love you.

Max and Jack Bartol, I count myself as the most fortunate person in the world to have you both in my life. Thank you for knowing when to let me write and when to rescue me from my computer.

Tamar Rydzinski, one of the best days of my life was when you agreed to be my agent. Thank you for always having my back.

Janet Wallace, you're inspirational. I love seeing what you create. Thank you for all of you help marketing Iniquity. I'm grateful.

Regina Wamba, you're an artist. Thank you for sharing your marketing genius with me.

Vilma Gonzalez, your support of this series has been mind-blowing. Thank you for being part of this journey.

Trish Brinkley, thank you for always including me in your circle!

Amber McLelland, thank you for your friendship.

Glossary

Aingeal – angel (Gaelic/Irish)
Aspire – angel significant other, similar to a human husband or wife (Angel)
Banjax – destroy (Gaelic/Irish)
Máistir – master (Gaelic/Irish)
Mo chroí – my heart (Gaelic/Irish)
Mo shíorghrá – my eternal love (Gaelic/Irish)
Reconnoître – black-winged nocturnal demon from Sheol who scouts and hunts prey – a messenger (Faerie)
Sclábhaí – slave (Gaelic/Irish)
Síorghrá - eternal love (Gaelic/Irish)
Sláinte – cheers (Gaelic/Irish)
Tristitiae – sorrow (Latin)
Wans – human women (Gaelic/Irish)
Werree – demons who steal body parts of other creatures to wear over their own shadowy figures (Faerie)
Wo gehst du hin? – Where are you going? (German)

About The Author

I live in Michigan with my husband and our two sons. My family is very supportive of my writing. When I'm writing, they often bring me the take-out menu so that I can call and order them dinner. They listen patiently when I talk about my characters like they're real. They rarely roll their eyes when I tell them I'll only be a second while I finish writing a chapter…and then they take off their coats. They ask me how the story is going when I surface after living for hours in a world of my own making. They have learned to accept my "writing uniform" consisting of a slightly unflattering pink fleece jacket, t-shirt, and black yoga pants. And they smile at my nerdy bookishness whenever I try to explain urban fantasy to them. In short, they get me, so they are perfect and I am blessed.

@Amy_A_Bartol
authoramyabartol

www.amyabartol.com
amyabartol@yahoo.com

Made in the USA
Lexington, KY
07 December 2015